SOUL MUSIC: THE ILLUSTRATED SCREENPLAY
WYRD SISTERS: THE ILLUSTRATED SCREENPLAY
MORT – THE PLAY (adapted by Stephen Briggs)
WYRD SISTERS – THE PLAY (adapted by Stephen Briggs)
MEN AT ARMS – THE PLAY (adapted by Stephen Briggs)
GUARDS! GUARDS! – THE PLAY (adapted by Stephen Briggs)
MASKERADE (adapted for the stage by Stephen Briggs)❖
CARPE JUGULUM (adapted for the stage by Stephen Briggs)❖
LORDS AND LADIES (adapted for the stage by Irana Brown)❖
INTERESTING TIMES (adapted by Stephen Briggs)◆
JINGO (adapted for the stage by Stephen Briggs)◆
THE FIFTH ELEPHANT (adapted by Stephen Briggs)◆
THE TRUTH (adapted by Stephen Briggs)◆
NIGHT WATCH (adapted for the stage by Stephen Briggs)◆
MONSTROUS REGIMENT (adapted for the stage by Stephen Briggs)◆
GOING POSTAL (adapted for the stage by Stephen Briggs)◆
THE SCIENCE OF DISCWORLD (with Ian Stewart and Jack Cohen)◉
THE SCIENCE OF DISCWORLD II: THE GLOBE
(with Ian Stewart and Jack Cohen)◉
THE SCIENCE OF DISCWORLD III: DARWIN'S WATCH
(with Ian Stewart and Jack Cohen)◉
THE NEW DISCWORLD COMPANION (with Stephen Briggs)¥
THE WIT AND WISDOM OF DISCWORLD (compiled by Stephen Briggs)
THE ART OF DISCWORLD (with Paul Kidby)¥
THE STREETS OF ANKH-MORPORK (with Stephen Briggs)
THE DISCWORLD MAPP (with Stephen Briggs)
A TOURIST GUIDE TO LANCRE – A DISCWORLD MAPP
(with Stephen Briggs and Paul Kidby)
DEATH'S DOMAIN (with Paul Kidby)
NANNY OGG'S COOKBOOK
THE PRATCHETT PORTFOLIO (with Paul Kidby)¥
THE LAST HERO (with Paul Kidby)¥
THE CELEBRATED DISCWORLD ALMANAK by Bernard Pearson
THE UNSEEN UNIVERSITY CUT OUT BOOK
WHERE'S MY COW?
GOOD OMENS
(with Neil Gaiman)
STRATA
THE DARK SIDE OF THE SUN
THE UNADULTERATED CAT (illustrated by Gray Jolliffe)¥

* also available in audio   ¥ published by Victor Gollancz
❖ published by Samuel French   ◆ published by Methuen Drama
◉ published by Ebury Press   ✱ published by Oxford University Press

TERRY PRATCHETT

WINTERSMITH

A STORY OF DISCWORLD

CORGI BOOKS

WINTERSMITH
A CORGI BOOK 978 0 552 15702 5

First published in Great Britain by Doubleday an imprint of
Random House Children's Books
A Random House Group Company

Doubleday edition published 2006
Corgi (RHCB) edition published 2007
Corgi (Transworld) edition published 2007

1 3 5 7 9 10 8 6 4 2

Corgi Books are published by Transworld Publishers Ltd,
61–63 Uxbridge Road, London W5 5SA

www.terrypratchett.co.uk
www.rbooks.co.uk

Addresses for Random House Group companies can be found at:
www.randomhouse.co.uk/offices.htm

THE RANDOM HOUSE GROUP Limited Reg. No. 954009

A CIP catalogue record for this book is available from the British Library.

Printed in the UK by CPI Bookmarque, Croydon, CR0 4TD

WINTERSMITH

INTRODUCTION

Bigjobs: human beings

Big Man: chief of the clan (usually the husband of the kelda)

Blethers: rubbish, nonsense

Boggin: to be desperate, as in 'I'm boggin for a cup of tea.'

Bunty: a weak person

Carlin: old woman

Cludgie: the privy

Crivens!: a general exclamation that can mean anything from 'My goodness!' to 'I've just lost my temper and there is going to be trouble.'

Dree your/my/his/her weird: facing the fate that is in store for you/me/him/her

Een: eyes

Eldritch: weird, strange. Sometimes means oblong, too, for some reason.

Fash: worry, upset

Geas: a very important obligation, backed up by tradition and magic. Not a bird.

Gonnagle: the bard of the clan, skilled in musical instruments, poems, stories and songs

Hag: a witch, of any age

Hag o' hags: a very important witch

Hagging/Haggling: anything a witch does

Hiddlins: secrets

Kelda: the female head of the clan, and eventually the mother of most of it. Feegle babies are very small, and a kelda will have hundreds in her lifetime.

Lang syne: long ago

Last World: The Feegles believe that they are dead. This world is so nice, they argue, that they must have been really good in a past life and then died and ended up here. Appearing to die here means merely going back to the Last World, which they believe is rather dull.

Mudlin: useless person

Pished: I am assured that this means 'tired'.

Schemie: an unpleasant person

Scuggan: a really unpleasant person

Scunner: a generally unpleasant person

Ships: woolly things that eat grass and go baa. Easily confused with the other kind.

Spavie: see Mudlin

Special Sheep Liniment: probably moonshine whisky, I am very sorry to say. No one knows what it'd do to sheep, but it is said that a drop of it is good for shepherds on a cold winter's night and for Feegles at any time at all. Do not try to make this at home.

Spog: a leather pouch, worn on the front of his belt, where a Feegle keeps his valuables and uneaten food, interesting insects, useful bits of twig, lucky dirt and so on. It is not a good idea to fish around in a spog.

Steamie: only found in the big Feegle mounds in the mountains, where there's enough water to allow regular bathing; it's a kind of sauna. Feegles on the Chalk tend to rely on the fact that you can only get so much dirt on you before it starts to fall off of its own accord.

Waily: a general cry of despair

CHAPTER 1

THE BIG SNOW

When the storm came, it hit the hills like a hammer. No sky should hold as much snow as this, and because no sky could, it fell; fell in a wall of white.

There was a small hill of snow where there had been, a few hours ago, a little cluster of thorn trees on an ancient mound. This time last year there had been a few early primroses; now there was just snow.

Part of the snow moved. A piece about the size of an apple rose up, with smoke pouring out around it. A hand no larger than a rabbit's paw waved the smoke away.

A very small, but very angry blue face, with the lump of snow still balanced on top of it, looked out at the sudden white wilderness.

'Ach, crivens!' it grumbled. 'Will ye no' look at this? 'Tis the work o' the wintersmith! Noo there's a scunner that willnae tak' "no" fra' a answer!'

Other lumps of snow were pushed up. More heads peered out.

'Oh waily, waily, waily!' said one of them. 'He's found the big wee hag again!'

The first head turned towards this head, and said, 'Daft Wullie?'

'Yes, Rob?'

'Did I no' tell ye to lay off that waily business?'

'Aye, Rob, ye did that,' said the head addressed as Daft Wullie.

'So why did ye just do it?'

'Sorry, Rob. It kinda bursted oot.'

'It's so dispiritin'.'

'Sorry, Rob.'

Rob Anybody sighed. 'But I fear ye're right, Wullie. He's come for the big wee hag, right enough. Who's watchin' over her doon at the farm?'

'Wee Dangerous Spike, Rob.'

Rob looked up at clouds so full of snow that they sagged in the middle.

'OK,' he said, and sighed again. 'It's time fra' the Hero.'

He ducked out of sight, the plug of snow dropping neatly back into place, and slid down into the heart of the Feegle mound.

It was quite big inside. A human could just about stand up in the middle, but they would then bend double with coughing because the middle was where there was a hole to let smoke out.

All around the inner wall were tiers of galleries, and every one of them was packed with Feegles. Usually the place was awash with noise, but now it was frighteningly quiet.

Rob Anybody walked across the floor to the fire, where his wife Jeannie was waiting. She stood up straight and proud, like a kelda should, but close up it seemed to him that she had been crying. He put his arm around her.

'All right, ye probably ken what's happenin',' he told the blue and red audience looking down on him. 'This is nae common storm. The wintersmith has found the big wee hag – now then, settle doon!'

He waited until the shouting and sword-rattling had died down, then went on:

'We cannae fight the wintersmith for her! That's her road! We cannae walk it for her! But the hag o' hags has set us on another path! It's a dark one, and dangerous!'

A cheer went up. Feegles liked the idea of this, at least.

'Right!' said Rob, satisfied at this. 'Ah'm awa' tae fetch the Hero!'

There was a lot of laughter at this, and Big Yan, the tallest of the Feegles, shouted, 'It's tae soon. We've only had time tae gi'e him a couple o' heroing lessons! He's still nae more than a big streak o' nothin'!'

'He'll be a hero for the big wee hag and that's an end o' it,' said Rob sharply. 'Noo, off ye go, the whole boilin' o' ye! Tae the chalk pit! Dig me a path tae the Underworld!'

It had to be the wintersmith, Tiffany Aching told herself, standing in front of her father in the freezing farmhouse. She could feel it out there. This wasn't normal weather even for midwinter, and this was springtime. It was a challenge. Or perhaps it was just a game. It was hard to tell, with the wintersmith.

Only it can't be a game because the lambs are dying. I'm only just thirteen, and my father, and a lot of other people older than me, want me to do something. And I can't. The wintersmith has found me again. He is here now, and I'm too weak.

It would be easier if they were bullying me, but no, they're begging. My father's face is grey with worry and he's begging. *My father is begging me.*

Oh no, he's taking his hat off. He's *taking off his hat* to speak to me!

They think magic comes free, when I snap my fingers. But if I can't do this for them now, what good am I? I can't let them see I'm afraid. Witches aren't allowed to be afraid.

And this is my fault. I: I started all this. I must finish it.

Mr Aching cleared his throat.

'. . . And, er, if you could . . . er, magic it away, uh, or something? For us . . . ?'

Everything in the room was grey, because the light from the windows was coming through snow. No one had wasted time digging the horrible stuff away from the houses. Every person who could hold a shovel was needed elsewhere, and still there were not enough of them. As it was, most people had been up all night, walking the flocks of yearlings, trying to keep the new lambs safe . . . in the dark, in the snow . . .

Her snow. It was a message to her. A challenge. A summons.

'All right,' she said. 'I'll see what I can do.'

'Good girl,' said her father, grinning with relief.

No, not a good girl, thought Tiffany. I brought this on us.

'You'll have to make a big fire, up by the sheds,' she said aloud. 'I mean a big fire, do you understand? Make it out of anything that will burn and you must keep it going. It'll keep trying to go out, but you must keep it going. Keep piling on the fuel, whatever happens. *The fire must not go out!*'

She made sure that the 'not!' was loud and frightening. She didn't want people's minds to wander. She put on the heavy brown woollen cloak that Miss Treason had made for her and grabbed the black pointy hat that hung on the back of the farm-house door. There was a sort of communal grunt from the people who'd crowded into the kitchen, and some of them backed away. We want a witch now, we need a witch now, but – we'll back away now, too.

That was the magic of the pointy hat. It was what Miss Treason called 'boffo'.

Tiffany Aching stepped out into the narrow corridor that had been cut through the snow-filled farmyard where the drifts were more than twice the height of a man. At least the deep snow kept off the worst of the wind, which was made of knives.

A track had been cleared all the way to the paddock, but it had been heavy-going. When there is fifteen feet of snow everywhere, how can you clear it? Where can you clear it to?

She waited by the cart sheds while the men hacked and scraped at the snow banks. They were tired to the soul by now; they'd been digging for hours.

The important thing was—

But there were lots of important things. It was important to look calm and confident, it was important to keep your mind clear, it was important not to show how pants-wettingly scared you were . . .

She held out a hand, caught a snowflake and took a good look at it. It wasn't one of the normal ones, oh no. It was one of his special snowflakes. That was nasty. He was taunting her. Now, she could hate him. She'd never hated him before. But he was killing the lambs.

She shivered, and pulled the cloak around her.

'This I choose to do,' she croaked, her breath leaving little clouds in the air. She cleared her throat and started again. 'This I choose to do. If there is a price, this I choose to pay. If it is my death, then I choose to die. Where this takes me, there I choose to go. I choose. This I choose to do.'

It wasn't a spell, except in her own head, but if you couldn't make spells work in your own head you couldn't make them work at all.

Tiffany wrapped her cloak around her against the clawing wind and watched dully as the men brought straw and wood. The fire started slowly, as if frightened to show enthusiasm.

She'd done this before, hadn't she? Dozens of times. The trick was not that hard when you got the feel of it, but she'd done it with time to get her mind right and, anyway, she'd never done it with anything more than a kitchen fire to warm her freezing feet. In theory it should be just as easy with a big fire and a field of snow, right?

Right?

The fire began to roar up. Her father put his hand on her shoulder. Tiffany jumped. She'd forgotten how quietly he could move.

'What was that about choosing?' he said. She'd forgotten what good hearing he had, too.

'It's a . . . witch thing,' she answered, trying not to look at his face. 'So that if this . . . doesn't work, it's no one's fault but mine.' And this is my fault, she added to herself. It's unfair, but no one said it wasn't going to be.

Her father's hand caught her chin and gently turned her head round. How soft his hands are, Tiffany thought. Big man's hands but soft as a baby's, because of the grease on the sheep's fleeces.

'We shouldn't have asked you, should we . . .' he said.

Yes, you should have asked me, Tiffany thought. The lambs are dying under the dreadful snow. And I should have said no, I should have said I'm not that good yet. But the lambs are dying under the dreadful snow!

There will be other lambs, said her Second Thoughts.

But these aren't those lambs, are they? These are the lambs that are dying, here and now. And they're dying because I listened to my feet and dared to dance with the wintersmith.

'I can do it,' she said.

Her father held her chin and stared into her eyes.

'Are you sure, jiggit?' he said. It was the nickname her grandmother had had for her – Granny Aching, who never lost a lamb to the dreadful snow. He'd never used it before. Why had it risen up in his mind now?

'Yes!' She pushed his hand away, and broke his gaze before she burst into tears.

'I . . . haven't told your mother this yet,' said her father, very slowly, as if the words required enormous care, 'but I can't find your brother. I think he was trying to help. Abe Swindell said he saw him with his little shovel. Er . . . I'm sure he's all right, but . . . keep an eye open for him, will you? He's got his red coat on.'

His face, with no expression at all, was heart-breaking to see. Little Wentworth, nearly seven years old, always running after the men, always wanting to be one of them, always trying to help . . . how easily a small body could get overlooked . . . The snow was still coming fast. The horribly wrong snowflakes were white on her father's shoulders. It's these little things you remember when the bottom falls out of the world, and you're falling—

That wasn't just unfair; that was . . . cruel.

Remember the hat you wear! Remember the job that is in front of you! Balance! Balance is the thing. Hold balance in the centre, hold the balance . . .

Tiffany extended her numb hands to the fire, to draw out the warmth.

'Remember, don't let the fire go out,' she said.

'I've got men bringing up wood from all over,' said her father. 'I told 'em to bring all the coal from the forge, too. It won't run out of feeding, I promise you!'

The flame danced and curved towards Tiffany's hands. The trick was, the trick, the trick . . . was to fold the heat somewhere close, draw it with you and . . . balance. Forget everything else!

'I'll come with—' her father began.

'No! Watch the fire!' Tiffany shouted, too loud, frantic with fear. 'You will do what I say!'

I am not your daughter today! her mind screamed. I am your witch! *I* will protect *you*!

21

She turned before he could see her face and ran through the flakes, along the track that had been cut towards the lower paddocks. The snow had been trodden down into a lumpy, hummocky path, made slippery with fresh snow. Exhausted men with shovels pressed themselves into the snow banks on either side rather than get in her way.

She reached the wider area where other shepherds were digging into the wall of snow. It tumbled in lumps around them.

'Stop! Get back!' her voice shouted, while her mind wept.

The men obeyed quickly. The mouth that had given that order had a pointy hat above it. You didn't argue with that.

Remember the heat, the heat, remember the heat, balance, balance . . .

This was witching cut to the bone. No toys, no wands, no boffo, no headology, no tricks. All that mattered was how good you were.

But sometimes you had to trick yourself. She wasn't the Summer Lady and she wasn't Granny Weatherwax. She needed to give herself all the help she could.

She pulled the little silver horse out of her pocket. It was greasy and stained, and she'd meant to clean it, but there had been no time, no time . . .

Like a knight putting on his helmet, she fastened the silver chain around her neck.

She should have practised more. She should have listened to people. She should have listened to herself.

She took a deep breath and held out her hands on either side of her, palms up. On her right hand, a white scar glowed.

'Thunder on my right hand,' she said. 'Lightning in my left hand. Fire behind me. Frost in front of me.'

She stepped forward until she was only a few inches away from the snow bank. She could feel its coldness already pulling the heat out of her. Well, so be it. She took a few deep breaths. This I choose to do . . .

'Frost to fire,' she whispered.

In the yard, the fire went white and roared like a furnace.

The snow wall spluttered, and then exploded into steam, sending chunks of snow into the air. Tiffany walked forward slowly. Snow pulled back from her hands like mist at sunrise. It melted in the heat of her, becoming a tunnel in the deep drift, fleeing from her, writhing around her in clouds of cold fog.

Yes! She smiled desperately. It was true. If you had the perfect centre, if you got your mind right, you could balance. In the middle of the see-saw is a place that never moves . . .

Her boots squelched over warm water. There was fresh green grass under the snow, because the awful storm had been so late in the year. She walked on, heading to where the lambing pens were buried.

Her father stared at the fire. It was burning white-hot, like a furnace, eating through the wood as if driven by a gale. It was collapsing into ashes in front of his eyes . . .

Water was pouring around Tiffany's boots.

Yes! But don't think about it! Hold the balance! More heat! Frost to fire!

There was a bleat.

Sheep could live under the snow, at least for a while. But as Granny Aching used to say, when the gods made sheep they must've left their brains in their other coat. In a panic, and sheep were always just an inch from panicking, they'd trample their own lambs.

Now ewes and lambs appeared, steaming and bewildered as the snow melted around them, as if they were sculptures left behind.

Tiffany moved on, staring straight ahead of her, only just aware of the excited cries of the men behind her. They were following her, pulling the ewes free, cradling the lambs . . .

Her father yelled at the other men. Some of them were hacking at a farm cart, throwing the wood down into the white-hot flames. Others were dragging furniture up from the house. Wheels, tables, straw bales, chairs – the fire took everything, gulped it down, and roared for more. And there wasn't any more.

No red coat. No red coat! Balance, balance. Tiffany waded on, water and sheep pouring past her. The tunnel ceiling fell in a splashing and slithering of slush. She ignored it. Fresh snowflakes fell down through the hole and boiled in the air above her head. She ignored that, too. And then, ahead of her . . . a glimpse of red.

Frost to fire! The snow fled, and there he was. She picked him up, held him close, sent some of her heat into him, felt him stir, whispered: 'It weighed at least forty pounds! At least forty pounds!'

He coughed, and opened his eyes. Tears falling like melting snow, she ran over to a shepherd and thrust the boy into his arms.

'Take him to his mother! *Do it now!*' The man grabbed the boy and ran, frightened of her fierceness. Today she was their witch!

Tiffany turned back. There were more lambs to be saved.

Her father's coat landed on the starving flames, glowed for a moment, then fell into grey ashes. The other men were ready; they grabbed the man as he went to jump after it and pulled him back, kicking and shouting.

The flint cobbles had melted like butter. They spluttered for a moment, then froze.

The fire went out.

Tiffany Aching looked up, into the eyes of the wintersmith.

And up on the roof of the cart shed the small voice belonging to Wee Dangerous Spike said, 'Ach, crivens!'

All this hasn't happened yet. It might not happen at all. The future is always a bit wobbly. Any little thing, like the fall of a snowflake or the dropping of the wrong kind of spoon, can send it spinning off along a new path. Or perhaps not.

Where it all *began* was last autumn, on the day with a cat in it . . .

CHAPTER 2

MISS TREASON

This is Tiffany Aching, riding a broomstick though the mountain forests a hundred miles away. It's a very old broomstick and she's flying it just above the ground; it's got two smaller broomsticks stuck on the back like trainer wheels, to stop it tipping up. It belongs, appropriately, to a very old witch called Miss Treason, who's even worse at flying than Tiffany and is 113 years old.

Tiffany is slightly more than one hundred years younger than that, taller than she was even a month ago, and not as certain of anything at all as she was a year ago.

She is training to be a witch. Witches usually wear black, but as far as she could tell the only reason that witches wore black was because they'd always worn black. This did not seem a good enough reason, so she tended to wear blue or green. She didn't laugh with scorn at finery, because she'd never seen any.

You couldn't escape the pointy hat, though. There was nothing magical about a pointy hat except that it said that the person underneath it was a witch. People paid attention to a pointy hat.

Even so, it was hard to be a witch in the village where you'd grown up. It was hard to be a witch to people who knew you as 'Joe Aching's girl' and had seen you running around with only your vest on when you were two years old.

Going away had helped. Most people Tiffany knew hadn't been more than ten miles away from the spot where they were born, so if you'd gone to mysterious foreign parts, that made you a bit mysterious, too. You came back slightly different. A witch needed to be different.

Witching was turning out to be mostly hard work and really short on magic of the 'zap! glingle-glingle-glingle' variety. There was no school and nothing that was exactly like a lesson. But it wasn't wise to try to learn witching all by yourself, especially if you had a natural talent. If you got it wrong you could go from ignorant to cackling in a week . . .

When you got right down to it, it was all about cackling. No one ever talked about this, though. Witches said things like 'You can never be too old, too skinny or too warty', but they never mentioned the cackling. Not properly. They watched out for it, though, all the time.

It was all too easy to become a cackler. Most witches

lived by themselves (cat optional) and might go for weeks without ever seeing another witch. In those times when people hated witches, they were often accused of talking to their cats. Of course they talked to their cats. After three weeks without an intelligent conversation that wasn't about cows, you'd talk to the *wall*. And that was an early sign of cackling.

'Cackling', to a witch, didn't just mean nasty laughter. It meant your mind drifting away from its anchor. It meant you losing your grip. It meant loneliness and hard work and responsibility and other people's problems driving you crazy a little bit at a time, each bit so small that you'd hardly notice it, until you thought that it was normal to stop washing and wear a kettle on your head. It meant you thinking that the fact you knew more than anyone else in your village made you better than them. It meant thinking that right and wrong were negotiable. And, in the end, it meant you 'going to the dark', as the witches said. That was a bad road. At the end of that road were poisoned spinning-wheels and gingerbread cottages.

What stopped this was the habit of visiting. Witches visited other witches all the time, sometimes travelling quite a long way for a cup of tea and a bun. Partly this was for gossip of course, because witches love gossip, especially if it's more exciting than truthful. But mostly it was to keep an eye on one another.

Today, Tiffany was visiting Granny Weatherwax, who was in the opinion of most witches (including

Granny's own) the most powerful witch in the mountains. It was all very polite. No one said, 'Not gone bats, then?' or, 'Certainly not! I'm as sharp as a spoon!' They didn't need to. They understood what it was all about, so they talked of other things. But when she was in a mood, Granny Weatherwax could be hard work.

She sat silently in her rocking-chair. Some people are good at talking, but Granny Weatherwax was good at silence. She could sit so quiet and still that she faded. You forgot she was there. The room became empty.

It upset people. It was probably meant to. But Tiffany had learned silence, too, from Granny Aching, her real grandmother. Now she was learning that if you made yourself really quiet you could become almost invisible.

Granny Weatherwax was an expert.

Tiffany thought of it as the 'I'm not here' spell, if it was a spell. She reasoned that everyone had something inside them that told the world they were there. That was why you could often sense when someone was behind you, even if they were making no sound at all. You were receiving their 'I am here!' signal.

Some people had a very strong one. They were the people who got served first in shops. Granny Weatherwax had an 'I am here' signal that bounced off the mountains when she wanted it to; when she walked into a forest, all the wolves and bears ran out the other side.

She could turn it off, too.

She was doing that now. Tiffany was having to concentrate to see her. Most of her mind was telling her that there was no one there at all.

Well, she thought, that's about enough of that. She coughed. Suddenly, Granny Weatherwax had always been there.

'Miss Treason is very well,' said Tiffany.

'A fine woman,' said Granny. 'Oh, yes.'

'She has her funny ways,' said Tiffany.

'We're none of us perfect,' said Granny.

'She's trying some new eyes,' said Tiffany.

'That's good.'

'They're a couple of ravens . . .'

'It's just as well,' said Granny.

'Better than the mouse she usually uses,' said Tiffany.

'I expect they are.'

There was a bit more of this, until Tiffany began to get annoyed at doing all the work. There was such a thing as common politeness, after all. Oh well, she knew what to do about it now.

'Mrs Earwig's written another book,' she said.

'I heard,' said Granny. The shadows in the room maybe grew a little darker.

Well, that explained the sulk. Even thinking about Mrs Earwig made Granny Weatherwax angry. Mrs Earwig was all wrong to Granny Weatherwax. She wasn't born locally, which was almost a crime to begin with. She wrote books, and Granny Weatherwax didn't trust books. And Mrs Earwig (pronounced 'Ahwij', at least by Mrs Earwig) believed in shiny wands and magical amulets and mystic runes and the power of the stars, while Granny Weatherwax believed in cups of tea, dry biscuits, washing every morning in cold water and, well, she believed mostly in Granny Weatherwax.

Mrs Earwig was popular among the younger witches, because if you did witchcraft her way you could wear so much jewellery that you could barely walk. Granny Weatherwax wasn't popular with anyone much—

– except when they needed her. When Death was standing by the cradle or the axe slipped in the woods and blood was soaking into the moss, you sent someone hurrying to the cold, gnarly little cottage in the clearing. When all hope was gone, you called for Granny Weatherwax, because she was the best.

And she always came. Always. But popular? No. Need is not the same as like. Granny Weatherwax was for when things were *serious*.

Tiffany did like her, though, in an odd kind of way. She thought Granny Weatherwax liked her, too. She let Tiffany call her Granny to her face, when all the other young witches had to call her Mistress Weatherwax. Sometimes Tiffany thought that if you were friendly to Granny Weatherwax she tested

32

you to see how friendly you would stay. Everything about Granny Weatherwax was a test.

'The new book is called *First Flights in Witchcraft*,' she went on, watching the old witch carefully.

Granny Weatherwax smiled. That is, her mouth went up at the corners.

'Hah!' she said. 'I've said it before and I'll say it again, you can't learn witchin' from books. Letice Earwig thinks you can become a witch by goin' shoppin'.' She gave Tiffany a piercing look, as if she was making up her mind about something. Then she said: 'An' I'll wager she don't know how to do *this*.'

She picked up her cup of hot tea, curling her hands around it. Then she reached out with her other hand and took Tiffany's hand.

'Ready?' said Granny.

'For wha—?' Tiffany began, and then she felt her hand get hot. The heat spread up her arm, warming it to the bone.

'Feelin' it?'

'Yes!'

The warmth died away. And Granny Weatherwax, still watching Tiffany's face, turned the teacup upside down.

The tea dropped out in one lump. It was frozen solid.

Tiffany was old enough not to say, 'How did you do that?' Granny Weatherwax didn't answer silly questions or, for that matter, many questions at all.

'You moved the heat,' she said. 'You took the heat

out of the tea and moved it through you to me, yes?'

'Yes, but it never touched me,' said Granny triumphantly. 'It's all about balance, do you see? Balance is the trick. Keep the balance and—' She stopped. 'You've ridden on a see-saw? One end goes up, one end goes down. But the bit in the middle, right in the middle, that stays where it is. Up-ness and down-ness go right through it. Don't matter how high or low the ends go, it keeps the balance.' She sniffed. 'Magic is mostly movin' stuff around.'

'Can I learn that?'

'I dare say. It's not hard, if you get your mind right.'

'Can you teach me?'

'I just have. I showed you.'

'No, Granny, you just showed me how to do it, not . . . *how* to do it!'

'Can't tell you that. I know how I do it. How you do it'll be different. You've just got to get your mind right.'

'How do I do that?'

'How should I know? It's your mind,' snapped Granny. 'Put the kettle on again, will you? My tea's gone cold.'

There was something almost spiteful about all this, but that was Granny. She took the view that if you were capable of learning, you'd work it out. There was no point in making it easy for people. Life wasn't easy, she said.

'An' I see you're still wearing that trinket,' said

Granny. And she didn't like trinkets, a word she used to mean anything metal a witch wore that wasn't there to hold up, shut or fasten. That was 'shoppin''.

Tiffany touched the little silver horse she wore around her neck. It was small, simple and meant a lot to her.

'Yes,' she said calmly. 'I still am.'

'What have you got in that basket?' Granny said now, which was unusually rude. Tiffany's basket was on the table. It had a present in it, of course. Everyone knew you took a small present along when you went visiting, but you were supposed to be surprised when you were given it, and say things like, 'Ooo, you shouldn't have.'

'I brought you something,' said Tiffany, swinging the big black kettle onto the fire.

'You've got no call to be bringing me presents, I'm sure,' said Granny sternly.

'Yes, well,' said Tiffany, and left it at that.

Behind her, she heard Granny lift the lid of the basket. There was a kitten in it.

'Her mother is Pinky, the Widow Cable's cat,' said Tiffany, to fill the silence.

'*You shouldn't have*,' growled the voice of Granny Weatherwax.

'It was no trouble.' Tiffany smiled at the fire.

'I can't be havin' with cats.'

'She'll keep the mice down,' said Tiffany, still not turning round.

'Don't have mice.'

Nothing for them to eat, thought Tiffany. Aloud, she said, 'Mrs Earwig's got six big black cats.' In the basket, the white kitten would be staring up at Granny Weatherwax with the sad, shocked expression of all kittens. You test me, I test you, Tiffany thought.

'I don't know what I shall do with it, I'm sure. It'll have to sleep in the goat shed,' said Granny Weatherwax. Most witches had goats.

The kitten rubbed up against Granny's legs and went 'meep'.

When she left, later on, Granny Weatherwax said goodbye at the door and very carefully shut the kitten outside.

Tiffany went across the clearing to where she'd tied up Miss Treason's broomstick.

But she didn't get on, not yet. She stepped back up against a holly bush, and went quiet until she wasn't there any more, until everything about her said: I'm not here.

Everyone could see pictures in the fire and in clouds. You just turned that the other way around. You turned off that bit of yourself that said you were there. You dissolved. Anyone looking at you would find you very hard to see. Your face became a bit of leaf and shadow, your body a piece of tree and bush. The other person's mind would fill in the gaps.

Looking like just another piece of holly bush, she watched the door. The wind had got up, warm but worrisome, shaking the yellow and red leaves off the sycamore trees and whirring them around the clearing. The kitten tried to bat a few of them out of the air and then sat there, making sad little mewling noises. Any minute now, Granny Weatherwax would think Tiffany had gone and would open the door and—

'*Forgot something?*' said Granny, by her ear.

She *was* the bush.

'Er . . . it's very sweet. I just thought you might, you know, grow to like it,' said Tiffany, but she was thinking: Well, she could have got there if she ran, but why didn't I see her? Can you run and hide at the same time?

'Never you mind about me, my girl,' said the witch. 'You run along back to Miss Treason and give her my best wishes, right now. But' – and her voice softened a little – 'that was good hiding you did just then. There's many as would not have seen you. Why, I hardly heard your hair growin'!'

When Tiffany's stick had left the clearing, and Granny Weatherwax had satisfied herself in other little ways that she had really gone, she went back inside, carefully ignoring the kitten again.

After a few minutes, the door creaked open a little. It may have been just a draught. The kitten trotted inside . . .

All witches were a bit odd. Tiffany had got used to odd, so that odd seemed quite normal. There was Miss

Level, for example, who had two bodies, although one of them was imaginary. Mistress Pullunder, who bred pedigree earthworms and gave them all names ... well, she was hardly odd at all, just a bit peculiar, and anyway earthworms were quite interesting in a basically uninteresting kind of way. And there had been Old Mother Dismass, who suffered from bouts of temporal confusion, which can be quite strange when it happens to a witch; her mouth never moved in time with her words, and sometimes her footsteps came down the stairs ten minutes before she did.

But when it came to odd, Miss Treason didn't just take the cake, but a packet of biscuits too, with sprinkles on the top, and also a candle.

Where to start, when things were wall to wall odd ...

Miss Eumenides Treason had gone blind when she was sixty years old. To most people that would have been a misfortune, but Miss Treason was skilled at Borrowing, a particular witch talent.

She could use the eyes of animals, reading what they saw right out of their minds.

She'd gone deaf when she was seventy-five, too, but she'd got the hang of it by now and used any ears she could find running around.

When Tiffany had first gone to stay with her, Miss Treason had used a mouse for seeing and hearing, because her old jackdaw had died. It was a bit worrying to see an old woman striding around the cottage with a mouse in her outstretched hand, and very worrying if you said something and the mouse was swung around to face you. It was amazing how creepy a little pink wriggly nose could be.

The new ravens were a lot better. Someone in one of the local villages had made the old woman a perch that fitted across her shoulders, one bird on each side, and with her long white hair the effect was very, well, witchy, although a bit messy down the back of her cloak by the end of the day.

Then there was her clock. It was heavy and made of rusty iron by someone who was more blacksmith than watchmaker, which was why it went **clonk-clank** instead of *tick-tock*. She wore it on her belt and could tell the time by feeling the stubby little hands.

There was a story in the villages that the clock was Miss Treason's heart, which she'd used ever since her first heart died. But there were lots of stories about Miss Treason.

You had to have a high threshold for odd to put up with her. It was traditional that young witches travelled around and stayed with older witches, to learn from a lot of experts in exchange for what Miss Tick the witch-finder called 'some help with the chores', which meant 'doing all the chores'. Mostly, they left Miss Treason's after one night. Tiffany had stuck it out for three months so far.

Oh . . . and sometimes, when she was looking for a pair of eyes to look through, Miss Treason would creep into yours. It was a strange prickly sensation, like having someone invisible looking over your shoulder.

Yes . . . perhaps Miss Treason didn't just take the cake, a packet of biscuits with sprinkles on the top, and a candle, but also the trifle, the sandwiches and a man who made amusing balloon animals afterwards.

She was weaving at her loom when Tiffany came in. Two beaks turned to face her.

'Ah, child,' said Miss Treason, in a thin, cracked voice. 'You have had a good day.'

'Yes, Miss Treason,' said Tiffany obediently.

'You have seen the girl Weatherwax and she is well.' *Click-clack* went the loom. **Clonk-clank** went the clock.

'Quite well,' said Tiffany. Miss Treason didn't ask questions. She just told you the answers. The girl Weatherwax, Tiffany thought, as she started to get their supper. But Miss Treason was very old.

And very scary. It was a fact. You couldn't deny it. She didn't have a hooked nose and she did have all her teeth, even if they were yellow, but after that she was a picture-book wicked witch. And her knees clicked when she walked. And she walked very fast, with the help of two sticks, scuttling around like a big spider. That was another strange thing: the cottage was full of cobwebs, which Miss Treason ordered Tiffany never to touch, but you never saw a spider.

Oh, and there was the thing about black, too. Most witches liked black, but Miss Treason even had black goats and black chickens. The walls were black. The floor was black. If you dropped a stick of liquorice, you'd never find it again. And, to Tiffany's dismay, she had to make her cheeses black, which meant painting the cheeses with shiny black wax. Tiffany was an excellent cheese-maker and it did keep them moist, but Tiffany distrusted black cheeses. They always looked as though they were plotting something.

And Miss Treason didn't seem to need sleep. She hadn't got much use for night and day, now. When the ravens went to bed she'd summon up an owl, and weave by owl-sight. An owl was particularly good, she said, because it'd keep turning its head to watch the shuttle of the loom. *Click-clack* went the loom, and **clonk-clank** went the clock, right back at it.

Miss Treason, with her billowing black cloak and bandaged eyes and wild white hair . . .

Miss Treason with her two sticks, wandering the cottage and garden in the dark and frosty night, smelling the memory of flowers . . .

All witches had some particular skill, and Miss Treason delivered Justice.

People would come from miles around to bring her their problems:

I know it's my cow but he says it's his!

She says it's her land but my father left it to me!

. . . and Miss Treason would sit at the click-clacking loom with her back to the room full of anxious people. The loom worried them. They watched it as though they were afraid of it, and the ravens watched them.

They would stutter out their case, um-ing and ah-ing, while the loom rattled away in the flickering candlelight. Oh, yes . . . the candlelight . . .

The candle-holders were two skulls. One had the word ENOCHI carved on it; the other had the word ATHOOTITA.

The words meant 'GUILT' and 'INNOCENCE'. Tiffany wished she didn't know that. There was no way that a girl brought up on the Chalk should know that, because the words were in a foreign language, and an ancient one, too. She knew them because of Dr Sensibility Bustle, D.M. Phil., B.El L., Patricius Professor of Magic at Unseen University, who was in her head.

Well, a tiny part of him, at least.

A couple of summers ago she had been taken over by a hiver, a . . . thing that had been collecting minds for millions of years. Tiffany managed to get it out of her head, but a few fragments had stayed tangled up in her brain. One of these was a tiny lump of ego and a tangle of memories that were all that remained of the late Dr Bustle. He wasn't much trouble, but if she looked at anything in a foreign language she could read it – or, rather, hear Dr Bustle's reedy voice translating it for her. (That seemed to be all that was left of him, but she tried to avoid getting undressed in front of a mirror.)

The candles had dripped wax all over the skulls, and

people would keep glancing at them the whole time they were in the room.

And then, when all the words had been said, the loom would stop with a shock of sudden silence, and Miss Treason would turn round in her big heavy chair, which had wheels on it, and remove the black blindfold from her pearly grey eyes and say:

'I have heard. Now I shall see. I shall see what is true.'

Some people would actually run away at this point, when she stared at them in the light from the skulls. Those eyes that could not see your face could somehow see your mind. When Miss Treason was looking right through you, you could only be truthful or very, very stupid.

So no one ever argued with Miss Treason.

Witches were not allowed to be paid for using their talents, but everyone who came to have a dispute settled by Miss Treason brought her a present, usually food but sometimes clean used clothing, if it was black, or a pair of old boots if they were her size. If Miss Treason gave judgement against you, it was really not a good idea (everyone said) to ask for your present back, as being turned into something small and sticky often offends.

They said if you lied to Miss Treason you would die horribly within a week. They said that kings and princes came to see Miss Treason at night, asking questions about great affairs of state. They said that in her cellar was a heap of gold, guarded by a demon with skin like fire and three heads that would attack anyone it saw and eat their noses.

Tiffany suspected that at least two of these beliefs were wrong. She knew the third one wasn't true, because one day she'd gone down into the cellar (with a bucket of water and a poker, just in case) and there was nothing there but piles of potatoes and carrots. And a mouse, watching her carefully.

Tiffany wasn't scared, much. For one thing, unless the demon was good at disguising itself as a potato, it probably didn't exist. And the other was that although Miss Treason looked bad and sounded bad and smelled like old locked wardrobes, she didn't feel bad.

First Sight and Second Thoughts, that's what a witch had to rely on: First Sight to see what's really there, and Second Thoughts to watch the First Thoughts to check that they were thinking right. Then there were the Third Thoughts, which Tiffany had never heard discussed and therefore kept quiet about; they were odd, seemed to think for themselves, and didn't usually turn up very often. Now they were telling her that there was more to Miss Treason than met the eye.

And then one day, when she was dusting, Tiffany knocked over the skull called Enochi.

. . . and suddenly, Tiffany knew a lot more about Miss Treason than Miss Treason probably wanted anyone to know.

Tonight, as they were eating their stew (with black

beans), Miss Treason said, 'The wind is rising. We must go soon. I would not trust the stick above the trees on a night like this. There may be strange creatures about.'

'Go? We're going out?' Tiffany asked. They never went out in the evenings, which was why the evenings always felt a hundred years long.

'Indeed we are. They will be dancing tonight.'

'Who will?'

'The ravens will not be able to see and the owl will get confused,' Miss Treason went on. 'I will need to use your eyes.'

'Who will be dancing, Miss Treason?' said Tiffany. She liked dancing, but no one seemed to dance up here.

'It is not far, but there will be a storm.'

So that was it; Miss Treason wasn't going to tell. But it sounded interesting. Besides, it would probably be an education to see anyone that Miss Treason thought was strange.

Of course, it did mean Miss Treason would put her pointy hat on. Tiffany hated this bit. She'd have to stand in front of Miss Treason and stare at her, and feel the little tingle in her eyes as the ancient witch used her as a kind of mirror.

The wind was roaring in the woods like a big dark animal by the time they'd finished supper. It barged the door out of Tiffany's hands when she opened it and blew around the room, making the cords hum on the loom.

'Are you sure about this, Miss Treason?' she said, trying to push the door shut.

'Don't you say that to me! You will not say that to me! The dance must be witnessed! I have never missed the dance!' Miss Treason looked nervous and edgy. 'We must go! And you must wear black.'

'Miss Treason, you *know* I don't wear black,' said Tiffany.

'Tonight is a night for black. You will wear my second-best cloak.'

She said it with a witch's firmness, as if the idea of anyone disobeying had never crossed her mind. She was 113 years old. She'd had a lot of practice. Tiffany didn't argue.

It's not that I have anything against black, Tiffany thought as she fetched the second-best cloak, but it's just not me. When people say witches wear black they actually mean that old ladies wear black. Anyway, it's not as if I'm wearing pink or something . . .

After that she had to wrap Miss Treason's clock in pieces of blanket, so that the **clonk-clank** became clonk-clank. There was no question of leaving it behind. Miss Treason always kept the clock close to her.

While Tiffany got herself ready, the old woman wound the clock up with a horrible graunching noise. She was always winding it up; sometimes she stopped to do it in the middle of a judgement, with a room full of horrified people.

There was no rain yet, but when they set out the air was full of twigs and flying leaves. Miss Treason sat side-saddle on the broom, hanging on for dear life, while Tiffany walked along towing it by means of a piece of clothesline.

The sunset sky was still red and a gibbous moon was high, but the clouds were being whipped across it, filling the woods with moving shadows. Branches knocked together, and Tiffany heard the creak and crash as, somewhere in the dark, one fell to the ground.

'Are we going to the villages?' Tiffany yelled above the din.

'No! Take the path through the forest!' shouted Miss Treason.

Ah, thought Tiffany, is this the famous 'dancing about without your drawers on' that I've heard so much about? Actually, not very much about, because as soon as anyone mentions it, someone else tells them to shut up, so I really haven't heard much about it at all, but haven't heard in a very meaningful way.

It was something people thought witches did, but witches didn't think they did it. Tiffany had to admit she could see why. Even hot summer nights weren't all that warm, and there were always hedgehogs and thistles to worry about. Besides, you just couldn't imagine someone like Granny Weatherwax dancing about without— Well, you just couldn't imagine it, because if you did, it would make your head explode.

The wind died down as she took the forest track, still towing the floating Miss Treason. But the wind had brought cold air with it and then left it behind. Tiffany was glad of the cloak, even if it was black.

She trudged on, taking different tracks when Miss Treason told her to, until she saw firelight through the trees, in a little dip in the land.

'Stop here and help me down, girl,' said the old witch. 'And listen carefully. There are rules. One, you will not talk; two, you will look only at the dancers; three, *you will not move until the dance is finished*. I will not tell you twice!'

'Yes, Miss Treason. It's very cold up here.'

'And will get colder.'

They headed for the distant light. What good is a dance you can only watch? Tiffany wondered. It didn't sound like much fun.

'It isn't meant to be fun,' said Miss Treason.

Shadows moved across the firelight, and Tiffany heard the sound of men's voices. Then, as they reached the edge of the sunken ground, someone threw water over the fire.

There was a hiss, and a cloud of smoke and steam rose among the trees. It happened in a moment, and left a shock behind. The only thing that had seemed alive here had died.

Dry fallen leaves crunched under her feet. The moon, in a sky swept clean now of clouds, made little silver shapes on the forest floor.

It was some time before Tiffany realized that there were six men standing in the middle of the clearing. They must have been wearing black; against the moonlight, they looked like man-shaped holes into nothing. They were in two lines of three, facing each other, but were so still that after a while Tiffany wondered if she was imagining them.

There was the thud of a drumbeat: *bom . . . bom . . . bom*.

It went on for half a minute or so, and then stopped. But in the silence of the cold woods the beat went on inside Tiffany's head, and perhaps that wasn't the only head it thundered in, because the men were gently nodding their heads, to keep the beat.

They began to dance.

The only noise was of their boots hitting the ground as the shadow men wove in and out. But then Tiffany, her head full of the silent drum, heard another sound. Her foot was tapping, all by itself.

She'd heard this beat before, she'd seen men dancing like this. But it had been on warm days in bright sunshine. They'd worn little bells on their clothes!

'This is a Morris dance!' she said, not quite under her breath.

'Shush!' hissed Miss Treason.

'But this isn't the right—'

'Be silent!'

Blushing and angry in the dark, Tiffany took her eyes off the dancers and defiantly looked around the clearing. There were other shadows crowding in, human or at least human-shaped, but she couldn't see them clearly and maybe that was just as well.

It was getting colder, she was sure. White frost was crackling across the leaves.

The beat went on. But it seemed to Tiffany that it wasn't alone now, but had picked up other beats, and echoes from inside her head.

Miss Treason could shush all she liked. It was a Morris dance. But it was out of time!

The Morris men came to the village some time in May. You could never be sure when, because they had to call at lots of villages along the Chalk, and every village had a pub, which slowed them down.

They carried sticks and wore white clothes with bells on them, to stop them creeping up on people. No one likes an unexpected Morris dancer. Tiffany would wait outside the village with the other children and dance behind them all the way in.

And then they used to dance on the village green to the beat of a drum, banging their sticks together in the air, and then everyone would go to the pub and summer would come.

Tiffany hadn't been able to work out how that last bit happened. The dancers danced, and then summer came – that was all anybody seemed to know. Her father said that there had once been a year when the dancers hadn't turned up, and a cold wet spring had turned into a chilly autumn, with the months between being filled with mists and rain and frosts in August.

The sound of the drums filled her head now, making her feel dizzy. They were wrong; there was something wrong—

And then she remembered the seventh dancer, the one they called the Fool. He was generally a small man, wearing a battered top hat and bright rags sewn all over his clothes. Mostly he wandered around holding out the hat and grinning at people until they gave him money for beer. But sometimes he'd put the hat down and whirl off into the dancers. You'd expect there to be a massive collision of arms and legs, but it never happened. Jumping and twirling among the sweating men, he always managed to be where the other dancers weren't.

The world was moving around her. She blinked. The drums in her head were like thunder now, and there was one beat as deep as oceans. Miss Treason was forgotten. So were the strange, mysterious crowd. Now there was only the dance itself.

It twisted in the air like a living thing. But there was a space in it, moving around. It was where she should be, she knew it. Miss Treason had said no, but that had been a long time ago and how could Miss Treason understand? What could she know? When did *she* last dance? The dance was in Tiffany's bones now, calling to her. Six dancers were not enough!

She ran forward and jumped into the dance.

The eyes of the dancing men glared at her as she

skipped and danced between them, always being where they weren't. The drums had her feet, and they went where the beat sent them.

And then . . .

. . . there was someone else there.

It was like the feeling of someone behind her – but it was also the feeling of someone in front of her, and beside her, and above her, and below her, all at once.

The dancers froze, but the world spun. The men were just black shadows, darker outlines in the darkness. The drumbeats stopped and there was one long moment as Tiffany turned gently and silently, arms out, feet not touching the ground, her face turned towards stars that were as cold as ice and sharp as needles. It felt . . . wonderful.

A voice said: 'Who Are You?' It had an echo, or perhaps two people had said it at almost the same time.

The beat came back, suddenly, and six men crashed into her.

A few hours later, in the small town of Dogbend, down on the plains, the citizens threw a witch in the river, with her arms and legs tied together.

This sort of thing never happened in the mountains, where witches had respect, but down on the wide plains there were still people dumb enough to believe the nastier stories. Besides, there wasn't much to do in the evenings.

However, it probably wasn't often that the witch was given a cup of tea and some biscuits before her ducking.

It had happened here because the people of Dogbend Did It By The Book.

The book was called: *Magavenatio Obtusis.**

The townspeople didn't know how the book had arrived. It had just turned up one day, on a shelf in one of the shops.

They knew how to read, of course. You had to have a certain amount of reading and writing to get on in the world, even in Dogbend. But they didn't trust books much, or the kind of people who read them.

This one, though, was a book on how to deal with witches. It looked pretty authoritative, too, without too many long (and therefore untrustworthy) words, like 'marmalade'. At last, they told one another, this is what we need. This is a sensible book. OK, it isn't what you'd expect, but remember that witch last year? We ducked her in the river and then tried to burn her alive? Only she was too soggy, and got away? Let's not go through that again!

They paid particular attention to this bit:

> It is very important, having caught your witch, not to harm her in any way (yet!). On no account set fire to her! This is an error beginners often fall into. It just makes them

* Er . . . *Witch-hunting for Dumb People.*

mad and they come back even stronger. As everyone knows, the other way to get rid of a witch is to throw her into a river or pond.

This is the best plan:

First, imprison her overnight in a moderately warm room and give her as much soup as she asks for. Carrot and lentil might do, but for best results we recommend leek and potato made with a good beef stock. This has been proven to seriously harm her magical powers. Do not give her tomato soup: it will make her very powerful.

To be on the safe side, put a silver coin in each of her boots. She will not be able to pull them out because they will burn her fingers.

Provide her with warm blankets and a pillow. This will trick her into going to sleep. Lock the door and see that no one enters.

About one hour before dawn, go into the room. Now, you might think the way to do this would be to rush in shouting. NOTHING COULD BE FURTHER FROM THE TRUTH. Tiptoe in gently, leave a cup of tea by the sleeping witch, tiptoe back to the doorway and cough quietly. This is important. If awakened suddenly, she could get very nasty indeed.

Some authorities recommend a chocolate biscuit with the tea; others say that a ginger biscuit will be enough. If you value your life, do not give her a plain biscuit, because sparks will fly out of her ears. When she awakes, recite this powerful mystic rune, which will stop her turning into a swarm of bees and flying away:

ITI SAPIT EYI MA NASS

When she has finished the tea and biscuits, tie her hands and feet with rope using No. 1 Bosun's knots and throw her in the water. IMPORTANT SAFETY NOTE: do this before it starts getting light. Do not stay to watch!

Of course, this time some people did. And what they saw was the witch sinking and not coming up again, while her wicked pointy hat floated away. Then they went home for breakfast.

In this particular river, nothing much happened for several minutes more. Then the pointy hat started to move towards a thick patch of reeds. It stopped there, and rose very slowly. A pair of eyes peered out from underneath the brim . . .

When she was sure that there was no one about, Miss Perspicacia Tick, teacher and witch-finder, crawled up the bank on her stomach and then legged it away at high speed into the woods just as the sun came up. She'd left a bag with a clean dress and some fresh underwear stuck in a badger's sett, along with a box of matches (she never carried matches in her pocket if there was a danger of being caught, in case it gave people ideas).

Well, she thought, as she dried out in front of a fire, things could have been worse. Thank goodness the village still had someone left who could read, or else she would have been in a pretty pickle. Maybe it was a good idea that she'd had the book printed in big letters.

It was in fact Miss Tick who had written *Witch-hunting for Dumb People*, and she made sure that copies of it found their way into those areas where people still believed that witches should be burned or drowned.

Since the only witch ever likely to pass through these days was Miss Tick herself, it meant that if things did go wrong she'd get a good night's sleep and a decent meal before being thrown into the water. The water was no problem at all to Miss Tick, who had been to the Quirm College for Young Ladies, where you had to have an icy dip every morning to build Moral Fibre. And a No. 1 Bosun's knot was very easy to undo with your teeth, even underwater.

Oh, yes, she thought, as she emptied her boots, and she'd got two silver sixpences, too. Really, the people of the village of Dogbend were getting very stupid indeed. Of course, that's what happened when you got rid of your witches. A witch was just someone who knew a bit more than you did. That's what the name meant. And some people didn't like anyone who knew more than they did, so these days the wandering teachers and the travelling librarians steered clear of the place. The way things were going, if the people of Dogbend wanted to throw stones at anyone who knew more than them, they'd soon have to throw them at the pigs.

The place was a mess. Unfortunately, there was a girl aged eight there who was definitely showing promise, and Miss Tick dropped in sometimes to keep an eye on her. Not as a witch, obviously, because although she liked a cold dip in the morning, you could have too much of a good thing. She disguised herself as a humble apple-seller, or a fortune-teller. (Witches don't usually do fortune-telling, because if they did they'd be too good at it. People don't want to know what's really going to happen, only that it's going to be nice. But witches don't add sugar.)

Unfortunately the spring on Miss Tick's stealth hat had gone wrong while she was walking down the main street and the point had popped up. Even Miss Tick hadn't been able to talk her way out of that one. Oh well, she'd have to make other arrangements now. Witch-finding was always dangerous. You had to do it, though. A witch growing up all alone was a sad and dangerous child . . .

She stopped, and stared at the fire. Why had she just thought about Tiffany Aching? Why now?

Working quickly, she emptied her pockets and started a shamble.

Shambles worked. That was about all you could say about them for certain. You made them out of some string and a couple of sticks and anything you had in your pocket at the time. They were a witch's equivalent of those knives with fifteen blades and three screwdrivers and a tiny magnifying glass and a thing for extracting earwax from chickens.

You couldn't even say precisely what they did,

although Miss Tick thought they were a way of knowing what things the hidden bits of your own mind
somehow knew. You had to make a shamble from
scratch every time, and only from things in your
pockets. There was no harm in having interesting
things in your pockets, though, just in case.

After less than a minute Miss Tick had crafted a
shamble, out of:

> One twelve-inch ruler
> One bootlace
> One piece of second-hand string
> Some black cotton
> One pencil
> One pencil-sharpener
> One small stone with a hole in it
> One matchbox containing a mealworm called
>   Roger, along with a scrap of bread for him to
>   eat, because every shamble must contain
>   something living
> About half a packet of Mrs Sheergold's
>   Lubricated Throat Lozenges
> A button

It looked like a cat's cradle, or maybe the tangled
strings of a very strange puppet.

Miss Tick stared at it, waiting for it to read her. Then
the ruler swung round, the throat sweets exploded in
a little cloud of red dust, the pencil shot away and

stuck in Miss Tick's hat and the ruler was covered in frost.

That was not supposed to happen.

Miss Treason sat downstairs in her cottage and watched Tiffany sleeping in the low bedroom above her. She did this through a mouse, which was sitting on the tarnished brass bedstead. Beyond the grey windows (Miss Treason hadn't bothered to clean them for fifty-three years and Tiffany hadn't been able to shift all the dirt), the wind howled among the trees, even though it was mid-afternoon.

He's looking for her, she thought, as she fed a piece of ancient cheese to another mouse on her lap. But he won't find her. She is safe here.

Then the mouse looked up from the cheese. It had heard something.

'I told yez! She's here somewhere, fellas!'

'I dinnae see why we cannae just talk tae the ol' hag. We get along fine wi' hags.'

'Mebbe, but this one is a terrrrrible piece o' work. They say she's got a fearsome demon in her tattie cellar.'

Miss Treason looked puzzled. 'Them?' she whispered to herself. The voices were coming from beneath the floor. She sent the mouse scurrying across the boards and into a hole.

'I dinnae want to disappoint ye, but we's in a cellar right here, and it's full o' tatties.'

After a while a voice said: 'So where izzit?'

'Mebbe it's got the day off?'

'What's a demon need a day off for?'

'Tae gae an' see its ol' mam an' dad, mebbe?'

'Oh, aye? Demons have mams, do they?'

'Crivens! Will ye lot stop arguin'! She might hear us!'

'Nae, she's blind as a bat and deaf as a post, they say.'

Mice have very good hearing. Miss Treason smiled as the hurrying mouse came out in the rough old stone wall of the cellar, near the floor.

She looked though its eyes. It could see quite well in the gloom, too.

A small group of little men were creeping across the floor. Their skins were blue and covered with tattoos and dirt. They all wore very grubby kilts, and each one had a sword, as big as he was, strapped to his back. And they all had red hair, a real orange-red, with scruffy pigtails. One of them wore a rabbit skull as a helmet. It would have been more scary if it hadn't kept sliding over his eyes.

In the room above, Miss Treason smiled again. So they'd heard of Miss Treason? But they hadn't heard enough.

As the four little men squirmed through an old rat hole to get out of the cellar, they were watched by two more mice, three different beetles and a moth. They tiptoed carefully across the floor, past an old witch who was clearly asleep – right up until she banged on the arms of her chair and bellowed:

'*Jings! I see you there, ye wee schemies!*'

The Feegles reacted in instant panic, colliding with one another in shock and awe.

'I dinnae remember tellin' ye tae move!' shouted Miss Treason. Grinning horribly.

'Oh, waily, waily, waily! She's got the knowin' o' the speakin'!' someone sobbed.

'Ye're Nac Mac Feegles, right? But I didnae ken the clan markin's. Calm doon, I ain't gonna deep-fry ye. You! What's your name?'

'Ah'm Rob Anybody, Big Man o' the Chalk Hill clan,' said the one with the rabbit-skull helmet. 'And—'

'Aye? Big Man, are ye? Then ye'll do me the courtesy an' tak' off yon bony bonnet 'ere ye speak tae me!' said Miss Treason, enjoying herself no end. 'An' stannit up straight! I will have nae slouchin' in this hoose!'

Instantly, all four Feegles stood to rigid attention.

'Right!' said Miss Treason. 'An' who are the rest o' yez?'

'This is my brother Daft Wullie, miss,' said Rob Anybody, shaking the shoulder of the Feegle who was an instant wailer. He was staring in horror at Enochi and Athootita.

'An' the other two of you . . . I mean, twa o' ye?' said Miss Treason. 'You, there. I mean ye. Ye have the mousepipes. Are ye a gonnagle?'

'Aye, mistress,' said a Feegle who looked neater and cleaner than the others, although it had to be said that there were things living under old logs that were cleaner and neater than Daft Wullie.

'And your name is . . . ?'

'Billy Bigchin, mistress.'

'You're staring hard at me, Billy Bigchin,' said Miss Treason. 'Are ye afraid?'

'No, mistress, I wuz admirin' ye. I' does my heart good tae see a witch so . . . witchy.'

'It does, does it?' said Miss Treason suspiciously. 'Are ye sure ye're no' afraid o' me, Mr Billy Bigchin?'

'No, mistress. But I will be if it makes ye happy,' said Billy carefully.

'Hah!' said Miss Treason. 'Well, I see we have— hae a clever one here. Who is your big friend, Mr Billy?'

Billy elbowed Big Yan in the ribs. Despite his size, which for a Feegle was huge, he was looking very nervous. Like a lot of people with big muscles, he got edgy about people who were strong in other ways.

'He's Big Yan, mistress,' Billy Bigchin supplied, while Big Yan stared at his feet.

'I see he's got a necklace o' big teeth,' said Miss Treason. 'Human teeth?'

'Aye, mistress. Four, mistress. One for every man he's knocked out.'

'Are you talking about human men?' asked Miss Treason in astonishment

'Aye, mistress,' said Billy Bigchin. 'Mostly he drops on 'em heid first oot o' a tree. He has a verrae tough heid,' he added, in case this wasn't clear.

Miss Treason sat back. 'And now you will kindly explain why ye were creepin' aboot here in my hoose,' she said. 'Come along, now!'

There was a tiny, tiny pause before Rob Anybody said happily, 'Oh, weel, that's easy. We wuz huntin' the haggis.'

'No, you weren't,' said Miss Treason sharply, 'because a haggis is a pudding of sheep's offal and meat, well spiced and cooked in a sheep's stomach.'

'Ah, that is only when ye cannae find the real thing, mistress,' said Rob Anybody carefully. ''Tis no' a patch on the real thing. Oh, a canny beast is the haggis, which makes its burrows in – tattie cellars . . .'

'And that's the truth? You were hunting the haggis? Is it, Daft Wullie?' said Miss Treason, her voice suddenly sharp. All eyes, including a pair belonging to an earwig, turned to the luckless Wullie.

'Er . . . aye . . . oooh . . . aarg . . . waily, waily, waily!' moaned Daft Wullie, and dropped to his knees. 'Please dinnae do somethin' horrible tae me, mistress!' he begged. 'Yon earwiggy is givin' me a dreadful look!'

'Very well, we shall start again,' said Miss Treason. She reached up and tore off her blindfold. The Feegles stepped back as she touched the skulls on either side of her.

'I do not need eyes to smell a lie when it comes

calling,' she said. 'Tell me why you are here. Tell me
. . . again.'

Rob Anybody hesitated for a moment. This was, in
the circumstances, very brave of him. Then he said:
' 'Tis aboot the big wee hag, mistress, we came.'

'The big wee— Oh, you mean Tiffany?'

'Aye!'

'We is under one o' them big birds,' said Daft Wullie,
keeping his eyes averted from the witch's blind stare.

'He means a geas, miss,' said Rob Anybody, glaring
at his brother. 'It's like a—'

'– a tremendous obligation that you cannot disobey,'
said Miss Treason. 'I ken what a geas is. But why?'

Miss Treason had heard a lot of things in 113 years,
but now she listened in astonishment to a story about
a human girl who had, for a few days at least, been the
kelda of a clan of Nac Mac Feegles. And if you were
their kelda, even for a few days, they'd watch over
you . . . for ever.

'An' she's the hag o' our hills,' said Billy Bigchin.
'She cares for them, keeps them safe. But . . .'

He hesitated, and Rob Anybody continued: 'Our
kelda is havin' dreams. Dreams o' the future. Dreams
o' the hills all froze an' everyone deid an' the big wee
hag wearin' a crown o' ice!'

'My goodness!'

'Aye, an' there wuz more!' said Billy, throwing out
his arms. 'She saw a green tree growin' in a land o' ice!
She saw a ring o' iron! She saw a man with a nail in

his heart! She saw a plague of chickens an' a cheese that walks like a man!'

There was silence, and then Miss Treason said: 'The first two, the tree and the ring, no problem there, good occult . . . symbolism. The nail, too, very metaphorical. I'm a bit doubtful about the cheese – could she mean Horace? – and the chickens . . . I'm not sure you can have a plague of chickens, can you?'

'Jeannie wuz very firm about them,' said Rob Anybody. 'She's dreamed many strange and worryin' things, so we thought we might just see how the big wee hag wuz gettin' along.'

'And so the four o' yez came all the way?' said Miss Treason.

'Oh, we brought a few o' the lads,' said Rob. 'We didnae want to bring 'em all at once, ye ken. They're oot in the woods.'

'How many of them are there, then?'

'Oh, aboot five hundred, gi' or tak' a spog.'

Miss Treason's various eyes stared at him. Rob Anybody stared back with an expression of ferocious honesty, and did not flinch.

'This seems an honourable enterprise,' she said. 'Why start by lying?'

'Oh, the lie wuz goin' tae be a lot more interestin',' said Rob Anybody.

'The truth of the matter seems quite interesting to *me*,' said Miss Treason.

'Mebbe, but I wuz plannin' on puttin' in giants an'

pirates an' magic weasels,' Rob declared. 'Real value for money!'

'Oh well,' said Miss Treason. 'When Miss Tick brought Tiffany to me she did say she was guarded by strange powers.'

'Aye,' said Rob Anybody proudly. 'That'd be us, right enough.'

'But Miss Tick is a rather bossy woman,' said Miss Treason. 'I am sorry to say I didn't listen much to what she said. She is always telling me that these gels are really keen to learn, but mostly they are just flibbertigibbets who want to be a witch to impress the young men, and they run away after a few days. This one doesn't, oh no! She runs towards things! Did you know she tried to dance with the wintersmith!'

'Aye. We ken. We were there,' said Rob Anybody.

'You were?'

'Aye. We followed yez.'

'No one saw you there. I would have known if they did,' Miss Treason said.

'Aye? Weel, we're good at no one seein' us,' said Rob Anybody, smiling. 'It's amazin', the people who dinnae see us.'

'She actually tried to dance with the wintersmith,' Miss Treason repeated. 'I told her not to.'

'Ach, people're always telling us no' tae do things,' said Rob Anybody. 'That's how we ken what's the most interestin' things tae do!'

Miss Treason stared at him with the eyes of one mouse, two ravens, several moths and an earwig.

'Indeed,' she said, and sighed. 'Yes. The trouble with being this old, you know, is that being young is so far away from me now that it seems sometimes that it happened to someone else. A long life is not what it's cracked up to be, that is a fact. It—'

'The wintersmith is seekin' for the big wee hag, mistress,' said Rob Anybody. 'We saw her dancin' wi' the wintersmith. Now he is seekin' her. We can hear him in the howl o' the wind.'

'I know,' said Miss Treason. She stopped, and listened for a moment. 'The wind has dropped,' she stated. 'He's *found* her.'

She snatched up her walking-sticks and scuttled towards the stairs, going up them with amazing speed. Feegles swarmed past her into the bedroom, where Tiffany lay on a narrow bed.

A candle burned in a saucer at each corner of the room.

'But *how* has he found her?' Miss Treason demanded. 'I had her hidden! You, blue men, fetch wood now!' She glared at them. 'I said, fetch—'

She heard a couple of thumps. Dust was settling. The Feegles were watching Miss Treason expectantly. And sticks, a lot of sticks, were piled in the tiny bedroom fireplace.

'Ye did well,' she said. 'An' not tae soon!'

Snowflakes were drifting down the chimney.

Miss Treason crossed her walking-sticks in front of her and stamped her foot hard.

'Wood burn, fire blaze!' she shouted. The wood in the grate burst into flame. But now frost was forming on the window, ferny white tendrils snapping across the glass with a crackling sound.

'I am not putting up with this at my age!' said the witch.

Tiffany opened her eyes, and said: 'What's happening?'

CHAPTER 3

THE SECRET OF BOFFO

It is not good, being in a sandwich of bewildered dancers. They were heavy men. Tiffany was Aching all over. She was covered in bruises, including one the shape of a boot that she wasn't going to show to *anyone*.

Feegles filled every flat surface in Miss Treason's weaving room. She was working at her loom with her back to the room, because she said that this helped her think, but since she was Miss Treason this didn't matter much. There were plenty of eyes and ears she could use after all. The fire burned hot, and there were candles everywhere. Black ones, of course.

Tiffany was angry. Miss Treason hadn't shouted, hadn't even raised her voice. She'd just sighed and said, 'Foolish child,' which was a whole lot worse, mostly because that's just what Tiffany knew she'd been. One of the dancers had helped bring her back to the cottage. She couldn't remember anything about that at all.

A witch didn't do things because they seemed a good idea at the time! That was practically cackling! You had to deal every day with people who were foolish and lazy and untruthful and downright unpleasant, and you could certainly end up thinking that the world would be considerably improved if you gave them a slap. But you didn't because, as Miss Tick had once explained: a) it would only make the world a better place for a very short time; b) it would then make the world a slightly worse place; and c) you're not supposed to be as stupid as they are.

Her feet had moved, and she'd listened to them. She ought to have been listening to her head. Now she had to sit by Miss Treason's fire with a tin hot water-bottle on her lap and a shawl around her.

'So the wintersmith is a kind of god?' she said.

'That kind o' thing, yes,' said Billy Bigchin. 'But not the prayin'-to kinda god. He just . . . makes winters. It's his job, ye ken.'

'He's an elemental,' said Miss Treason from her loom.

'Aye,' said Rob Anybody. 'Gods, elementals, demons, spirits . . . sometimes it's hard to tell 'em apart wi'oot a map.'

'And the dance is to welcome winter?' said Tiffany. 'That doesn't make sense! The Morris dance is to welcome the coming of the summer, yes, that's—'

'Are you an infant?' said Miss Treason. 'The year is round! The wheel of the world must spin! That is why

70

up here they dance the Dark Morris, to balance it. They welcome the winter because of the new summer deep inside it!'

Clack-clack went the loom. Miss Treason was weaving a new cloth, of brown wool.

'Well, all right,' said Tiffany. 'We welcomed it . . . him. That doesn't mean he's supposed to come looking for me!'

'Why did you join the dance?' Miss Treason demanded.

'Er . . . There was a space, and—'

'Yes. A space. A space not intended for you. Not for you, foolish child. You danced with him, and now he wants to meet such a bold girl. I have never heard of such a thing! I want you to fetch the third book from the right on the second shelf from the top of my bookcase.' She handed Tiffany a heavy black key. 'Can you manage to do even that?'

Witches didn't need to slap the stupid, not when they had a sharp tongue that was always ready.

Miss Treason also had several shelves of books, which was unusual for one of the older witches. It was high up, the books looked big and heavy, and up until now Miss Treason had forbidden Tiffany to dust them, let alone unlock the big black iron band that secured them to the shelves. People who came here always gave them a nervous look. Books were dangerous.

Tiffany unlocked the bands and wiped away the dust. Ah . . . the books were, like Miss Treason, not everything they seemed. They looked like magic books, but they had names like *An Encyclopaedia of Soup*. There was a dictionary. Next to it, the book Miss Treason had asked for was covered in cobwebs.

Still blushing with shame and anger, she got the book down, fighting to get it free of the webs. Some of them went *pling!* as they snapped, and dust fell off the top of the pages. When she opened it, it smelled old and parchmenty, like Miss Treason. The title, in gold lettering that had almost rubbed away, was *Chaffinch's Ancient and Classical Mythology*. It was full of bookmarks.

'Pages eighteen and nineteen,' said Miss Treason, her head not moving. Tiffany turned to them.

'The Dacne of the Sneasos?' she said. 'Is that supposed to be the Dance of the Seasons?'

'Regrettably, the artist Don Weizen de Yoyo, whose famous masterpiece that was, did not have the same talent with letters as he had with painting,' said Miss Treason. 'They worried him, for some reason. I notice you mention the words before the pictures. You are a bookish child.'

The pictures were . . . strange. They showed two figures. Tiffany hadn't seen fancy dress. There wasn't the money at home for that sort of thing. But she'd read about it and this was pretty much what she'd imagined.

The page showed a man and a woman – or, at least, things that looked like a man and a woman. The woman was labelled 'Summer' and was tall and blonde and beautiful, and therefore to the short brown-haired Tiffany a figure of immediate distrust. She was carrying what looked like a big basket shaped like a shell or horn, which was full of fruit.

The man, 'Winter', was old and bent and grey. Icicles glittered on his beard.

'Ach, that's wha' the wintersmith would look like, sure enough,' said Rob Anybody, strolling across the page. 'Ol' Frosty.'

'Him?' said Tiffany. '*That's* the wintersmith? He looks a hundred years old!'

'A youngster, eh?' said Miss Treason nastily.

'Dinnae let him kiss ye, or yer nose might turn blue and fall off!' said Daft Wullie cheerfully.

'Daft Wullie, don't you dare say things like that!' said Tiffany.

'I wuz just tryin' to lighten the mood, ye ken,' said Wullie, looking sheepish.

'That's an artist's impression, of course,' said Miss Treason.

'What does that mean?' said Tiffany, staring at the picture. *It was wrong.* She knew it. This wasn't what he was like at all . . .

'It means he made it up,' said Billy Bigchin. 'He wouldnae ha' seen him, noo, would he? No one's seen the wintersmith.'

'Yet!' said Daft Wullie.

'Wullie,' said Rob Anybody, turning to his brother,

'you ken I told ye aboot makin' tactful remarks?'

'Aye, Rob, I ken weel,' said Wullie obediently.

'What ye just said wuz not one o' them,' said Rob.

Wullie hung his head. 'Sorry, Rob.'

Tiffany clenched her fists. 'I didn't mean all this to happen!'

Miss Treason turned her chair and removed her grey bandage with some solemnity.

'Then what did you mean? Will you tell me? Did you dance out of youth's inclination to disobey old age? To mean is to think. Did you think at all? Others have joined in the dance before now. Children, drunkards, youths for a silly bet . . . nothing happened. The spring and autumn dances are . . . just an old tradition, most people would say. Just a way of marking when ice and fire exchange their dominion over the world. Some of us think we know better. We think something happens. For you, the dance became real, and something *has* happened. And now the wintersmith is seeking you.'

'Why?' Tiffany managed

'I don't know. When you were dancing, did you see anything? Hear anything?'

How could you describe the feeling of being everywhere and everything? Tiffany wondered. She didn't try.

'I . . . thought I heard a voice, or maybe two voices,' she mumbled. 'Er, they asked me who I was.'

'Int-ter-rest-ting,' said Miss Treason. 'Two voices? I

will consider the implications. What I can't understand is how he found you. I will think about that. In
the meantime, I expect it would be a good idea to wear
warm clothing.'

'Aye,' said Rob Anybody, 'the wintersmith cannae
abide the heat. Oh, I'd be forgettin' my ain head next!
We brought a wee letter from that hollow tree down
in the forest. Gi' it to the big wee hag, Wullie. We
picked it up on the way past.'

'A letter?' said Tiffany, as the loom clacked behind
her and Daft Wullie began to pull a grubby rolled-up
envelope from his spog.

'It's from that wee heap o' jobbies at the castle back
hame,' Rob went on, as his brother hauled. 'He says
he bides fine and hopes ye do likewise, an' he's lookin'
forward to you bein' back hame soon, an' there's lots
o' stuff about how the ships are doin' an' suchlike, no'
verrae interesting in ma opinion, an' he's writ
S.W.A.L.K. on the bottom, but we havenae worked
out what that means yet.'

'You read my letter?' said Tiffany, in horror.

'Oh, aye,' said Rob with pride. 'Nae problem. Billy
Bigchin here gave me a wee hint with some o' the
longer words, but it was mostly me, aye.' He beamed,
but the grin faded as he watched Tiffany's expression.
'Ach, I ken ye're a wee bitty upset that we opened yon
envelope thingy,' he explained. 'But that's OK, 'cuz
we glued it up again wi' slug. Ye wouldnae ever know
it'd been read.'

He coughed, because Tiffany was still glaring at him. All women were a bit scary to the Feegles, and witches were the worst. At last, when he was really nervous, Tiffany said: 'How did you know where that letter would be?'

She glanced sideways at Daft Wullie. He was chewing the edge of his kilt. He only ever did this when he was frightened.

'Er . . . would you accept a wee bitty lie?' Rob said.

'No!'

'It's interestin'. There's dragons an' unicorns in it—'

'No. I want the truth!'

'Ach, it's so boring. We go to the Baron's castle an' read the letters you send him, an' ye said the postman knows to leave letters tae you in the hollow tree by the waterfall,' said Rob.

If the wintersmith had got into the cottage, the air couldn't have got any colder.

'He keeps the letters fra' you in a box under his—' Rob began, and then shut his eyes as Tiffany's patience parted with a twang even louder than Miss Treason's strange cobwebs.

'Don't you know it's wrong to read other people's letters?' she demanded.

'Er . . .' Rob Anybody began.

'And you broke into the Baron's cast—'

'Ah, ah, ah, no, no, no!' said Rob, jumping up and down. 'Ye cannae get us on that one! We just walked

in through one of them little wee slits for the firin' o'
the arrows—'

'And then you read my personal letters sent
personally to Roland?' said Tiffany. 'They were
personal!'

'Oh, aye,' said Rob Anybody. 'But dinnae fash
yersel', we willnae tell anyone what was in 'em.'

'We ne'er tell a soul what's in your diary, after all,'
said Daft Wullie. 'Not e'en the bits wi' the flowers ye
draw aroound them.'

Miss Treason is grinning to herself behind me,
Tiffany thought. I just know she is. But she'd run out
of nasty tones of voice. You did that after talking to the
Feegles for any length of time.

You were their Kelda, her Second Thoughts
reminded her. They think they have a solemn duty to
protect you. It doesn't matter what you think. They're
going to make your life sooo complicated.

'Don't read my letters,' she said, 'and don't read my
diary, either.'

'OK,' said Rob Anybody.

'Promise?'

'Oh, aye.'

'But you promised last time!'

'Oh, aye.'

'Cross your heart and hope to die?'

'Oh, aye, nae problemo.'

'And that's the promise of an untrustworthy, lying,
stealing Feegle, is it?' said Miss Treason. 'Because ye

believe ye're deid already, do ye no'? That's what ye people think, right?'

'Oh, aye, mistress,' said Rob Anybody. 'Thank ye for drawing my attention tae that.'

'In fact, Rob Anybody, ye ha' nae intention o' keepin' any promise at all!'

'Aye, mistress,' said Rob proudly. 'Not puir wee weak promises like that. Becuz, ye see, 'tis oor solemn destiny to guard the big wee hag. We mus' lay doon oor lives for her if it comes to it.'

'How can ye do that when ye're deid already?' said Miss Treason sharply.

'That's a bit o' a puzzler, right enough,' said Rob, 'so probably we'll lay down the lives o' any scunners who do wrong by her.'

Tiffany gave up, and sighed. 'I'm almost thirteen,' she said. 'I can look after myself.'

'Hark at Miss Self-Reliant,' said Miss Treason, but not in a particularly nasty way. 'Against the wintersmith?'

'What does he want?' said Tiffany.

'I told you. Perhaps he wants to find out what kind of girl was so forward as to dance with him?' said Miss Treason.

'It was my feet! I said I didn't mean to!'

Miss Treason turned round in her chair. How many eyes is she using? Tiffany's Second Thoughts wondered. The Feegles? The ravens? The mice? All of them? How many of me is she seeing? Is she using the insects, with dozens of glittery eyes?

'Oh, that's all right then,' said Miss Treason. 'Once again, you didn't mean it. A witch takes responsibility! Have you learned *nothing*, child?'

Child. That was a terrible thing to say to anyone who was almost thirteen. Tiffany felt herself going red again. The horrible hotness spread inside her head.

That's why she walked across the room, opened the front door and stepped outside.

A fluffy snow was falling, very gently. When Tiffany looked into the pale grey sky she saw the flakes drifting down in soft, feathery clusters; it was the kind of snow that people back home on the Chalk called 'Granny Aching shearing her sheep'.

Tiffany felt them melting on her hair as she walked away from the cottage. Miss Treason was shouting from the doorway but she walked on, letting the melting snow cool her blushes.

Of course this is stupid, she told herself. But being a witch is stupid. Why do we do it? It's hard work for not much reward. What's a good day for Miss Treason? When someone brings her a second-hand pair of old boots that fit properly! What does she know about anything?

Where is the wintersmith, then? Is he here? I've only got Miss Treason's word for it! That and a made-up picture in a book!

'Wintersmith!' she shouted.

You could hear the snow falling. It made a strange little noise, like a faint, cold sizzle.

'Wintersmith!'

There was no reply.

Well, what had she expected? A big booming voice? Mr Spiky the icicle man? There was nothing but the softness of white snow falling patiently among dark trees.

She felt a bit silly now, but satisfied, too. This was what a witch did! She faced what she was afraid of, and then it held no more fear! She was good at this!

She turned, and saw the wintersmith.

Remember this, said her Third Thoughts, cutting in. Every little detail is important.

The wintersmith was . . .

. . . nothing. But the snow outlined him. It flowed round him in lines, as if travelling on an invisible skin. He was just shape, and nothing more, except perhaps for two tiny pale purple-grey dots in the air, where you might expect to find eyes.

Tiffany stood still, her mind frozen, her body waiting to be told what to do.

The hand made of falling snow was reaching towards her now, but very slowly, as you would reach out towards an animal you do not want to frighten. There was . . . something, some strange sense of things unsaid because there was no voice to say them, a sense of striving, as if the thing was putting heart and soul into this moment, even if it did not know the meaning of heart or soul.

The hand stopped about a foot away from her. It was

formed into a fist, and now it turned over and the fingers opened.

Something gleamed. It was the white horse, made of silver, on a fine silver chain.

Tiffany's hand flew to her throat. But she'd had it on last night! Before she went . . . to . . . watch . . . the . . . dance . . .

It must have come off! And he'd found it!

That's interesting, said her Third Thoughts, that busied themselves with the world in their own way. You can't see what's hidden inside an invisible fist. How does that work? And why are those little purple-grey blurs in the air where you'd expect to find eyes? Why aren't *they* invisible?

That's Third Thoughts for you. When a huge rock is going to land on your head, they're the thoughts that think: Is that an igneous rock, such as granite, or is it sandstone?

That part of Tiffany's brain that was a little less precise at the moment watched the silver horse dangle on its chain.

Her First Thought was: Take it.

Her Second Thought was: Don't take it. It's a trap.

Her Third Thought was: Really don't take it. It will be colder than you can imagine.

And then the rest of her over-ruled the thoughts entirely and said: Take it. It's part of who you are. Take it. When you hold it you think of home. Take it!

She held out her right hand.

The horse dropped into it. Instinctively she closed her fingers over it. It was indeed colder than she could have imagined, and it burned.

She screamed. The wintersmith's snowy outline became a flurry of flakes. The snow around her feet erupted with a cry of 'Crivens!' as a mass of Feegles grabbed her feet and carried her, upright, across the clearing and back in through the cottage's doorway.

Tiffany forced her hand open and, with trembling fingers, pulled the silver horse off her palm. It left a perfect print, a white horse on pink flesh. It wasn't a burn, it was a . . . freeze.

Miss Treason's chair rumbled around on its wheels.

'Come here, child,' she ordered.

Still clasping her hand, trying to force back the tears, Tiffany walked over to her.

'Stand right here by my chair, this instant!'

Tiffany did so. This was no time to be disobedient.

'I wish to look in your ear,' said Miss Treason. 'Brush your hair aside.'

Tiffany held back her hair, and winced when she heard the tickle of mouse whiskers. Then the creature was taken away.

'Ah, I am surprised,' said Miss Treason. 'I can see nothing.'

'Er . . . what were you expecting to see?' Tiffany ventured.

'Daylight!' snapped Miss Treason, so loudly that the mouse scuttled away. 'Have you no brains at all, child?'

'Ah dunno if anyone is interested,' said Rob Anybody, 'but I think yon wintersmith has offski'd. An' it's stopped snowin'.'

No one was listening. When witches row, they concentrate.

'It was mine!' Grabbing up the horse and chain again.

'A trinket!'

'No!'

'O' course, this may not be the best time tae tell ye . . .' Rob went on miserably.

'You think you need it to be a witch?'

'Yes!'

'A witch needs no devices!'

'You've used shambles!'

'Used, yes! Don't need. Not *need*!'

'Ah mean, it's quite meltin' awa—' Rob said, smiling nervously.

Anger grabbed Tiffany's tongue. How dare this stupid old crone talk about not needing things!

'Boffo!' she shouted. 'Boffo, Boffo, Boffo!'

Silence slammed down. After a while Miss Treason looked past Tiffany and said: 'You wee Feegle schemies! Get oot o' here right noo! Ah'll ken it if ye don't! This is hag business!'

The room filled with a sort of whooshing noise and the door to the kitchen slammed shut.

'So,' said Miss Treason, 'you know about Boffo, do you?'

'Yes,' said Tiffany, breathing heavily. 'I do.'

'Very well. And have you told anyone—?' Miss Treason paused and raised a finger to her lips. Then she banged a stick on the floor. 'Ah said get oot, ye scunners! Off intae the woods wi' ye! Check that he's really gang awa'! I'll see yer guilt through yer own een if ye defy me!'

From below there was the sound of a lot of potatoes rumbling as the Feegles scrambled out through the little ventilation grille.

'Now they've gone,' said Miss Treason. 'They'll stay gone, too. Boffo will see to that.'

Somehow, in the space of a few seconds, Miss Treason had become more human and a lot less scary. Well . . . slightly less scary.

'How did you find out? Did you go looking for it? Did you go prowling and rummaging?' said Miss Treason.

'No! I'm not like that! I found out by accident one day when you were having a nap!' Tiffany rubbed her hand.

'Does that hurt a lot?' said Miss Treason, leaning forwards. She might be blind, but – like all the senior witches who knew what they were doing – she noticed *everything*.

'No, not now. It did, though. Look, I—'

'Then you will learn to listen! Do you think the wintersmith has gone?'

'He just seemed to vanish— I mean, vanish even

more. I think he just wanted to give me back my necklace.'

'Do you think that is the sort of thing the spirit of winter, who commands the blizzard and the frost, would really do?'

'I don't know, Miss Treason! He's the only one I've met!'

'You danced with him.'

'I didn't know I was going to!'

'Nevertheless.'

Tiffany waited, and then said: 'Nevertheless what?'

'Just general neverthelessness. The little horse led him to you . . . But he's not here now, you're right about that. I'd know if he was.'

Tiffany walked up to the front door, hesitated for just a moment, and then opened it and went out into the clearing. There was a bit of snow here and there, but the day was turning into just another one of those grey-skied winter days.

I'd know if he was, too, she thought. And he isn't. And her Second Thoughts said: Oh? How do you know?

'We've both touched the horse,' she said, under her breath.

She looked around at the empty branches and the sleeping trees, fiddling with the silver chain in her hand. The forests were curling in on themselves, ready for the winter.

He's out there, but not close. He must be very busy, with a whole winter to make . . .

She said, 'Thank you!' automatically, because her mother had always said that politeness cost nothing, and went back inside. It was very hot inside now, but Miss Treason always had a huge log pile . . . built by the Secret of Boffo. The local woodcutters always kept the pile high. A chilly witch might get nasty.

'I should like a cup of black tea,' said the old woman as Tiffany walked back in, looking thoughtful.

She waited until Tiffany was washing out the cup, then said: 'Have you heard the stories about me, child?' The voice was kindly. There had been shouts, there had been things said that might have been better put, there had been temper and defiance. But they were there together, with nowhere else to go. The quiet voice was a peace offering, and Tiffany was glad of it.

'Er, that you have a demon in the cellar?' Tiffany answered, her mind still full of puzzles. 'And you eat spiders? And get visited by kings and princes? And that any flower planted in your garden blooms black?'

'Oh, do they say so?' said Miss Treason, looking delighted. 'I haven't heard that last one. How nice. And did you hear that I walk around at night in the dark time of the year and reward those who have been good citizens with a purse of silver? But, if they have

86

been bad, I slit open their bellies with my thumbnail like this?'

Tiffany leaped backwards as a wrinkled hand twisted her round and Miss Treason's yellow thumbnail scythed past her stomach. The old woman looked terrifying.

'No! No, I haven't heard that one!' she gasped, pressing up against the sink.

'What? And it was a wonderful story, with real historical antecedents!' said Miss Treason, her vicious scowl becoming a smile. 'And the one about me having a cow's tail?'

'A cow's tail? No!'

'Really? How very vexing,' said Miss Treason, lowering her finger. 'I fear the art of story-telling has got into a pretty bad way in these parts. I really shall have to do something.'

'This is just another kind of boffo, right?' said Tiffany. She wasn't totally sure. Miss Treason had looked pretty scary with that thumbnail. No wonder girls left so quickly.

'Ah, you do have a brain, after all. Of course it is. Boffo, yes. A good name for it. Boffo, indeed. The art of expectations. Show people what they want to see, show 'em what they think should be there. I have a reputation to keep up, after all.'

Boffo, Tiffany thought. Boffo, Boffo, Boffo.

She went over to the skulls, picked one up and read the label underneath, just like she'd done a month ago:

Ghastly Skull No. 1 Price $2.99
The Boffo Novelty and Joke Shop
No 4, Tenth Egg Street, Ankh-Morpork
"If it's a laugh … it's a Boffo!"

'Very lifelike, aren't they,' said Miss Treason, clicking back to her chair, 'if you can say that about a skull, of course! The shop sold a wonderful machine for making spider webs. You poured in this sticky stuff, d'you see, and with practice quite good webs could be made. Can't abide creepy-crawlies, but of course I've got to have the webs. Did you notice the dead flies?'

'Yes,' said Tiffany, glancing up. 'They're currants. I thought you had vegetarian spiders.'

'Well done. Nothing wrong with your eyes, at least. I got my hat from there, too. Wicked Old Witch Number Three, A Must For Scary Parties, I think it was. I've still got their catalogue somewhere, if you're interested.'

'Do all witches buy from Boffo?' said Tiffany.

'Only me, at least around here. Oh, and I believe Old Mistress Breathless over in Two Falls used to buy warts from there.'

'But . . . why?' said Tiffany

'She couldn't grow them. Just couldn't grow them at all, poor woman. Tried everything. Face like a baby's bottom, her whole life.'

'No, I meant, why do you want to seem so' – Tiffany hesitated, and went on – 'awful?'

'I have my reasons,' said Miss Treason.

'But you don't do those things the stories say you do, do you? Kings and princes don't come to consult you, do they?'

'No, but they might do,' said Miss Treason stoutly. 'If they got lost, for example. Oh, I know all about those stories. I made up most of them!'

'You made up stories about *yourself*?'

'Oh, yes. Of course. Why not? I couldn't leave something as important as that to *amateurs*.'

'But people say you can see a man's soul!'

Miss Treason chuckled. 'Yes. Didn't make that one up! But I'll tell you, for some of my parishioners I'd need a magnifying glass! I see what they see, I hear with their ears. I knew their fathers and grandfathers and great-grandfathers. I know the rumours and the secrets and the stories and the truths. And I am Justice to them, and I am fair. Look at me. See me.'

Tiffany looked – and looked past the black cloak and the skulls and the rubber cobwebs and the black flowers and the blindfold and the stories, and saw a little half-deaf and blind old lady.

Boffo made the difference . . . not just the silly party stuff, but Boffo-thinking – the rumours and the stories. Miss Treason had power because they thought she did. It was like the standard witch's hat. But Miss Treason was taking Boffo much, much further.

'A witch needs no devices, Miss Treason,' she said.

'Don't get smart with me, child. Didn't the girl Weatherwax tell you all this? Oh, yes, you don't need a wand or a shamble or even a pointy hat to *be* a witch. But it helps a witch to put on a show! People expect it. They'll believe in you. I didn't get where I am today by wearing a woolly bobble hat and a gingham apron! I look the part. I—'

There was a crash from outside, in the direction of the dairy.

'Our little blue friends?' said Miss Treason, raising her eyebrows.

'No, they're absolutely forbidden to go into any dairy I work in,' Tiffany began, heading for the door. 'Oh dear, I hope it's not Horace . . .'

'I told you he'd be nothing but trouble, did I not?' Miss Treason shouted as she hurried away.

It *was* Horace. He'd squeezed out of his cage again. He could make himself quite runny when he wanted to.

There was a broken butter dish on the floor, but although it had been full of butter there was none there now. There was just a greasy patch.

And, from the darkness under the sink, there came a sort of high-speed grumbling noise, a kind of *mnnamnamnam* . . .

'Oh, you're after butter now, are you, Horace?' said Tiffany, picking up the dairy broom. 'That's practically cannibalism, you know.'

Still, it was better than mice, she had to admit. Finding little piles of mouse bones on the floor was a bit distressing. Even Miss Treason had not been able to work that one out. A mouse she happened to be looking through would be trying to get at the cheeses and then it would all go dark.

That was because Horace was a cheese.

Tiffany knew that Lancre Blue cheeses were always a bit on the lively side, and sometimes had to be nailed down, but . . . well, she was highly skilled at cheese-making, even though she said it herself, and Horace was definitely a champion. The famous blue streaks that gave the variety its wonderful colour were really pretty, although Tiffany wasn't sure they should glow in the dark.

She prodded the shadows with the end of the broom. There was a crack, and when she pulled the stick out again two inches were missing from the end. Then there was a *ptooi!* noise and the missing piece of handle bounced off the wall on the other side of the room.

'No more milk for you, then,' said Tiffany, straightening up, and thought:

The wintersmith came to give me the Horse back. He took the trouble to do that.

Um . . .

That is quite . . . impressive, when you think about it.

I mean, he's got to organize avalanches and gales

and come up with new shapes for snowflakes and everything, but he spared a bit of time just to come and give me my necklace back. Um . . .

And he just stood there.

And then he just vanished – I mean, vanished even more.

Um . . .

She left Horace muttering under the sink and made tea for Miss Treason, who was back at her weaving. Then she quietly went up to her room.

Tiffany's diary was three inches thick. Annagramma, another local trainee witch and one of her friends (more or less), said that she should really call it her Book of Shadows and write it on vellum using one of the special magical inks sold at ZakZak Stronginthearm's Magical Emporium at popular prices – at least, prices that were popular with ZakZak.

Tiffany couldn't afford one. You could only trade witchcraft, you weren't supposed to sell it. Miss Treason didn't mind her selling cheeses, but even so, paper was expensive up here and the wandering pedlars never had very much to sell. They usually had an ounce or two of green copperas, though, which could make a decent ink if you mixed it with crushed oak-galls or green walnut shells.

The diary was now as thick as a brick with extra pages Tiffany had glued in. She'd worked out she could make it last two more years if she wrote small.

On the leather cover she had, with a hot skewer,

drawn the words 'Feegles Keep Out!!' It had never worked. They looked upon that sort of thing as an invitation. She wrote parts of the diary in code these days. Reading didn't come naturally to the Chalk Hill Feegles, so surely they'd never get the hang of a code.

She looked around carefully, in any case, and unlocked the huge padlock that secured a chain around the book. She turned to today's date, dipped her pen in the ink and wrote:

Met t ❄

Yes, a snowflake would be a good code for the wintersmith.

He just stood there, she thought.

And he ran away because I screamed.

Which was a good thing, obviously.

Um . . .

But . . . I wish I hadn't screamed.

She opened her hand. The image of the horse was still there, as white as chalk, but there was no pain at all.

Tiffany gave a little shiver and pulled herself together. So? She had met the spirit of the winter. She was a witch. It was the sort of thing that sometimes happened. He'd politely given her back what was hers, and then he'd gone. There was no call to get soppy about it. There were things to do.

Then she wrote: 'Ltr frm R.'

She very carefully opened the letter from Roland, which was easy because slug slime isn't much of a glue. With any luck she could even re-use the envelope. She hunched over the letter so that no one could read it over her shoulder. Finally, she said: 'Miss Treason, will you get out of my face, please? I need to use my eyeballs privately.'

There was a pause and then a mutter from down-stairs, and the tickling behind her eyes went away.

It was always . . . good to get a letter from Roland. Yes, they were often about the sheep, and other things of the Chalk, and sometimes there'd be a dried flower inside, a harebell or a cowslip. Granny Aching wouldn't have approved of that; she always said that if the hills had wanted people to pick the flowers they would have grown more of them.

The letters always made her homesick.

One day, Miss Treason had said, 'This young man who writes to you . . . is he your beau?' and Tiffany had changed the subject until she had time to look up the word in the dictionary and stop blushing.

Roland was . . . well, the thing about Roland was . . . the main thing about . . . well, the point was . . . he was there.

OK, when she'd first really met him he'd been a rather useless, rather stupid lump, but what could you expect? He'd been the prisoner of the Queen of the Fairies for a year, to start with, fat as butter and half-crazy on sugar and despair. Besides, he'd been brought up by a couple of haughty aunts, his father – the Baron – being mostly more interested in horses and dogs.

He'd more and less changed since then: more thoughtful, less rowdy, more serious, less stupid. He'd also had to wear glasses, the first ever seen on the Chalk.

And he had a library! More than a hundred books! Actually, it belonged to the castle, but no one else seemed interested in it.

Some of the books were huge and ancient, with wooden covers and huge black letters and coloured pictures of strange animals and far-off places. There was Waspmire's *Book of Unusual Days*, Crumberry's *Why Things Are Not Otherwise*, and all but one volume of *The Ominous Encyclopaedia*. Roland had been astonished to find that Tiffany could read foreign words, and she'd been careful not to tell him it was all done with the help of what remained of Dr Bustle.

The thing was ... the fact was ... well, who else had they got? Roland couldn't, just *couldn't* have friends among the village kids, what with him being the son of the Baron and everything. But Tiffany had the pointy hat now, and that counted for something. The people of the Chalk didn't like witches much, but she was Granny Aching's grand-daughter, right? No tellin' what she learned from the ol' girl, up at the shepherding hut. And they do say she showed those witches up in the mountains what witchin's all about, eh? Remember the lambing last year? She prit near brought dead lambs back to life just by lookin' at 'em! And she's an Aching, and they've got these hills in their bones. She's all right. She's ours, see?

And that was fine, except that she didn't have any old friends any more. Kids back home who'd been friendly were now . . . respectful, because of the hat. There was a kind of wall, as if she'd grown up and they hadn't. What could they talk about? She'd been to places they couldn't even imagine. Most of them hadn't even been to Twoshirts, which was only half a day away. And this didn't worry them at all. They were going to do the jobs their fathers did, or raise children like their mothers did. And that was fine, Tiffany added hurriedly to herself. But they hadn't decided. It was just happening to them, and they didn't notice.

It was the same up in the mountains. The only people of her own age that she could actually talk to were other witches-in-training like Annagramma and the rest of the girls. It was useless trying to have a real conversation with people in the villages, especially the boys. They just looked down and mumbled and shuffled their feet, like people at home when they had to talk to the Baron.

Actually, Roland did that, too, and he went red every time she looked at him. Whenever she visited the castle, or walked on the hills with him, the air was full of complicated silences . . . just like it had been with the wintersmith.

She read the letter carefully, trying to ignore the grubby Feegle fingerprints all over it. He'd been kind enough to include several spare sheets of paper.

She smoothed one out, very carefully, stared at the wall for a while and then began to write.

Down in the scullery,* Horace the cheese had come out from behind the slop bucket. Now he was in front of the back door. If a cheese ever looked thoughtful, Horace looked thoughtful now.

In the tiny village of Twoshirts, the driver of the mail coach was having a bit of a problem. A lot of mail from the countryside around Twoshirts ended up at the souvenir shop there, which also acted as the post office.

Usually the driver just picked up the mailbag, but today there was a difficulty. He frantically turned over the pages of the book of Post Office Regulations.

Miss Tick tapped her foot. This was getting on his nerves.

---

* A room off a kitchen for washing pans and doing other wet and messy chores. Although Miss Treason had skulls, she did not keep them in the scullery. It would have been quite amusing, though, if she did.

'Ah, ah, ah,' said the coachman triumphantly. 'Says here no animals, birds, dragons or fish!'

'And which one of them do you think I am?' said Miss Tick icily.

'Ah, well, right, well, human is kind of like animal, right? I mean, look at monkeys, right?'

'I have no wish to look at monkeys,' said Miss Tick. 'I have seen the sort of things they do.'

The coachman clearly spotted that this was a road not to go down, and turned the pages furiously. Then he beamed.

'Ah, ah, ah!' he said. 'How much do you weigh, miss?'

'Two ounces,' said Miss Tick. 'Which by chance is the maximum weight of letter that can be sent to the Lancre and Near Hinterland area for ten pence.' She pointed to the two stamps gummed to her lapel. 'I have already purchased my stamps.'

'You never weigh two ounces!' said the coachman. 'You're a hundred and twenty pounds at least!'

Miss Tick sighed. She'd wanted to avoid this, but Twoshirts wasn't Dogbend, after all. It lived on the highway, it watched the world go past. She reached up and pressed the button that worked her hat.

'Would you like me to forget you just said that?' she said.

'Why?' said the coachman.

There was a pause while Miss Tick stared blankly at him. Then she turned her eyes upwards.

'Excuse me,' she said. 'This is always happening, I'm

afraid. It's the duckings, you know. The spring rusts.'

She reached up and banged the side of the hat. The hidden pointy bit shot up, scattering paper flowers.

The coachman's eyes followed it. 'Oh,' he said.

And the thing about pointy hats was this: the person under it was definitely a witch or a wizard. Oh, someone who wasn't could probably get a pointy hat and go out wearing it, and they'd be fine right up until the moment when they met a real pointy-hat owner. Wizards and witches didn't like impostors. They also don't like being kept waiting.

'How much do I weigh now, pray?' she asked.

'Two ounces!' said the coachman quickly.

Miss Tick smiled. 'Yes. And not one scruple more! A scruple being, of course, a weight of twenty grains or one twenty-fourth of an ounce. I am in fact . . . unscrupulous!'

She waited to see if this extremely teachery joke was going to get a smile, but didn't mind when it didn't. Miss Tick rather liked being smarter than other people.

She got on the coach.

As the coach climbed up into the mountains, snow started to fall. Miss Tick, who knew that no two snowflakes are alike, didn't pay them any attention. If she had done so, she'd have felt slightly less smart.

Tiffany slept. A fire glowed in the bedroom grate. Downstairs, Miss Treason's loom weaved its way through the night . . .

Small blue figures crept across the bedroom floor and, by forming a Feegle pyramid, reached the top of the little table Tiffany used as a desk.

Tiffany turned over in bed and made a little *snfgl* noise. The Feegles froze, just for a moment, and then the bedroom door swung gently shut behind them.

A blue and red blur raised a trail of dust on the narrow stairs, across the loom-room floor, out into the scullery and through a strange cheese-shaped hole in the outside door. From then on it was a trail of disturbed leaves deep into the woods, where a small fire burned. It lit the faces of a horde of Feegles, although it may not have wanted to.

The blur stopped and became about six Feegles, two of them carrying Tiffany's diary.

They laid it down carefully.

'We're well oot o' that hoose,' said Big Yan. 'Di'a see dem bigjob skulls? There's a hag ye wouldnae want tae cross in a hurry!'

'Ach, I see she's got one of they paddly locks again,' said Daft Wullie, walking around the diary.

'Rob, I cannae help thinkin' that it's no' right to read this,' said Billy Bigchin, as Rob put his arm into the keyhole. 'It's pers'nal!'

'She's oor hag. What's pers'nal to her is pers'nal to us,' said Rob matter-of-factly, fishing around inside the lock. 'Besides, she must want someone tae read it, cuz she wrote things doon. Nae point in writin' stuff doon if ye dinnae want it read! It's a sheer waste o' pencil!'

'Mebbe she wanted tae read it hersel',' said Billy doubtfully.

'Oh, aye? Why'd she want tae do that?' said Rob scornfully. 'She already kens what's in it. An' Jeannie wants tae know what she's thinkin' aboot the Baron's lad . . .'

There was a click, and the padlock opened. The assembled feeglehood watched carefully.

Rob turned the rustling pages, and grinned.

'Ach, she's writ here: *Oh, the dear Feegles ha' turned up again*,' he said. This met with general applause.

'Ach, what a kind girl she is tae write that,' said Billy Bigchin. 'Can I see?'

He read: *Oh dear, the Feegles have turned up again*.

'Ah,' he said. Billy Bigchin had come with Jeannie all the way from the Long Lake clan. The clan there was more at home with reading and writing, and since he was the gonnagle he was expected to be good at both.

The Chalk Hill Feegles, on the other hand, were more at home with the drinkin', stealin' and fightin', and Rob Anybody was good at all three. But he'd learned to read and write because Jeannie had asked him to. He did them with a lot more optimism than accuracy, Billy knew. When he was faced with a long sentence he tended to work out a few words and then have a great big guess.

'The art o' readin' is all aboot understandin' whut the wurds is *tryin'* tae say, right?' said Rob.

'Aye, mebbe,' said Big Yan, 'but is there any wurd there to tell us that the big wee hag is sweet on that heap o' jobbies doon in the stone castle?'

'Ye ha' a verrae ro-mantic nature,' said Rob. 'And the answer is: I cannae tell. They writes some bits of their letters in them wee codies. That's a terrible thing tae do to a reader. It's hard enough readin' the normal words, wi'oot somebody jumblin' them all up.'

'It'll be a baaaad look-oot fra' us all if the big wee hag starts mindin' boys instead o' gettin' the knowin' o' the hagglin',' said Big Yan.

'Aye, but the boy willnae be interested in marryin',' said Slightly Mad Angus.

'He might be, one day,' said Billy Bigchin, who'd made a hobby of watching humans. 'Most bigjob men get married.'

'They do?' said a Feegle, in astonishment.

'Oh, aye.'

'They want tae get married?'

'A lot o' them do, aye,' said Billy.

'So there's nae more boozin', stealin' an' fighting?'

'Hey, ah'm still allowed some boozin' an' stealin' an' fightin'!' said Rob Anybody.

'Aye, Rob, but we cannae help noticin' ye also have tae do the Explainin', too,' said Daft Wullie.

There was a general nodding from the crowd. To Feegles, Explaining was a dark art. It was just so *hard*.

'Like, when we come back from boozin', stealin' an' fightin', Jeannie gives ye the pursin' o' the lips,' Daft Wullie went on.

A moan went up from all the Feegles: 'Ooooh, save us from the pursin' o' the lips!'

'An' there's the foldin' o' the arms,' said Wullie, because he was even scaring himself.

'Oooooh, waily, waily, waily, the foldin' o' the arms!' the Feegles cried, tearing at their hair.

'Not tae mention the tappin' o' the feets . . .' Wullie stopped, not wanting to mention the tappin' o' the feets.

'Aargh! Ooooo! No' the tappin' o' the feets!' Some of the Feegles started to bang their heads on trees.

'Aye, aye, aye, BUT,' said Rob Anybody desperately, 'what youse dinnae ken is that this is part o' the hiddlins o' husbandry.'

Feegles looked at one another. There was silence except for the creak of a small tree as it fell over.

'We never heard o' any sich thing, Rob,' said Big Yan.

'Well, an' ah'm no' surprised! Who'd tell ye? Ye ain't married! Ye dinnae get the po-et-ic symi-tree o' the whole thing. Gather roound till I tell ye . . .'

Rob looked around to see if anyone apart from about five hundred Feegles was watching him, and went on: 'See . . . first ye get the boozin' an' the fightin' an' the stealin', OK. An' when you get back tae the mound it's time for the tappin' o' the feets—'

'Ooooooo!'

'– an' the foldin' o' the arms—'

'Aaaargh!'

'– an', o' course, the pursin' o' the lips and— *will ye scunners knock it off wi' the groanin' before I starts bangin' heids together! Right?*'

All the Feegles fell silent, except for one:

'Oh, waily, waily, waily! Ohhhhhhh! Aaarrgh! The pursin' . . . o' . . . the—'

He stopped, and looked around in embarrassment.

'Daft Wullie?' said Rob Anybody, with icy patience.

'Aye, Rob?'

'Ye ken I told yez there wuz times ye should listen to whut I was sayin'?'

'Aye, Rob?'

'That wuz one o' them times.'

Daft Wullie hung his head. 'Sorry, Rob.'

'Aye! Now, where wuz I . . . ? Oh, aye . . . we get the lips an' the arms an' the feets, OK? An' then—'

'I's time for the Explainin'!' said Daft Wullie.

'Aye!' snapped Rob Anybody. 'Any one o' youse mudlins want to be the one who dares tae do the Explainin'?'

He looked around.

The Feegles shuffled backwards.

'Wi' the kelda a-pursin' an' a-foldin' an' a-tappin',' Rob went on in a voice of Doom. 'An' that look in her bonny eye that says: "This Explanation had better be really guid"? Well? Do ye?'

By now Feegles were crying and chewing the edges of their kilts in terror.

'No, Rob,' they murmured.

'No, aye!' said Rob Anybody triumphantly. 'Ye wouldnae! That's because you don't have the knowin' o' the husbandry!'

'I heard Jeannie say you come up with Explanations no other Feegle in all the world would try,' said Daft Wullie admiringly.

'Aye, that's quite likely,' said Rob, swelling with pride. 'And Feegles has got a fine tradition o' huge Explanations!'

'She said some of your Explainin' is so long an' twisty, by the time ye've got to the end, she cannae recall how they started,' Daft Wullie went on.

'It's a nat'ral gift, I wouldnae wantae boast,' said Rob, waving his hand modestly.

'I can't see bigjobs bein' good at Explainin',' said Big Yan. 'They're verrae slow thinkers.'

'They still get wed, though,' said Billy Bigchin.

'Aye, and yon boy in the big castle is bein' too friendly wi' the big wee hag,' said Big Yan. 'His da' is gettin' old an' sick and soon yon boy will own a big stone castle and the wee bittie papers that says that he owns the hills.'

'Jeannie's afeared that if he's got the wee bittie papers that says he owns the hills,' Billy Bigchin continued, 'he might go daft and think they belong to him. An' we know where that'll lead, right?'

'Aye,' said Big Yan. 'Ploughin'.'

It was a dreaded word. The old baron had once planned to plough a few of the flatter areas of the Chalk, because corn was fetching high prices and there was no money in sheep, but Granny Aching had been alive then and had changed his mind for him.

But some pastures around the Chalk were being ploughed up already. There *was* money in corn. The Feegles took it for granted that Roland would take to the plough, too. Wasn't he brought up by a couple of vain, scheming and unpleasant aunts?

'I dinnae trust him,' said Slightly Mad Angus. 'He reads books an' such. He disnae care about the land.'

'Aye,' said Daft Wullie, 'but if he wuz wed tae the big wee hag, he'd no' think o' the plough, cuz the big wee hag would soon gi'e him the pursin' o' the arms—'

'It's the *foldin*' o' the arms!' snapped Rob Anybody.

All the Feegles looked around fearfully.

'Ooooooh, not the foldin' o' th—'

'Shut up!' Rob yelled. 'Ah'm ashamed o' yez! It's up tae the big wee hag tae marry who she wants tae! Is that no' so, gonnagle?'

'Hmm?' said Billy, looking upwards. He caught another snowflake.

'I said, the big wee hag can wed who she wants, right?'

Billy was staring at the snowflake.

'Billy?' said Rob.

'What?' he said, as if waking up. 'Oh . . . yes. Do ye think she wants to marry the wintersmith?'

'The wintersmith?' said Rob. 'He cannae marry anyone. He's like a spirit, there's nothin' tae him!'

'She danced with him. We saw her,' said Billy, catching another flake and inspecting it.

'Just girlish high spirits! Anyway, why should the big wee hag think anything o' the wintersmith?'

'I have reason tae believe,' said the gonnagle slowly, as more flakes danced down, 'that the wintersmith is thinkin' a lot aboot the big wee hag . . .'

CHAPTER 4

SNOWFLAKES

They say that there can never be two snowflakes that are exactly alike, but has anyone checked lately?

Snow fell gently in the darkness. It piled up on rooftops, it kissed its way though the branches of trees, it settled on the forest floor with a gentle sizzle and smelled sharply of tin.

Granny Weatherwax always checked the snow. She stood at her doorway, with the candlelight streaming out around her, and caught flakes on the back of a shovel.

The white kitten watched the snowflakes. That's all it did. It didn't bat them with a paw, it just watched, very intently, each flake spiral down until it landed. Then the kitten would watch it some more, until it was sure the entertainment was over, before it looked up and selected another flake.

It was called You, as in 'You! Stop that!' and 'You! Get off there!' When it came to names, Granny Weatherwax didn't do fancy.

Granny looked at the snowflakes and smiled in her not-exactly-nice way.

'Come back in, You,' she said, and shut the door.

Miss Tick was shivering by the fire. It wasn't very big – just big enough. However, there was the smell of bacon and pease pudding coming from a small pot on the embers, and beside it was a much larger one from which came the smell of chicken. Miss Tick didn't often get chicken, so she lived in hope.

It had to be said that Granny Weatherwax and Miss Tick did not get on well with each other. Senior witches often don't. You could tell that they didn't by the way they were extremely polite all the time.

'The snow is early this year, Mistress Weatherwax,' said Miss Tick.

'Indeed it is, Miss Tick,' said Granny Weatherwax. 'And so . . . interesting. Have you looked at it?'

'I've seen snow before, Mistress Weatherwax,' said Miss Tick. 'It was snowing all the way out up here. I had to help push the mail coach! I saw altogether too much snow! But what are we going to do about Tiffany Aching?'

'Nothing, Miss Tick. More tea?'

'She is rather our responsibility.'

'No. She's hers, first and last. She's a witch. She danced the Winter Dance. I saw her do it.'

'I'm sure she didn't mean to,' said Miss Tick.

'How can you dance and not mean it?'

'She's young. The excitement probably ran away

with her feet. She didn't know what was going on.'

'She should have found out,' said Granny Weatherwax. 'She should have listened.'

'I'm sure you always did what you were told when you were almost thirteen, Mistress Weatherwax,' said Miss Tick with just a hint of sarcasm.

Granny Weatherwax stared at the wall for a moment. 'No,' she said. 'I made mistakes. But I didn't make excuses.'

'I thought you wanted to help the child?'

'I'll help her to help herself. That is my way. She's danced her way into the oldest story there is, and the only way out is through the other end. The only way, Miss Tick.'

Miss Tick sighed. Stories, she thought. Granny Weatherwax believes the world is all about stories. Oh well, we all have our funny little ways. Except me, obviously.

'Of course. It's just that she's so . . . normal,' she said aloud. 'When you consider what she's done, I mean. And she thinks so much. And now she's come to the attention of the wintersmith, well . . .'

'She fascinates him,' said Granny Weatherwax.

'That's going to be a big problem.'

'Which she will have to solve.'

'And if she can't?'

'Then she's not Tiffany Aching,' said Granny Weatherwax firmly. 'Ah, yes, she's in the story now, but she don't know it! Look at the snow, Miss Tick.

They say that no two snowflakes are alike. How could they know something like that? Oh, they think they're so smart! I've always wanted to catch 'em out. An' I have done! Go outside now, and look at the snow. Look at the snow, Miss Tick! Every flake the same!'

Tiffany heard the knocking and opened the tiny bedroom window with difficulty. Snow had built up on the sill, soft and fluffy.

'We didnae want tae wake ye,' said Rob Anybody, 'but Wee Billy said you ought tae see this.'

Tiffany yawned. 'What am I looking for?' she muttered.

'Catch some o' yon flakes,' said Rob. 'No, not on yer hand, they'll melt tae soon.'

In the gloom, Tiffany felt around for her diary. It wasn't there. She looked on the floor, in case she'd knocked it off. Then a match flared as Rob Anybody lit a candle, and there was the diary, looking as though it had always been there but, she noticed, also being suspiciously cold to the touch. Rob looked innocent, a sure sign of guilt.

Tiffany saved the questions for later, and poked the diary out of the window. Flakes settled on it, and she lifted it closer to her eyes.

'They look just like any ordin—' she began, and then stopped, and then said, 'Oh, no . . . this must be a trick!'

'Aye? Well, ye could call it that,' said Rob. 'But it's *his* trick, ye ken.'

Tiffany stared at the falling flakes, drifting in the light of the candle.

Every one of them was Tiffany Aching. A little, frozen, sparkling Tiffany Aching.

Downstairs, Miss Treason burst out laughing.

The doorknob on the door to the tower bedroom was rattled angrily. Roland de Chumsfanleigh (pronounced Chuffley; it wasn't his fault) carefully paid it no attention.

'What are you doing in there, child?' said a muffled voice, peevishly.

'Nothing, Aunt Danuta,' said Roland, without turning round from his desk. One of the advantages of living in a castle was that rooms were easy to lock; his door had three iron locks and two bolts that were as thick as his arm.

'Your father is calling out for you, you know!' said another voice, with even more peeve.

'He whispers, Aunt Araminta,' Roland said calmly, carefully writing an address on an envelope. 'He only cries out when you set the doctors on him.'

'It's for his own good!'

'He cries out,' Roland repeated, and then licked the flap on the envelope.

Aunt Araminta rattled the doorknob again.

'You are a very ungrateful child! You will starve, you

know! We will get the guards to batter this door down!'

Roland sighed. The castle had been built by people who did not like to have their doors battered down, and anyone trying to do that here would have to carry the battering ram up a narrow spiral staircase with no room at the top to turn round, and then find a way to knock down a door four planks thick and made of oak timbers so ancient it was like iron. One man could defend this room for months, if he had provisions. He heard some more grumbling outside and then the echo of the aunts' shoes as they went down the tower. Then he heard them screaming at the guards again.

It wouldn't do them much good. Sergeant Roberts and his guards* were edgy about taking orders from the aunts. Everyone knew though that, if the Baron died before the boy was twenty-one, the aunts would legally run the estate until he *was*. And while the Baron was very ill, he was not dead. It was not a happy time to be a disobedient guard, but the sergeant and his men survived the anger of the aunts by being, when their orders justified it, deaf, stupid, forgetful, confused, ill, lost or – in the case of Kevin – foreign.

For now, Roland kept his excursions for the small hours, when no one was around and he could pillage the kitchen. That's when he went in to see his father. The doctors kept the old man dosed with something,

* Kevin and Neville and Trevor.

but he held his hand for a while for the comfort that it gave. If he found jars of wasps or leeches, he threw them into the moat.

He stared at the envelope. Perhaps he ought to tell Tiffany about this, but he didn't like to think about it. It would worry her and she might try to rescue him again, and that wouldn't be right. This was something he had to face. Besides, *he* wasn't locked in. *They* were locked out. While he held the tower, there was a place where they couldn't poke and pry and steal. He'd got what was left of the silver candlesticks under his bed, along with what remained of the antique silver cutlery ('gone to be valued', they'd said) and his mother's jewel box. He'd been a bit late finding that; it was missing her wedding ring and the silver and garnet necklace his grandmother had left to her.

But tomorrow he'd get up early and ride over to Twoshirts with the letter. He liked writing them. They turned the world into a nicer place, because you didn't have to include the bad bits.

Roland sighed. It would have been nice to tell her that in the library he'd found a book called *Sieges and Survival* by the famous General Callus Tacticus (who invented 'tactics', which was interesting). Who'd have thought such an ancient book could be so useful? The general had been very firm about having provisions, so Roland had plenty of small beer, large sausage and heavy dwarf bread, which was handy to drop on people.

He glanced across the room, where there was a

portrait of his mother that he had carried up from the cellar where *they* had left it (it was 'waiting to be cleaned', they said). Right beside it, if you knew what you were looking for, an area of wall about the size of a small door looked lighter than the rest of the stones. The candlestick next to it looked slightly lopsided, too.

There were lots of advantages to living in a castle.

Outside, it began to snow.

The Nac Mac Feegles peered out at the fluffy flakes from the thatch of Miss Treason's cottage. By the light that managed to leak out from the grubby windows below, they watched the tiny Tiffanys whirl past.

'Say it wi' snowflakes,' said Big Yan. 'Hah!'

Daft Wullie snatched a spiralling flake. 'Ye gotta admit he's done the wee pointy hat really well,' he said. 'He must like the big wee hag a lot . . .'

'It disnae make any *sense*!' said Rob Anybody. 'He's the winter! He's all the snow an' ice an' storms an' frosts. She's just a wee big girl! Ye cannae say that's an ideal match! Whut do ye say, Billy? Billy?'

The gonnagle was chewing the end of his mousepipes while staring at the flakes with a faraway look in his eyes. But somehow Rob's voice broke into his thoughts, because he said: 'Whut does he ken aboot people? He's no' as alive as a wee insect yet he's as powerful as the sea. An' he's sweet on the big wee hag. Why? What can she be to him? What will he do next? I tell ye this: snowflakes is just the beginning.

We must watch oot, Rob. This may become verrae bad . . .'

Up in the mountains, 990,393,072,007 Tiffany Achings landed lightly on the old packed snow on a ridge and began an avalanche which carried away more than a hundred trees and a hunting lodge. This wasn't her fault.

It wasn't her fault that people slipped on packed layers of her, or couldn't open the door because she was piled up outside it, or got hit by handfuls of her thrown by small children. Most of her had melted by breakfast-time next day, and besides, no one noticed anything strange, except witches who don't take people's word for things, and a lot of kids who no one listened to.

Even so, Tiffany woke up feeling very embarrassed.

Miss Treason didn't help at all.

'At least he likes you,' she said while she ferociously wound up her clock.

'I wouldn't know about that, Miss Treason,' said Tiffany, really not wanting this conversation at all. She was washing the dishes at the sink, her back to the old woman, and she was glad that Miss Treason could not see her face – and, if it came to it, that she couldn't see Miss Treason's face, either.

'What will your young man say about it? I wonder.'

'What young man is that, Miss Treason?' said Tiffany, as stonily as she could manage.

'He writes you letters, girl!'

And I expect you read them with my eyes, Tiffany thought. 'Roland? He's just a friend . . . sort of,' she said.

'A *sort* of friend?'

I'm not going into this, Tiffany thought. I bet she's grinning. It's not her business, anyway.

'Yes,' she said, 'that's right, Miss Treason. A sort of friend.'

There was a long silence, which Tiffany used to scrub out the bottom of an iron saucepan.

'It is important to have friends,' said Miss Treason, in a voice that was somehow smaller than it had been. It sounded as though Tiffany had won. 'When you have finished, dear, please be kind enough to fetch me my shamble bag.'

Tiffany did so, and hurried off into the dairy. It was always good to get in there. It reminded her of home, and she could think better. She—

There was a cheese-shaped hole in the bottom of the door, but Horace was back in his broken cage, making a very faint *mnmnmnmn* noise which may have been cheese snores. She left him alone, and dealt with the morning's milk.

At least it wasn't snowing. She felt herself blushing, and tried to stop herself from even thinking about it.

And there was going to be a coven meeting tonight. Would the other girls know? Hah! Of course they would. Witches paid attention to snow, especially if it was going to be embarrassing for somebody.

'Tiffany? I wish to speak with you,' Miss Treason called out.

Miss Treason had hardly ever called her Tiffany before. It was quite worrying to hear her say the name.

Miss Treason was holding up a shamble. Her seeing-eye mouse was dangling awkwardly among the bits of bone and ribbon.

'This is so inconvenient,' she said, and raised her voice. 'Ach, ye mudlins! C'mon oot! I ken ye're there! I can see ye lookin' at me!'

Feegle heads appeared from behind very nearly everything.

'Good! Tiffany Aching, sit down!' Tiffany sat down quickly.

'At a time like this, too,' said Miss Treason, laying down the shamble. 'This is so inconvenient. But there is no doubt.' She paused for a moment and said: 'I will die the day after tomorrow. On Friday, just before half past six in the morning.'

It was an impressive statement, and did not deserve this reply: 'Oh, that's a shame, tae be missin' the weekend like that,' said Rob Anybody. 'Are ye going somewhere nice?'

'But . . . but . . . you can't die!' Tiffany burst out. 'You're a hundred and thirteen years old, Miss Treason!'

'You know, that is very probably the reason, child,' said Miss Treason calmly. 'Didn't anyone tell you that

118

witches have forewarning of when they're going to die? Anyway, I like a good funeral.'

'Oh aye, ye cannae beat a good wake,' said Rob Anybody. 'Wi' lots o' boozin' an' dancin' an' greetin' an feastin' an' boozin'.'

'There may be some sweet sherry,' said Miss Treason. 'As for feasting, I always say you cannot go far wrong with a ham roll.'

'But you can't just—' Tiffany began, and stopped as Miss Treason turned her head fast, like a chicken does.

'– leave you like this?' she said. 'Is that what you were going to say?'

'Er, no,' Tiffany lied.

'You'll have to move in with someone else, of course,' said Miss Treason. 'You're not really senior enough to take on a cottage, not when there's older girls waiting—'

'You know I don't want to spend my life in the mountains, Miss Treason,' Tiffany said quickly.

'Oh yes, Miss Tick did tell me,' said the old witch. 'You want to go back to your little chalk hills.'

'They're not little!' Tiffany snapped, louder than she'd meant to.

'Yes, this has been a bit of a trying time all round,' said Miss Treason, very calmly. 'I shall write some letters which you will take down to the village, and then you shall have your afternoon off. We shall hold the funeral tomorrow afternoon.'

'Sorry? You mean *before* you die?' said Tiffany.

'Why, of course! I don't see why I shouldn't have some fun!'

'Good thinkin'!' said Rob Anybody. 'That's the kind of sensible detail people usually fail tae consider.'

'We call it a going-away party,' said Miss Treason. 'Just for witches, of course. Other people tend to get a bit nervous, I can't think why. And on the bright side, we've got that splendid ham that Mr Armbinder gave us last week for settling the ownership of the chestnut tree, and I'd love to try it.'

An hour later Tiffany set out, with her pockets full of notes to butchers and bakers and farmers in the local villages.

She was a bit surprised at the reception she got. They seemed to think it was all a joke.

'Miss Treason's not going to go dying at her time of life,' said a butcher, weighing out sausages. 'I heard that Death's come for her before and she slammed the door on him!'

'Thirteen dozen sausages, please,' said Tiffany. 'Cooked and delivered.'

'Are you sure she's going to die?' said the butcher, uncertainty clouding his face.

'No. But *she* is,' said Tiffany.

And the baker said, 'Don't you know about that clock of hers? She had it made when her heart died. It's like a clockwork heart, see?'

'Really?' said Tiffany. 'So, if her heart died, and she

had a new one made of clockwork, how did she stay alive while the new heart was being made?'

'Oh, that'd be by magic, obviously,' said the baker.

'But a heart pumps blood, and Miss Treason's clock is outside her body,' Tiffany pointed out. 'There's no . . . tubes . . .'

'It pumps the blood by magic,' said the baker, speaking slowly. He gave her an odd look. 'How can you be a witch if you don't know this stuff?'

It was the same everywhere else. It was as if the idea of there being no Miss Treason was the wrong shape to put in anyone's head. She was 113 years old, and they argued that it was practically unheard of for anyone to die aged 113. It was a joke, they said, or she'd got a scroll signed in blood that meant she'd live for ever, or you'd have to steal her clock before she'd die, or every time the Grim Reaper came for her she lied about her name or sent him to another person, or maybe she was just feeling a bit unwell . . .

By the time Tiffany was finished she was wondering if it really *was* going to happen. Yet Miss Treason had seemed so certain. And at 113, the amazing thing wasn't that you were going to die tomorrow, but that you were still alive today.

With her head full of gloomy thoughts, she set out to the coven meeting.

Once or twice she thought she could feel Feegles watching her. She never knew how she could feel this; it was a talent you learned. And you learned to put up with it, most of the time.

All the other young witches were there by the time she arrived, and had even got a fire lit.

Some people think that 'coven' is a word for a group of witches, and it's true that's what the dictionary says. But the real word for a group of witches is 'an argument'.

In any case, most of the witches Tiffany had met never used the word. Mrs Earwig did, though, almost all the time. She was tall and thin and rather chilly, and wore silver spectacles on a little chain, and used words like 'avatar' and 'sigil'. And Annagramma, who ran the coven because she'd invented it and had the tallest hat and sharpest voice, was her star pupil (and her only one).

Granny Weatherwax always said that what Mrs Earwig did was wizard magic with a dress on, and Annagramma certainly dragged a lot of books and wands along to the meetings. Mostly, the girls did a few ceremonies to keep her quiet, because for them the real purpose of the coven was to meet friends, even if they were friends simply because they were really the only people you could talk to freely as they had the same problems and would understand what you were moaning about.

They always met out in the woods, even in the snow. There was always enough wood lying around for a fire, and they all dressed up warm as a matter of course. Even in the summer, comfort on a broomstick at any height meant more layers of underclothing than anyone would dare guess at, and sometimes a couple of hot water-bottles held on with string.

At the moment three small fireballs circled the fire. Annagramma had made them. You could slay enemies with them, she'd said. They made the others uneasy. It was wizard magic, showy and dangerous. Witches would prefer to cut enemies dead with a look. There was no sense in killing your enemy. How would she know you'd won?

Dimity Hubbub had brought a huge tray of Inside-out cake. It was just the thing to put a coating on your ribs against the cold.

Tiffany said: 'Miss Treason told me she's going to die on Friday morning. She said she just knows.'

'That's a shame,' said Annagramma, in a that's-not-really-a-shame tone of voice. 'She was very old, though.'

'She still is,' said Tiffany.

'Um, it's called The Call,' said Petulia Gristle. 'Old witches know when they're going to die. No one knows how it works. They just do.'

'Has she still got those skulls?' said Lucy Warbeck, who today had her hair piled up on her head with a knife and fork stuck in it. 'I couldn't stand them. They seemed to be, like, looking at me all the time!'

'It was her using me as a mirror that made me leave,' said Lulu Darling. 'Does she still do that?'

Tiffany sighed. 'Yes.'

'I said flatly that I wouldn't go,' said Gertruder

Tiring, poking the fire. 'Did you know that if you leave a witch without permission, no other witch will take you on, but if you leave Miss Treason even after only one night, no one says anything about it and they just find you another place?'

'Mrs Earwig says things like skulls and ravens are going far too far,' said Annagramma. 'Everyone around there is literally frightened out of their lives!'

'Um, what's going to happen to you?' said Petulia to Tiffany.

'I don't know. I suppose I'll go somewhere else.'

'Poor you,' said Annagramma. 'Miss Treason didn't say who'll take over the cottage, by any chance?' she added, as if she'd only just thought of the question.

The sound that followed was the silence made by half a dozen pairs of ears listening so hard they were nearly creaking. There were not a lot of young witches coming up, it was true, but witches lived a long time and getting your own cottage was the prize. That's when you started getting respect.

'No,' said Tiffany.

'Not even a hint?'

'No.'

'She didn't say it was going to be you, did she?' said Annagramma sharply. Her voice could be really annoying. It could make 'hello' sound like an accusation.

'No!'

'Anyway, you're too young.'

'Actually, there's no, you know, actual age limit,'

said Lucy Warbeck. 'Nothing written down, anyway.'

'How do you know that?' Annagramma snapped.

'I asked Old Mrs Pewmire, said Lucy.

Annagramma's eyes narrowed. 'You *asked* her? Why?'

Lucy rolled her eyes. 'Because I wanted to know, that's all. Look, everyone knows you're the oldest and the . . . you know, most trained. Of course you'll get the cottage.'

'Yes,' said Annagramma, watching Tiffany suspic-iously. 'Of course.'

'That's, um, sorted out, then,' said Petulia, more loudly than necessary. 'Did you have a lot of snow last night? Old Mother Blackcap said it was unusual.'

Tiffany thought: Oh dear, here we go . . .

'No, we often get it this early up here,' said Lucy.

'I thought it was a bit fluffier than usual,' said Petulia. 'Quite pretty, if you like that sort of thing.'

'It was just snow,' said Annagramma. 'Hey, did any of you hear what happened to the new girl who started with Old Miss Tumult? Ran away screaming after an hour?' She smiled, not very sympathetically.

'Um, was it the frog?' said Petulia.

'No, not the frog. She didn't mind the frog. It was Unlucky Charlie.'

'He can be scary,' Lucy agreed.

And that was it, Tiffany realized, as the gossip ran on. Someone who was practically a kind of god had made billions of snowflakes that looked like her – and they hadn't noticed!

. . . which was a good thing, obviously . . .

Of course it was. The last thing she wanted was teasing and stupid questions, of course. Well, of course . . .

. . . but . . . well . . . it would have been nice if they'd known, if they'd said 'Wow!' if they'd been jealous or frightened or impressed. And she couldn't tell them, or at least she couldn't tell Annagramma, who'd make a joke of it and almost but not exactly say that she was making it up.

The wintersmith had visited her and been . . . impressed. It was a bit sad if the only people who knew about this were Miss Treason and hundreds of Feegles, especially since – she shuddered – by Friday morning it would only be known by hundreds of little blue men.

To put it another way: if she didn't tell someone else who was at least the same size as her and alive, she would burst.

So she told Petulia, on the way home. They had to go the same way and they both flew so slowly that at night it was easier to walk, since you didn't hit so many trees.

Petulia was plump and reliable and already the best pig witch in the mountains, a fact that means a lot where every family owns a pig. And Miss Treason had said that soon the boys would be running after her, because a girl who knows her pigs would never want for a husband.

The only problem with Petulia was that she always agreed with you and always said what she thought you wanted to hear. But Tiffany was a bit cruel, and just told her all the facts. She got a few wows, which she was pleased with.

After a while Petulia said: 'That must have been very, um, interesting.' And that was Petulia for you.

'What shall I do?'

'Um . . . do you need to do anything?' said Petulia.

'Well, sooner or later people are going to notice that all snowflakes are shaped like me!'

'Um, are you worried that they won't?' said Petulia, so innocently that Tiffany laughed.

'But I've got this feeling that it's not going to stop with snowflakes! I mean, he is everything to do with wintertime!'

'And he ran away when you screamed . . .' said Petulia thoughtfully.

'That's right.'

'And then he did something sort of . . . silly.'

'What?'

'The snowflakes,' said Petulia helpfully

'Well, I wouldn't say that, exactly,' said Tiffany, a bit hurt. 'Not exactly *silly*.'

'Then it's all obvious,' said Petulia. 'He's a boy.'

'What?'

'A boy. You know what they are?' said Petulia. 'Blush, grunt, mumble, wibble? They're pretty much all the same.'

'But he's millions of years old and he acts like he's never seen a girl before!'

'Um, I don't know. *Has* he ever seen a girl before?'

'He must have done! What about Summer?' said Tiffany. 'She's a girl. Well, a woman. According to a book I've seen, anyway.'

'I suppose all you can do is wait to see what he does next, then. Sorry. I've never had snowflakes made in my honour . . . er, we're here . . .'

They'd reached the clearing where Miss Treason lived, and Petulia began to look a bit nervous.

'Um . . . all these stories about her . . .' she said, looking at the cottage. 'Are you all right there?'

'Was one of them about what she can do with her thumbnail?' said Tiffany.

'Yes!' said Petulia, shuddering.

'She made that one up. Don't tell anyone, though.'

'Why would anyone make up a story like that about themselves?'

Tiffany hesitated. Pigs couldn't be fooled by boffo, so Petulia hadn't run across it. And she was amazingly honest, which Tiffany was coming to learn was a bit of a drawback in a witch. It wasn't that witches were actually *dishonest*, but they were careful about what kind of truth they told.

'I don't know,' she lied. 'Anyway, you have to cut through quite a lot of a person before anything falls out. And skin is quite tough. I don't think it's possible.'

Petulia looked alarmed. 'You tried?'

'I practised with my thumbnail on a big ham this morning, if that's what you mean,' said Tiffany. You have to check things, she thought to herself. I heard the story that Miss Treason has wolf's teeth, and people tell that to one another even though they've seen her.

'Um . . . I'll come and help tomorrow, of course,' said Petulia, nervously looking at Tiffany's hands in case there were going to be any more thumbnail experiments. 'Going Away parties can be quite jolly, really. But, um, if I was you, I'd tell Mr Wintersmith to go away. That's what I did when Davey Lummock started getting, um, too romantic. And I told him that I was, um, walking out with Makky Weaver – *don't tell the others*!'

'Isn't he the one who talks about pigs all the time?'

'Well, pigs are very interesting,' said Petulia reproachfully. 'And his father, um, has got the biggest pig-breeding farm in the mountains.'

'That's something worth thinking about, definitely,' said Tiffany. 'Ouch.'

'What happened?' said Petulia.

'Oh, nothing. My hand really twinged there for a moment.' Tiffany rubbed it. 'Part of the healing, I suppose. See you tomorrow.'

Tiffany went indoors. Petulia carried on through the forest.

From up near the roof came the sounds of a conversation.

'Didja hear what the fat girl said?'

'Aye, but pigs are no' that interestin'.'

'Oh, I dinnae ken aboot that. A verrae useful animal is the pig. You can eat every part o' it, ye ken, except for the squeal.'

'Ach, ye're wrong there. Ye can use the squeal.'

'Dinnae be daft!'

'Aye, ye can so! Ye make up a pie crust, right, an' ye put in a lot o' ham, right, an' then ye catch the squeal, put the top on the pie before he can escape, right, an' bung it straight in the oven.'

'I ne'er heard o' such a thing as that!'

'Have ye no'? It's called squeal and ham pie.'

'There's nae such thing!'

'Why not? There's bubble-and-squeak, right? An' a squeak is wee compared tae a squeal. I reckon you could—'

'If youse mudlins dinnae listen I'll put ye inna pie!' yelled Rob Anybody. The Feegles muttered into silence.

And on the other side of the clearing, the wintersmith watched with purple-grey eyes. He watched until a candle was lit in an upstairs room, and watched the orange glow until it went out.

Then, walking unsteadily on new legs, he went towards the flower patch where, in the summer, roses had grown.

If you went to Zakzak Stronginthearm's magical emporium, you'd see crystal balls of all sizes but more or less only one price, which was A Great Deal Of Money. Since most witches, and particularly the good ones, had Not Much Money At All, they made use of other things, like the glass floats off old fishing nets or a saucer of black ink.

There was a puddle of black ink on Granny Weatherwax's table now. It had been in the saucer, but things had wobbled a bit when Granny and Miss Tick had banged their heads together through trying to look in the saucer at the same time.

'Did you hear that?' said Granny Weatherwax. 'Petulia Gristle asked the important question, and she just didn't think about it!'

'I'm sorry to say I missed it too,' said Miss Tick. You, the white kitten, jumped up onto the table, walked carefully through the puddle of ink and dropped into Miss Tick's lap.

'Stop that, You,' said Granny Weatherwax in a vague sort of way, as Miss Tick stared down at her dress.

'It hardly shows up,' said Miss Tick, but in fact four perfect cat footprints were very clear. Witches' dresses start out black but soon fade to shades of grey because of frequent washings or, in the case of Miss Tick, regular dips in various ponds and streams. They got threadbare and ragged, too, and their owners liked that. It showed you were a working witch, not a witch for show. Four black kitten footprints in the middle of your dress suggested you were a bit wussy, though. She lowered the cat to the floor, where it trotted over to Granny Weatherwax, rubbed up against her and tried to 'meep' more chicken into existence.

'What was the important thing?' said Miss Tick.

'I'm asking you as one witch to another, Perspicacia Tick: has the wintersmith ever *met* a girl?'

'Well,' said Miss Tick, 'I suppose the classic representation of Summer might be called a—'

'But do they ever *meet*?' said Granny Weatherwax.

'In the dance, I suppose. Just for a moment,' said Miss Tick.

'And at that moment, that very moment, in dances Tiffany Aching,' said Granny Weatherwax. 'A witch who won't wear black. No, it's blue and green for her, like green grass under a blue sky. She calls to the strength of her hills, all the time. An' they calls to her! Hills that was once alive, Miss Tick! They feels the rhythm of the dance, an' so in her bones does she, if she did but know it. And this shapes her life, even here! She could not help but tap her feet! The *land* taps its feet to the dance of the seasons!'

'But she—' Miss Tick began, because no teacher likes to hear anyone else talk for very long.

'What happened in that moment?' Granny Weatherwax went on, unstoppably. 'Summer, Winter and Tiffany. One spinning moment! And then they part. Who knows what got tangled? Suddenly, the wintersmith is acting so stupid he might even be a wee bit . . . human?'

'What *has* she got herself into?' said Miss Tick.

'The Dance, Miss Tick. The dance never ends. An' she can't change the steps, not yet. She has to dance to his tune for a while.'

'She's going to be in a lot of danger,' Miss Tick said.

'She has the strength of her hills,' said Granny.

'Soft hills, though,' said Miss Tick. 'Easily worn down.'

'But the heart of the chalk is flint, remember. It cuts sharper than any knife.'

'Snow can cover the hills,' said Miss Tick.

'Not for ever.'

'It did once,' said Miss Tick, fed up with playing games. 'For thousands of years, at least. An age of ice. Great beasts wallowed and sneezed across the world.'

'That's as may be,' said Granny Weatherwax, a glint in her eye. 'O' course, I wasn't around then. In the meantime, we must watch our girl.'

Miss Tick sipped her tea. Staying with Granny Weatherwax was a bit of a trial. Last night's pot of chicken scraps had turned out to be not for her but for You. The witches had good thick pease pudding and bacon soup without – and this was important – the bacon. Granny kept a big lump of fat bacon on a string and had taken it out, carefully dried it and put it away for another day. Despite her hunger, Miss Tick was impressed. Granny could shave the skin off a second.

'I hear that Miss Treason has heard her Call,' she said.

'Yes. Funeral tomorrow,' said Granny Weatherwax.

'That's a difficult steading over there,' said Miss Tick. 'They've had Miss Treason for a long, long time. It'll be a tricky task for a new witch.'

'She'll be a difficult . . . act to follow, indeed,' said Granny Weatherwax.

'Act?' said Miss Tick.

'I meant life, of course,' said Granny Weatherwax.

'Whom will you put in there?' said Miss Tick, because she liked to be first with the news. She also made a point of saying 'whom' whenever she could. She felt it was more literate.

'Miss Tick, that is not up to me,' said Granny sharply. 'We have no leaders in witchcraft, you know that.'

'Oh indeed,' said Miss Tick, who also knew that the leader the witches did not have was Granny Weatherwax. 'But I know that Mrs Earwig will be proposing young Annagramma, and Mrs Earwig has quite a few followers these days. It's probably those books she writes. She makes witchcraft sound exciting.'

'You know I don't like witches who try to impose their will on others,' said Granny Weatherwax.

'Quite,' said Miss Tick, trying not to laugh.

'I shall, however, drop a name into the conversation,' said Granny Weatherwax.

With a clang, I expect, thought Miss Tick. 'Petulia Gristle has shaped up very well,' she said. 'A good all-round witch.'

'Yes, but mostly all round pigs,' said Granny Weatherwax. 'I was thinking about Tiffany Aching.'

'What?' said Miss Tick. 'Don't you think that child has enough to cope with?'

Granny Weatherwax smiled briefly. 'Well, Miss Tick, you know what they say: if you want something done, give it to someone who's busy! And young Tiffany might be very busy soon,' she added.

'Why do you say that?' said Miss Tick.

'Hmm. Well, I can't be sure, but I will be very interested to see what happens to her feet . . .'

Tiffany didn't sleep much on the night before the funeral. Miss Treason's loom had clicked and clacked all through the night, because she had an order for bed sheets she wanted to complete.

It was just getting light when Tiffany gave up and got up, in that order. At least she could get the goats mucked out and milked before she tackled the other chores. There was snow, and a bitter wind was blowing it across the ground.

It wasn't until she was carting a barrowload of muck to the compost heap, which was steaming gently in the grey light, that she heard the tinkling. It sounded a bit like the wind chimes Miss Pullunder had around her cottage, only they were tuned to a note that was uncomfortable for demons.

It was coming from the place where the rose bed was in summer. It grew fine, old roses, full of scent and so red they were nearly, yes, black.

The roses were blooming again. But they—

'*How do you like them, sheep girl?*' said a voice. It didn't arrive in her head, it wasn't her thoughts, any of them, and Dr Bustle didn't wake up until at least ten. It was her own voice, from her own lips. But she hadn't thought it, and she hadn't meant to say it.

Now she was running back to the cottage. She hadn't decided to do that either, but her legs had taken over. It wasn't fear, not exactly; it was just that she very much wanted to be somewhere other than in the garden with the sun not up and the snow blowing and filling the air with ice crystals as fine as fog.

She ran through the scullery door and collided with a dark figure, which said, 'Um, sorry,' and therefore was Petulia. She was the kind of person who apologized if you trod on her foot. Right now, there was no sight more welcome.

'Sorry, I was called out to deal with a difficult cow and, um, it wasn't worth going back to bed,' she said, and then added: 'Are you all right? You don't look it!'

'I heard a voice in my mouth!' said Tiffany.

Petulia gave her an odd look and might just have stepped an inch or so backward.

'You mean in your head?' she said.

'No! I can deal with *those*! My mouth said them all by itself! And come and see what's grown in the rose garden! You won't believe it!'

There were roses. They were made of ice so fragile

that, if you breathed on them, they melted away and left nothing but the dead stalks they'd grown on. And there were dozens of them, waving in the wind.

'Even the heat of my hand near them makes them drip,' said Petulia. 'Do you think it's your wintersmith?'

'He's not mine! And I can't think of any other way they'd turn up!'

'And you think he, um, spoke to you?' said Petulia, plucking another rose. Ice particles as fine as sugar slid off her hat every time she moved.

'No! It was me! I mean, my voice! But it didn't sound like him, like him . . . I mean, like I think he'd sound! It was a bit snide, like Annagramma when she's in a mood! But it was my voice!'

'How *do* you think he'd sound?' said Petulia.

The wind gusted across the clearing, making the pine trees shake and roar.

'. . . Tiffany . . . be mine . . .'

After a little while, Petulia coughed and said: 'Um, was it just me, or did that sound like—?'

'Not just you,' whispered Tiffany, standing very still.

'Ah,' said Petulia, in a voice as bright and brittle as a rose of ice. 'Well, I think we should get indoors now, yes? Um, and get all the fires lit and some tea made, yes? And then start getting things ready, because quite soon *a lot of people will be turning up*.'

A minute later they were in the cottage, with the doors bolted and every candle spluttering into life.

They didn't talk about the wind or the roses. What would be the point? Besides, there was a job to be done. Work, that's what helped. Work and think and talk later, don't gabble now like frightened ducks. They even managed to get another layer of grime off the windows.

All through the morning people arrived from the village with the things Miss Treason had ordered. People were walking across the clearing. The sun was out, even if it was as pale as a poached egg. The world was belonging to . . . normality. Tiffany caught herself wondering if she was wrong about things. Were there roses? There were none now; the petals had not survived even the dawn's weak light. Had the wind spoken? Then she met Petulia's gaze. Yes, it had happened. But for now, there was a funeral to feed.

The girls had already got to work on the ham rolls, with three sorts of mustard, but however far wrong you couldn't go with a ham roll, if that was all you were giving seventy or eighty hungry witches, you were going all the way past Wrong and were heading into Absolute Party Disaster. So barrows were arriving with loaves and joints of beef, and jars of pickled cucumbers so big that they looked like drowned whales. Witches are very keen on pickles, as a rule, but the food they like best is free food. Yes, that's the diet for your working witch: lots of food that someone else is paying for, and so much of it that there is enough to shove in your pockets for later.

As it turned out, Miss Treason wasn't paying for it either. No one would take any money. They wouldn't leave, either, but hung about by the back door looking worried until they could have a word with Tiffany. The conversation, when she could spare the time from slicing and spreading, would go something like this:

'She's not really dying, is she?'

'Yes. At around half past six tomorrow morning.'

'But she's very old!'

'Yes. I think that's sort of why, you see.'

'But what will we do without her?'

'I don't know. What did you do before she was here?'

'She was *always* here! She knew everything! Who's going to tell us what to do now?'

And then they'd say: 'It's not going to be you, is it?' and give her a Look which said: We hope not. You don't even wear a black dress.

After a while Tiffany got fed up with this and in a very sharp voice asked the next person, a woman delivering six cooked chickens: 'What about all those stories about her slitting open bad people's bellies with her thumbnail, then?'

'Er, well, yes, but it was never anyone we knew,' said the woman virtuously.

'And the demon in the cellar?'

'So they say. O' course, I never saw it pers'nally.' The woman gave Tiffany a worried look. 'It is down there, isn't it?'

You want it to be, Tiffany thought. You actually want there to be a monster in the cellar!

But as far as Tiffany knew, what was in the cellar this morning was a lot of snoring Feegles who had been boozin'. If you put a lot of Feegles in a desert, within twenty minutes they'd find a bottle of something dreadful to drink.

'Believe me, madam, you wouldn't want to wake what's down there now,' she said, giving the woman a worried smile.

The woman seemed satisfied with that, but suddenly looked concerned again.

'And the spiders? She really eats spiders?' she said.

'Well, there's lots of webs,' said Tiffany, 'but you never see a spider!'

'Ah, right,' said the woman, as if she'd been let into a big secret. 'Say what you like, Miss Treason's been a real witch. With skulls! I expect you have to polish 'em, eh? Ha! She could spit your eye out as soon as look at you!'

'She never did, though,' said a man delivering a huge tray of sausages. 'Not to anyone local, anyway.'

'That's true,' the woman admitted reluctantly. 'She was very gracious in that respect.'

'Ah, she was a proper old-time witch, Miss Treason,' said the sausage man. 'Many a man has widdled in his boots when she's turned the sharp side of her tongue on him. You know that weaving she's always doing? She weaves your name into the loom, that's what she does! And if you tell her a lie, your thread breaks and you drop down dead on the spot!'

'Yes, that happens all the time,' said Tiffany, thinking: This is amazing! Boffo has a life of its own!

'Well, we don't get witches like her these days,' said a man delivering four dozen eggs. 'These days it's all airy-fairy and dancin' about without your drawers on.'

They all looked enquiringly at Tiffany.

'It's wintertime,' she said coldly. 'And I've got to get on with my work. The witches will be here soon. Thank you very much.'

When they were putting the eggs on to boil, she told Petulia about it. It didn't come as a surprise.

'Um, they're proud of her,' she said. 'I've heard them boasting about her up at the pig market in Lancre.'

'They boast?'

'Oh, yes. Like: you think old Mistress Weatherwax is tough? Ours has got skulls! And a demon! She's gonna live for ever 'cos she's got a clockwork heart she winds up every day! And she eats spiders, sure of it! How d'you like them poisoned apples, huh?'

Boffo works all by itself, Tiffany thought, once you get it started. Our baron is bigger than your baron, our witch is witchier than your witch . . .

CHAPTER 5

MISS TREASON'S BIG DAY

The witches started arriving at four o'clock, and Tiffany went out into the clearing to do air traffic control. Annagramma arrived by herself, looking very pale and wearing more occult jewellery than you could imagine. And there was a difficult moment when Mrs Earwig and Granny Weatherwax arrived at the same time, and circled in a ballet of careful politeness as each waited for the other to land. In the end, she directed them into different corners of the clearing and hurried away.

There was no sign of the wintersmith, and she was sure she'd know if he was near. He'd gone far away, she hoped, arranging a gale or conducting a blizzard. The memory of that voice in her head remained, awkward and worrying. Like any oyster dealing with a piece of grit, Tiffany coated it with people and hard work.

Now the day was just another pale, dry, early winter's day. Apart from the food, nothing else at the

funeral had been arranged. Witches arrange themselves. Miss Treason sat in her big chair, greeting old
friends and old enemies alike.* The cottage was far too
small for them all, so they spilled out into the garden
in gossiping groups, like a flock of old crows or,
possibly, chickens. Tiffany didn't have much time to
talk, because she was kept too busy carrying trays.

But something was going on, she could tell. Witches
would pause and turn to watch her as she staggered
past, and then turn back to their group and the level
of hubbub in the group would rise a bit. Groups would
come together and separate again. Tiffany recognized
this. The witches were making a Decision.

Lucy Warbeck sidled up to her while she was bringing out a tray of tea, and whispered, as if it was a guilty
secret: 'Mistress Weatherwax has suggested *you*, Tiff.'

'No!'

'It's true! They're talking about it! Annagramma's
having a fit!'

'Are you sure?'

'Positive. Honestly! Best of luck!'

'But I don't want the—' Tiffany pushed the tray into
Lucy's arms. 'Look, can you take that around for me,
please? They'll just grab as you go past. I've got to get
the, er, put the things in, er . . . got things to do . . .'

She hurried down the steps to the cellar, which was

---

* It says something about witches that an old friend and an old
enemy could quite often be the same person.

suspiciously empty of Feegles, and leaned against the wall.

Granny Weatherwax must be cackling, rules or no rules! But the Second Thoughts crept up to whisper: You could do it, though. She may be right. Annagramma annoys people. She talks to them as if they are children. She's interested in magic (sorry, magick with a K), but people get on her nerves. She'll make a mess of it, you know she will. She just happens to be tall and wears lots of occult jewellery and looks impressive in a pointy hat . . .

Why would Granny suggest Tiffany? Oh, she was good. She knew she was good. But didn't everyone know she didn't want to spend her life up here? Well, it had to be Annagramma, didn't it? Witches tended to be cautious and traditional, and she was the oldest of the coven. OK, a lot of witches didn't like Mrs Earwig, but Granny Weatherwax didn't exactly have many friends, either.

She went back upstairs before she was missed, and tried to be inconspicuous as she sidled through the crowd.

She saw Mrs Earwig at the centre of one group, with Annagramma; the girl looked worried, and hurried over when she caught sight of Tiffany. She was red in the face.

'Have you heard anything?' she demanded.

'What? No!' said Tiffany, starting to pile up used plates.

'You're trying to take the cottage away from me, aren't you?' Annagramma was nearly crying.

'Don't be silly! Me? I don't want a cottage at all!'

'So you say. But some of *them* are saying you should get it! Miss Level and Miss Pullunder have spoken up for you!'

'What? I couldn't possibly follow Miss Treason!'

'Well, of course that's what Mrs Earwig is telling everyone,' said Annagramma, settling down a bit. 'Completely unacceptable, she says.'

I took the hiver through the Dark Door, Tiffany thought, as she viciously scraped food scraps onto the garden for the birds. The White Horse came out of the hill for me. I got my brother and Roland back from the Queen of the Fairies. And I danced with the wintersmith, who turned me into ten billion snow-flakes. No, I don't want to be in a cottage in these damp woods; I don't want to be a kind of slave to people who can't be bothered to think for themselves; I don't want to wear midnight and make people afraid of me. There is no name for what I want to be. But I was old enough to do all those things, and I was *acceptable*.

But she said: 'I don't know what this is about!'

At which point, she felt someone looking at her and she knew, if she turned round, that it would be Granny Weatherwax.

Her Third Thoughts – the ones that paid attention out of the corner of her ear and the edge of her eye all the time – told her: Something is going on. All you can do about it is be yourself. Don't look round.

'You're really not interested?' said Annagramma uncertainly.

'I've come up here to learn witching,' said Tiffany stiffly. 'And then I'm going to go home. But . . . are you *sure* you want the cottage?'

'Well, of course! Every witch wants a cottage!'

'But they've had years and years of Miss Treason,' Tiffany pointed out.

'Then they'll just have to get used to me,' said Annagramma. 'I expect they'll be pretty glad to see the back of skulls and cobwebs and being frightened! I know she's got the local people really scared of her.'

'Ah,' said Tiffany.

'I'll be a new broom,' said Annagramma. 'Frankly, Tiffany, after that old woman just about anyone would be popular.'

'Er, yes . . .' said Tiffany. 'Tell me, Annagramma, have you ever worked with any other witch?'

'No, I've always been with Mrs Earwig. I'm her first pupil, you know,' Annagramma added proudly. 'She's very exclusive.'

'And she doesn't go around the villages much, does she?' said Tiffany.

'No. She concentrates on the Higher Magick.' Annagramma wasn't particularly observant and was very vain even by the standard of witches, but now she looked a little less confident. 'Well, someone has to. We can't all tramp around bandaging cut fingers, you know,' she added. 'Is there a problem?'

'Hmm? Oh, no. I'm sure you'll get on well,' said Tiffany. 'Er . . . I know my way around the place, so if you need any help, just ask.'

'Oh, I'm sure I'll get things sorted out to my liking,' said Annagramma, whose boundless self-confidence couldn't stay squashed for long. 'I'd better go. By the way, it looks as though the food is running low.'

She swept away.

The big vats on the trestle table just inside the door were indeed looking a bit empty. Tiffany saw one witch stuff four hard-boiled eggs into her pocket.

'Good afternoon, Miss Tick,' she said loudly.

'Ah, Tiffany,' said Miss Tick smoothly, turning round without the least sign of embarrassment. 'Miss Treason has just been telling us how well you have been doing here.'

'Thank you, Miss Tick.'

'She says you have a fine eye for hidden detail,' Miss Tick went on.

Like the labels on skulls, Tiffany thought. 'Miss Tick,' she said, 'do you know anything about people wanting me to take over the cottage?'

'Oh, that's all been decided,' said Miss Tick. 'There was some suggestion that it should be you, since you're already here, but really, you are still young and Annagramma has had much more experience. I'm sorry, but—'

'That's not fair, Miss Tick,' said Tiffany.

'Now, now, Tiffany, that's not the sort of thing a witch says—' Miss Tick began.

'I don't mean not fair on me, I mean unfair on Annagramma. She's going to make a mess of it, isn't she?'

Just for the skin of a moment, Miss Tick looked guilty. It really was a very short space of time indeed, but Tiffany spotted it.

'Mrs Earwig is certain that Annagramma will do a very good job,' said Miss Tick.

'Are you?'

'Remember who you are talking to, please!'

'I'm talking to you, Miss Tick! This is . . . wrong!' Tiffany's eyes blazed.

She saw movement out of the corner of her eye. An entire plate of sausages was moving across the white cloth at very high speed.

'And *that* is stealing,' she growled, leaping after it.

She chased after the dish as, skimming a few feet above the ground, it rounded the cottage and disappeared behind the goat shed. She plunged after it.

There were several plates lying on the leaves behind the shed. There were jacket potatoes, oozing butter, and a dozen ham rolls, and a pile of hard-boiled eggs and two cooked chickens. Everything except the sausages in the dish, which was now stationary, had a gnawed look.

There was absolutely no sign of the Feegles. That

was how she could tell they were there. They always hid from her when they knew she was angry.

Well, this time she was really angry. Not at the Feegles (much), although the stupid hiding trick got on her nerves, but at Miss Tick and Granny Weatherwax and Annagramma and Miss Treason (for dying), and the wintersmith himself (for a lot of reasons she hadn't had time to sort out yet).

She stepped back and went quiet.

There was always a feeling of sinking slowly and peacefully, but this time it was like a dive into darkness.

When she opened her eyes, it felt as if she was look-ing through windows into a huge hall. Sound seemed to be coming from a long way away and there was an itching between her eyes.

Feegles appeared, from under leaves, behind twigs, even from under plates. Their voices sounded as though they were under water.

'Ach, crivens! She's done some big hagglin' on us!'

'She's ne'er done that before!'

Hah, I'm hiding from you, thought Tiffany. Bit of a change, eh? Hmm, I wonder if I can move? She took a step sideways. The Feegles didn't seem to see it.

'She's gonna jump oot on us any moment! Ooohhh, waily—'

Ha! If I could walk up to Granny Weatherwax like this she'd have to be so impressed—

The itch on Tiffany's nose was getting worse, and

there was a feeling that was similar to, but fortunately not yet the same as, the need to visit the privy. It meant: Something is going to happen soon, so it would be a good idea to be ready for it.

The sound of the voices began to get clearer and little blue and purple spots ran across her vision.

And then there was something that, if it had made a noise, would have gone *Wwwhamp!* It was like the popping you got in your ears after a high broomstick flight. She reappeared in the middle of the Feegles, causing immediate panic.

'Stop stealing the funeral meats right now, you wee scuggers!' she shouted.

The Feegles stopped and stared at her. Then Rob Anybody said: 'Socks wi'oot feets?'

There was one of those moments – you got a lot of them around the Feegles – when the world seems to have got tangled up and it was so important to unravel the knot before you can go any further.

'What are you talking about?' said Tiffany.

'Scuggers,' said Rob Anybody. 'They're like socks wi'out feets in 'em. For keepin' yer legs warm, ye ken?'

'You mean like legwarmers?' said Tiffany.

'Aye, aye, that would be a verrae guid name for 'em, it bein' what they do,' said Rob. 'In point o' fact, mebbe the term ye meant to use wuz "thievin' scunners", which means—'

'– Us,' said Daft Wullie helpfully.

'Oh. Yes. Thank you,' said Tiffany quietly. She folded her arms and then shouted, 'Right, you thieving scunners! How dare you steal Miss Treason's funeral meats!'

'Oh, waily waily, it's the foldin' o' the arms, the foooldin' o' the aaaarmss!' cried Daft Wullie, dropping to the ground and trying to cover himself with leaves. Around him Feegles started to wail and cower and Big Yan began to bang his head on the rear wall of the dairy.

'Now then, ye must all stay calm!' yelled Rob Anybody, turning round and waving his hand desperately at his brothers.

'There's the pursin' o' the lips!' a Feegle shouted, pointing a shaking finger at Tiffany's face. 'She's got the knowin' o' the pursin' o' the lips! 'Tis doom come upon us a'!'

The Feegles tried to run, but since they were panicking again they mostly collided with one another.

'I'm waiting for an explanation!' said Tiffany.

The Feegles froze, and every face turned towards Rob Anybody.

'An explanation?' he said, shifting uneasily. 'Oh, aye. An Explanation. Nae problemo. An Explanation. Er . . . what kind would you like?'

'What kind? I just want the truth!'

'Aye? Oh. The truth? Are you sure?' Rob ventured, rather nervously. 'I can do much more interestin' Explanations than that—'

'Out with it!' snapped Tiffany, tapping her foot.

'Ach, crivens, the tappin' o' the feets has started!' moaned Daft Wullie. 'There's gonna be witherin' scoldin' at any moment!'

And that was it. Tiffany burst out laughing. You couldn't look at a bunch of frightened Nac Mac Feegles and not laugh. They were so bad at it. One sharp word and they were like a basket of frightened puppies, only smellier.

Rob Anybody gave her a lopsided, nervous grin.

'Weel, all the big hags is doin' it too,' he said. 'The wee fat one's thieved fifteen ham rolls!' he added admiringly.

'That'd be Nanny Ogg,' said Tiffany. 'Yes, she always carries a string bag up her knicker leg.'

'Ach, this is no' a proper wake,' said Rob Anybody. 'There should be singin' an' boozin' an' the flexin' o' the knees, no' all this standin' arroond gossipin'.'

'Well, gossiping's part of witchcraft,' said Tiffany. 'They're checking to see if they've gone batty yet. What is the flexin' o' the knees?'

'The dancin', ye ken,' said Rob. 'The jigs an' reels. 'Tis no' a good wake unless the hands is flingin' an' the feets is twinklin' an' the knees is flexin' an' the kilts is flyin'.'

Tiffany had never seen the Feegles dance, but she had heard them. It sounded like warfare, which was probably how they ended up. The flyin' o' the kilts sounded a bit worrying, though, and reminded her of a question she'd never quite dared to ask up until now.

'Tell me . . . is there anything worn under the kilt?'

From the way the Feegles went quiet again, she got the feeling that this was not a question they liked being asked.

Rob Anybody narrowed his eyes. The Feegles held their breath.

'Not necessarily,' he said.

At last the funeral was over, possibly because there was nothing left to eat and drink. Many of the departing witches were carrying small packages. That was another tradition. A lot of things in the cottage were the property of the cottage, and would pass on to the next witch, but everything else got passed on to the soon-to-be-late-witch's friends. Since the old witch would be alive when this happened, it saved squabbling.

That was the thing about witches. They were, according to Granny Weatherwax, 'people what looks up'. She didn't explain. She seldom explained. She didn't mean people who looked at the sky; everyone did that. She probably meant that they looked up above the everyday chores and wondered, What's all this about? How does it work? What should I do? What am I for? And possibly even: Is there anything worn under the kilt? Perhaps that was why odd, in a witch, was normal . . .

. . . but they'd squabble like polecats over a silver spoon that wasn't even silver. As it was, several were waiting impatiently by the sink for Tiffany to wash up some big dishes that Miss Treason had promised to them, and which had held the funeral roast potatoes and sausage rolls.

At least there was no problem with leftovers. Nanny Ogg, a witch who'd invented Leftover Sandwiches Soup, was waiting in the scullery with her big string bag and a bigger grin.

'We were going to have the rest of the ham with potatoes for supper,' said Tiffany, severely but with a certain amount of interest. She'd met Nanny Ogg before and quite liked her, but Miss Treason had said, darkly, that Nanny Ogg was 'a disgusting old baggage'. That sort of comment attracts your attention.

'Fair enough,' said Nanny Ogg as Tiffany placed her hand on the meat. 'You did a good job here today, Tiff. People notice that.'

She was gone before Tiffany could recover. One of them had very nearly said thank you! Amazing!

Petulia helped her bring the big table indoors and finish the tidying up. She hesitated, though, before she left.

'Um . . . you will be all right, will you?' she said. 'It's all a bit . . . strange.'

'We're supposed to be no strangers to strangeness,' said Tiffany primly. 'Anyway, you've sat up with the dead and dying, haven't you?'

'Oh, yes. Mostly pigs, though. Some humans. Um . . . I don't mind staying, if you like,' Petulia added, in a leaving-as-soon-as-possible voice.

'Thank you. But, after all, what's the worst that can happen?'

Petulia stared at her, and then said, 'Well, let me think . . . a thousand vampire demons, each one with enormous—'

'I'll be fine,' said Tiffany quickly. 'Don't you worry at all. Goodnight.'

She shut the door and then leaned on it with her hand over her mouth until she heard the gate click. She counted to ten to make sure that Petulia had got some distance and then risked taking her hand away. By then the scream that had been patiently waiting to come out had dwindled to something like 'Unk!'

This was going to be a very strange night.

People died. It was sad, but they did. What did you do next? People expected the local witch to know. So you washed the body and did a few secret and squelchy things and dressed them in their best clothes and laid them out with bowls of earth and salt beside them (no one knew why you did this bit, not even Miss Treason, but it had always been done) and you put two pennies on their eyes 'for the ferryman' and you sat with them the night before they were buried, because they shouldn't be left alone.

Exactly why was never properly explained, although everyone had been told the story of the old man who was slightly less dead than everyone thought and rose up off the spare bed in the middle of the night and got back into bed with his wife.

The real reason was probably a lot darker that that. The start and finish of things was always dangerous, lives most of all.

But Miss Treason was a wicked ol' witch. Who knew what might happen? Hang on, Tiffany told herself; don't you believe the boffo. She was really just a clever old lady with a catalogue!

In the other room Miss Treason's loom stopped.

It often did. But, this evening, the sudden silence it made was louder than usual.

Miss Treason called out: 'What do we have in the larder that needs eating up?'

Yes, this is going to be a very odd night, Tiffany told herself.

Miss Treason went to bed early. It was the first time Tiffany had ever known her not to sleep in a chair. She'd put on a long white nightdress, too, the first time Tiffany had seen her not in black.

There was a lot still to do. It was traditional that the cottage should be left sparkling clean for the next witch, and although it was hard to make black sparkle, Tiffany did her best. Actually, the cottage was always pretty clean, but Tiffany scraped and scrubbed and polished because it put off the moment when she'd have to go and talk to Miss Treason. She even took down the fake spider webs and threw them on the fire, where they burned with a nasty blue flame. She wasn't sure what to do with the skulls. Finally, she wrote down everything she could remember about the local villages: when babies were due, who was very ill and what with, who was feuding, who was 'difficult' and just about every other local detail she thought might be helpful to Annagramma. Anything to just put off the moment . . .

At last there was nothing for it but to climb the narrow stairs and say: 'Is everything all right, Miss Treason?'

The old woman was sitting up in bed, scribbling. The ravens were perched on the bed posts.

'I'm just writing a few thank-you letters,' she said. 'Some of those ladies today came quite a long way and will be having a chilly ride back.'

'"Thank you for coming to my funeral" letters?' said Tiffany weakly.

'Indeed. And they're not often written, you may be sure of that. You know the girl Annagramma Hawkin will be the new witch here? I am sure she would like you to stay on. At least for a while.'

'I don't think that would be a good idea,' said Tiffany.

'Quite,' said Miss Treason, smiling. 'I suspect the girl Weatherwax has arrangements in mind. It will be interesting to see how Mrs Earwig's brand of witchcraft suits my silly people, although it may be best to observe events from behind a rock. Or, in my case, under it.'

She put the letters aside, and both the ravens turned to look at Tiffany.

'You have been here with me only three months.'

'That's right, Miss Treason.'

'We have not talked, woman to woman. I should have taught you more.'

'I've learned a lot, Miss Treason.' And that was true.

'You have a young man, Tiffany. He sends you letters and packages. You go into Lancre Town every week to send letters to him. I fear you live not where you love.'

Tiffany said nothing. They'd been through this before. Roland seemed to fascinate Miss Treason.

'I was always too busy to pay attention to young men,' said Miss Treason. 'They were always for later and then later was too late. Pay attention to your young man.'

'Erm . . . I did say, he's not actually my—' Tiffany began, feeling herself start to blush.

'But do not become a strumpet like Mrs Ogg,' said Miss Treason.

'I'm not very musical,' said Tiffany uncertainly.

Miss Treason laughed. 'You have a dictionary, I believe,' she said. 'A strange but useful thing for a girl to have.'

'Yes, Miss Treason.'

'On my bookshelf you will find a rather larger dictionary. An unexpurgated dictionary. A useful thing for a young woman to have. You may take it, and one other book. The others will remain with the cottage. You may also have my broomstick. Everything else, of course, belongs to the cottage.'

'Thank you very much, Miss Treason. I'd like to take that book about mythology.'

'Ah, yes. Chaffinch. A very good choice. It has been a great help to me, and will, I suspect, be of *particular* assistance to you. The loom must stay, of course. Annagramma Hawkin will find it useful.'

Tiffany doubted this. Annagramma wasn't very practical at all. But it was probably not the time to say so.

Miss Treason leaned back against the cushions.

'They think you wove names into your cloth,' said Tiffany.

'That? Oh, it's true. There's nothing magical about it. It's a very old trick. Any weaver can do it. You won't be able to read it, though, without knowing how it was done.' Miss Treason sighed. 'Oh, my silly people. Anything they don't understand is magic. They think I can see into their hearts, but no witch can do that. Not without surgery, at least. No magic is needed to read their little minds, though. I've known them since they were babes. I remember when their grandparents were babes! They think they're so grown up! But they're still no better than babies in the sandpit, squabbling over mud pies. I see their lies and excuses and fears. They never grow up, not really. They never look up and open their eyes. They stay children their whole lives.'

'I'm sure they'll miss you,' said Tiffany.

'Ha! I'm the wicked ol' witch, girl. They feared me, and did what they were told! They feared joke skulls and silly stories. I chose fear. I knew they'd never love me for telling 'em the truth, so I made certain of their fear. No, they'll be relieved to hear the witch is dead. And now I shall tell you something vitally important. It is the secret of my long life.'

Ah, thought Tiffany, and leaned forward.

'The important thing,' said Miss Treason, 'is to stay the passage of the wind. You should avoid rumbustious fruits and vegetables. Beans are the worst, take it from me.'

'I don't think I understand—' Tiffany began.

'Try not to fart, in a nutshell.'

'In a nutshell I imagine it would be pretty unpleasant!' said Tiffany nervously. She couldn't believe she was being told this.

'This is no joking matter,' said Miss Treason. 'The human body only has so much air in it. You have to make it last. One plate of beans can take a year off your life. I have avoided rumbustiousness all my days. I am an old person and that means what I say is wisdom!' She gave the bewildered Tiffany a stern look. 'Do you understand, child?'

Tiffany's mind raced. Everything is a test! 'No,' she said. 'I'm not a child and that's nonsense, not wisdom!'

The stern look cracked into a smile. 'Yes,' said Miss Treason. 'Total gibberish. But you've got to admit it's a corker, all the same, right? You definitely believed it, just for a moment? The villagers did, last year. You should have seen the way they walked about for a few weeks! The strained looks on their faces quite cheered me up! How are things with the wintersmith? All gone quiet, has it?'

The question was like a sharp knife in a slice of cake, and arrived so suddenly that Tiffany gasped.

'I woke up early and wondered where you were,' said Miss Treason. It was so easy to forget that she used other people's ears and eyes all the time, in an absent-minded sort of way.

'Did you see the roses?' said Tiffany. She hadn't felt the tell-tale tickle, but she hadn't exactly had much time for anything but worry.

'Yes. Fine things,' said Miss Treason. 'I wish I could help you, Tiffany, but I'm going to be otherwise occupied. And romance is an area where I cannot offer much advice.'

'Romance?' said Tiffany, shocked

'The girl Weatherwax and Miss Tick will have to guide you,' Miss Treason went on. 'I must say, though, that I suspect that neither of them has jousted much in the lists of love.'

'Lists of love?' said Tiffany. It was getting worse!

'Can you play poker?' Miss Treason asked.

'Pardon?'

'Poker. The card game. Or Cripple Mr Onion? Chase My Neighbour Up the Passage? You must have sat up with the dead and dying before?'

'Well, yes. But I've never played cards with them! Anyway, I don't know how to play!'

'I'll teach you. There's a pack of cards in the bottom drawer of the dresser. Go and fetch them.'

'Is this like gambling?' said Tiffany. 'My father said that people shouldn't gamble.'

Miss Treason nodded. 'Good advice, my dear. Don't worry. The way I play poker isn't like gambling at all . . .'

When Tiffany awoke with a jolt, playing cards sliding off her dress and onto the floor, the cold grey light of morning filled the room.

She peered at Miss Treason, who was snoring like a pig.

What was the time? Gone six at least! What should she do?

Nothing. There was nothing to do.

She picked up the Ace of Wands and stared at it. So that was poker, was it? Well, she hadn't been too bad at it, once she'd worked out that it was all about making your face tell lies. For most of the time the cards were just something to do with your hands.

Miss Treason slept on. Tiffany wondered if she should get some breakfast, but it seemed such a—

'The ancient kings of Djelibeybi, who are buried in pyramids,' said Miss Treason, from the bed, 'used to believe that they could take things with them into the next world. Such things as gold and precious stones and even slaves. On that basis, please make me a ham sandwich.'

'Er . . . you mean . . . ?' Tiffany began.

'The journey after death is quite a long one,' said Miss Treason, sitting up. 'I may get hungry.'

'But you'll just be a soul!'

'Well, perhaps a ham sandwich has a soul, too,' said Miss Treason, as she swung her skinny legs out of the bed. 'I'm not sure about the mustard, but it's worth a try. Hold still there!' This was because she had picked up her hairbrush and was using Tiffany as a mirror. The fiercely concentrated glare a few inches away was as much as Tiffany could bear on a morning like this.

'Thank you, you may go and make the sandwich,' said Miss Treason, laying the brush aside. 'I will now get dressed.'

Tiffany hurried out and washed her face in the basin in her room; she always did that after the eyeballing, but she'd never plucked up the courage to object and now certainly wasn't the time to start.

As she dried her face, she thought she heard a muffled sound outside and went over to the window. There was frost on—

163

Oh, no . . . oh . . . no . . . no! He was at it again!

The frost ferns spelled the word: *Tiffany*. Over and over again.

She grabbed the flannel and wiped them off, but the ice only formed again, thicker.

She hurried downstairs. The ferns were all over the windows, and when she tried to wipe them off, the flannel froze to the glass. It creaked when she pulled at it.

Her name, all over the window. Over all the windows. Maybe over all the windows in all the mountains. Everywhere.

He'd come back. That was dreadful!

But also, just a bit . . . cool . . .

She didn't think the word, because as far as Tiffany knew it meant 'slightly cold'. But she thought the thought, even so. It was a hot little thought.

'In my day young men would just carve the girl's initials on a tree,' said Miss Treason, coming down the stairs one careful step at a time. Too late, Tiffany felt the tickle behind her eyes.

'It's not funny, Miss Treason! What shall I do?'

'I don't know. If possible, be yourself.'

Miss Treason bent down creakily, and opened her hand. The seeing-eye mouse hopped down onto the floor, turned and stared at her with tiny black eyes for a moment. She prodded it with a finger. 'Go on, off you go. Thank you,' she said and then it scuttled off to a hole.

Tiffany helped her upright, and the old witch said: 'You're starting to snivel, aren't you . . .'

'Well, it's all a bit—' Tiffany began. The little mouse had looked so lost and forlorn.

'Don't cry,' said Miss Treason. 'Living this long's not as wonderful as people think. I mean, you get the same amount of youth as everyone else, but a great big extra helping of being very old and deaf and creaky. Now, blow your nose and help me on with the ravens' perch.'

'He might still be out there . . .' Tiffany mumbled, as she eased the perch onto the thin shoulders.

Then she rubbed at the window again, and saw shapes and movement.

'Oh . . . they came . . .' she said.

'What?' said Miss Treason. She stopped. 'There's lots of people out there!'

'Er . . . yes,' said Tiffany.

'What do you know about this, my girl?'

'Well, you see, they kept asking when—'

'Fetch my skulls! They mustn't see me without my skulls! How does my hair look?' said Miss Treason, frantically winding up her clock.

'It looks nice—'

'Nice? *Nice?* Are you mad? Mess it up this minute!' Miss Treason demanded. 'And fetch my most raggedy cloak! This one's far too clean! Move yourself, child!'

It took several minutes to get Miss Treason ready, and a lot of the time was spent convincing her that taking the skulls out in daylight might be dangerous, in case they got dropped and someone saw the labels. Then Tiffany opened the door.

A murmur of conversation crashed into silence.

There were people in a crowd all around the door. As Miss Treason stepped forward, it parted to leave a clear path.

To her horror, Tiffany saw a dug grave on the other side of the clearing. She hadn't expected that. She wasn't sure what she had expected, but a dug grave wasn't it.

'Who dug—?'

'Our blue friends,' said Miss Treason. 'I asked them to.'

And then the crowd started to cheer. Women hurried forward with big bunches of yew, holly and mistletoe, the only green things growing. People were laughing. People were crying. They clustered around the witch, forcing Tiffany out to the edge of the crowd. She went quiet, and listened.

'We don't know what we'll do without you, Miss Treason' . . . 'I don't think we'll get another witch as good as you, Miss Treason!' . . . 'We never thought you'd go, Miss Treason, you brought my ol' granddad into the world' . . .

Walking into the grave, Tiffany thought. Well, that's style. That's . . . solid gold boffo. They'll remember that for the rest of their lives—

'In that case you shall keep all the puppies but

one—' Miss Treason had stopped to organize the crowd. 'The custom is to give that one to the owner of the dog. You should have kept the bitch in, after all, and minded your fences. And your question, Mister Blinkhorn?'

Tiffany stood up straight. They were bothering her! Even this morning! But she . . . wanted to be bothered. Being bothered was her life.

'Miss Treason!' she snapped, pushing her way through the mob. 'Remember you have an appointment!'

It wasn't the best thing to say, but a lot better than: 'You said you were going to die in about five minutes' time!'

Miss Treason turned, and looked uncertain for a moment.

'Oh, yes,' she said. 'Yes, indeed. We had better get on.' Then, still talking to Mr Blinkhorn about some complex problem concerning a fallen tree and someone's shed, and with the rest of the crowd trailing after her, she let Tiffany walk her gently to the graveside.

'Well, at least you've got a happy ending, Miss Treason,' Tiffany whispered. It was a silly thing to say and deserved what it got.

'We make happy endings, child, day to day. But, you see, for the witch there are no happy endings. There are just endings. And here we are . . .'

Best not to think, thought Tiffany. Best not to think you're climbing down an actual ladder into an actual grave. Try not to think about helping Miss Treason down the ladder onto the leaves which are piled up at one end. Do not let yourself know you're standing in a grave.

Down here, the horrible clock seem to clank even louder: *clonk, clank, clonk, clank* . . .

Miss Treason trod the leaves down a bit and said, cheerfully, 'Yes, I can see myself being quite comfortable here. Listen, child, I told you about the books, did I not? And there is a small gift for you under my chair. Yes, this seems adequate. Oh, I forgot . . .'

Clonk, clank, clonk, clank . . . went the clock, sounding much louder down there.

Miss Treason stood on tiptoe and poked her head over the edge of the hole. 'Mister Easy! You owe two months rent to the widow Langley! Understand? Mr Plenty, the pig belongs to Mrs Frumment, and if you don't give it back to her I shall come back and groan under your window! Mistress Fullsome, the Dogelley family have had Right of Passage over the Turnwise pasture since even I cannot remember, and you must . . . you must . . .'

Clon . . . k.

There was a moment, one long moment, when the sudden silence of the clock not ticking any more filled the clearing like thunder.

Slowly, Miss Treason sagged down onto the leaves.

It took a few dreadful seconds for her brain to stop working again, and then Tiffany screamed at the people clustered above: 'Go back, all of you! Give her some air!'

She knelt down as they backed hurriedly away.

The smell of the raw soil was sharp in the air. At least Miss Treason seemed to have died with her eyes shut. Not everyone did. Tiffany hated having to shut them for people; it was like killing them all over again . . .

'Miss Treason?' she whispered. That was the first test. There were a lot of them and you had to do them all: speak to them, raise an arm, check the pulses including the one behind the ear, check for breath with a mirror . . . and she'd always been so nervous about getting them wrong that the first time she'd had to go out to deal with someone who looked dead – a young man who'd been in a horrible sawmill accident – she done every single test, even though she'd had to go and find his head.

There were no mirrors in Miss Treason's cottage.

In that case she—

– should think! This is Miss Treason here! And I heard her wind her clock up only a few minutes ago!

She smiled.

'Miss Treason!' she said, very close to the woman's ear. 'I know you're in there!'

And that's when the morning, which had been sad, weird, odd and horrible, became . . . boffo all the way.

Miss Treason smiled.

'Have they gone?' she enquired.

'Miss Treason!' said Tiffany sternly. 'That was a terrible thing to do!'

'I stopped my clock with my thumbnail,' said Miss Treason proudly. 'Couldn't disappoint them, eh? Had to give 'em a show!'

'Miss Treason,' said Tiffany severely, 'did you make up the story about your clock?'

'Of course I did! And it's a wonderful bit of folklore, a real corker. Miss Treason and her clockwork heart! Might even become a myth, if I'm lucky. They'll remember Miss Treason for thousands of years!'

Miss Treason closed the eye.

'I'll certainly remember you, Miss Treason,' said Tiffany. 'I will really, because—'

The world had gone grey, and was getting greyer. And Miss Treason had gone very still.

'Miss Treason?' said Tiffany, nudging her. 'Miss Treason?'

MISS EUMENIDES TREASON, AGED ONE HUNDRED AND ELEVEN?

Tiffany heard the voice inside her head. It didn't seem to have come through her ears. And she'd heard it before, making her quite unusual. Most people hear the voice of Death only once.

Miss Treason stood up, without the creak of even one bone. And she looked just like Miss Treason, solid and smiling. What now lay on the dead leaves was, in this strange light, just a shadow.

But a very tall dark figure was standing beside her.

It was Death himself. Tiffany had seen him before, in his own land beyond the Dark Door, but you didn't need to have met him before to know who he was. The scythe, the long hooded robe and of course the bundle of hourglasses were all clues.

'Where are your manners, child?' said Miss Treason.

Tiffany looked up and said: 'Good morning.'

GOOD MORNING, TIFFANY ACHING, AGED THIRTEEN, said Death, in his no-voice. I SEE YOU ARE IN GOOD HEALTH.

'A little curtsey would be in order, too,' said Miss Treason.

To Death? thought Tiffany. Granny Aching wouldn't have liked that. Never bend the knee to tyrants, she would say.

AT LAST, MISS EUMENIDES TREASON, WE MUST WALK TOGETHER. Death took her gently by the arm.

'Hey, wait a minute!' said Tiffany. 'Miss Treason is one hundred and thirteen!'

'Er . . . I adjusted it slightly for professional reasons,' said Miss Treason. 'One hundred and eleven sounds so . . . adolescent.' As if to hide her ghostly embarrassment, she plunged her hand into her pocket and pulled out the spirit of the ham sandwich.

'Ah, it worked,' she said. 'I know I— Hey, where has the mustard gone?'

MUSTARD IS ALWAYS TRICKY, said Death as they began to fade.

'No mustard? What about pickled onions?'

PICKLES OF ALL SORTS DON'T SEEM TO MAKE IT. I'M SORRY.

Behind them, the outline of a door appeared.

'No relishes in the next world? That's dreadful! What about chutneys?' said the vanishing Miss Treason.

THERE'S JAM. JAM WORKS.

'Jam? Jam! With ham?'

And they were gone. The light went back to normal. Sound came back. Time came back.

Once again, the thing to do was not to think too deeply, just keep her thoughts nice and level and focused on what she had to do.

Watched by the people still hovering around the clearing, Tiffany went and got some blankets, bundling them up so that when she carried them back to the grave no one would notice that the two Boffo skulls and the spider web-making machine were tucked inside. Then, with Miss Treason and the secret of boffo safely tucked away, she filled in the grave, and at this point a couple of men ran and helped her, right up until there came, from under the soil:

Clonk clank. Clonk.

The men froze. So did Tiffany, but her Third Thoughts cut in with: Don't worry! Remember, she stopped it! A falling stone or something must have started it going again!

She relaxed and said sweetly: 'That was probably just her saying goodbye.'

The rest of the soil got shovelled in really quickly.

And now I'm part of the boffo, Tiffany thought, as

the people hurried back to their villages. But Miss Treason worked very hard for them. She deserves to be a myth, if that's what she wants. And I'll bet, I bet that on dark nights they'll hear her : . .

But now there was nothing but the wind in the trees.

She stared at the grave.

Someone should say something. Well? She was the witch, after all.

There wasn't much religion on the Chalk or in the mountains. The Omnians came and had a prayer meeting about once a year, and sometimes a priest from the Nine Day Wonderers or the See of Little Faith or the Church of Small Gods would come by on a donkey. People went along to listen, if a priest sounded interesting or went red and shouted, and they sang the songs if they had a good tune. And then they went home again.

'We are small people,' her father had said. 'It ain't wise to come to the attention of the gods.'

Tiffany remembered the words he had said over the grave of Granny Aching, what seemed like a lifetime ago. On the summer turf of the downlands, with the buzzards screaming in the sky, they had seemed to be all there was to say. So she said them now:

    'If any ground is Consecrate, this ground is.
    If any day is Holy, it is this day.'

She saw a movement, and then Billy Bigchin the gonnagle scrambled onto the turned earth of the grave. He gave Tiffany a solemn look, then unslung his mousepipes and began to play.

Humans could not hear the mousepipes very well because the notes were too high, but Tiffany could feel them in her head. A gonnagle could put many things into his music, and she felt sunsets, and autumns, and the mist on hills and the smell of roses so red they were nearly black . . .

When he had finished, the gonnagle stood in silence for a moment, looked at Tiffany again, then vanished.

Tiffany sat on a stump and cried a bit, because it needed to be done. Then she went and milked the goats, because someone had to do that, too.

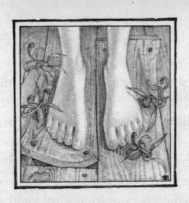

CHAPTER 6

FEET AND SPROUTS

In the cottage, the beds were airing, the floors had been swept and the log basket was full. On the kitchen table the inventory was laid out: so many spoons, so many pans, so many dishes, all lined up in the dingy light. Tiffany packed some of the cheeses, though. She'd made them, after all.

The loom was silent in its room; it looked like the bones of some dead animal, but under the big chair was the package Miss Treason had mentioned, wrapped in black paper. Inside it was a cloak woven of brown wool so dark that it was almost black. It looked warm.

That was it, then. Time to go. If she lay down and put her ear to a mouse hole, she could hear widespread snoring coming from the cellar. The Feegles believed that after a really good funeral, everyone should be lying down. It wasn't a good idea to wake them. They'd find her. They always did.

Was that everything? Oh, no, not quite. She took down *The Unexpurgated Dictionary* and Chaffinch's *Mythology*, with 'The Dacne of the Sneasos' in it, and went to tuck them into a bag under the cheeses. As she did so the pages flipped like cards and several things dropped out onto the stone floor. Some of them were faded old letters, which she tucked back inside for now.

There was also the Boffo catalogue. The cover had a grinning clown on it, and the words:

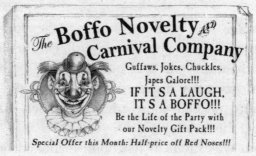

The **Boffo Novelty** *and* **Carnival Company**

Guffaws. Jokes. Chuckles.
Japes Galore!!!
IF IT'S A LAUGH,
IT'S A BOFFO!!!
Be the Life of the Party with
our Novelty Gift Pack!!!

Special Offer this Month: Half-price off Red Noses!!!

Yes, you could spend years trying to be a witch or you could spend a lot of money with Mr Boffo and be one as soon as the postman arrived.

Fascinated, Tiffany turned the pages. There were skulls (Glow in the Dark, $8 Extra) and fake ears and pages of hilarious noses (Ghastly Dangling Bogey free on noses over $5) and masks, as Boffo would say, Galore!!! Mask No. 19, for example, was: Wicked Witch De-luxe, with Mad Greasy Hair, Rotting Teeth and Hairy Warts (supplied loose, stick them where you like!!!). Miss Treason had obviously stopped short of buying one of these, possibly because the nose looked like a carrot but probably because the skin was bright green. She could also have bought Scary Witch Hands ($8 a pair, with green skin and black fingernails) and Smelly Witch Feet ($9).

Tiffany tucked the catalogue back into the book. She couldn't leave it for Annagramma to find, or the secret of Miss Treason's boffo would be out.

And that was it: one life ended and neatly tidied away. One cottage, clean and empty. One girl, wondering what was going to happen next. 'Arrangements' would be made.

Clonk-clank.

She didn't move, didn't look round. I'm not going to be boffo'd, she told herself. There's an explanation for that noise which isn't to do with Miss Treason. Let's see . . . I cleaned the fireplace, right? And I leaned the poker next to it. But unless you get it just right, it always falls over sooner or later in a sneaky kind of way. That's it. When I turn and look behind me, I'll see that the poker has fallen over and is lying in the grate and therefore the noise wasn't caused by any kind of ghostly clock at all.

She turned round slowly. The poker was lying in the grate.

And now, she thought, it would be a good idea to go outside in the fresh air. It's bit sad and stuffy in here. That's why I want to go out, because it's sad and stuffy. It's not at all because I'm afraid of any imaginary noises. I'm not superstitious. I'm a witch. Witches aren't superstitious. We are what people are super-stitious of. I just don't want to stay. I felt safe here when she was alive – it was like sheltering under a huge tree – but I don't think it is safe any more. If the wintersmith makes the trees shout my name, well, I'll cover my ears. The house feels like it's dying and I'm going *outside*.

There was no point in locking the door. The local people were nervous enough about going inside even when Miss Treason was alive. They certainly wouldn't set foot inside now, not until another witch had made the place her own.

A weak, runny-egg kind of sun was showing through the clouds now, and the wind had blown the frost away. But a brief autumn turned to winter quickly up here; from now on there would always be the smell of snow in the air. Up in the mountains the winter never ended. Even in the summer the water in the streams was ice-cold from the melting snow.

Tiffany sat down on the old stump with her ancient suitcase and the sack and waited for the Arrange-ments. Annagramma would be here pretty soon, you could bet on that.

From here, the cottage already looked abandoned. It seemed like—

It was her birthday. The thought pushed itself to the front. Yes, it would be today. Death had got it right. The one big day in the year that was totally hers, and she had forgotten about it in all the excitement and now it was already two-thirds over.

Had she ever told Petulia and the others when it was? She couldn't remember.

Thirteen years old. But she'd been thinking of herself as 'nearly thirteen' for months now. Pretty soon she'd be 'nearly fourteen'.

She was just about to enjoy a bit of self pity when there was a stealthy rustling behind her. She turned so quickly that Horace the cheese leaped backwards.

'Oh, it's you,' said Tiffany. 'Where have you been, you naughty bo— cheese? I was worried sick!'

Horace looked ashamed, but it was quite hard to see how he managed it.

'Are you going to come with me?' she said.

Horace was immediately surrounded by a feeling of yesness.

'All right, you must get in the sack.' Tiffany opened it, but Horace backed away.

'Well, if you are going to be a naughty chee—' she began, and stopped. Her hand was itching. She looked up . . . at the wintersmith.

It had to be him. At first he was just swirling snow in the air, but as he strode across the clearing he seemed to come together, become human, become a young man with a cloak billowing out behind him and snow on his hair and shoulders. He wasn't transparent this time, not entirely, but something like ripples ran across him and Tiffany thought she could see the trees behind him, like shadows.

She took a few hurried steps backwards, but the wintersmith was crossing the dead grass with the speed of a skater. She could turn and run, but that would mean she was, well, turning and running, and why should she do that? She hadn't been the one scribbling on people's windows!

What should she say? What should she say?

'Now, I really appreciated you finding my necklace,' she said, backing away again. 'And the snowflakes and roses were really very . . . it was very sweet. But . . . I don't think that we . . . well, you're made of cold and I'm not . . . I'm a human, made of . . . human things . . .'

'You must be her,' said the wintersmith. 'You were in the dance! And now you are here, in my winter.'

The voice wasn't right. It sounded . . . fake, somehow, as if the wintersmith had been taught to say the sound of words without understanding what they were.

'I'm a her,' she said uncertainly. 'I don't know about "must be". Er . . . please, I'm *really* sorry about the dance, I didn't mean to, it just seemed so . . .'

He'd still got the same purple-grey eyes, she noticed. Purple-grey, in a face sculpted from freezing fog. A handsome face, too. 'Look, I never meant to make you think—' she began.

'Meant?' said the wintersmith, looking astonished. 'But we don't *mean*. We are!'

'What do you . . . mean?'

'Crivens!'

'Oh, no . . .' muttered Tiffany as Feegles erupted from the grass.

The Feegles didn't know the meaning of the word 'fear'. Sometimes Tiffany wished they'd read a dictionary. They fought like tigers, they fought like demons, they fought like giants. What they didn't do was fight like something with more than a spoonful of brain.

They attacked the wintersmith with swords, heads and feet, and the fact that everything went through him as if he was a shadow didn't seem to bother them. If a Feegle aimed a boot at a misty leg and ended up kicking himself in his own head, then it had been a good result.

The wintersmith ignored them, like a man paying no attention to butterflies.

'Where is your power? Why are you dressed like this?' the wintersmith demanded. 'This is not as it should be!'

He stepped forward and grabbed Tiffany's wrist hard, much harder than a ghostly hand should be able to do.

'It is wrong!' he shouted. Above the clearing, the clouds were moving fast.

Tiffany tried to pull away. 'Let me go!'

'You are her!' the wintersmith shouted, pulling her towards him.

Tiffany hadn't known where the shout came from, but the slap came from her hand, thinking for itself. It caught the figure on the cheek so hard that for a moment the face blurred, as if she'd smeared a painting.

'Don't come near me! Don't touch me!' she screamed.

There was a flicker behind the wintersmith. Tiffany couldn't see it clearly because of the icy haze and her own anger and terror, but something blurred and dark was moving towards them across the clearing, wavering and distorted like a figure seen though ice. It loomed behind the transparent figure for one dark moment, and then became Granny Weatherwax, in the same space as the wintersmith . . . inside him.

He screamed for a second, and exploded into a mist.

Granny stumbled forward, blinking.

'Urrrgh. It'll take a while to get the taste of that out of my head,' she said. 'Shut your mouth, girl, something might fly into it.'

Tiffany shut her mouth. Something might fly into it.

'What . . . what did you do to him?' she managed.

'*It!*' snapped Granny, rubbing her forehead. 'It's an it, not a he! An it that thinks it's a he! Now give me your necklace!'

'What! But it's mine!'

'Do you think I want an argument?' Granny Weatherwax snapped. 'Does it say on my face I want an argument? Give it to me now! Don't you dare defy me!'

'I won't just—'

Granny Weatherwax lowered her voice, and in a piercing hiss much worse than a scream said: 'It's how it finds you. Do you want it to find you again? It's just a fog now. How solid do you think it will become?'

Tiffany thought about that strange face, not moving like a real one should, and that strange voice, putting words together as if they were bricks . . .

She undid the little silver clasp and held up the necklace.

It's just boffo, she told herself. Every stick is a wand, every puddle is a crystal ball. This is just a . . . a thing. I don't need it to be me.

Yes, I do.

'You must *give* it to me,' said Granny softly. 'I can't take it.'

She held out her hand, palm up.

Tiffany dropped the horse into it, and tried not to see Granny Weatherwax's fingers as a closing claw.

'Very well,' said Granny, satisfied. 'Now we must go.'

'You were watching me,' said Tiffany sullenly.

'All morning. You could have seen me if you'd thought to look,' said Granny. 'But you didn't do a bad job at the burial, I'll say that.'

'I did a good job!'

'That's what I said.'

'No,' said Tiffany, still trembling. 'You didn't.'

'I've never held with skulls and suchlike,' said

Granny, ignoring this. 'Artificial ones, at any rate. But Miss Treason—'

She stopped, and Tiffany saw her stare at the treetops.

'Is that him again?' she said.

'No,' said Granny, as if this was something to be disappointed about. 'No, that's young Miss Hawkin. And Mrs Letice Earwig. Didn't hang about, I see. And Miss Treason hardly cooled down.' She sniffed. 'Some people might have had the common decency not to snatch.'

The two broomsticks landed a little way off. Annagramma looked nervous. Mrs Earwig looked like she always did: tall, pale, very well dressed, wearing lots of occult jewellery and an expression that said you were slightly annoying her but she was being gracious enough not to let it show. And she always looked at Tiffany, when she ever bothered to look at her at all, as if she was some kind of strange creature that she didn't quite understand.

Mrs Earwig was always polite to Granny, in a formal and chilly way. It made Granny Weatherwax mad, but that was the way of witches. When they really disliked one another they were as polite as duchesses.

As the other two approached, Granny bowed low and removed her hat. Mrs Earwig did the same thing, only the bow was a little lower.

Tiffany saw Granny glance up, and then bow lower still, by about an inch.

Mrs Earwig managed to go half an inch further down.

Tiffany and Annagramma exchanged a hopeless glance over the straining backs. Sometimes this sort of thing could go on for hours.

Granny Weatherwax gave a grunt and straightened up. So did Mrs Earwig, red in the face.

'Blessin's be upon our meetin',' said Granny, in a calm voice. Tiffany winced. This was a declaration of hostilities. Yelling and prodding with the fingers was perfectly ordinary witch arguing, but speaking carefully and calmly was open warfare.

'How kind of you to greet us,' said Mrs Earwig.

'I hopes I sees you in good health?'

'I keep well, Miss Weatherwax.' Annagramma shut her eyes. That was a kick in the stomach, by witch standards.

'It's Mistress Weatherwax, Mrs Earwig,' said Granny. 'As I believes you know?'

'Why, yes. Of course it is. I am so sorry.'

These vicious blows having been exchanged, Granny went on: 'I trust Miss Hawkin will find everything to her likin'.'

'I'm sure that—' Mrs Earwig stared at Tiffany, her face a question.

'Tiffany,' said Tiffany helpfully.

'Tiffany. Of course. What a lovely name . . . I'm sure that Tiffany has done her very best,' said Mrs Earwig. 'However, we shall shrive and consecrate the cottage, in case of . . . influences.'

I already scrubbed and scrubbed everything! Tiffany thought.

'Influences?' said Granny Weatherwax, and even the wintersmith could not have managed a voice so icy.

'And disquieting vibrations,' said Mrs Earwig.

'Oh, I know about *those*,' said Tiffany. 'It's the loose floorboard in the kitchen. If you tread on it, it makes the dresser wobble.'

'There has been talk of a demon,' said Mrs Earwig, gravely ignoring this. 'And . . . skulls.'

'But—' Tiffany began, and Granny's hand squeezed her shoulder so hard she stopped.

'Deary, deary me,' said Granny, still holding on tightly. 'Skulls, eh?'

'There are some very disturbing stories,' said Mrs Earwig, watching Tiffany. 'Of the darkest nature, Mistress Weatherwax. I feel that the people in this steading have been very badly served, indeed. Dark forces have been unleashed.'

Tiffany wanted to yell: No! It was all stories! It was all boffo! She watched over them! She stopped their stupid arguments, she remembered their laws, she scolded their silliness! She couldn't do that if she was just a frail old lady! She had to be a myth! But Granny's grip kept her silent.

'Strange forces are certainly at work,' said Granny Weatherwax. 'I wish you well in your endeavours, Mrs Earwig. If you will excuse me?'

'Of course, Mis—tress Weatherwax. May good stars attend you.'

'May the road slow down to meet your feet,' said Granny. She stopped gripping Tiffany so hard but nevertheless almost dragged her around the side of the cottage. The late Miss Treason's broomstick was leaning against the wall.

'Tie your stuff on quickly!' she commanded. 'We must move!'

'Is he going to come back?' said Tiffany, struggling to tie the sack and the old suitcase onto the bristles.

'Not yet. Not soon, I think. But he will be looking for you. And he will be stronger. Dangerous to you, I believe, and those around you! You have such a lot to learn! You have such a lot to do!'

'I thanked him! I tried to be nice to him! Why is he still interested in me?'

'Because of the dance,' said Granny.

'I'm sorry about that!'

'Not good enough. What does a storm know of sorrow? You must make amends. Did you really think that space was left there for you? Oh, this is so tangled! How are your feet?'

Tiffany, angry and bewildered, stopped with one leg half over the stick.

'My feet? What about my feet?'

'Do they itch? What happens when you take your boots off?'

'Nothing! I just see my socks! What have my feet got to do with anything?'

'We shall find out,' said Granny, infuriatingly. 'Now, come along.'

Tiffany tried to get the stick to rise, but it barely cleared the dead grass. She looked round. The bristles were covered with Nac Mac Feegles.

'Dinnae mind us,' said Rob Anybody. 'We'll hold on tight!'

'An' dinnae make it too bumpy 'cos I feel like the top o' mah heid's come off,' said Daft Wullie.

'Do we get meals on this flight?' said Big Yan. 'I'm fair boggin' for a wee drink.'

'I can't take you all!' said Tiffany. 'I don't even know where I'm going!'

Granny Weatherwax glared at the Feegles. 'You'll have to walk. We're travellin' to Lancre Town. The address is: Tir Nani Ogg, The Square.'

'Tir Nani Ogg,' said Tiffany. 'Isn't that—?'

'It means Nanny Ogg's Place,' said Granny, as Feegles dropped off the broomstick. 'You'll be safe there. Well, more or less. But we must make a stop on the way. We must put that necklace as far away from you as we can. And I know how to do that! Oh, yes!'

The Nac Mac Feegle jogged through the afternoon woods. Local wildlife had found out about Feegles, so the fluffy woodland creatures had all dived for their burrows and climbed high in the trees, but after a while Big Yan called a halt and said: 'There's somethin' trackin' us!'

'Don't be daft,' said Rob Anybody. 'There's nothin' left in these woods that's mad enough tae hunt Feegles!'

'I know what I'm sensin',' said Big Yan stubbornly. 'I can feel it in my watter. There's somethin' creepin' up on us right noo!'

'Weel, I'm not one tae argue wi' a man's watter,' said Rob wearily. 'OK, lads, spread oot inna big circle!'

Swords drawn, the Feegles spread out, but after a few minutes there was a general muttering. There was nothing to see, nothing to hear. A few birds sang, at a safe distance. Peace and quiet, unusual in the vicinity of Feegles, was everywhere.

'Sorry, Big Yan, but I'm thinkin' yer watter is no' on the button this time,' said Rob Anybody.

It was at this point that Horace the cheese dropped from a branch onto his head.

A lot of water flowed under the big bridge at Lancre, but from up here you could barely see it because of the spray coming up from the waterfalls a little further on, spray which hovered in the freezing air. There was white water all through the deep gorge, and then the river leaped the waterfall like a salmon and hit the plains below like a thunderstorm. From the base of the falls you could follow the river all the way past the Chalk, but it moved in wide, lazy curves and it was quicker to fly in a straight line.

Tiffany had flown up it just once, when Miss Level had first brought her up into the mountains. Since then she'd always taken the long way down, cruising just above the zig-zagging coach road. Flying out over the edge of that furious torrent into a sudden drop full of cold damp air and then pointing the stick almost straight down was pretty high on her list of things she never intended to do, ever.

Now Granny Weatherwax stood on the bridge, the silver horse in her hand.

'It's the only way,' she said. 'It'll end up at the bottom of the deep sea. Let the wintersmith look for you there!'

Tiffany nodded. She wasn't crying, which is not the same as, well, not crying. People walked around not crying all the time and didn't think about it at all. But now, she did. She thought: I'm not crying . . .

It made sense. Of course it made sense. It was all boffo! Every stick is a wand, every puddle is a crystal ball. No thing had any power that you didn't put there. Shambles and skulls and wands were like . . . shovels and knives and spectacles. They were like . . . levers. With a lever you could lift a big rock, but the lever didn't do any work.

'It has to be your choice,' said Granny. 'I can't make it for you. But it's a small thing, and while you have it, it will be dangerous.'

'You know, I don't think he wanted to hurt me. He was just upset,' said Tiffany.

'Really? Do you want to meet it upset again?'

Tiffany thought about that strange face. There had been the shape of a human there – more or less – but it was as if the wintersmith had heard of the idea of being human but hadn't found out how to do it yet.

'You think he'll harm other people?' she said.

'He is the winter, child. It's not all pretty snowflakes, is it?'

Tiffany held out her hand. 'Give it back to me, please.'

Granny handed it over, with a shrug.

It lay in Tiffany's hand, on the strange white scar. It was the first thing she had ever been given that wasn't useful, that wasn't supposed to do something.

I don't need this, she thought. My power comes from the Chalk. But is that what life's going to be like? Nothing that you don't need?

'We should tie it to something that's light,' she said, in a matter-of-fact voice; 'otherwise it will get caught on the bottom.'

After some rooting around in the grass near the bridge she found a stick and wrapped the silver chain around it.

It was noon. Tiffany had invented the word noon-light, because she liked the sound of it. Anyone could be a witch at midnight, she'd thought, but you'd have to be really good to be a witch by noonlight.

Good at being a witch, anyway, she thought as she

walked back onto the bridge. Not good at being a happy person.

She threw the necklace off the bridge.

She didn't make a big thing of it. It would have been nice to say that the silver horse glittered in the light, seemed to hang in the air for a moment before falling the long fall. Perhaps it did, but Tiffany didn't look.

'Good,' said Granny Weatherwax.

'Is it all over now?' said Tiffany.

'No! You danced into a story, girl, one that tells itself to the world every year. It's the story about ice and fire, summer and winter. You've made it wrong. You've got to stay to the end and make sure it turns out right. The horse is just buyin' you time, that's all.'

'How much time?'

'I don't know. This hasn't happened before. Time to think, at least. How are your feet?'

The wintersmith was also moving through the world without, in any human sense, moving at all. Wherever winter was, he was too.

He was trying to think. He'd never had to do this before, and it hurt. Up until now, humans had just been parts of the world that moved around in strange ways and lit fires. Now he was spinning himself a mind, and everything was new.

A human . . . made of human stuff . . . that was what she had said.

Human stuff. He had to make himself of human

stuff for the beloved. In the chill of morgues and the wreckage of ships the wintersmith rode the air searching for human stuff. And what was it? Dirt and water, mostly. Leave a human long enough and even the water would go, and there would be nothing but a few handfuls of dust that blew away in the wind.

So, since water did not think, all the work was being done by the dust.

The wintersmith was logical, because ice was logical. Water was logical. Wind was logical. There were rules. So what a human was all about was . . . the right kind of dust!

And, while he was searching for it, he could show her how strong he was.

That evening, Tiffany sat on the edge of her new bed, the clouds of sleep rising in her brain like thunderheads, and yawned and stared at her feet.

They were pink, and had five toes each. They were pretty good feet, considering.

Normally, when people met you they'd say things like 'How are you?' Nanny Ogg had just said: 'Come on in. How're your feet?'

Suddenly, everyone was interested in her feet. Of course, feet were important, but what did people expect to happen to them?

She swung them back and forth on the end of her legs. They didn't do anything strange, so she got into bed.

She hadn't slept properly for two nights. She hadn't really understood that until she'd reached Tir Nani Ogg, when her brain had started to spin of its own accord. She'd talked to Mrs Ogg, but it was hard to remember what about. Voices had banged in her ears. Now, at last, she had nothing to do but sleep.

It was a good bed, the best she'd ever slept in. It was the best room she'd ever been in, although she'd been too tired to explore it much. Witches didn't go in much for comfort, especially in spare bedrooms, but Tiffany had grown up on an ancient bed where the springs went *gloing* every time she moved, and with care she could get them to play a tune.

This mattress was thick and yielding. She sank into it as if it was a very soft, very warm, very slow quicksand.

The trouble is, you can shut your eyes but you can't shut your mind. As she lay in the dark, it squiggled pictures inside her head, of clocks that went **clank-clonk**, of snowflakes shaped like her, of Miss Treason striding through the night-time forest, seeking bad people with her yellow thumbnail ready.

Myth Treason . . .

She fell through these scrambled memories into dull whiteness. But it got brighter, and took on detail, little areas of black and grey. They began to move gently from side to side . . .

Tiffany opened her eyes, and everything became clear. She was standing on a . . . a boat, no, a big sailing ship. There was snow on the decks, and icicles hung from the rigging. It was sailing in the washing-up-water light of dawn, in a silent grey sea full of floating ice and clouds of fog. The rigging creaked, the wind sighed in the sails. There was no one to be seen.

'Ah. This appears to be a dream. Let me out, please,' said a familiar voice.

'Who are you?' said Tiffany.

'You. Cough, please.'

Tiffany thought: Well, if this is a dream . . . and coughed.

A figure grew up out of the snow on the deck. It was her, and she was looking around thoughtfully.

'Are you me too?' Tiffany said. Strangely, here on the freezing deck, it didn't seem that, well, strange.

'Hmm. Oh, yes,' said the other Tiffany, still staring intently at things. 'I'm your Third Thoughts. Remember? The part of you that never stops thinking? The bit that notices little details? It's good to be out in fresh air. Hmm.'

'Is there something wrong?'

'Well, this clearly appears to be a dream. If you would care to look, you'll see that the steersman in yellow oilskins up there at the wheel is the Jolly Sailor off the wrappers of the tobacco that Granny Aching used to smoke. He always comes into our mind when we think about the sea, yes?'

Tiffany looked up at the bearded figure, who gave her a cheerful wave.

'Yes, that's certainly him!' she said.

'But I don't think this is our dream, exactly,' said the Third Thoughts. 'It's too . . . real.'

Tiffany reached down and picked up a handful of snow.

'Feels real,' she said. 'Feels cold.' She made a snowball and threw it at herself.

'I really wish I wouldn't do that,' said the other Tiffany, brushing the snow off her shoulder. 'But you see what I mean? Dreams are never as . . . well, non-dreamlike as this.'

'I know what I mean,' said Tiffany. 'I think they're going to be real, and then something weird turns up.'

'Exactly. I don't like it all. If this is a dream, then something horrible is going to happen . . .'

They looked ahead of the ship. There was a dismal, dirty bank of fog there, spreading out across the sea.

'There's something in the fog!' said the Tiffanys, together.

They turned and scurried up the ladder to the man at the wheel.

'Keep away from the fog! Please don't go near it!' she shouted.

The Jolly Sailor took his pipe out of his mouth and looked puzzled.

'A Good Smoke in Any Weather?' he said to Tiffany.

'What?'

'It's all he can say!' said her Third Thoughts,

grabbing the wheel. 'Remember? That's what he says on the label!'

The Jolly Sailor pushed her away, gently. 'A Good Smoke in Any Weather,' he said soothingly. 'In Any Weather.'

'Look, we only want to—' Tiffany began, but her Third Thoughts, without a word, put a hand on her head and turned her round.

Something was coming out of the fog.

It was an iceberg, a large one, at least three times as high as the ship, as majestic as a swan. It was so big that it was causing its own weather. It seemed to be moving slowly; there was white water around its base. Snow fell around it. Streamers of fog trailed behind it.

The Jolly Sailor's pipe dropped out of his mouth as he stared.

'A Good Smoke!' he swore.

The iceberg was Tiffany. It was a Tiffany hundreds of feet high, formed of glittering green ice, but it was still a Tiffany. There were seabirds perched on her head.

'It can't be the wintersmith doing this!' said Tiffany. 'I threw the horse away!' She cupped her hands to her mouth and shouted: 'I THREW THE HORSE AWAY!'

Her voice echoed off the huge ice figure. A few birds took off from the huge cold head, screaming. Behind Tiffany, the ship's wheel spun. The Jolly Sailor stamped a foot and pointed to the white sails above them.

'A Good Smoke in Any Weather!' he commanded.

'I'm sorry, I don't know what you mean!' said Tiffany desperately.

The man pointed to the sails and made frantic pulling motions with his hands.

'A Good Smoke!'

'Sorry, I just can't understand you!'

The sailor snorted and ran off towards a rope which he hauled on, in a great hurry.

'It's got weird,' said her Third Thoughts quietly.

'Well, yes, I should think a huge iceberg shaped like me is a—'

'No, that's just strange. This is weird,' said the Third Thoughts. 'We've got passengers. Look.' She pointed.

Down on the main deck there was a row of hatches with big iron grids on them; Tiffany hadn't noticed them before.

Hands, hundreds of them, pale as roots under a log, groping and waving, were thrusting through the grids.

'Passengers?' Tiffany whispered in horror. 'Oh, no . . .'

And then the screaming started. It would have been better, but not a lot better, if it had been cries of 'Help!' and 'Save us!' but instead it was just screaming and wailing, just the sounds of people in pain and fear—

No!

'Come back inside my head,' she said grimly. 'It's too distracting to have you running around outside. Right now.'

'I'll walk in from behind you,' said her Third Thoughts. 'Then it won't seem so—'

Tiffany felt a twinge of pain, and a change in her mind, and thought: Well, I suppose it could have been a lot messier.

OK. Let me think. Let all of me think.

She watched the desperate hands, waving like weeds underwater, and thought: I'm in something like a dream, but I don't think it's mine. I'm on a ship, and we're going to get killed by an iceberg that's a giant figure of me.

I think I liked it better when I was snowflakes . . .

Whose dream is this?

'What is this about, wintersmith?' she said, and her Third Thoughts, back where they should be, commented: It's amazing, you can even see your own breath in the air . . .

'Is this a warning?' Tiffany shouted. 'What do you want?'

You for my bride, said the wintersmith. The words just arrived in her memory.

Tiffany's shoulders sank.

You know this isn't real, said her Third Thoughts. But it may be the shadow of something real . . .

I shouldn't have let Granny Weatherwax send Rob Anybody away like that—

'Crivens! Shiver me timber!' shouted a voice behind her. And then there was the usual clamour:

'It's "timbers", ye dafty!'

'Aye? But I can only find one!'

'Splice the big plank! Daft Wullie's just walked intae the watter!'

'The big puddin'! I told him, just the one eyepatch!'

'With a yo hoho and a ho yoyo—'

Feegles erupted from the cabin behind Tiffany, and Rob Anybody stopped in front of her as the rest streamed past. He saluted.

'Sorry we're a wee bitty late, but we had to find the black patches,' he said. 'There's sich a thing as style, ye ken.'

Tiffany was speechless, but only for a moment. She pointed.

'We've got to stop this ship hitting that iceberg!'

'Just that? No problemo!' Rob looked past her to the looming ice giantess and grinned. 'He's got your nose just right, eh?'

'Just stop it! Please?' Tiffany pleaded.

'Aye-aye! C'mon, lads!'

Watching the Feegles working was like watching ants, except that ants didn't wear kilts and shout 'Crivens!' all the time. Maybe it was because they could make one word do so much work that they seemed to have no problem at all with the Jolly Sailor's orders. They swarmed across the deck like . . . well, a swarm. Mysterious ropes were pulled. Sails moved and billowed to a chorus of 'A Good Smoke!' and 'Crivens!'

Now the wintersmith wants to marry me, Tiffany thought. Oh, dear.

She'd sometimes wondered if she'd get married one day, but she was definite that now was too soon for 'one day'. Yes, her mother had been married when she was still fourteen, but that was the sort of thing that happened in the olden days. There *were* a lot of things to be done before Tiffany ever got married, she was very clear about that.

Besides, when you thought about it . . . yuk. He wasn't even a person. He'd be too—

Thud! went the wind in the sails. The ship creaked, and leaned over, and everyone was shouting at her. Mostly they shouted, 'The wheel! Grab the wheel right noo!' although there was also a desperate, 'A Good Smoke in Any Weather!' in there too.

Tiffany turned to see the wheel spinning in a blur. She made a snatch at it and got thumped across the fingers by the spokes, but there was a length of rope coiled nearby and she managed to lasso the wheel with a loop and jerk it to a halt without sliding along the deck too much. Then she grabbed it and tried to turn it the other way. It was like pushing a house, but it did move, very slowly at first and then faster as she put her back into it.

The ship came around. She could feel it moving, beginning to head a little bit away from the iceberg, not directly for it. Good! Things were going right at last! She spun the wheel some more, and now the huge cold wall was sliding past, filling the air with mist. Everything was going to be all right after—

The ship hit the iceberg.

It started with a simple *crack!* as a spar caught on an outcrop, but then others smashed as the ship scraped along the side of the ice. Then there were some sharp splintering noises as the ship ground onward, and bits of plank shot up on columns of foaming water. The top of a mast broke off, dragging sails and rigging with it. A lump of ice smashed onto the deck a few feet away from Tiffany, showering her with needles.

'This isn't how it's supposed to go!' she panted, hanging onto the wheel.

Marry me, said the wintersmith.

Churning white water roared across the foundering ship. Tiffany held on for a moment longer, then the cold surf covered her . . . except that it was suddenly not cold, but warm. But it was still stopping her from breathing. In the darkness she tried to fight her way to the surface, until the blackness was suddenly pulled aside, her eyes filled with light and a voice said: 'I'm sure these mattresses are far too soft, but you can't tell Mrs Ogg a thing.'

Tiffany blinked. She was in bed, and a skinny woman with worried hair and a rather red nose was standing by it.

'You were tossing and turning like a mad thing,' the woman said, putting a steaming mug on the small table by the bed. 'One day someone will suffikate, mark my words.'

Tiffany blinked again. I'm supposed to think: Oh, it

was just a dream. But it wasn't just a dream. Not my dream.

'What time is it?' she managed.

'About seven,' said the woman.

'Seven!' Tiffany pushed the sheets back. 'I've got to get up! Mrs Ogg will be wanting her breakfast!'

'I shouldn't think so. I took it to her in bed not ten minutes ago,' said the woman, giving Tiffany a Look. 'And I'm off home.' She sniffed. 'Drink your tea before it gets cold.' And with that she marched towards the door.

'Is Mrs Ogg ill?' said Tiffany, looking everywhere for her socks. She'd never heard of anyone who wasn't really old or very ill having a meal in bed.

'Ill? I don't think she's had a day's illness in her life,' said the woman, managing to suggest that in her opinion this was unfair. She shut the door.

Even the bedroom floor was smooth – not made smooth by centuries of feet that had worn down the planks and taken all the splinters out, but because someone had sanded and varnished it. Tiffany's bare feet stuck to it slightly. There was no dust to be seen, no spider webs anywhere. The room was bright and fresh and exactly unlike any room in a witch's cottage ought to be.

'I'm going to get dressed,' she said to the air. 'Are there any Feegles in here?'

'Ach, no,' said a voice from under the bed.

There was some frantic whispering and the voice

said: 'That is tae say, there's hardly any o' us here at a'.'

'Then shut your eyes,' said Tiffany.

She got dressed, taking occasional sips of the tea as she did so. Tea brought to your bedside when you weren't ill? That sort of thing happened to kings and queens!

And then she noticed the bruise on her fingers. It didn't hurt at all, but the skin was blue where the ship's wheel had hit it. Right . . .

'Feegles?' she said.

'Crivens, ye'll nae be foolin' us a second time,' said the voice from under the bed.

'Get out here where I can see you, Daft Wullie!' Tiffany commanded.

'It's real hagglin', miss, the way ye always ken it's me.'

After some more urgent whispering, Daft Wullie – for it was indeed he – trooped out with two more Feegles and Horace the cheese.

Tiffany stared. All right, he was a blue cheese, so he was about the same colour as a Feegle. And he acted like a Feegle, no doubt about that. Why, though, had he got a grubby strip of Feegle tartan around him?

'He kinda found us,' said Daft Wullie, putting his arm around as much of Horace as was possible. 'Can I keep him? He understands evera word I say!'

'That's amazing, because I don't,' said Tiffany. 'Look, were we in a shipwreck last night?'

'Oh, aye. Sorta.'

'Sort of? Was it real or wasn't it?'

'Oh, aye,' said the Feegle nervously.

'Which?' Tiffany insisted.

'Kinda real, and kinda not real, in a real unreal sorta way,' said Daft Wullie, squirming a bit. 'I don't have the knowin' o' the right wurdies . . .'

'Are all you Feegles OK?'

'Oh aye, miss,' said Daft Wullie, brightening up. 'Nae problemo. It wuz only a dream ship on a dream sea, after a'.'

'And a dream iceberg?' said Tiffany.

'Ach, no. The iceberg was real, mistress.'

'I thought so! Are you sure?'

'Aye. We're good at the knowin' o' stuff like that,' said Daft Wullie. 'That's so, eh, lads?' The other two Feegles, in total awe of being in the presence of the big wee hag without the safety of hundreds of brothers around them, nodded at Tiffany and then tried to shuffle behind each other.

'A real iceberg shaped like me is floating around on the sea?' said Tiffany, in horror. 'Getting in the way of shipping?'

'Aye. Could be,' said Daft Wullie.

'I'm going to get into so much trouble!' said Tiffany, standing up.

There was a snapping noise, and the end of one of the floorboards leaped out of the floor and hung there, bouncing up and down with a rocking-chair noise. It had ripped out two long nails.

'And now this,' said Tiffany weakly. But the Feegles and Horace had vanished.

Behind Tiffany, someone laughed, although it was maybe more of a chuckle, deep and real and with just a hint that maybe someone had told a rude joke.

'Those little devils can't half run, eh?' said Nanny Ogg, ambling into the room. 'Now then, Tiff, I wants you to turn round slowly and go and sit on your bed with your feet off the ground. Can you do that?'

'Of course, Mrs Ogg,' said Tiffany. 'Look, I'm sorry about—'

'Poo, what's a floorboard more or less?' said Nanny Ogg. 'I'm much more worried about Esme Weatherwax. She said there might be something like this! Ha, she was right and Miss Tick was wrong! There'll be no living with her after this! She'll have her nose so far in the air her feet won't touch the ground!'

With a *spioioioiiing!* sound, another floorboard sprang up.

'And it might be a good idea if yours didn't either, miss,' Nanny Ogg added. 'I'll be back in half a tick.'

That turned out to be the same length of time as twenty-seven seconds, when Nanny returned carrying a pair of violently pink slippers with bunny rabbits on them.

'My second best pair,' she said as, behind her, a board went *plunk!* and hurled four big nails into the far wall. The boards that had already sprung up were beginning to sprout what looked a lot like leaves. They were thin and weedy, but leaves were what they were.

'Is it me doing this?' asked Tiffany nervously.

'I daresay Esme will want to tell you all about it herself,' said Nanny, helping her feet into the slippers. 'But what you've got here, miss, is a bad case of Ped Fecundis.' In the back of Tiffany's memory Dr Sensibility Bustle, D.M. Phil., B.El. L., stirred in his sleep for a moment and took care of the translation.

'Fertile Feet?' said Tiffany.

'Well done! I didn't expect anything to happen to floorboards, mind you, but it makes sense, when you think about it. They're made of wood, after all, so they're tryin' to grow.'

'Mrs Ogg?' said Tiffany.

'Yes?'

'Please? I haven't got a clue what you're talking about! I keep my feet very clean! And I think I'm a giant iceberg!'

Nanny Ogg gave her a slow, kind look. Tiffany stared into dark, twinkling eyes. Don't try to trick her or hold anything back from those, said her Third Thoughts. Everyone says she's been Granny Weatherwax's best friend since they were girls. And that means that under all those wrinkles must be nerves of steel.

'Kettle's on downstairs,' said Nanny brightly. 'Why don't you come down and tell me all about it?'

Tiffany had looked up 'strumpet' in *The Unexpurgated Dictionary*, and found it meant 'a woman who is no better than she should be' and 'a lady of easy virtue'. This, she decided after some working out, meant that Mrs Gytha Ogg, known as Nanny, was a very respectable person. She found virtue easy, for one thing. And if she was no better than she should be then she was just as good as she ought to be.

She had a feeling that Miss Treason hadn't meant this, but you couldn't argue with logic.

Nanny Ogg was good at listening, at least. She listened like a great big ear, and before Tiffany realized it she was telling her everything. Everything. Nanny sat on the opposite side of the big kitchen table, puffing gently at a pipe with a hedgehog carved on it. Sometimes she'd ask a little question, like 'Why was that?' or 'And then what happened?' and off they'd go again. Nanny's friendly little smile could drag out of you things you didn't know you knew.

While they talked, Tiffany's Third Thoughts scanned the room out of the corners of her eyes.

It was wonderfully clean and bright, and there were ornaments everywhere – cheap, jolly ones, the sort that have things like 'To the World's Best Mum' on them. And where there weren't ornaments there were pictures, of babies and children and families.

Tiffany had thought that only grand folk lived in homes like this. There were oil lamps! There was a bath, made of tin, hanging conveniently on a hook outside the privy! There was a pump actually indoors!

But Nanny ambled around in her rather worn black dress, not grand at all.

From the best chair in the room of ornaments, a large grey cat watched Tiffany with a half-open eye that glinted with absolute evil. Nanny had referred to him as 'Greebo . . . don't mind him, he's just a big old softie,' which Tiffany knew enough to interpret as 'He'll have his claws in your leg if you go anywhere near him.'

Tiffany talked as she hadn't talked to anyone before. It must be a kind of magic, the Third Thoughts concluded. Witches soon picked up ways of controlling people with their voice, but Nanny Ogg listened at you.

'This lad Roland who is not your young man,' said Nanny, when Tiffany had paused for breath. 'Thinking of marrying him, are you?'

Don't lie, the Third Thoughts insisted.

'I . . . well, your mind comes up with all kinds of things when you're not paying attention, doesn't it?' said Tiffany. 'It's not like thinking. Anyway, all the other boys I've met just stare at their stupid feet! Petulia says it's because of the hat.'

'Well, taking it off helps,' said Nanny Ogg. 'Mind you, so did a low-cut bodice, when I was a girl. Stopped 'em lookin' at their stupid feet, I don't mind telling you!'

Tiffany saw the dark eyes locked onto her. She burst out laughing. Mrs Ogg's face broke into a huge grin that should have been locked up for the sake of public decency, and for some reason Tiffany felt a lot better. She'd passed some kind of test.

'Mind you, that probably wouldn't work with the wintersmith, of course,' said Nanny, and the gloom came down again.

'I didn't mind the snowflakes,' said Tiffany. 'But the iceberg – I think that was a bit much.'

'Showing off in front of the girls,' said Nanny, puffing at her hedgehog pipe. 'Yes, they do that.'

'But he can kill people!'

'He's winter. It's what he does. But I reckon he's in a bit of a tizzy because he's never been in love with a human before.'

'In love?'

'Well, he probably thinks he is.'

Once again the eyes watched her carefully.

'He's an elemental, and they're simple, really,' Nanny Ogg went on. 'But he's trying to be human. And that's complicated. We're packed with stuff he doesn't understand – can't understand, really. Anger, for example. A blizzard is never angry. The storm don't hate the people who die in it. The wind is never cruel. But the more he thinks about you, the more he's having to deal with feelings like this, and there's none can teach him. He's not very clever. He's never had to be. And the interesting thing is that you are changin' too—'

There was a knocking at the door. Nanny Ogg got up

and opened it. Granny Weatherwax was there, with Miss Tick peering over her shoulder.

'Blessings be upon this house,' said Granny, but in a voice which suggested that if blessings needed to be taken away she could do that, too.

'Quite probably,' said Nanny Ogg.

'It's Ped Fecundis, then?' Granny nodded at Tiffany.

'Looks like a bad case. The floorboards started growing after she walked over them in bare feet.'

'Ha! Have you given her anything for it?' said Granny.

'I prescribed a pair of slippers.'

'I really don't see how avatarization could be taking place, not when we're talking about elementals – it makes no—' Miss Tick began.

'Do stop wittering, Miss Tick,' said Granny Weatherwax. 'I notices you witter when things goes wrong and it is not being a help.'

'I don't want to worry the child, that's all,' said Miss Tick. She took Tiffany's hand, patted it and said, 'Don't you worry, Tiffany, we'll—'

'She's a witch,' said Granny sternly. 'We just have to tell her the truth.'

'You think I'm turning into a . . . a goddess?' said Tiffany.

It was worth it to see their faces. The only mouth not in an O now was the one belonging to Granny Weatherwax, which was smirking. She looked like someone whose dog has just done a rather good trick.

'How did you work that out?' she said.

Dr Bustle had a guess: Avatar, an incarnation of a god. But I'm not going to tell you that, Tiffany thought. 'Well, is it?' she said.

'Yes,' said Granny Weatherwax. 'The wintersmith thinks you are . . . oh, she's got a lot of names. The Lady of the Flowers is a nice one. Or the Summer Lady. She makes the summertime, just like he makes the winter. He thinks you're her.'

'All right,' said Tiffany. 'But we know he's wrong, don't we?'

'Er . . . not as quite as wrong as we'd like,' said Miss Tick . . .

Most of the Feegles had camped out in Nanny Ogg's barn, where they were holding a council of war, except that it was about something that isn't quite the same thing.

'What we've got here,' Rob Anybody pronounced, 'is a case o' Romance.'

'What's that, Rob?' said a Feegle.

'Aye, is it like how wee babies are made?' said Daft Wullie. 'Ye told us about that last year. It waz verrae interestin', although a bit far-fetched tae my mind.'

'No' exactly,' said Rob Anybody. 'An' it's kinda hard tae describe. But I reckon yon wintersmith wants to romance the big wee hag and she disnae ken what tae do aboot it.'

'So it *is* like how babbies are made?' said Daft Wullie.

'No, 'cos even beasties know that but only people know aboot Romancin',' said Rob. 'When a bull coo meet a lady coo he disnae have tae say, "My heart goes bang-bang-bang when I see your wee face," 'cos it's kinda built in tae their heads. People have it more difficult. Romancin' is verrae important, ye ken. Basically it's a way the boy can get close to the girl wi'oot her attackin' him and scratchin' his eyes oot.'

'I dinnae see how we can teach her any o' that stuff,' said Slightly Mad Angus.

'The big wee hag reads books,' said Rob Anybody. 'When she sees a book she just cannae help herself. And I,' he added proudly, 'have a Plan.'

The Feegles relaxed. They always felt happier when Rob had a Plan, especially since most plans of his boiled down to screaming and rushing at something.

'Tell us aboot the Plan, Rob,' said Big Yan.

'Ah'm glad ye asked me,' said Rob. 'The Plan is: we'll find her a book aboot Romancing.'

'And how will we find this book, Rob?' asked Billy Bigchin uncertainly. He was a loyal gonnagle, but he was also bright enough to get nervous whenever Rob Anybody had a Plan.

Rob Anybody airily waved a hand. 'Ach,' he said. 'We ken this trick! A' we need is a big hat an' coat an' a coathanger an' a broom handle!'

'Oh aye?' said Big Yan. 'Bags I not bein' doon in the knee again!'

* * *

With witches, everything is a test. That's why they tested Tiffany's feet.

I bet I'm the only person in the world about to do this, she thought as she lowered both her feet into a tray of soil that Nanny had hastily shovelled up. Granny Weatherwax and Miss Tick were both sitting on bare wooden chairs, despite the fact that the grey cat Greebo was occupying the whole of one big saggy armchair. You didn't want to wake up Greebo when he wanted to sleep.

'Can you feel anything?' asked Miss Tick.

'It's a bit cold, that's all – oh . . . something's happening . . .'

Green shoots appeared around her feet, and grew quickly. Then they went white at the base and gently pushed Tiffany's feet aside as they began to swell.

'Onions?' said Granny Weatherwax scornfully.

'Well, they were the only seeds I could find quickly,' said Nanny Ogg, poking at the glistening white bulbs. 'Good size. Well done, Tiff.'

Granny looked shocked. 'You're not going to eat those, are you, Gytha?' she said accusingly. 'You are, aren't you? You're going to eat them!'

Nanny Ogg, standing up with a bunch of onions in each podgy hand, looked guilty, but only for a moment.

'Why not?' she said stoutly. 'Fresh vegetables are

not to be sneezed at in the winter. And anyway, her feet are nice and clean.'

'It's not seemly,' said Miss Tick.

'It didn't hurt,' said Tiffany. 'All I had to do was put my feet on the tray for a moment.'

'Yes, she says it didn't hurt,' Nanny Ogg insisted. 'Now, I think I might have some old carrot seeds in the kitchen drawer—' She saw the expressions on the faces of the others. 'All right, all right, then, there's no need to look like that,' she said. 'I was just tryin' to point out the silver lining, that's all.'

'Someone *please* tell me what is happening to me?' Tiffany wailed.

'Miss Tick is going to give you the answer in some long words,' said Granny. 'But they boils down to this. It's the Story happening. It's making you fit into itself.'

Tiffany tried not to look like someone who didn't understand a word that she had just heard.

'I could do with a little bit of the fine detail, I think,' she said.

'I think I'll get some tea brewed,' said Nanny Ogg.

CHAPTER 7

ON WITH THE DANCE

The Wintersmith and the Summer Lady . . . danced. The dance never ended.

Winter never dies. Not as people die. It hangs on in late frost and the smell of autumn in a summer evening, and in the heat it flees to the mountains.

Summer never dies. It sinks into the ground; in the depths of winter buds form in sheltered places and white shoots creep under dead leaves. Some of it flees into the deepest, hottest deserts, where there is a summer that never ends.

To animals they were just the weather, just part of everything. But humans arose and gave them names, just as they filled the starry sky with heroes and monsters, because this turned them into stories. And humans loved stories, because once you're turned things into stories you could change the stories. And there was the problem, right there.

Now the Lady and the Wintersmith danced around

the year, changing places in the spring and autumn, and it had worked for thousands of years, right up until the time some girl couldn't control her feet and had arrived in the dance at exactly the wrong time.

But the Story had life, too. It was like a play, now. It would roll on around the year, and if one of the players wasn't the real actress but just some girl who'd wandered onto the stage, well, that was too bad. She'd have to wear the costume and speak the lines and hope that there was going to be a happy ending. Change the story, even if you don't mean to, and the story changes you.

Miss Tick used a lot more words than this, like 'anthropomorphic personification', but this was what ended up in Tiffany's head.

'So . . . I'm not a goddess?' she said.

'Oh, I wish I had a blackboard,' sighed Miss Tick. 'They really don't survive the water, though, and of course the chalks get so soggy . . .'

'What we *think* happened in the dance,' Granny Weatherwax began, in a loud voice, 'is that you and the Summer Lady got . . . mixed up.'

'Mixed up?'

'You may have some of her talents. The myth of the Summer Lady says that flowers grow wherever she walks,' said Granny Weatherwax.

'*Where e'er*,' said Miss Tick primly.

'What?' snapped Granny, who was now pacing up and down in front of the fire.

'It's where e'er she walks, in fact,' said Miss Tick. 'It's more . . . poetical.'

'Hah,' Granny said. 'Poetry!'

'Am I going to get into trouble about this?' Tiffany wondered. 'And what about the *real* Summer Lady? Is she going to be angry?'

Granny Weatherwax stopped pacing up and down and looked at Miss Tick, who said: 'Ah, yes . . . er . . . we are exploring every possibility—'

'That means we don't know,' said Granny. 'That's the truth of it. This is about gods, see? But yes, since you ask, they can be a bit touchy.'

'I didn't *see* her in the dance,' said Tiffany.

'Did you *see* the wintersmith?'

'Well . . . no,' said Tiffany. How could she describe that wonderful, endless, golden, spinning moment? It went beyond bodies and thoughts. But it *had* sounded as though two people had said: 'Who are you?' She pulled her boots back on. 'Er . . . where is she now?' she asked as she tied the laces. Perhaps she'd have to run.

'She's probably gone back underground for the winter. The Summer Lady doesn't walk above ground in winter.'

'Up until now,' said Nanny Ogg cheerfully. She seemed to be enjoying this.

'Aah, Mrs Ogg has put her finger on the *other* problem,' said Miss Tick. 'The, er, wintersmith and the Summer Lady are, uh, that is, they've never—' She looked imploringly at Nanny Ogg.

'They've never met except in the Dance,' said Nanny. 'But now here you are, and you feel like the Summer Lady to him, walking around as bold as brass in the wintertime, so you might be . . . how shall I put it . . . ?'

'. . . exciting his romantic propensities,' said Miss Tick quickly.

'I wasn't going to describe it quite like that,' said Nanny Ogg.

'Yes, I suspects you weren't!' said Granny. 'I suspects you was going to use Language!'

Tiffany definitely heard the capital 'L', which entirely suggested that the language she was thinking of was not to be uttered in polite company.

Nanny stood up and tried to look haughty, which is hard to do when you have a face like a happy apple.

'I was actually going to draw Tiff's attention to this,' she said, taking an ornament off the crowded mantelpiece. It was a little house. Tiffany had glanced at it before; it had two little doorways at the front and, at the moment, a tiny little wooden man with a top hat.

'It's called a weather house,' she said, handing it to Tiffany. 'I don't know how it works – there's a bit of special string or something – but there's a little wooden man who comes out if it's going to rain and a little wooden woman who comes out when it's going to be sunny. But they're on a little pivot-y thing, see? They can *never* be out at the same time, see? Never.

An' I can't help wonderin', when the weather's changin', if the little man sees the little woman out of the corner of his eye and wonders—'

'Is this about sex?' said Tiffany.

Miss Tick looked at the ceiling. Granny Weatherwax cleared her throat. Nanny gave a huge laugh that would have embarrassed even the little wooden man.

'Sex?' she said. 'Between summer and winter? Now there's a thought.'

'Don't . . . think . . . it,' said Granny Weatherwax sternly. She turned to Tiffany. 'He's fascinated by you, that's what it is. And we don't know how much of the Summer Lady's power is in you. She might be quite weak. You'll have to be a summer in winter until winter ends,' she added flatly. 'That's justice. No excuses. You made a choice. You get what you chose.'

'Couldn't I just go and find her and say I'm sorry—?' Tiffany began.

'No. The old gods ain't big on "sorry",' said Granny, pacing up and down again. 'They know it's *just* a word.'

'You know what I think?' said Nanny. 'I think she's watchin' you, Tiff. She's sayin' to herself, "Who's this hoity-toity young madam steppin' into my shoes? Well, let's make her walk a mile in 'em and see how she likes it!"'

'Mrs Ogg may have something there,' said Miss Tick, who was leafing through Chaffinch's *Mythology*. 'The gods expect you to *pay* for your mistakes.'

Nanny Ogg patted Tiffany's hand. 'If she wants to see what you can do, *show* her what you can do, Tiff, eh? That's the way! Surprise her!'

'You mean the Summer Lady?' said Tiffany.

Nanny winked. 'Oh, and the Summer Lady, too!'

There was what sounded very much like the start of a laugh from Miss Tick before Granny Weatherwax glared at her.

Tiffany sighed. It was all very well to talk about choices, but she had no choice here.

'All right. What else can I expect apart from . . . well, the feet?'

'I'm, er, checking,' said Miss Tick, still thumbing through the book. 'Ah . . . it says here that she was, I mean *is*, fairer than all the stars in heaven . . .'

They all looked at Tiffany.

'You could try doing something with your hair,' said Nanny Ogg, after a while.

'Like what?' said Tiffany.

'Like anything, really.'

'Apart from the feet and doing something about my hair,' said Tiffany sharply, 'is there anything else?'

'Says here, quoting a very old manuscript: "She waketh the grasses in Aprill and filleth the behives with honey swete,"' Miss Tick reported.

'How do I do that?'

'I don't know, but I suspect that happens anyway,' said Miss Tick.

'And the Summer Lady gets the credit?'

'I think she just has to exist for it to happen, really,' said Miss Tick.

'Anything else?'

'Er, yes. You have to make sure the winter ends,' said Miss Tick. 'And, of course, deal with the wintersmith.'

'And how do I do *that*?'

'We think that you just have to . . . be there,' said Granny Weatherwax. 'Oh, perhaps you'll know what to do when the time comes.'

'Meep?'

'Be where?' said Tiffany.

'Everywhere. Anywhere.'

'Granny, your hat squeaked,' said Tiffany. 'It went meep!'

'No it didn't,' Granny said sharply.

'It did, you know,' said Nanny Ogg. 'I heard it, too.'

Granny Weatherwax grunted and pulled off her hat. The white kitten, curled around her tight bun of hair, blinked in the light.

'I can't help it,' Granny muttered. 'If I leave the dratted thing alone it goes under the dresser and cries and cries.' She looked around at the others as if daring them to say anything. 'Anyway,' she added, 'it keeps m' head warm.'

On his chair, the yellow slit of Greebo's left eye opened lazily.

'Get down, You,' said Granny, lifting the kitten off her head and putting it on the floor. 'I dare say Mrs Ogg has got some milk in the kitchen.'

'Not much,' said Nanny. 'I'll swear something's been drinking it!'

Greebo's eye opened all the way and he began to growl softly.

'You sure you know what you're doing, Esme?' said Nanny Ogg, reaching for a cushion to throw. 'He's very protective of his territory.'

You the kitten sat on the floor and washed her ears. Then, as Greebo got to his feet, she fixed him with an innocent little stare and took a flying leap onto his nose, landing on it with all her claws out.

'So is she,' said Granny Weatherwax as Greebo erupted from the chair and hurtled around the room before disappearing into the kitchen. There was a crash of saucepans followed by the *gloioioioing* of a saucepan lid spinning into silence on the floor.

The kitten padded back into the room, hopped into the empty chair and curled up again.

'He brought in half a wolf last week,' said Nanny Ogg. 'You haven't been hexperimenting* on that poor kitten, have you?'

'I wouldn't dream of such a thing,' said Granny. 'She just knows her own mind, that's all.' She turned to Tiffany. 'I don't reckon the wintersmith will be worrying about you too much for a while,' she said. 'The big winter weather will be on us soon. That'll

---

* Hexperiment: to use magic just to see what happens.

keep him busy. In the meantime, Mrs Ogg will teach you . . . things she knows.'

And Tiffany thought: I wonder how embarrassing this is going to be?

Deep in the snow, in the middle of a windswept moorland, a small band of travelling librarians sat around their cooling stove and wondered what to burn next.

Tiffany had never been able to find out much about the librarians. They were a bit like the wandering priests and teachers who went even into the smallest, loneliest villages to deliver those things – prayers, medicine, facts – that people could do without for weeks at a time but sometimes needed a lot of all at once. The librarians would loan you a book for a penny, although they often would take food or good second-hand clothes. If you gave them a book, you got ten free loans.

Sometimes you'd see two or three of their wagons parked in some clearing and could smell the glues they boiled up to repair the oldest books. Some of the books they loaned were so old that the printing had been worn grey by the pressure of people's eyeballs reading it.

The librarians were mysterious. It was said they could tell what book you needed just by looking at you, and they could take your voice away with a word.

But here they were searching the shelves for

T. H. Mouseholder's famous book *Survival in the Snow*.

Things were getting desperate. The oxen that pulled the wagon had broken their tethers and run off in the blizzard, the stove was nearly out and, worst of all, they were down to their last candle, which meant that soon they would not be able to read books.

'It says here in K. Pierpoint Poundsworth's *Among the Snow Weasels* that the members of the ill-fated expedition to Whale Bay survived by making soup of their own toes,' said Deputy Librarian Grizzler.

'That's interesting,' said Senior Librarian Swinsley, who was rummaging on the shelf below. 'Is there a recipe?'

'No, but there may be something in Superflua Raven's book *Cooking in Dire Straits*. That's where we got yesterday's recipe for Nourishing Boiled Socks Surprise—' There was a thunderous knocking at the door. It was a two-part door which allowed only the top half to be opened, so that a ledge on the bottom half could be a sort of small desk for stamping books. Snow came through the crack as the knocking continued.

'I hope that's not the wolves again,' said Mr Grizzler. 'I got no sleep at all last night!'

'Do they knock? We could check in *The Habits of Wolves* by Captain W. E. Lightly,' said Senior Librarian Swinsley, 'or perhaps you could just open the door? Quickly! The candles are going out!'

Grizzler opened the top half of the door. There was

a tall figure on the steps, hard to see in the fitful, cloud-strained moonlight.

'Ah'm lookin' for Romance,' it rumbled.

The Deputy Librarian thought for a moment, and then said, 'Isn't it a bit chilly out there?'

'Aren't ye the people wi' all dem books?' the figure demanded.

'Yes, indeed . . . oh, Romance! Yes, certainly!' said Mr Swinsley, looking relieved. 'In that case, I think you'll want Miss Jenkins. Forward please, Miss Jenkins.'

'It looks like youse freezin' in here,' said the figure. 'Dem's icicles hanging from der ceilin'.'

'Yes. However, we have managed to keep them off the books,' said Mr Swinsley. 'Ah, Miss Jenkins. The, er, gentleman is looking for Romance. Your department, I think.'

'Yes, sir,' said Miss Jenkins, stepping out from the shelves. 'What kind of romance were you looking for?'

'Oh, one w' a cover on, ye ken, and wi' pages wi' all wurdies on 'em,' said the figure.

Miss Jenkins, who was used to this sort of thing, disappeared into the gloom at the other end of the wagon.

'Dese scunners are total loonies!' said a new voice. It appeared to come from somewhere on the person of the dark book-borrower, but much lower than the head.

'Pardon?' said Mr Swinsley.

'Ach, nae problemo,' said the figure quickly. 'Ah'm sufferin' from a grumblin' knee, 'tis an old trouble—'

'Why don't they be burnin' all dem books, eh?' the unseen knee grumbled.

'Sorry aboot this, ye know how knees can let a man doon in public. I'm a martyr to dis one,' said the stranger.

'I know how it is. My elbow plays me up in wet weather,' said Mr Swinsley. There was some sort of fight going on in the nether regions of the stranger, who was shaking like a puppet.

'That will be one penny,' Miss Jenkins said. 'And I will need your name and address.'

The dark figure shuddered. 'Oh, I— we ne'er give out oour name an' address!' it said quickly. 'It is against oor religion, ye ken. Er . . . I dinnae wanta be a knee aboot this, but why is ye all here freezin' tae death?'

'Our oxen wandered off and, alas, the snow's too deep to walk through,' said Mr Swinsley.

'Aye. But youse got a stove and all them dry ol' books,' said the dark figure.

'Yes, we know,' said the librarian, looking puzzled.

There was the kind of wretched pause you get when two people aren't going to understand each other's point of view at all. Then:

'Tell ye what, me an' – ma knee – will go and fetch yer cows for ye, eh?' said the mysterious figure.

'Got tae be worth a penny, eh? Big Yan, you'll feel the rough side o' my hand in a minit!'

The figure dropped out of sight. Snow flew up in the moonlight. For a moment it sounded as if a scuffle was going on, and then a sound like 'Crivens!' disappearing into the distance.

The librarians were about to shut the door when they heard the terrified bellows of the oxen, getting louder very quickly.

Two curling waves of snow came across the glittering moors. The creatures rode them like surfers, yelling at the moon. The snow settled down a few feet away from the wagon. There was a blue and red blur in the air, and the romantic book was whisked away.

But what was really odd, the librarians agreed, was that when the oxen had come speeding towards them, they had appeared to be travelling *backwards*.

. . . It was hard to be embarrassed by Nanny Ogg, because her laugh drove it away. She wasn't embarrassed about anything.

Today Tiffany, with extra pairs of socks on to avoid unfortunate floral incidents, went with her 'Around the houses', as it was known to witches.

'You did this for Miss Treason?' asked Nanny as they stepped out. There were big fat clouds massing around the mountains; there would be a lot more snow tonight.

'Oh yes. And for Miss Level and Miss Pullunder.'

'Enjoyed it, did you?' said Nanny, wrapping her cloak around her.

'Sometimes. I mean, I know why we do it, but sometimes you get fed up with people being stupid. I quite like doing the medicine stuff.'

'Good with the herbs, are you?'

'No. I'm very good with the herbs.'

'Oh, there's a bit of swank, eh?' said Nanny.

'If I didn't know I was good with herbs, I'd be stupid, Mrs Ogg.'

'That's right. Good. It's good to be good at something. Now, our next little favour is—'

– giving an old lady a bath, as much as was possible with a couple of tin basins and some flannels. And that was witchcraft. Then they looked in on a woman who'd just had a baby, and that was witchcraft, and a man with a very nasty leg injury that Nanny Ogg said was doing very well, and that was witchcraft, too, and then in an out-of-the-way group of huddled little cottages, they climbed the cramped wooden stairs to a tiny little bedroom where an old man shot at them with a crossbow.

'You old devil, ain't you dead yet?' said Nanny. 'You're looking well! I swear, the man with the scythe must've forgotten where you live!'

'I'm a-waitin' for him, Mrs Ogg!' said the old man cheerfully. 'If I'm gonna go, I'll take 'im with me!'

'This is my girl Tiff, she's learnin' the witchin',' said

Nanny, raising her voice. 'This is Mr Hogparsley, Tiff
. . . Tiff?' She snapped her fingers in front of Tiffany's
eyes.

'Huh?' said Tiffany. She was still staring in horror.

The twang of the bow as Nanny opened the door
had been bad enough, but for a fraction of a second
she could have sworn that an arrow had gone right
through Nanny Ogg and stuck in the doorframe.

'Shame on you for firing at a young lady, Bill,' said
Nanny severely, plumping up his pillows. 'And Mrs
Dowser says you've been shootin' at her when she
comes up to see you,' she added, putting her basket
down by the bed. 'That's no way to treat a respectable
woman who brings you your meals, is it? For shame!'

'Sorry, Nanny,' muttered Bill. 'It's just that she's
skinny as a rake and wears black. 'Tis an easy mistake
to make in poor light.'

'Mr Hogparsley here is lying in wait for Death, Tiff,'
said Nanny. 'Mistress Weatherwax helped you make
the special traps and arrows, ain't that right, Bill?'

'Traps?' whispered Tiffany. Nanny just nudged her
and pointed down. The floorboards were covered in
ferociously spiked mantraps.

They were all drawn in charcoal.

'I said, isn't that right, Bill?' Nanny repeated, raising
her voice. 'She helped you with the traps!'

'She did that!' said Mr Hogparsley. 'Hah! I wouldn't
want to get on the wrong side o' her!'

'Right, so no shootin' arrows at anyone except

Death, right? Otherwise Mistress Weatherwax won't help you any more,' said Nanny, putting a bottle on the old wooden box that was Mr Hogparsley's bedside table. 'Here's some of your jollop, freshly mixed up. Where did she tell you to keep the pain?'

'It's sitting up here on my shoulder, missus, being no trouble.'

Nanny touched the shoulder, and seemed to think for a moment. 'It's a brown and white squiggle? Sort of oblong?'

'That's right, missus,' said Mr Hogparsley, pulling at the cork on the bottle. 'It wiggles away there and I laughs at it.' The cork popped out. Suddenly, the room smelled of apples.

'It's gettin' big,' said Nanny. 'Mistress Weatherwax will be along tonight to take it away.'

'Right you are, missus,' said the old man, filling a mug to the brim.

'Try not to shoot her, all right? It only makes her mad.'

It was snowing again when they stepped out of the cottage, big feathery flakes that meant business.

'I reckon that's it for today,' Nanny announced. 'I've got things to see to over in Slice, but we'll take the stick tomorrow.'

'That arrow he fired at us—' said Tiffany.

'Imaginary,' said Nanny Ogg, smiling.

'It looked real for a moment!'

Nanny Ogg chuckled. 'It's amazing what Esme Weatherwax can make people imagine!'

'Like traps for Death?'

'Oh, yes. Well, it gives the old boy an interest in life. He's on his way to the Door. But at least Esme's seen to it that there's no pain.'

'Because it's floating over his shoulder?' said Tiffany.

'Yep. She put it just outside his body for him, so it don't hurt,' said Nanny, the snow crunching under her feet.

'I didn't know you could do that!'

'I can do it for small stuff, toothaches and the like. Esme's the champion for it, though. We're none of us too proud to call her in. Y'know, she's very good at people. Funny, really, 'cos she doesn't like 'em much.'

Tiffany glanced at the sky, and Nanny was the kind of inconvenient person who notices *everything*.

'Wondering if lover boy is goin' to drop in?' she said, with a big grin.

'Nanny! Really!' said Tiffany, shocked.

'But you are, aren't you,' said Nanny, who knew no shame. 'O' course, he's *always* around, when you think about it. You're walking through him, you feel him on your skin, you stamp him off your boots when you go indoors—'

'Just don't talk like that, please?' said Tiffany.

'Besides, what's time to an elemental?' Nanny chattered. 'And I suppose snowflakes don't just make themselves, especially when you've got to get the arms and legs right . . .'

She's looking at me out of the corner of her eye to see if I'm going red, Tiffany thought. I know it.

Then Nanny nudged her in the ribs and laughed one of her laughs that would make a rock blush.

'Good for you!' she said. 'I've had a few boyfriends myself that I'd have *loved* to stamp off my boots!'

Tiffany was just getting ready for bed that night when she found a book under her pillow.

The title, in fiery red letters, was *PASSION'S PLAY-THING* by Marjory J. Boddice, and in smaller print were the words: *Gods and Men said their love was not to be, but they would not listen!! A tortured tale of a tempestuous romance by the author of* Sundered Hearts!!!

The cover showed, up close, a young woman with dark hair and clothes that were a bit on the skimpy side in Tiffany's opinion, both hair and clothes blowing in the wind. She looked desperately determined, and also a bit chilly. A young man on a horse was watching her some distance away. It appeared that a thunderstorm was blowing up.

Strange. There was a library stamp inside and Nanny didn't use the library. Well, it wouldn't hurt to read a bit before blowing the candle out.

Tiffany turned to page one. And then to page two. When she got to page nineteen she went and fetched *The Unexpurgated Dictionary*.

She had older sisters and she knew some of this, she told herself. But Marjory J. Boddice had got some things laughably wrong. Girls on the Chalk didn't often run away from a young man who was rich enough to own his own horse – or not for long and not without giving him a chance to catch up. And Megs, the heroine of the book, clearly didn't know a thing about farming. No young man would be interested in a woman who couldn't dose a cow or carry a piglet. What kind of help would she be around the place? Standing around with lips like cherries wouldn't get the cows milked or the sheep sheared!

And that was another thing. Did Marjory J. Boddice know *anything* about sheep? This was a sheep farm in the summertime, wasn't it? So when did they shear the sheep? The second most important occasion in a sheep farm's year and it wasn't worth mentioning?

Of course, they might have a breed like Habbakuk Polls or Lowland Cobbleworths, which didn't need shearing, but these were rare and any sensible author would surely have mentioned it.

And the scene in chapter five, where Megs left the sheep to fend for themselves while she went gathering nuts with Roger . . . well, how stupid was that? They could have wandered anywhere, and they were really stupid to think they'd find nuts in June.

She read on a bit further, and thought: Oh. I see. Hmm. Hah. Not nuts at all, then. On the Chalk, we call that sort of thing 'looking for cuckoo nests'.

She stopped there to go downstairs to fetch a fresh

candle, got back into bed, let her feet warm up again, and went on reading.

Should Megs marry sulky dark-eyed William, who already owned two and a half cows, or should she be swayed by Roger, who called her 'my proud beauty' but was clearly a bad man because he rode a black stallion and had a moustache?

Why did she think she had to marry either of them? Tiffany wondered. Anyway, she spent too much time leaning meaningfully against things and pouting. Wasn't anyone doing any work? And if she always dressed like that, she'd catch a chill.

It was amazing what those men put up with. But it made you think.

She blew out the candle and sank gently under the eiderdown, which was as white as snow.

Snow covered the Chalk. It fell around the sheep, making them look a dirty yellow. It covered the stars, but glowed by its own light. It stuck to the windows of the cottages, blotting out the orange candlelight. But it would never cover the castle. It stood on a mound a little way from the village, a tower of stone ruling all those thatched homes. They looked as if they had grown from the land, but the castle nailed it down. It said: I Own.

In his room, Roland wrote carefully. He ignored the hammering from outside.

Annagramma, Petulia, Miss Treason— Tiffany's

letters were full of faraway people with strange-sounding names. Sometimes he tried to imagine them, and wondered if she was making them up. The whole witchcraft business seemed . . . well, not as advertised. It was more like—

'Do you hear this, you wicked boy?' Aunt Danuta sounded triumphant. 'Now it's barred from this side too! Hah! This is for your own good, you know. You will stay in there until you are ready to apologize!'

– like hard work, to be honest. Worthy, though, visiting the sick and everything, but very busy and not very magical. He'd heard of 'dancing about without your drawers on' and tried his best not to imagine it, but in any case there didn't seem to be anything like that. Even broomstick rides sounded—

'And we know about your secret passage now, oh yes! It's being walled up! No more cocking a snook at people who are doing their very best for you!'

– dull. He paused for a moment, staring blankly at the carefully stacked piles of loaves and sausages beside his bed. I ought to get some onions tonight, he thought. General Tacticus says they are unsurpassable for the proper operation of the digestive system if you can't find fresh fruit.

What to write, what to write . . . yes! He'd tell her about the party. He'd only gone because his father, in one of his good moments, had asked him to. It was important to keep in with the neighbours *but not with the relatives*! It'd been quite nice to get out, and he'd been able to leave his horse at Mr Gamely's stable where the aunts wouldn't think of looking for it. Yes . . . she'd enjoy hearing about the party.

The aunts were shouting again, about locking the door to his father's room. And they were blocking the secret passage. That meant that all he was left with was the loose stone that came out behind the tapestry in the next room, the wobbly flagstone that could let him drop down into the room below and, of course, the chain outside the window which let him climb all the way down to the ground. And on his desk, on top of Gen. Tacticus's book, was a complete set of shiny new castle keys. He'd got Mr Gamely to make them for him. The blacksmith was a thoughtful man who could see the sense in being friendly to the next baron.

He could come and go as he liked, whatever they did. They could bully his father, they could shout all they pleased, but they would never own *him*.

You could learn a lot from books.

The wintersmith was learning. It was a hard, slow task when you have to make your brain out of ice. But he had learned about snowmen. They were built by the smaller kinds of humans. That was interesting. Apart from the ones in pointy hats, the bigger humans didn't seem to hear him. They knew invisible creatures didn't speak to them out of the air.

The small ones, though, hadn't found out what was impossible.

In the big city was a big snowman.

Actually, it would be more honest to call it a slushman. *Technically* it was snow, but by the time it had spiralled down through the big city's fogs, smogs and smokes it was already a sort of yellowish grey, and then most of what ended up on the pavement was what had been thrown up from the gutter by cart wheels. It was, at best, a mostly-snowman. But three grubby children were building it anyway, because building something that you could call a snowman was what you did. Even if it was yellow.

They'd done their best with what they could find, and had given him two horse apples* for eyes and a dead rat for a nose.

At which point, the snowman spoke to them, in their heads.

Small humans, why do you do that?

The boy who might have been the oldest boy looked at the girl who might have been the oldest girl. 'I'll tell you I heard that if you say you heard it too,' he said.

The girl was still young enough not to think 'snowmen can't talk' when one of them had just spoken to her, so she said to it: 'You have to put them in to make you a snowman, mister.'

Does that make me human?

'No, 'cos . . .' She hesitated.

---

* So called because you get them from horses and they are about the size of apples . . .

'You ain't got innards,' said the third and smallest child, who might have been the youngest boy or the youngest girl, but who was spherical with so many layers of clothing that it was quite impossible to tell. It did have a pink woolly hat with a bobble on it, but that didn't mean anything. Someone did care about it, though, because they'd embroidered 'R' and 'L' on its mittens, 'F' and 'B' on the front and back of its coat, 'T' on top of the bobble hat and probably 'U' on the underside of its rubber boots. That meant that while you couldn't know what it was, you could be certain it was the right way up and which way it was facing.

A cart went by, throwing up another wave of slush.

Innards? said the secret voice of the snowman. *Made of special dust, yes! But what dust?*

'Iron,' said the possibly older boy promptly. 'Enough iron to make a nail.'

'Oh, yeah, that's right, that's how it goes,' said the possibly older girl. 'We used to skip to it. Er . . . "Iron enough to make a nail, water enough to drown a cow—"'

'A dog,' said the possibly older boy. 'It's "Water enough to drown a dog, sulphur enough to kill the fleas." It's "poison enough to kill a cow."'

What is this? the wintersmith asked.

'It's . . . like . . . an old song,' said the possibly older boy.

'More like a sort of poem. Everyone knows it,' said the possibly older girl.

''S called "These Are the Things That Make a Man",' said the child who was the right way up.

Tell me the rest of it, the wintersmith demanded, and on the freezing pavement they did, as much as they knew.

When they'd finished, the possibly older boy said hopefully, 'Is there any chance you can take us flying?'

No, said the wintersmith. *I have things to find! Things that make a man!*

One afternoon, when the sky was growing cold, there was a frantic knocking on Nanny's door. It turned out to be caused by Annagramma, who almost fell into the room. She looked terrible, and her teeth were chattering.

Nanny and Tiffany stood her by the fire, but she started talking before her teeth had warmed up.

'Skkkkulls!' she managed.

Oh dear, thought Tiffany.

'What about them?' she said, as Nanny Ogg hurried in from the kitchen with a hot drink.

'Mmmmmiss Trrreason's Skkkkulls!'

'Yes? What about them?'

Annagramma took a swig from the mug. 'What did you do with them?' she gasped, cocoa dribbling down her chin.

'Buried them.'

'Oh, no! Why?'

'They were skulls. You can't just leave skulls lying about!'

Annagramma looked around wildly. 'Can you lend me a shovel, then?'

'Annagramma! You can't dig up Miss Treason's grave!'

'But I need some skulls!' Annagramma insisted. 'The people there – well, it's like the olden days! I whitewashed that place with my own hands! Have you any idea how long it takes to whitewash over black? They complained! They won't have anything to do with crystal therapy, they just frown and say Miss Treason gave them sticky black medicine that tasted horrible but worked! And they keep on asking me to sort out stupid little problems, and I don't have a clue what they're on about. And this morning there was this old man who's dead and I've got to lay him out and sit up with him tonight. Well, I mean, that's so . . . yuk . . .'

Tiffany glanced at Nanny Ogg, who was sitting in her chair and puffing gently on her pipe. Her eyes were gleaming. When she saw Tiffany's expression she winked and said: 'I'll leave you girls to have a little chat, shall I?'

'Yes please, Nanny. And please don't listen at the door.'

'To a private conversation? The very idea!' said Nanny, and went into the kitchen.

'Will she listen?' whispered Annagramma. 'I'll just die if Mistress Weatherwax finds out.'

Tiffany sighed. Did Annagramma know anything? 'Of course she'll listen,' she said. 'She's a witch.'

'But she said she wouldn't!'

241

'She'll listen but she'll pretend she hasn't and she won't tell anyone,' said Tiffany. 'It's her cottage, after all.'

Annagramma looked desperate. 'And on Tuesday I've probably got to go and deliver a baby out in some valley somewhere! An old woman came and gabbled at me about it!'

'That'll be Mrs Owslick's baby,' said Tiffany. 'I *did* leave some notes, you know. Didn't you read them?'

'I think perhaps Mrs Earwig tidied them away,' said Annagramma.

'You should have looked at them! It took me an hour to write them all down!' said Tiffany reproachfully. 'Three pieces of paper! Look, calm down, will you? Didn't you learn anything about midwifery?'

'Mrs Earwig said giving birth is a natural action and nature should be allowed to take its course,' said Annagramma, and Tiffany was sure she heard a snort from behind the kitchen door. 'I know a soothing chant, though.'

'Well, I expect that will be a help,' said Tiffany weakly.

'Mrs Earwig said the village women know what to do,' said Annagramma hopefully. 'She says to trust in their peasant wisdom.'

'Well, Mrs Obble was the old woman who called and what she has got is simple peasant ignorance,' said Tiffany. 'She puts leaf mould on wounds if you don't watch her. Look, just because a woman's got no teeth doesn't mean she's wise. It might just mean she's been stupid for a very long time. Don't let her anywhere near Mrs Owlslick until after the baby. It's not going to be an easy birth as it is.'

'Well, I know plenty of spells that will help—'

'No! No magic! Only to take away pain! Surely you know that?'

'Yes, but Mrs Earwig says—'

'Why don't you go and ask Mrs Earwig to help you then?'

Annagramma stared at Tiffany. That sentence had come out a bit louder than intended. And then Annagramma's face slid into what she probably thought was a friendly expression. It made her look slightly mad.

'Hey, I've got a great idea!' she said, as bright as a crystal that was about to shatter. 'Why don't you come back to the cottage and work for me?'

'No. I've got other work to do.'

'But you're so good at the messy stuff, Tiffany,' said Annagramma in a syrupy voice. 'It seems to come naturally to you.'

'I started at the lambing when I was small, that's why. Small hands can get inside and untangle things.'

And now Annagramma had that hunted look she got when she was dealing with anything she didn't immediately understand.

'Inside the sheep? You mean up its . . .'

'Yes. Of course.'

'*Untangle things?*'

'Sometimes the lambs try to get born backwards,' said Tiffany.

'Backwards,' muttered Annagramma weakly.

'And it can be worse if there's twins.'

'Twins . . .' Then Annagramma said, as if spotting the flaw: 'But look, I've seen lots of pictures of shepherds and sheep and there's never anything like that. I thought it was all just . . . standing around and watching the sheep eat grass.'

There were times when you could feel that the world would be a better place if Annagramma got the occasional slap around the ear. The silly unthinking insults, her huge lack of interest in anyone other than herself, the way she treated everyone as if they were slightly deaf and a bit stupid . . . it could make your blood boil. But you put up with it because every once in a while you saw through it all. Inside there was this worried, frantic little face watching the world like a bunny watching a fox, and screaming at it in the hope that it would go away and not hurt her. And a meeting of witches, who were supposed to be clever, had handed her this steading which would be a hard job for anyone.

It didn't make sense.

No, it didn't make sense.

'It only happens when there's a difficult lambing,' said Tiffany, while her mind raced. 'And that means it's out in the dark and cold and the rain. Artists never seem to be around then. It's amazing.'

'Why are you looking at me like that?' said Annagramma. 'Like I'm not here!'

Tiffany blinked. All right, she thought. How am I supposed to deal with this?

'Look, I'll come and help you with the laying-out,' she said, as calmly as she could manage. 'And I expect I can help with Mrs Owslick. Or ask Petulia. She's good. But you'll have to do the watching by yourself.'

'Sitting up all night with a dead person?' said Annagramma, and shivered.

'You can take a book to read,' said Tiffany.

'I suppose I could draw a circle of protection around the chair . . .' Annagramma muttered.

'No,' said Tiffany. 'No magic. Mrs Earwig must have told you this?'

'But a circle of protection—'

'It draws attention. Something might turn up to see why it's there. Don't worry, it's just to make the old people happy.'

'Er . . . when you say something might turn up . . .' Annagramma began.

Tiffany sighed. 'All right, I'll sit up with you, just this once,' she said. Annagramma beamed.

'And as for skulls,' said Tiffany, 'just wait a moment.' She went upstairs and got the Boffo catalogue, which she'd hidden in her old suitcase. She came back with it carefully rolled up and handed it over. 'Don't look at it now,' she said. 'Wait until you're alone. You might find it gives you ideas.

OK? I'll come and meet you around seven tonight.'

When Annagramma had gone, Tiffany sat and counted under her breath. When she'd got to five, Nanny Ogg came and vigorously dusted a few ornaments before saying: 'Oh, has your little friend gone?'

'Do you think I'm being silly?' said Tiffany.

Nanny stopped pretending to do housework. 'I don't know what you're talkin' about, not havin' listened,' she said, 'but if I had been listenin' I'd think you won't get any thanks, that's what I'd think.'

'Granny shouldn't have meddled,' said Tiffany.

'Shouldn't have, eh?' said Nanny, her face blank.

'I'm not stupid, Nanny,' said Tiffany. 'I've worked it out.'

'Worked it out, have you? There's a clever girl,' said Nanny Ogg, sitting down in her chair. 'And what is it you've worked out then?'

This was going to get difficult. Nanny was usually cheerful all the time. When she went solemn, like she was now, it could make you nervous. But Tiffany pressed on.

'I couldn't take on a cottage,' she said. 'Oh, I can do most of the everyday stuff, but you need to be older to run a steading. There's things people won't tell you if you're thirteen, hat or not. But Granny put it about that she was suggesting me, and so everyone saw it as a contest between me and Annagramma, right? And they chose her because she's older and sounds really competent. And now it's all falling apart. It's not her fault she was taught magic instead of witchcraft. Granny just wants her to fail so that everyone will know that Mrs Earwig is a bad teacher. And I don't think that's good.'

'I wouldn't be too quick to decide what it is Esme Weatherwax wants, if I was you,' said Nanny Ogg. 'I won't say a word, mind you. You go off and help your friend if you want, but you've still got to work for me, OK? That's only fair. How's the feet?'

'They feel fine, Nanny. Thank you for asking.'

More than a hundred miles away, Mr Fusel Johnson knew nothing about Tiffany, Nanny Ogg or, indeed, anything very much except for clocks and watches, which he made for a living. He also knew how to lime-wash a kitchen, which was an easy and cheap way to get a nice white look even if the stuff was a bit runny. And therefore he had no idea why several handfuls of the white powder fountained up out of the mixing bowl before he could add the water, hung in the air for a moment like a ghost and vanished up the chimney. In the end, he put it down to too many trolls moving into the area. This wasn't very logical, but such beliefs generally aren't.

And the wintersmith thought: Lime enough to make a man!

That night she sat up with Annagramma and old Mr

Tissot, except that he was lying down because he was dead. Tiffany had never liked watching over the dead. It wasn't exactly something you could like. It was always a relief when the sky turned grey and the birds started to sing.

Sometimes, in the night, Mr Tissot made little noises. Except, of course, it wasn't Mr Tissot, who'd met Death hours ago. It was just the body he'd left behind, and the sounds it made were really no different from the noises made by an old house as it cooled down.

It was important to remember these things around two o'clock in the morning. Vitally important, when the candle flickered.

Annagramma snored. No one with a nose that small should be able to make a snore that loud. It was like ripping planks. Whatever evil spirits might be around on this night, that sound would probably scare them away.

It wasn't the *Gnh gnh gnh* part that was so bad, and Tiffany could live with the *Bloooooorrrrt!* It was the gap between them, after the *Gnh gnh gnh* had wound up but before the long let-down of the *Bloooooorrrrt!* That really got on her nerves. It was never the same length twice. Sometimes there was *Gnh gnh gnh Bloooooorrrrt!* one right after the other, and then there might be such a huge gap after *Gnh gnh gnh* that Tiffany found herself holding her breath while she waited for the *Bloooooorrrrt!* It wouldn't have been so bad if Annagramma had stuck to one length of pause.

Sometimes she stopped altogether, and there was blessed silence until a festival of blorts began, usually with a faint *mni mni* lip-smacking sound as Annagramma shifted position in her chair.

Where are you, Flower Lady? What are you? You should be sleeping!

The voice was so faint that Tiffany might not have heard it at all if she hadn't been all tensed up waiting for the next *Gnh gnh gnh*. And here it came—

Gnh gnh gnh!

Let me show you my world, Flower Lady. Let me show you all the colours of ice!

BLOOOOOORRRRT!

About three quarters of Tiffany thought: Oh, no! Will he find me if I reply? No. If he could find me, he'd be here. My hand isn't itching.

The other quarter thought: A god or god-like being is talking to me and I could really do without the snoring, Annagramma, thank you so much.

Gnh gnh gnh!

'I said I was sorry,' she whispered into the dancing candlelight. 'I saw the iceberg. It was very . . . er . . . nice of you.'

I have made many more.

BLOOOOOORRRRT!

Many more icebergs, thought Tiffany. Great big freezing, floating mountains that look like me, dragging fog banks and snowstorms behind them. I wonder how many ships run into them?

'You shouldn't have gone to all that trouble,' she whispered.

Now I am growing stronger! I am listening and learning! I am understanding humans!

Outside the cottage window a thrush began to sing. Tiffany blew out the candle, and grey light crept into the room.

Listening and learning . . . how could a blizzard understand things?

Tiffany, Flower Lady! I am making myself a man!

There was a complicated grunting as Annagramma's *Gnh gnh gnh* and *Blooooooorrrrt!* ran into each other and she woke up.

'Ah,' she said, stretching her arms and yawning. She looked around. 'Well, that seemed to go well.'

Tiffany stared at the wall. What did he mean, making himself a man? Surely he—

'You didn't fall asleep, did you, Tiffany?' said Annagramma in what she probably thought was a playful voice. 'Not even for one tiny little second?'

'What?' said Tiffany, glaring at the wall. 'Oh . . . no. I didn't!'

People were moving around downstairs. After a little while there was a creaking on the stairs and the low door was pushed open. A middle-aged man, looking sheepishly at the floor, uttered, 'Mam says would you ladies like some breakfast?'

'Oh, no, we couldn't possibly take what little you have—' Annagramma began.

'Yes please, we would be grateful,' said Tiffany, louder and quicker. The man nodded, and shut the door.

'Oh, how could you say that?' said Annagramma, as his footsteps creaked down. 'These are poor people! I thought you would—'

'Shut up, will you?' snapped Tiffany. 'Just shut up and wake up! These are real people! They're not some kind of, of, of *idea*! We will go down there and we will eat breakfast and we'll say how good it is and then we will thank them and they will thank us and we will go! And that will mean everyone has done the right thing by custom and that will be what's important to them. Besides, they don't think they're poor, because everyone around here is poor! But they're not so poor they can't afford to do the right things! That *would* be poor!'

Annagramma was staring at her with her mouth open.

'Be careful what you say next,' said Tiffany, breathing heavily. 'In fact, don't say anything.'

Breakfast was ham and eggs. It was eaten in polite silence. After that, in the same silence except that it was outdoors, they flew back to what people would probably always think of as Miss Treason's cottage.

There was a small boy loitering outside. As soon as they landed he blurted out, 'Mrs Obble says the baby's on the way an' she said you'd give me a penny for goin'.'

'You've got a bag, have you?' said Tiffany, turning to Annagramma.

'Yes, er, lots.'

'I mean a call-out bag. You know, you keep it by the door with everything in it that you'll need if . . .'

Tiffany saw the terrified look on the girl's face. 'OK, so you haven't got a bag. We'll just have to do the best we can. Give him a penny and let's go.'

'Can we get anyone to help if it goes wrong?' said Annagramma as they left the ground.

'We *are* the help,' said Tiffany simply. 'And since this is your steading, I'm giving you the really tough job—'

– which was keeping Mrs Obble occupied. Mrs Obble wasn't a witch, although most people thought she was. She looked like one – that is, she looked like someone who'd bought everything in the Boffo catalogue on the day of the Special Offer on hairy warts – and she was mildly crazy and should not have been allowed within a mile of any mother who was going to have her first baby, since she would very conscientiously tell them (or cackle at them, anyway) about everything that could go wrong in a way that made it sound as if they would all go wrong. She wasn't a bad nurse, though, once you stopped her putting a leaf-mould poultice on everything.

Things went noisily and with a certain amount of fuss, but nothing like Mrs Obble had predicted, and the result was a baby boy, who was not a bouncing baby but only because Tiffany caught him; Anna-gramma didn't know how to hold babies.

She did look good in a pointy hat, though, and since she was clearly older than Tiffany and did hardly any of the work the other women assumed she was in charge.

Tiffany left her holding the baby (the right way up, this time) and looking proud, and began the long flight back though the woods to Tir Nani Ogg. It was a crisp evening but there was a bit of wind which blew sting-ing snow crystals off the trees. It was an exhausting journey and very, very cold. He can't know where I am, she repeated to herself as she flew back in the dusk. And he's not very clever. Winter has to end sometime, right?

Er . . . how? said her Second Thoughts. Miss Tick says you just have to be there, but surely you have to do something else?

I suppose I'll have to walk around with my shoes off, Tiffany thought.

Everywhere? the Second Thoughts wondered, as she swerved between the trees.

It's probably like being a queen, her Third Thoughts said. She just has to sit in a palace and maybe do a bit of driving around in a big coach and waving, and all over a huge kingdom monarching is going on.

But as she avoided more trees she also tried to avoid the little scurrying thought that was trying to creep into her mind: Sooner or later, one way or the other, he will find you . . . and how can he make himself a man?

Assistant Postmaster Groat did not believe in doctors. They made you ill, he thought. So he put sulphur in his socks every morning and he was proud to say that he had never had a day's illness in his life. This may have been because not many people cared to come very close to him, because of the smell. Something did come close, though. A gale roared into his post office when he was opening the door one morning and blew his socks clean off.*

And no one heard the wintersmith say: 'Sulphur enough to make a man!'

Nanny Ogg was sitting by the fire when Tiffany came in, stamping snow off her boots.

'You look frozen all through,' she said. 'You need a glass of hot milk with a drop of brandy in it, that's what you need.'

'Ooh, y-yess . . .' Tiffany managed through chattering teeth.

'Get me one too, then, will you?' said Nanny. 'Only joking. You get warmed up, I'll see to the drink.'

Tiffany's feet felt like blocks of ice. She knelt by the

---

* This was reported in the newspapers, and shortly afterwards a widow wrote to him saying how much she admired a man who really understood about hygiene. They were later seen walking together, so it's an ill wind, as they say . . .

fire and stretched out her hand to the stockpot on its big black hook. It bubbled all the time.

Get your mind right, and balance. Reach out and cup your hands around it, and concentrate, concentrate, on your freezing boots.

After a while her toes felt warm and then—

'Ow!' Tiffany pulled her hands away and sucked at her fingers.

'Didn't have your mind right,' said Nanny Ogg from the doorway.

'Well, you know, that's just a bit difficult when you've had a long day and you didn't sleep much and the wintersmith is looking for you,' snapped Tiffany.

'The fire doesn't care,' said Nanny, shrugging. 'Hot milk coming up.'

Things were a little better when Tiffany had warmed up. She wondered how much brandy Nanny had added to the milk. Nanny had done one for herself, with probably some milk added to the brandy.

'Isn't this nice and cosy,' said Nanny after a while.

'Is this going to be the talk about sex?' said Tiffany.

'Did anyone say there was going to be one?' said Nanny innocently.

'I kind of got the feeling,' said Tiffany. 'And I know where babies come from, Mrs Ogg.'

'I should hope so.'

'I know how they get there, too. I live on a farm and I've got a lot of older sisters.'

'Ah, right,' said Nanny. 'Well, I see you're pretty

well prepared for life, then. Not much left for me to tell you, I expect. And I've never had a god pay any attention to me, as far as I can recall. Flattered, are you?'

'No!' Tiffany looked into Nanny's smile. 'Well, a bit,' she admitted.

'And frightened of him?'

'Yes.'

'Well, the poor thing hasn't quite got it right yet. He started off so well with the ice roses and everything, and then he wanted to show you his muscles. Typical. But you shouldn't be frightened of him. He should be frightened of you.'

'Why? Because I'm pretending to be the flower woman?'

'Because you're a girl! It's a poor lookout if a bright girl can't wind a boy around her little finger. He's smitten with you. You could make his life a misery with a word. Why, when I was a girl, a young man nearly threw himself off the Lancre bridge because I spurned his advances!'

'He did? What happened?'

'I unspurned 'em. Well, he looked so pretty standing there, and I thought, That's a good-looking bum on him if ever I saw one.' Nanny sat back. 'And think about poor ol' Greebo. He'll fight anything. But Esme's little white kitten leaped straight at him and now the poor dear won't come into this room without peering round the door to check she's not here. You should see his poor little face when he does, too. It's all wrinkled up. O' course, he could tear her into bits with one claw, but he can't now 'cos she's fixed his head.'

'You're not saying I should try to tear the wintersmith's face off, are you?'

'No, no, you don't have to be as blunt as that. Give him a little hope. Be kind but firm—'

'He wants to marry me!'

'Good.'

'*Good?*'

'That means he wants to stay friendly. Don't say no, don't say yes. Act like a queen. He's got to learn to show you some respect. What are you doing?'

'Writing this down,' said Tiffany, scribbling in her diary.

'You don't need to write it down, love,' said Nanny. 'It's written down in you, somewhere. On a page you haven't read yet, I reckon. Which reminds me, these came when you were out.' Nanny felt down among the seat cushions and fished out a couple of envelopes. 'My boy Shawn is the postman, so he knew you'd moved.'

Tiffany nearly snatched them out of her hand. Two letters! 'Like him, do you? Your young man in the castle?' said Nanny.

'He's a friend who writes to me,' said Tiffany haughtily.

'That's right, that's just the look and voice you need to deal with the wintersmith!' said Nanny, looking delighted. 'Who does he think he is, daring to talk to you? That's the way!'

'I shall read them in my room,' said Tiffany.

Nanny nodded. 'One of the girls did us a lovely casserole,' she said (famously, Nanny never remembered the names of her daughters-in-law). 'Yours is in the oven. I'm off to the pub. Early start tomorrow!'

Alone in her room, Tiffany read the first letter.

To the unaided eye, not much happened on the Chalk. It had avoided History. It was a place of small things. Tiffany enjoyed reading about them.

The second letter seemed to be much the same as the first one – until the bit about the ball. He'd gone to a ball! It was at the house of Lord Diver, who was a neighbour! He'd danced with his daughter, who was called Iodine because Lord Diver thought that was a nice name for a girl! They'd had three dances!! And ice cream!! Iodine had shown him her water-colours!!!

How could he sit there and write such things?!!!

Tiffany's eyes moved on, over everyday news like the bad weather and what had happened to old Aggie's leg, but the words didn't enter her head because it was on fire.

Who did he think he was, dancing with another girl?

You danced with the wintersmith, her Third Thoughts said.

All right, but what about the water-colours?

The wintersmith showed you the snowflakes, said the Third Thoughts.

But I was just being polite!

Perhaps he was just being polite, too.

All right, but I know those aunts, Tiffany thought furiously. They've never liked me, because I'm only a farm girl! And Lord Diver's very rich and his daughter is his only child! They're scheming!

How could he sit there and write as if eating ice creams with another girl was a perfectly normal thing to do! That was as bad as – well, something pretty bad, at least!

As for looking at her water-colours . . .

He's just a boy you happen to write to, said the Third Thoughts.

Yes, well . . .

Yes, well . . . what? the Third Thoughts persisted. They were getting on Tiffany's nerves. Your own brain ought to have the decency to be on your side!

Just, 'Yes, well . . .' OK? she thought angrily.

You're not being very sensible about this.

Oh, really? Well, I've been sensible all day! I've been sensible for years! I think I'm owed five minutes of being really unreasonably angry, don't you?

There's some casserole downstairs and you haven't eaten since breakfast, said the Third Thoughts. You'll feel better after you've eaten something.

How can I eat stew when people are looking at water-colours? How dare he look at water-colours!

But the Third Thoughts were right – not that this made things any better. If you're going to be angry and miserable, you might as well be so on a full stomach. She went downstairs and found the casserole in the oven. It smelled good. Nothing but the best for dear ol' Mum.

She opened the cutlery drawer for a spoon. It stuck. She rattled it, pulled at it and swore a few times, but it stayed stuck.

'Oh, yes, go ahead,' said a voice behind her. 'See how much help that is. Don't be sensible and stick your hand under the top and carefully free up the stuck item. Oh no. Rattle and curse, that's the way!'

Tiffany turned.

There was a skinny, tired-looking woman standing by the kitchen table. She seemed to be wearing a sheet draped around her and was smoking a cigarette. Tiffany had never seen a woman smoke a cigarette before, but especially never a cigarette that burned with a fat red flame and gave off sparks.

'Who are you and what are you doing in Mrs Ogg's kitchen,' she said sharply.

This time it was the woman who looked surprised.

'You can hear me?' she said. 'And see me?'

'Yes!' Tiffany snarled. 'And this is a food preparation area, you know!'

'You're not supposed to be able to see me!'

'Well, I'm looking at you!'

'Hold on a minute,' said the woman, frowning at

260

Tiffany. 'You're not just a human, are you . . . ?' She squinted oddly for a moment and then said, 'Oh, you're *her*. Am I right? The new Summer?'

'Never mind me, who are you?' said Tiffany. 'And it was only one dance!'

'Anoia, Goddess of Things That Get Stuck in Drawers,' said the woman. 'Pleased to meet you.' She took another puff at the flaming cigarette, and there were more sparks. Some of them dropped on the floor, but didn't seem to do any damage.

'There's a goddess just for that?' said Tiffany.

'Well, I find lost corkscrews and things that roll under furniture,' said Anoia, off-handedly. 'Sometimes things that get lost under sofa cushions, too. They want me to do stuck zips, and I'm thinking about that. But mostly I manifest whensoever people rattle stuck drawers and call upon the gods.' She puffed on her cigarette. 'Got any tea?'

'But I didn't call on anyone!'

'You did,' said Anoia, blowing more sparks. 'You cussed. Sooner or later, every curse is a prayer.' She waved the hand that wasn't holding the cigarette and something in the drawer went *pling*. 'It'll be all right now. It was the fish slice. Everyone has one, and no one knows why. Did anyone in the world ever knowingly go out one day and buy a fish slice? I don't think so.'

Tiffany tried the drawer. It slid out easily.

'About that tea . . . ?' said Anoia, sitting down.

Tiffany put the kettle on. 'You know about me?' she said.

'Oh, yes,' said Anoia. 'It's been quite some time since a god fell in love with a mortal. Everyone wants to see how it turns out.'

'Fell in love?'

'Oh, yes.'

'And you mean the gods are watching?'

'Well, of course,' said Anoia. 'Most of the big ones don't do anything else these days! But I'm supposed to do zips, oh yes, and my hands get very stiff in this weather!'

Tiffany glanced at the ceiling, which was now full of smoke.

'They're watching all the time?' she said, aghast.

'I heard you're getting more interest than the war in Klatchistan, and that was pretty popular,' said Anoia, holding out her red hands. 'Look, chilblains. Not that they care, of course.'

'Even when I'm having a . . . wash?' said Tiffany.

The goddess laughed nastily. 'Yes. And they can see in the dark, too. Best not to think about it.'

Tiffany looked up the ceiling again. She had been hoping for a bath tonight.

'I'll try not to,' she said darkly, and added: 'Is it . . . hard, being a goddess?'

'It has its good days,' said Anoia. She stood with her cigarette cupped at the elbow by her other hand, holding the flaming, sparking thing close to her face. Now she took a sharp pull, raised her head and blew a cloud of smoke out to join the smog on the ceiling. Sparks fell out of it like rain. 'I haven't been doing drawers long. I used to be a volcano goddess.'

'Really?' said Tiffany. 'I'd never have guessed.'

'Oh, yes. It was good work, apart from the screaming,' said Anoia, and then added, in a bitter tone of voice: 'Ha! And the god of storms was always raining on my lava. That's men for you, dear. They rain on your lava.'

'And look at water-colours,' said Tiffany.

Anoia's eyes narrowed. 'Someone else's water-colours?'

'Yes!'

'Men! They're all the same,' said Anoia. 'Take my advice, dear, and show Mr Wintersmith the door. He's only an elemental, after all.'

Tiffany glanced at the door.

'Give him the boot, dear, send him packing and change the locks. Let's have summer all year round like the hot countries do. Grapes all over the place, eh? Coconuts on every tree! Hah, when I was in the volcano game I couldn't move for mangoes. Kiss goodbye to snow and fog and slush. Have you got the thingy yet?'

'The thingy?' said Tiffany, looking worried.

'It'll turn up, I daresay,' said Anoia. 'I hear it can be a bit tricky to— Oops, I hear rattling, must fly, don't worry, I won't tell him where you are—'

She vanished. So did the smoke.

Not knowing what else to do, Tiffany ladled out a plate of hearty meat and vegetables, and ate it. So . . . she could see gods now? And they knew about her? And everyone wanted to give her advice.

It was not a good idea to come to the attention of those in high places, her father had said.

But it was impressive. In love with her, eh? And telling everyone? But he was really an elemental, not a proper god at all. All he knew was how to move wind and water around!

Even so . . . huh! Some people have elementals running after them! Oh yes! How about that? If people were stupid enough to dance around with girls who painted water-colours to lead honest men to their Doom, well, she could be haughty to people who were almost gods. She ought to mention that in a letter, except that of course she wasn't going to be writing to him *now*. Hah!

And a few miles away Old Mother Blackcap, who made her own soap out of animal fat and the potash that came, indeed, from plant ashes, felt a bar snatched from her hand just as she was about to boil some sheets. The tub of water froze solid, too.

Being a witch, she immediately said: 'There's a strange thief about!'

And the wintersmith said: 'Potash enough to make a man!'

CHAPTER 8

THE HORN OF PLENTY

That night, after Nanny Ogg had gone to bed, Tiffany did have the bath she'd been looking forward to. It was not something to be taken lightly. First, the tin bath had to be fetched from its hook on the back of the privy, which was at the bottom of the garden, and then dragged through the dark, freezing night to a place of honour in front of the fire. Kettles had to be heated over the fire and on the black kitchen stove, and getting even six inches of warm water was an effort. Afterwards, the water all had to be scooped out and into the sink and the bath moved into a corner, ready to be taken outside in the morning. When you had to do all that, you might as well scrub every inch.

Tiffany did one extra thing: she wrote 'PRIVATE!!' on a piece of cardboard and wedged it in the hanging lamp in the centre of the room so that it could only be read from above. She wasn't sure it would put off any inquisitive gods, but she felt better for doing it.

That night she slept without dreaming. In the morning fresh snow had put a coating on the drifts, and a couple of Nanny Ogg's grandchildren were building her a snowman on the lawn. They came in after a while and demanded a carrot for the nose and two lumps of coal for the eyes.

Nanny took her to the isolated village of Slice, where people were always glad and surprised to see someone they weren't related to. Nanny Ogg ambled from cottage to cottage along the paths cut in the snow, drinking enough cups of tea to float an elephant and doing witchcraft in small ways. Mostly, it seemed to just consist of gossip, but once you got the hang of it, you could hear the magic happening. Nanny Ogg changed the way people thought, even if it was only for a few minutes. She left people thinking they were slightly better people. They weren't, but as Nanny said, it gave them something to live up to.

Then there was another night without dreams, but Tiffany woke up with a snap at half-past five, feeling . . . odd.

She rubbed the frost off the window, and saw the snowman by moonlight.

Why do we do it? she wondered. As soon as there's snow, we build snowmen. We do worship the wintersmith, in a way. We make the snow human . . . We give him coal eyes and a carrot nose to bring him alive. Oh, and I see the children gave him a scarf.

That's what a snowman needs, a scarf to keep him warm . . .

She went down into the silent kitchen, and for want of anything else to do scrubbed the table. Doing something with her hands helped her think.

Something had changed, and it was her. She'd been worrying about what he would do and what he would think, as if she was just a leaf being blown about by the wind. She dreaded hearing his voice in her head, where he had no right to be.

Well, not now. Not any more.

He ought to be worried about her.

Yes, she'd made a mistake. Yes, it was her fault. But she wasn't going to be bullied. You couldn't let boys go around raining on your lava and ogling other people's water-colours.

Find the story, Granny Weatherwax always said. She believed that the world was full of story shapes. If you let them, they controlled you. But if you studied them, if you found out about them . . . you could use them, you could change them . . .

Miss Treason had known all about stories, yes? She'd spun them like a spider's web, to give herself power. And they worked because people wanted to believe them. And Nanny Ogg told a story, too. Fat, jolly Nanny Ogg, who liked a drink (and another drink, thank you kindly) and was everyone's favourite grandmother . . . but those twinkling little eyes could bore into your head and read all your secrets.

Even Granny Aching had a story. She'd lived in the old shepherding hut, high on the hills, listening to the wind blowing over the turf. She was mysterious, alone – and the stories floated up and gathered around her, all those stories about her finding lost lambs even though she was dead, all those stories about her, still, watching over people . . .

People wanted the world to be a story, because stories had to sound right and they had to make sense. People wanted the world to make sense.

Well, her story wasn't going to be the story of a little girl who got pushed around. There was no sense in that.

Except . . . he's not actually bad. The gods in the *Mythology*, they seemed to get the hang of being human – a bit too human, sometimes – but how could a snowstorm or a gale ever find out? He was dangerous and scary – but you couldn't help feeling sorry for him . . .

Someone hammered on Nanny Ogg's back door. It turned out to be a tall figure in black.

'Wrong house,' said Tiffany. 'No one here is even a bit sick.'

A hand raised the black hood and from its depths a voice hissed: 'It's me, Annagramma! Is she in?'

'Mrs Ogg's not up yet,' said Tiffany.

'Good. Can I come in?'

At the kitchen table, over a cup of warming tea, Annagramma revealed all. Life in the woods was not going well.

'Two men came to see me about some stupid cow they both think they own!' she said.

'That'll be Joe Broomsocket and Shifty Adams. I left you a note about them, too,' said Tiffany. 'Whenever one or other of them gets drunk, they argue about that cow.'

'What am I supposed to do about it?'

'Nod and smile. Wait until the cow dies, Miss Treason always said. Or one of the men,' said Tiffany. 'It's the only way.'

'And a woman came to see me with a sick pig!'

'What did you do about it?'

'I told her I don't do pigs! But she burst into tears, so I tried Bangle's Universal Nostrum on it.'

'You used that on a pig?' said Tiffany, shocked.

'Well, the pig-witch uses magic, so I don't see why—' Annagramma began defensively.

'*She* knows what works!' said Tiffany.

'It was perfectly all right when I got it down out of the tree! She didn't have to make all that fuss! I'm sure the bristles will grow back! In time!'

'It wasn't a spotted pig, was it? And a woman with a squint?' Tiffany asked.

'Yes! I think so! Does it matter?'

'Mrs Stumper is very attached to that pig,' said Tiffany reproachfully. 'She brings him up to the cottage about once a week. It's usually just an upset stomach. She feeds him too much.'

'Really? Then I won't open the door to her next time,' said Annagramma firmly.

'No, let her in. Really, it's all because she's lonely and wants to chat.'

'Well, I should think I've got better things to do with my time than listen to an old lady who just wants to talk,' said Annagramma indignantly.

Tiffany looked at her. Where did you start, apart from banging the girl's head on the table until the brain started working?

'Listen very carefully,' she said. 'I mean to her, not just to me. You've got no better use of your time than to listen to old ladies who want to talk. Everyone tells things to witches. So listen to everyone and don't say much and think about what they say and how they say it and watch their eyes . . . it becomes like a big jigsaw, but you're the only one who can see all the pieces. You'll know what they want you to know, and what they don't want you to know, and even what they think no one knows. That's why we go around the houses. That's why you *will* go around the houses, until you're part of their lives.'

'All this just to get some power over a crowd of farmers and peasants?'

Tiffany spun round and kicked a chair so hard that it broke a leg. Annagramma backed away quickly.

'What did you do that for?'

'You're clever, you guess!'

'Oh, I forgot . . . your father is a shepherd . . .'

'Good! You remembered!' Tiffany hesitated. Certainty was pouring into her brain, courtesy of her

Third Thoughts. Suddenly, she knew Annagramma.

'And *your* father?' she asked.

'What?' Annagramma instinctively drew herself up. 'Oh, he owns several farms—'

'Liar!'

'Well, perhaps I should say he is a farmer—' the girl began, nervousness beginning to show.

'Liar!'

Annagramma backed away. 'How dare you talk to me like—'

'How dare you not tell me the truth!'

In the pause that opened, Tiffany heard everything – the faint crackle of wood in the stove, the sound of mice in the cellar, her own breathing roaring like the sea in a cave . . .

'He works for a farmer, all right?' said Annagramma quickly, and then looked shocked at her own words. 'We don't have any land, we don't even own the cottage. There's the truth, if you want it. Happy now?'

'No. But thank you,' said Tiffany.

'Are you going to tell the others?'

'No. It doesn't matter. But Granny Weatherwax wants you to make a mess of all this, do you understand? She's got nothing against you . . .' Tiffany hesitated, then went on, 'I mean, nothing more than she has against everyone. She just wants people to see that Mrs Earwig's style of witchcraft doesn't work. This is just like her! She's not said a word against you, she's just let you have exactly what you wanted. It's like a story. Everyone knows that if you get exactly what you wish for, it all goes bad. And you wished for a cottage. And you're going to mess it up.'

'I just need another day or two to get the hang—'

'Why? You're a witch with a cottage. You're supposed to be able to deal with it! Why take it on if you couldn't do it?'

You're supposed to be able to deal with it, sheep girl! Why take it on if you couldn't do it?

'So you're not going to help me?' Annagramma glared at Tiffany and then her expression, most unusually, softened a bit and she said, 'Are you all right?'

Tiffany blinked. It's horrible to have your own voice echo back at you from the other side of your mind.

'Look, I haven't got time,' she said weakly. 'Maybe the others can . . . help out?'

'I don't want them to know!' Panic cut its curves on Annagramma's face.

She can do magic, Tiffany thought. She's just not good at witchcraft. She'll make a mess of it. She'll make a mess of *people*.

She gave in. 'All right, I can probably spare some time: there's not many chores to do at Tir Nani Ogg. And I'll explain things to the others. They'll have to know. They'll probably help. You learn fast, you could pick up the basic stuff in a week or so.'

Tiffany watched Annagramma's face. She was actually *thinking* about it! If she was drowning and you threw her a rope she'd complain if it was the wrong colour . . .

'Well, if they are just *helping* me . . .' Annagramma said, brightening up.

You could almost admire the girl for the way she could rearrange the real world in her head. Another story, thought Tiffany; it's all about Annagramma.

'Yes, we'll be helping you,' she sighed.

'Perhaps we could even tell people that you girls are coming to me to learn things?' said Annagramma hopefully.

People said that you should always count up to ten before losing your temper. But if it was Annagramma you were dealing with, you had to know some bigger numbers, like perhaps a million.

'No,' said Tiffany, 'I don't think we'll do that. You are the one doing the learning.'

Annagramma opened her mouth to argue, saw the look on Tiffany's face and decided not to.

'Er, yes,' she said. 'Of course. Er . . . thank you.'

That was a surprise.

'They probably will help,' said Tiffany. 'It won't look good if one of us fails.'

To her amazement, the girl really was crying. 'It's just that I didn't really think they were my friends . . .'

'I don't like her,' said Petulia, who was knee-deep in pigs. 'She calls me the pig-witch.'

'Well, you are a pig-witch,' said Tiffany, who was

273

standing outside the pig pen. The big shed was full of pigs. The noise was nearly as bad as the smell. Fine snow, like dust, was falling outside.

'Yes, but when she says it, there's a good deal too much pig and not enough witch,' said Petulia. 'Every time she opens her mouth I think I've done something wrong.' She waved a hand in a pig's face and muttered a few words. The animal's eyes crossed and it opened its mouth. It got a large dose of green liquid from a bottle.

'We can't just leave her to struggle,' said Tiffany. 'People might get hurt.'

'Well, that wouldn't be our fault, would it?' said Petulia, dosing another pig. She cupped her hands and shouted over the din to a man at the other end of the pens: 'Fred, this lot's done!' Then she climbed out of the pen and Tiffany saw that she'd got her dress tucked up to her waist and was wearing a pair of heavy leather britches under it.

'They're making a real fuss this morning,' she said. 'Sounds like they're getting a bit frisky.'

'Frisky?' said Tiffany. 'Oh . . . yes.'

'Listen, you can hear the boars yelling in their shed,' said Petulia. 'They can smell the spring.'

'But it's not even Hogswatch yet!'

'It's the day after tomorrow. Anyway the springtime sleeps under the snow, my dad always says,' said Petulia, washing her hands in a bucket.

No Ums, said Tiffany's Third Thoughts. When she's

working, Petulia never says 'um'. She's certain of things when she's working. She stands up straight. She's in charge.

'Look, it *will* be our fault if we can see something wrong and don't do anything about it,' said Tiffany.

'Oh, Annagramma again,' said Petulia. She shrugged. 'Look, I can go over there maybe once a week after Hogswatch and show her some of the basic stuff. Will that make you happy?'

'I'm sure she'll be grateful.'

'I'm sure she won't be. Have you asked any of the others?'

'No, I thought that if they knew you'd agreed, they probably would, too,' said Tiffany.

'Hah! Well, I suppose that at least we can say we tried. You know, I used to think Annagramma was really clever because she knew a lot of words and could do sparkly spells. But show her a sick pig and she's useless!'

Tiffany told her about Mrs Stumper's pig and Petulia looked shocked.

'We can't have that sort of thing,' she said. 'In a tree? Perhaps I'll try to drop in this afternoon, then.' She hesitated. 'You know Granny Weatherwax won't be happy about this. Do we want to be caught between her and Mrs Earwig?'

'Are we doing the right thing or not?' said Tiffany. 'Anyway, what's the worst she could do to us?'

Petulia gave a short laugh with no humour in

it at all. 'Well,' she said, 'first, she could make our—'

'She won't.'

'I wish I was as sure as you,' said Petulia. 'All right, then. For Mrs Stumper's pig.'

Tiffany flew above the treetops, so that the occasional high twig brushed against her boots. There was just enough winter sunshine to make the snow crisp and glittery, like a frosted cake.

It had been a busy morning. The coven hadn't been very interested in helping Annagramma. The coven itself seemed a long time ago. It had been a busy winter.

'All we did was muck about while Annagramma bossed us around,' Dimity Hubbub had said, while grinding minerals and very carefully tipping them, a bit at a time, into a tiny pot being heated by a candle. 'I'm too busy to mess around with magic. It never did anything useful. You know her trouble? She thinks you can be a witch by buying enough things.'

'She just needs to learn how to deal with people,' said Tiffany. At this point, the pot exploded.

'Well, I think we can safely say that wasn't your everyday toothache cure,' said Dimity, picking bits of pot out of her hair. 'All right, I can spare the odd day, if Petulia's doing it. But it won't do much good.'

Lucy Warbeck was lying full length and fully clothed in a tin bath full of water when Tiffany called. Her head was right under the surface, but when she saw

Tiffany peering in she held up a sign saying: I'M NOT DROWNING! Miss Tick had said she would make a good witch-finder, so she was training hard.

'I don't see why we should help Annagramma,' she said as Tiffany helped her get dry. 'She just likes putting people down with that sarcastic voice of hers. Anyway, what's it to you? You know she doesn't like you.'

'I thought we've always got on . . . more or less,' said Tiffany.

'Really? You can do stuff she can't even attempt! Like that thing where you go invisible . . . you do it and you make it look easy! But you come along to the meetings and act like the rest of us and help clear up afterwards and that drives her mad!'

'Look, I don't understand what you're going on about . . .'

Lucy picked up another towel. 'She can't stand the idea that someone's better than her but doesn't crow about it.'

'Why should I do that?' said Tiffany, bewildered.

'Because that's what she'd do, if she was you,' said Lucy, carefully pushing the knife and fork back into her piled-up hair.* 'She thinks you're laughing at her. And now, oh my word, she's got to depend on you. You might as well have pushed pins up her nose.'

---

* All witches are a bit odd. It's best to get your oddness sorted out early.

But Petulia had signed up, and so Lucy and the rest of them did, too. Petulia had become the big success story since she'd won the Witch Trials with her famous Pig Trick two years ago. She'd been laughed at – well, by Annagramma, and everyone else had sort of grinned awkwardly – but she'd stuck to what she was good at and people were saying that she'd got skills with animals that even Granny Weatherwax couldn't match. She'd got solid respect, too. People didn't understand a lot of what witches did, but anyone who could get a sick cow back on its feet . . . well, that person was someone you looked up to. So, for the whole coven, after Hogswatch, it was going to be All About Annagramma time.

Tiffany flew back to Tir Nani Ogg with her head spinning. She'd never thought anyone could be envious of her. OK, she'd picked up one or two things, but anyone could do them. You just had to be able to switch yourself off.

She'd sat on the sand of the desert behind the Door, she'd faced dogs with razor teeth . . . they weren't things she wanted to remember. And on top of all that, there was the wintersmith.

He couldn't find her without the horse, everyone was sure of that. He could speak in her head, and she could speak to him, but that was a kind of magic and didn't have anything to do with maps.

He'd been quiet for a while. He was probably building icebergs.

She landed the broomstick on a small bald hill amongst the trees. There was no cottage to be seen.

She climbed off the stick but held onto it, just in case.

The stars were coming out. The wintersmith liked clear nights. They were colder.

And the words came. They were her words in her voice and she knew what they meant, but they had a sort of echo.

'Wintersmith! I command you!'

As she blinked at the high-toned way the words had sounded, the reply came back.

The voice was all around her.

Who commands the wintersmith?

'I am the Summer Woman.' Well, she thought, I'm a sort of stand-in.

'Then why do you hide from me?'

'I fear your ice. I fear your chill. I run from your avalanches. I hide from your storms.' Ah, right. This is goddess talk.

'Live with me in my world of ice!'

'How dare you order me! Don't you dare to order me!'

'But you chose to dwell in my winter . . .' The wintersmith sounded uncertain.

'I go where I please. I make my own way. I seek the leave of no man. In your country you will honour me – or there will be a reckoning!' And that bit is mine, Tiffany thought, pleased to get a word in.

There was a long silence, filled with uncertainty and puzzlement. Then the wintersmith said: 'How may I serve you, my lady?'

'No more icebergs looking like me. I don't want to be a face that sinks a thousand ships.'

'And the frost? May we share the frosts? And the snowflakes?'

'Not the frosts. You must not write my name on windows. That can only lead to trouble.'

'But I may be permitted to honour you in snowflakes?'

'Er . . .' Tiffany stopped. Goddesses shouldn't say 'er', she was sure of that.

'Snowflakes will be . . . acceptable,' she said. After all, she thought, it's not as though they have my name on them. I mean, most people won't notice and if they do they won't know it's me.

Then there will be snowflakes, my lady, until the time we dance again. And we will, for I am making myself a man!

The voice of the wintersmith . . . went.

Tiffany was alone again among the trees.

Except . . . she wasn't.

'I know you're still there,' she said, her breath leaving a sparkle in the air. 'You are, aren't you? I can feel you. You're not my thoughts. I'm not imagining you. The wintersmith has gone. You can speak with my mouth. Who are you?'

The wind made snow fall from the trees nearby. The stars twinkled. Nothing else moved.

'You *are* there,' said Tiffany. 'You've put thoughts in my head. You've even made my own voice speak to me. That's not going to happen again. Now I know the feeling, I *can* keep you out. If you have anything to say to me, say it now. When I leave here, I *will* shut my mind to you. I will not let—'

How does it feel to be so helpless, sheep girl?

'You are Summer, aren't you?' said Tiffany.

And you are like a little girl dressing in her mother's clothes, little feet in big shoes, dress trailing in the dirt. The world will freeze because of a silly child—

Tiffany did . . . something that it would be impossible for her to describe, and the voice ended up like a distant insect.

It was lonely on the hill, and cold. And all you could do was keep going. You could scream, cry and stamp your feet, but apart from making you feel warmer it wouldn't do any good. You could say it was unfair, and that was true, but the universe didn't care because it didn't know what 'fair' meant. That was the big problem about being a witch. It was up to you. It was always up to you.

Hogswatch came, with more snow and some presents. Nothing from home, though, even though some coaches were getting through. She told herself there was probably a good reason, and tried to believe it.

It was the shortest day of the year, which was convenient because it fitted neatly with the longest night. This was the heart of winter, but Tiffany didn't expect the present that arrived next day.

It had been snowing hard, but the evening sky was pink and blue and freezing.

It came out of the pink evening sky with a whistling noise and landed in Nanny Ogg's garden, throwing up a shower of dirt and leaving a big hole.

'Well, that's goodbye to the cabbages,' said Nanny, looking out of the window.

Steam was rising from the hole when they went outside and there was a strong smell of sprouts.

Tiffany peered through the steam. Dirt and stalks covered the thing, but she could make out something rounded.

She let herself slide further into the hole, right down amongst the mud and steam and the mysterious thing. It wasn't very hot now, and as she scraped stuff away she began to have a nasty feeling that she knew what it was.

It was, she was sure, the thingy that Anoia had talked about. It looked mysterious enough. And as it emerged from the mud, she knew she'd seen it before . . .

'Are you all right down there? I can't see you for all this steam!' Nanny Ogg called down. By the sound of it, the neighbours had come running; there was some excited chattering.

Tiffany quickly scraped mud and mashed cabbages over the arrival and called up, 'I think this might explode. Tell everyone to get indoors! And then reach down and grab my hand, will you?'

There was some shouting above her and the sound of running feet. Nanny Ogg's hand appeared, waving around in the fog, and between them they got Tiffany out of the hole.

'Shall we hide under the kitchen table?' said Nanny as Tiffany tried to brush mud and cabbage off her dress. Then Nanny winked. 'If it *is* going to explode?'

Her son Shawn came round the house with a bucket of water in each hand and stopped, looking disappointed that there was nothing to do with them.

'What was it, Mum?' he panted.

Nanny looked at Tiffany, who said: 'Er . . . a giant rock fell out of the sky.'

'Giant rocks can't stay up in the sky, miss!' said Shawn.

'I expect that's why this one fell down, lad,' said Nanny briskly. 'If you want to do something useful, you can stand guard and make sure nobody comes near it.'

'What shall I do if it explodes, Mum?'

'Come and tell me, will you?' said Nanny.

She hurried Tiffany into the cottage, shut the door behind them and said: 'I'm a dreadful ol' liar, Tiff, and it takes one to know one. What's down there?'

'Well, I don't think it's going to explode,' said Tiffany. 'And if it did, I think the worst that'll happen is that we'd be covered in coleslaw. I think it's the Cornucopia.'

There was the sound of voices outside and the door was flung open.

'Blessings be upon this house,' said Granny Weatherwax, stamping snow off her boots. 'Your boy said I shouldn't come in, but I think he was wrong. I came as quick as I could. What's happened?'

'We've got cornucopias,' said Nanny Ogg, 'whatever *they* are.'

It was later that evening. They'd waited until it was dark before pulling the Cornucopia out of the hole. It was a lot lighter than Tiffany had expected; in fact it had an air about it of something very, very heavy which, for reasons of its own, had become light just for a while.

Now it was on the kitchen table, wiped clean of mud and cabbages. Tiffany thought it looked vaguely alive. It was warm to the touch and seemed to vibrate slightly under her fingers.

'According to Chaffinch,' she said, with the *Mythology* open on her lap at the picture of the Summer Lady, 'the god Blind Io created the Cornucopia from a horn of the magical goat Almeg to feed his two children by the Goddess Bisonomy, who was later turned into a shower of oysters by Epidity, god of things shaped like potatoes, after insulting Resonata, goddess of weasels, by throwing a mole at her shadow. It is now the badge of office of the Summer Goddess.'

'I always said there used to be far too much of that sort of thing in the old days,' said Granny Weatherwax.

The witches stared at the thing. It did look a bit like a goat horn, but much larger.

'How does it work?' said Nanny Ogg. She stuck her head inside it and shouted, 'Hello!' Hellos came back, echoing for a long time, as if they had gone much further than you would expect them to.

'Looks like a great big seashell to *me*,' was the opinion of Granny Weatherwax. The kitten You padded around the giant thing, sniffing daintily at it (Greebo was hiding behind the saucepans on the top shelf. Tiffany checked).

'I don't think anyone knows,' she said. 'But the other name for it is the Horn of Plenty.'

'A horn? Can you play a tune on it?' asked Nanny.

'I don't think so,' said Tiffany. 'It contains . . . er . . . things.'

'What sort of things?' said Granny Weatherwax.

'Well, technically . . . everything,' said Tiffany. 'Everything that grows.'

She showed them the picture in the book. All sorts of fruits, vegetables and grain were spilling from the Cornucopia's wide mouth.

'Mostly fruit, though,' said Nanny. 'Not many carrots, but I suppose they're up in the pointy end. They'd fit better there.'

'Typical artist,' said Granny. 'He just painted the

showy stuff in the front. Too proud to paint an honest potato!' She poked at the page with an accusing finger. 'And what about these cherubs? We're not going to get them too, are we? I don't like to see little babies flying though the air.'

'They turn up a lot in old paintings,' said Nanny Ogg. 'They put them in to show it's Art and not just naughty pictures of ladies with not many clothes on.'

'Well, they're not fooling *me*,' said Granny Weatherwax.

'Go on, Tiff, give it a go,' said Nanny Ogg, walking round the table.

'I don't know how!' said Tiffany. 'There aren't any instructions!'

And then, too late, Granny shouted: 'You! Come out of there!'

But with a flick of her tail, the white kitten trotted inside.

They banged on the horn. They held it upside down and shook it. They tried shouting down it. They put a saucer of milk in front of it and waited. The kitten didn't return. Then Nanny Ogg prodded gently inside the Cornucopia with a mop, which to no one's great surprise went further inside the Cornucopia than there was Cornucopia on the outside.

'She'll come out when she's hungry,' she said reassuringly.

'Not if she finds something to eat in there,' said Granny Weatherwax, peering into the dark.

'I shouldn't think she'll find cat food,' said Tiffany, examining the picture closely. 'There may be milk, though.'

'You! Come out of there this minute!' Granny commanded, in a voice fit to shake mountains.

There was a distant 'meep'.

'Perhaps she's got stuck?' said Nanny. 'I mean, it's like a spiral, growing smaller at the end, right? Cats ain't very big at goin' backwards.'

Tiffany saw the look on Granny's face and sighed.

'Feegles?' she said to the room in general. 'I *know* there are some of you in this room. Come out, please!'

Feegles appeared from behind every ornament. Tiffany tapped the Cornucopia.

'Can you get a little kitten out of here?' she said.

'Just that? Aye, nae problemo,' said Rob Anybody. 'I wuz hopin' it was gonna be something *difficult*!'

The Nac Mac Feegles disappeared into the horn at a trot. Their voices died away. The witches waited.

They waited some more.

And some more.

'Feegles!' shouted Tiffany into the hole. She thought she heard a very distant, very faint 'Crivens!'

'If it can produce grain, they might have found beer in there,' said Tiffany. 'And that means they'll only run out when the beer runs out too!'

'Cats can't feed on beer!' snapped Granny Weatherwax.

'Well, I'm fed up with waiting,' said Nanny. 'Look,

there's a little hole in the pointy end, too. I'm going to blow into it!'

She tried to, at least. Her cheeks went big and red and her eyes bulged and it was pretty clear that if the horn didn't blow up then she would – at which point, the horn gave up. There was a distant and un-mistakably *curly* rumbling noise, which got louder and louder.

'I can't see anything yet,' said Granny, looking into the wide mouth of the horn.

Tiffany pulled her away just as You galloped out of the Cornucopia with her tail straight out and her ears flattened. She skidded across the table, leaped onto Granny Weatherwax's dress, scrambled onto her shoulder and turned and spat defiance.

With a cry of 'Crivvvvvvvvens!' Feegles poured out of the horn.

'Behind the sofa, everyone!' yelled Nanny. 'Run!'

Now the rumble was like thunder. It grew and grew and then—

– stopped.

In the silence, three pointy hats rose from behind the sofa. Small blue faces arose from behind everything.

Then there was a noise very similar to *pwat!* and something small and wizened rolled out of the end of the horn and dropped onto the floor. It was a very dried-up pineapple.

Granny Weatherwax brushed some dust off her dress. 'You'd better learn to use this,' she said to Tiffany.

'How?'

'Don't you have *any* idea?'

'No!'

'Well, it's turned up for you, madam, and it's dangerous!'

Tiffany gingerly picked up the Cornucopia, and again there was that definite feeling of some hugely heavy thing pretending, very successfully, to be light.

'Maybe it needs some magic word,' suggested Nanny Ogg. 'Or there's somewhere special that you press . . .'

As Tiffany turned it in the light, something gleamed for a moment.

'Hold on, these look like words,' she said. She read: Π'ΑΝΤΑ Π'Ο'Υ ΕΠΙΘ'ΕΙΣ, ΧΑΠ'ΙΖΩ Ε'ΙΟ 'ΕΝΑ 'ΟΝΟΜΑ

All that you desire, I give upon a name, murmured the memory of Dr Bustle.

The next line said: ΜΕΓΑΛΩΝΩ ΣΥΣΤΕΛΛΟΜΙ

I Grow, I Shrink, Dr Bustle translated.

'I think I might have an idea,' she said, and in memory of Miss Treason she declared: 'Ham sandwich! With mustard!'

Nothing happened.

Then Dr Bustle lazily translated, and Tiffany said: 'Ένα σαντουιτς του ζαμπον με μουταρδι!'

With a *fwlap* a ham sandwich sailed out of the mouth of the Cornucopia and was expertly caught by Nanny, who bit into it.

'Not bad at all!' she announced. Try a few more.'

'δωσε μσμ πολλα σαυισυιτζ χαμπωυ!' said Tiffany, and there was the kind of sound you get when you disturb a cave full of bats.

'Stop!' she yelled, but nothing stopped. Then Dr Bustle whispered and she shouted: 'Μην περισσοτερο σαντουιτς των ζαμπον!'

There were a *lot* of sandwiches. The pile reached the ceiling, in fact. Only the tip of Nanny Ogg's hat was visible, but there were some muffled noises further down the heap.

An arm thrust out, and Nanny Ogg forced her way through the wall of bread and sliced pig, chewing thoughtfully.

'No mustard, I notice. Hmm. Well, at least we can see that everyone around here has a good supper tonight,' she said. 'And I can see I'm going to have to make an awful lot of soup, too. Best not to try it again in here, though, all right?'

'I don't like it at all,' snapped Granny Weatherwax. 'Where does all that stuff come from, eh? Magic food never fed anyone properly!'

'It's not magic, it's a god thing,' said Nanny Ogg. 'Like manners from heaven, that sort of stuff. I expect it's made out of raw firmament.'

In fact it's merely a living metaphor for the boundless fecundity of the natural world, whispered Dr Bustle in Tiffany's head.

'You don't get manners from heaven,' said Granny.

'This was in foreign parts, a long time ago,' said Nanny, turning to Tiffany. 'If I was you, dear, I'd take it out into the woods tomorrow and see what it can do. Although, if you don't mind, I could really do with some fresh grapes right now.'

'Gytha Ogg, you can't use the Cornucopia of the Gods as a . . . a larder!' said Granny. 'The feet business was bad enough!'

'But it is one,' said Nanny Ogg innocently. 'It's *the* larder. It's, like, everything waiting to grow next spring.'

Tiffany put it down very carefully. There was something . . . alive about the Cornucopia. She wasn't at all sure that it was just some magical tool. It seemed to be listening.

As it touched the tabletop it began to shrink, until it was the size of a small vase.

'Scuse me?' said Rob Anybody. 'But does it do beer?'

'Beer?' said Tiffany, without thinking.

There was a trickling noise. All eyes turned to look at the vase. Brown liquid was foaming over the lip.

Then all the eyes turned to Granny Weatherwax, who shrugged.

'Don't look at me,' she said sourly. 'You're going to drink it *anyway*!'

It *is* alive, Tiffany thought, as Nanny Ogg hurried off to find some more mugs. It learns. It's learned my language . . .

* * *

Around midnight, Tiffany woke up because a white chicken was standing on her chest. She pushed it off and reached down for her slippers, and found only chickens. When she got the candle alight, she saw half a dozen chickens on the end of the bed. The floor was covered in chickens. So were the stairs. So was every room down below. In the kitchen, chickens had over-flowed into the sink.

They weren't making much noise, just the occasional 'werk' a chicken makes when it's a bit un-certain about things, which is more or less all the time.

The chickens were shuffling along patiently, to make room. 'Werk.' They were doing this because the Cornucopia, now grown just a bit bigger than a full-grown chicken, was gently firing out a chicken every eight seconds. 'Werk.'

As Tiffany watched, another one landed on the mountain of ham sandwiches. 'Werk.'

Marooned on top of the Cornucopia was You, look-ing very puzzled. 'Werk.' And in the middle of the floor Granny Weatherwax snored gently in the big armchair, surrounded by fascinated hens. 'Werk.' Apart from the snoring, the chorus of 'werks' and the rustle of shuffling chickens, it was all very peaceful in the candlelight. 'Werk.'

Tiffany glared at the kitten. She rubbed up against things when she wanted to be fed, didn't she? 'Werk.' And made 'meep' noises? 'Werk.' And the Cornucopia could work out languages, couldn't it? 'Werk.'

Now she whispered: 'No more chickens,' and, after a few seconds the flow of chickens ceased. 'Werk.'

But she couldn't really leave it like that. She shook Granny by the shoulder and, as the old woman awoke, she said: 'The good news is, a lot of the ham sandwiches have gone . . . er . . .'

'Werk.'

CHAPTER 9

GREEN SHOOTS

It was much colder next morning, a numb dull coldness that could practically freeze the flames on a fire.

Tiffany let the broomstick settle between the trees a little way from Nanny Ogg's cottage. The snow hadn't drifted much here, but it came up to her knees and cold had put a crispness on it that crackled like a stale loaf when Tiffany trod it.

In theory she was out in the woods to get the hang of the Cornucopia, but really she was there to keep it out of the way. Nanny Ogg hadn't been too upset about the chickens. After all, she now owned five hundred hens, which were currently standing around in her shed going 'werk'. But the floors were a mess, there were chicken doo-dahs even on the banisters, and, as Granny had pointed out (in a whisper), supposing someone had said 'sharks'?

The Cornucopia lay on her lap while she sat on a stump among snow-covered trees. Once, the forest had been pretty. Now it was hateful. Dark trunks against snowdrifts, a striped world of black and white, bars against the light. She longed for horizons.

Funny . . . the Cornucopia was always very slightly warm, even out here, and seemed to know in advance what size it ought to be. I Grow, I Shrink, thought Tiffany. And I'm feeling pretty small.

What next? What now? She'd kept hoping that the . . . the power would drop on her, just like the Cornucopia had done. It hadn't.

There was life under the snow. She felt it in her fingertips. Somewhere down there, out of reach, was the real Summer. Using the Cornucopia as a scoop, she scraped away at the snow until she reached dead leaves. There was life down there in the white webs of fungi and pale, new roots. A half-frozen worm crawled slowly away and burrowed under a leaf skeleton, fine as lace. Beside it was an acorn.

The woods weren't silent. They were holding their breath. They were all waiting for her, and she didn't know what to do.

I'm not the Summer Lady, she told herself. I can never be her. I'm in her shoes, but I can never be her. I might be able to make a few flowers grow, but I can never be her. She'll walk across the world, and oceans of sap will rise in these dead trees and a million tons of grass will grow in a second. Can I do that? No. I'm a stupid child with a handful of tricks, that's all. I'm just Tiffany Aching, and I'm aching to go home.

Feeling guilty about the worm, she breathed some warm air on the soil and then pulled the leaves back to cover it. As she did so there was a wet little sound, like the snapping of a frog's fingers, and the acorn split. A white shoot escaped from it and grew more than half an inch as she watched it.

Hurriedly, she made a hole in the mould with her fingers, pushed the acorn in and patted the soil back again.

Someone was watching her. She stood up and turned round quickly. There was no one to be seen, but that didn't mean a thing.

'I know you're there!' she said, still turning round. 'Whoever you are!'

Her voice echoed among the black trees. Even to her, it sounded thin and scared.

She found herself raising the Cornucopia.

'Show yourself,' she quavered, 'or—'

What? she wondered. Fill you full of fruit?

Some snow fell off a tree with a thump, making her jump and then feel even more foolish. Now she was flinching at the fall of a handful of snowflakes! A witch ought never to be frightened in the darkest forest, Granny Weatherwax had once told her, because she should be sure in her soul that the most terrifying thing in the forest was her.

She raised the Cornucopia and said, half-heartedly: 'Strawberry . . .'

Something shot out of the Cornucopia with a *pfut*

and made a red stain on a tree twenty feet away. Tiffany didn't bother to check; it always delivered what you asked for.

Which was more than she could say for herself.

And on top of everything else, it was her day to visit Annagramma. Tiffany sighed deeply. She'd probably get that wrong, too.

Slowly, astride her broomstick, she disappeared among the trees.

After a minute or two, a green shoot thrust up from the patch of soil that she had breathed on, grew to a height of about six inches, and put out two green leaves.

Footsteps approached. They were not as crunchy as footsteps on frozen snow usually are.

There was a crunch now, though, of someone kneeling on the frosted snowdrifts.

A pair of skinny but powerful hands gently dragged and sculpted the snow and dead leaves together to make a tall, thin wall around the shoot, enclosing it and protecting it from the wind like a soldier in a castle.

A small white kitten tried to nuzzle at it and was carefully lifted out of the way.

Then Granny Weatherwax walked back into the woods, leaving no footprints. You never teach anyone else *everything* you know.

Days went by. Annagramma learned, but it was a struggle. It was hard to teach someone who wouldn't admit that there was anything she didn't know, so there were conversations like this:

'You know how to prepare placebo root, do you?'

'Of course. Everyone knows that.' And this was not the time to say, 'OK then, show me,' because she'd mess around for a while and then say she had a headache. This was the time to say, 'Good, watch me to see if I'm doing it right,' and then do it perfectly. And you'd add things like: 'As you know, Granny Weatherwax says that practically anything works instead of placebo root, but it's best to use the real thing if you can get it. If prepared in syrup it's an amazing remedy for minor illnesses, but of course you already know this.'

And Annagramma would say: 'Of course.'

A week later, in the forests, it was so cold some older trees exploded in the night. They hadn't seen that for a long time, the older people said. It happened when the sap froze, then tried to expand.

Annagramma was as vain as a canary in a room full of mirrors and panicked instantly when faced with anything she didn't know, but she was sharp at picking things up, and very good at appearing to know more than she really did, which is a valuable talent for a witch. Once, Tiffany noticed the Boffo catalogue open on the table with some things ringed around. She asked no questions. She was too busy.

A week after that, wells froze.

Tiffany went around the villages with Annagramma

a few times, and knew that she would make it, eventually. She'd got built-in boffo. She was tall and arrogant and acted as if she knew everything even when she didn't have a clue. That would get her a long way. People listened to her.

They needed to. There were no roads open now; between cottages, people had cut tunnels full of cold blue light. Anything that needed to be moved was moved by broomstick. That included old people. They were lifted, bedclothes, walking-sticks and all, and moved into other houses. People packed together stayed warmer, and could pass the time by reminding one another that, however cold this was, it wasn't as cold as the cold you got when they were young.

After a while, they stopped saying that.

Sometimes it would thaw, just a little, and then freeze again. That fringed every roof with icicles. At the next thaw, they stabbed the ground like daggers.

Tiffany didn't sleep; at least, she didn't go to bed. None of the witches did. The snow got trampled down into ice that was like rock, so a few carts could be moved about, but there still weren't enough witches to go around or enough hours in the day. There weren't enough hours in the day and the night put together. Petulia had fallen asleep on her stick and ended up in a tree two miles away. Tiffany slid off once and landed in a snowdrift.

Wolves entered the tunnels. They were weak with hunger, and desperate. Granny Weatherwax put a stop to them and never told anyone how she'd done it.

The cold was like being punched, over and over again, day and night. All over the snow were little dark dots that were dead birds, frozen out of the air. Other birds had found the tunnels and filled them with twittering, and people fed them scraps because they brought a false hope of spring to the world . . .

. . . *because there was food. Oh, yes, there was food. The Cornucopia ran day and night.*

And Tiffany thought: I should have said no to snowflakes . . .

There was a shack, old and abandoned. And there was, in the rotted planks, a nail. If the wintersmith had fingers, they would have been shaking.

This was the last thing! There had been so much to learn! It had been so hard, so hard! Who would have thought a man was made of stuff like chalk and soot and gases and poisons and metals? But now, ice formed under the rusty nail, and the wood groaned and squeaked as the ice grew and forced it out.

It spun gently in the air, and the voice of the wintersmith could be heard in the wind that froze the treetops: 'IRON ENOUGH TO MAKE A MAN!'

High up in the mountains, the snow exploded. It mounded up into the air as if dolphins were playing under it, shapes forming and disappearing . . .

Then, as suddenly as it had risen, the snow settled again. But now there was a horse there, white as snow, and on its back a rider, glittering with frost. If the greatest sculptor the world had ever known had been told to build a snowman, this is what it would have looked like.

Something was still going on. The shape of the horse and man still crawled with movement as they grew more and more lifelike. Details settled. Colours crept in, always pale, never bright.

And there was a horse, and there was a rider, shining in the comfortless light of the mid-winter sun.

The wintersmith extended a hand and flexed his fingers. Colour is, after all, merely a matter of reflection; the fingers took on the colour of flesh.

The wintersmith spoke. That is, there were a variety of noises, from the roar of a gale to the rattle of the sucking of the surf on a shingle shore after a wrecking storm at sea. Somewhere among them all was a tone that seemed right. He repeated it, stretched it, stirred it around and turned it into speech, playing with it until it sounded right.

He said: 'Tasbnlerizwip? Ggokyziofvva? Wiswip? Nananana . . . Nyip . . . nap . . . Ah . . . Ah! It is to speak!' The wintersmith threw back his head and sang the Overture to 'Überwald Winter' by the composer Wotua Doinov. He'd overheard it once when driving a roaring gale around the rooftops of an opera house, and had been astonished to find that a human being, nothing more really than a bag of dirty water on legs, could have such a wonderful understanding of snow.

'СНОВА ПОХОЛОДАЛО!' he sang to the freezing sky.

The only slight error the wintersmith made, as his horse trotted through the pine trees, was in singing the instruments as well as the voices. He sang, in fact, the whole thing, and rode like a travelling orchestra, making the sounds of the singers, the drums and the rest of the orchestra all at once.

To smell the trees! To feel the pull of the ground! To be solid! To feel the darkness behind your eyes and know it was you! To be – and know yourself to be – a man!

He had never felt like this before. It was exhilarating. There was so much of . . . of everything, coming at him from every direction. The thing with the ground, for example. It tugged, all the time. Standing upright took a lot of thinking about. And the birds! The wintersmith had always seen them as nothing more than impurities in the air, interfering with the flow of the weather, but now they were living things just like him. And they played with the tug and the wind, and owned the sky.

The wintersmith had never seen before, never felt before, never heard before. You could not do those things unless you were . . . apart, in the dark behind the eyes. Before, he hadn't been apart; he'd been a part, a part of the whole universe of tug and pressure, sound and light, flowing, dancing. He'd run storms against mountains for ever, but he'd never known what a mountain was until today.

The dark behind the eyes . . . what a precious thing. It gave you your . . . you-ness. Your hand, with those laughable waggly things on it, gave you touch; the holes on either side of your head let in sound; the holes at the front let in the wonderful smell. How clever of holes to know what to do! It was amazing! When you were an elemental, everything happened all together, inside and outside, in one big . . . thing.

Thing. That was a useful word . . . thing. Thing was anything the wintersmith couldn't describe. Everything was . . . things, and they were exciting.

It was good to be a man! Oh, he was mostly made of dirty ice, but that was just better organized dirty water, after all.

Yes, he was human. It was so easy. It was just a matter of organizing *things*. He had senses, he could move among humans, he could . . . search. That was how to search for humans. You become one! It was so hard to do it as an elemental; it was hard even to recognize a human in the churning thing-ness of the physical world. But a human could talk to other humans with the hole for the sound. He could talk to them and they would not suspect!

And now he was human, there would be no going back. King Winter!

All he needed was a queen.

Tiffany woke up because someone was shaking her.

'Tiffany!'

She'd gone to sleep in Nanny Ogg's cottage with her head against the Cornucopia. From somewhere close there was a strange *pif* noise, like a dry drip. Pale blue snowlight filled the room.

As she opened her eyes, Granny Weatherwax was gently pushing her back into her chair.

'You've been sleeping since nine o'clock, my girl,' she said. 'Time to go home, I think.'

Tiffany looked around. 'I am here, aren't I?' she said, feeling dizzy.

'No, this is Nanny Ogg's house. And this is a bowl of soup—'

Tiffany woke up. There was a blurry bowl of soup in front of her. It looked . . . familiar.

'When did you last sleep in a bed?' said a wavering, shadowy figure.

Tiffany yawned. 'What day is this?'

'Tuesday,' said Granny Weatherwax.

'Mmm . . . what's a Tuesday?'

Tiffany woke up for the third time, and was grabbed and pulled upright.

'There,' said the voice of Granny Weatherwax. 'This time, stay awake. Drink soup. Get warm. You need to go home.'

This time Tiffany's stomach took control of a hand and a spoon and, by degrees, Tiffany warmed up.

Granny Weatherwax sat opposite, the kitten You on her lap, watching Tiffany until the soup was gone.

'I expected too much from you,' she said. 'I'd hoped

that as the days grew longer you'd find more power. That ain't no fault of yours.'

The *pif* noises were getting more frequent. Tiffany looked down and saw corn dripping out of the Cornucopia. The number of grains increased even as she watched.

'You set it on corn before you fell asleep,' said Granny. 'It slows right down when you're tired. Just as well, really, otherwise we'd have been eaten alive by chickens.'

'It's about the only thing I've got right,' said Tiffany.

'Oh, I don't know. Annagramma Hawkin seems to be showing promise. Lucky in her friends, from what I hears.' If Miss Treason had tried to play poker against Granny Weatherwax's face, she would have lost.

The patter of the new corn suddenly became much louder in the silence.

'Look I—' Tiffany began.

Granny sniffed. 'I'm sure no one has to explain themselves to *me*,' she said virtuously. 'Will you promise me that you'll go home? A couple of coaches got through this morning and I hear it's not too bad yet, down on the plains. You go back to your Chalk country. You're the only witch they've got.'

Tiffany sighed. She did want to go home, more than anything. But it would be like running away.

'It might be like running to,' said Granny, picking up

her old habit of replying to something that hadn't actually been said.

'I'll go tomorrow then,' said Tiffany.

'Good.' Granny stood up. 'Come with me. I wants to show you something.'

Tiffany followed her through a snow tunnel that came out near the edge of the forest. The snow had been packed down here by people dragging firewood home and, once you got a little way from the edge of the forest, the drifts weren't too bad; a lot of snow hung in the trees, filling the air with cold blue shadows.

'What are we looking for?' said Tiffany.

Granny Weatherwax pointed.

There was a splash of green in the white and grey. It was young leaves on an oak sapling a couple of feet high. When Tiffany crunched her way through the snow crust and reached out to touch it, the air felt warm.

'Do you know how you managed that?' said Granny.

'No!'

'Me neither. I couldn't do it. You did, girl. Tiffany Aching.'

'It's just one tree,' said Tiffany.

'Ah, well. You have to start small, with oak trees.'

They stared in silence at the tree for a few moments. The green seemed to reflect off the snow around it. Winter stole colour, but the tree glowed.

'And now, we've all got things to do,' said Granny, breaking the spell. 'You, I believe, would normally be heading for Miss Treason's old place about now. I'd expect no less of you . . .'

There was a coaching inn. It was busy, even at this time in the morning. The fast mail coach had made a quick stop for fresh horses after the long haul into the mountains, and another one, bound for down on the plains, was waiting for the passengers. The breath of the horses filled the air with steam. Drivers stamped their feet. Sacks and packages were being loaded. Men bustled around with nosebags. Some bandy-legged men just hung around, smoking and gossiping. In fifteen minutes the inn's yard would be empty again, but for now everyone was too busy to pay much attention to one more stranger.

Afterwards, they all told different stories, contradicting one another at the tops of their voices. Probably the most accurate account came from Miss Dymphnia Stoot, the innkeeper's daughter, who was helping her father serve breakfast:

'Well, he, like, came in, and right there I could see he was odd. He walked funny, you know, lifting his legs like a trotting horse does. Also, he was kind of, like, shiny. But we get all sorts here; it does not pay to make pers'nal remarks; we had a bunch of werewolves in here last week and they were just like you

and me except we had to put their plates on the floor
. . . all right, yes, this man . . . well, he sat down at a
table and said: "I am a human just like you!" He came
out with it, just like that!

'Of course, no one else paid attention, but I told him
I was glad to hear it and what did he want to eat,
because the sausages was particular fine this morning,
and he said he could only eat cold food, which was
funny 'cos everyone was grumbling about how cold it
was in the room now, and it's not like there wasn't a
big fire burning. Anyway . . . actually we did have
some cold sausage left in the pantry and they were a
bit on the turn, if you know what I mean, so I gave
them to him, and he chewed one for a bit and then he
says, with his mouth full if you please, "This is not
what I expected. What do I do now?" and I said, "You
swallow," and he said, "Swallow?" and I said, "Yes,
you swallow it down into your stomach, right," and
he said, spraying bits of sausage all over the place,
"Oh, a hollow bit!" and sort of like wavers and then he
says, "Ah, I am a human, I have successfully eaten
human sausages!" and I said there was no need to be
like that, they were made of mostly pig, same as
always.

'Then he says what is he supposed to do with them
now and I says it's not my place to tell him and that
will be two pennies please and he puts down a gold
coin so I curtsey because, well, you never know. Then
he says, "I am a human just like you. Where are the

pointy humans who fly though the sky?" which was a funny way of putting it to my mind, but I told him if it was witches he wanted, there was plenty of 'em over the Lancre bridge, and he said, "Name of Treason?" and I said I heard she was dead but with witches who can say. And off he went. All the time he had this, like, smile, all shiny and a bit worrying. Something wrong with his clothes, too, like they were stuck to him or something. But you can't be too choosy in this business. We had some trolls in here yesterday. They can't eat our food, you know, being kind of like walking rocks, but we gave them a slap-up meal of broken cups and grease. But he was a rum 'un. The place got a lot warmer after he left, too.'

Expect no less of you . . .

The words kept Tiffany warm as she flew over the trees. The fire in her head burned with pride, but contained one or two big crackly logs of anger.

Granny had known! Had she planned it? Because it looked good, didn't it? All the witches would know. Mrs Earwig's pupil couldn't cope, but Tiffany Aching organized all the other girls to help out and didn't tell anyone. Of course, among witches, not telling anyone was a sure way of getting things found out. Witches were very good at listening to what you weren't saying. So Annagramma held onto her cottage, and Mrs Earwig was embarrassed and Granny would be smug. All that work and rushing around, to let Granny feel smug. Well, and for Mrs Stumper's pig and everyone else, of course. That made it complicated. If you could, you did what needed to be done. Poking your nose in was basic witchcraft. She knew it. Granny *knew* she knew it. So Tiffany had scurried around like a little clockwork mouse . . .

There would be a reckoning!

The clearing was full of snow in great icy drifts, but a path had been worn to the cottage, she was pleased to see.

There was something new. There were people standing by Miss Treason's grave, and some of the snow had been scraped off.

Oh no, Tiffany thought as she circled down, please say she hasn't gone looking for the skulls!

It turned out to be, in some ways, worse.

She recognized the people around the grave. They were villagers, and they gave Tiffany the defiant, worried stares of people scared half to death by the small but possibly angry pointy hat in front of them. And there was something about the very deliberate way they weren't looking at the mound that instantly drew her attention to it. It was covered in little torn scraps of paper, pinned down with sticks. They fluttered in the wind.

She snatched up a couple:

Miss Treason please Keep my boy Joe save at see.

Miss treason, I'm goin bald please help.

Miss Treason, please find our girl Becky what run away I'm sorry.

There were more. And just as she was about to speak sharply to the villagers for *still* bothering Miss Treason, she remembered the packets of Jolly Sailor tobacco that the shepherds even now left on the turf where the old shepherding hut had been. They didn't write their petitions down, but they were there, all the same, floating in the air:

'Granny Aching, who herds the clouds in the blue sky, please watch my sheep. Granny Aching, cure my son. Granny Aching, find my lambs.'

They were the prayers of small people, too afraid to bother the gods in their high places. They trusted in what they knew. They weren't right or wrong. They were just . . . hopeful.

Well, Miss Treason, she thought, you're a myth now, as sure as anything. You might even make it to goddess. It's not much fun, I can tell you.

'And has Becky been found?' she said, turning to the people.

A man avoided her gaze as he said: 'I reckon Miss Treason'll understand why the girl won't be wantin' to come home any time soon.'

Oh, thought Tiffany, one of *those* reasons.

'Any news of the boy, then?' she said.

'Ah, that one worked,' said a woman. 'His mum got a letter yesterday sayin' he'd been in a dreadful shipwreck but was picked up alive, which only goes to show.'

Tiffany didn't ask what it was that it went to show. It was enough that it had gone to show it.

'Well, that's good,' she said.

'But lots of poor seamen got drownded,' the woman went on. 'They hit an iceberg in the fog. A big floating mountain of ice shaped like a woman, they said. What d'you think of that?'

'I expect if they'd been at sea long enough, anything would look like a woman, eh?' said the man and chuckled. The women gave him a Look.

'He didn't say who she— if she looked like, you know . . . anyone?' said Tiffany, trying to sound nonchalant.

'Depends where they were looking—' the man began cheerfully.

'You ought to wash your brain out with soap and water,' said the woman, prodding him sharply in the chest.

'Er, no, miss,' he said, looking down at his feet. 'He just said her head was all covered with seagull— poo, miss.'

This time, Tiffany tried not to sound relieved. She looked down at the fluttering bits of paper on the grave and back to the woman, who was trying to hide what might be a fresh request behind her back.

'Do you believe in this stuff, Mrs Carter?'

The woman suddenly looked flustered. 'Oh no, miss, of course not. But it's just that . . . well, you know . . .'

It makes you feel better, thought Tiffany. It's something you can do when there's nothing more to be done. And who knows, it might work. Yes, I know. It's—

Her hand itched. And now she realized that it had been itching for a while.

'Oh yes?' she said, under her breath. 'You dare?'

'Are you all right, miss?' said the man. Tiffany ignored him. A rider was approaching and snow followed after him, spreading and widening behind him like a cloak, soundless as a wish, thick as fog.

Without taking her eyes off him, Tiffany reached into her pocket and gripped the tiny Cornucopia. Hah!

She walked forward.

The wintersmith dismounted from his snow-white horse when it had drawn level with the old cottage.

Tiffany stopped about twenty feet away, her heart pounding.

'My lady,' said the wintersmith, and bowed.

He looked . . . better, and older.

'I warn you! I've got a Cornucopia and I'm not afraid to use it!' said Tiffany. But she hesitated. He did look almost human, except for that fixed, strange grin. 'How did you find me?' she said.

'For you I have learned,' said the figure. 'I learned how to search. I am human!'

Really? But his mouth doesn't look right, said her Third Thoughts. It's pale inside, like snow. That's not a boy there. It just thinks it is.

One big pumpkin, her Second Thoughts urged. They get really hard at this time of year. Shoot him now!

Tiffany herself, the one on the outside, the one who could feel the air on her face, thought: I can't just do that! All he's doing is standing there talking. All this is my fault!

He wants never-ending winter, said the Third Thoughts. Everyone you know will die!

She was sure the eyes of the wintersmith could see right into her mind.

The summer kills the winter, the Third Thoughts insisted. That's how it works!

But not like this, Tiffany thought. I know it's not supposed to be like this! It feels wrong. It's not the right . . . story. The king of winter can't be killed by a flying pumpkin!

The wintersmith was watching her carefully.

Thousands of Tiffany-shaped flakes were falling around him.

'We will finish the dance now?' he said. 'I am human, just like you!' He held out a hand.

'Do you know what human is?' said Tiffany.

'Yes! Easy! Iron enough to make a nail!' said the wintersmith promptly. He beamed, as if he'd done a successful trick. 'And now, please, we dance . . .'

He took a step forward. Tiffany backed away.

If you dance now, her Third Thoughts warned, that will be the end of it. You'll be believing in yourself and trusting in your star, and big twinkly things thousands of miles up in the sky don't care if they twinkle on everlasting snow.

'I'm . . . not ready,' Tiffany said, hardly above a whisper.

'But time is passing,' said the wintersmith. 'I am human, I know these things. Are you not a goddess in human form?'

The eyes bored into her.

No, I'm not, she thought. I'll always be just . . . Tiffany Aching.

The wintersmith drew closer, his hand still out-stretched.

'Time to dance, Lady. Time to finish the dance.'

Thoughts leaked out away from Tiffany's grasp. The eyes of the wintersmith filled her mind with nothing but whiteness, like a field of pure snow . . .

'Aaaiiiiieeeee!'

The door of old Miss Treason's cottage flew open and . . . something came out, staggering through the snow.

It was a witch. You could not mistake it. She – it was probably a she, but some things are so horrible that worrying about how to address a letter to them is silly – had a hat with a point that curled like a snake. It was on top of dripping strands of mad, greasy hair, which was perched on a nightmare of a face. It was green, like the hands which waved black fingernails that were really terrible claws.

Tiffany stared. The wintersmith stared. The people stared.

As the horrible screaming, lurching thing drew nearer, the details got clearer, like the brown rotting teeth and the warts. Lots of warts. Even the warts on the warts had warts.

Annagramma had sent off for *everything*. Part of Tiffany wanted to laugh, even now, but the wintersmith snatched at her hand—

– and the witch grabbed his shoulder.

'Don't you take hold of her like that! How dare you! I'm a witch, you know!'

Annagramma's voice wasn't easy on the ear at the best of times, but when she was frightened or angry it had a whine that bored right into the head.

'Let go of her, I say!' screamed Annagramma, and the wintersmith looked stunned. Having to listen to Annagramma in a rage was hard for someone who hadn't had ears for very long.

'Let her go!' she yelled. Then she threw a fireball.

She missed. Possibly she meant to. A ball of flaming gas whizzing nearby usually makes most people stop what they are doing. But most people don't melt.

The wintersmith's leg dropped off.

Later, on the journey through the blizzard, Tiffany wondered how the wintersmith *worked*. He was made of snow, but he could make it walk and talk. That must mean he had to *think* about it all the time. He had to. Humans didn't have to think about their bodies all the time, because their bodies knew what to do. But snow doesn't even know how to stand up straight.

Annagramma was glaring at him as if he'd done something really annoying.

He looked around, as if puzzled, cracks appearing across his chest, and then he was just crumbling snow, collapsing into glittering crystals.

The snow began to pour down now, as if the clouds were being squeezed.

Annagramma pulled the mask to one side and stared first at the heap and then at Tiffany.

'All right,' she said, 'what just happened? Was he *supposed* to do that?'

'I was coming to see you and . . . that's the wintersmith!' was all that Tiffany could manage at that point.

'You mean like . . . the *wintersmith*?' said Annagramma. 'Isn't he just a story? What is he after *you* for?' she added accusingly.

'It's . . . he . . . I . . .' Tiffany began, but there was nowhere to start. 'He's real! I've got to get away from him!' she said. 'I've got to get away! It takes too long to explain!'

For a horrible moment she thought Annagramma was still going to demand the whole story, but she reached out and grabbed Tiffany's hand with a black rubber claw.

'Then get out of here right now! Oh, no, you've *still* got Miss Treason's old broom? Totally useless! Use mine!' She dragged Tiffany towards the cottage, as the snowflakes thickened.

'"Iron enough to make a nail"!' said Tiffany, trying to keep up. She couldn't think of anything else to say, and it was suddenly very important. 'He thought he was human—'

'I've only knocked over his snowman, you fool. He'll be back!'

'Yes, but iron enough, you see, to—'

A green hand slapped her face, but this hurt less than it might because of the rubber.

'Don't babble! I thought you were clever! I really don't know what this is about, but if I had that thing after me I wouldn't stand around babbling!' Annagramma pulled across the Wicked Witch De-Luxe Mask With Free Dangling Bogey, adjusted the hang of the bogey and turned to the villagers, who'd been rooted to the spot all this time. 'What are you all staring at? Haven't you ever seen a witch before?' she shouted. 'Go back home! Oh, and I'll be down tomorrow with some physic for your little boy, Mrs Carter!'

They stared at the green face, the rotted teeth, the stinking hair and the huge bogey, made in fact of glass, and fled.

Still drunk with terror and relief, Tiffany rocked gently, muttering, 'Iron enough to make a nail!' until Annagramma shook her. The thick flakes were dropping so fast that it was hard to see her face.

'Tiffany, broomstick. Broomstick fly,' said Annagramma. 'Fly a long way! Do you hear me! Somewhere safe!'

'But he . . . the poor thing thinks that . . .'

'Yes, yes, I'm sure it's all very important,' said Annagramma, dragging her towards the cottage wall, where her broomstick leaned. She half-pushed, half-lifted Tiffany onto it and looked up. Snow was pouring out of the sky like a waterfall now.

'He's coming back!' she snapped, and said a few words under her breath. The broomstick shot straight up and disappeared into the fading, snow-filled light.

CHAPTER 10

GOING HOME

Granny Weatherwax looked up from the saucer of ink, in which a tiny Tiffany was disappearing into the whiteness of the blizzard. She was smiling, but with Granny Weatherwax this did not necessarily mean that something nice was happening.

'We could ha' taken him doon easy,' said Rob Anybody reproachfully. 'Ye should ha' let us.'

'Perhaps. Or perhaps he'd have frozen you solid?' said Granny. 'Besides, there's a bigger task ahead of the Nac Mac Feegles. Your big wee hag needs you to do two things. One of them is hard, the other one is very hard.'

The Feegles cheered up when they heard this. They were everywhere in Mrs Ogg's kitchen. Some were perched on Nanny Ogg herself, and Miss Tick looked very uncomfortable surrounded by them. Unlike Miss Tick, Feegles rarely had an opportunity for a bath.

'Firstly,' said Granny, 'she will need you to go into the . . . Underworld, to fetch the Real Summer Lady.'

The significant pause did not seem to bother the Feegles at all.

'Oh aye, we can do that,' said Rob Anybody. 'We can get into anywhere. An' that's the verrae hard bit, is it?'

'And out again?' said Granny.

'Oh, aye,' said Rob firmly. 'Mostly we get thrown oot!'

'The very hard part,' said Granny, 'will be finding a Hero.'

'That's no' hard,' said Rob. 'We're a' heroes here!' A cheer went up.

'Really?' said Granny. 'Are you frightened to go into the Underworld, Rob Anybody?'

'Me? No!' Rob Anybody looked around at his brothers and grinned hugely.

'Spell the word "marmalade", then.' Granny Weatherwax pushed a pencil across Nanny Ogg's table and sat back in her chair. 'Go on. Right now. And no one is to help you!'

Rob backed away. Granny Weatherwax was the hag o' all hags, he knew that. There was no telling what she might do to an errant Feegle.

He picked up the pencil nervously, and placed the pointy end against the wood of the table. Other Feegles clustered around, but under Granny's frown no one dared to even cheer him on.

Rob stared upwards, his lips moving and sweat beading his forehead.

'Mmmmaa . . .' he said.

'One,' said Granny.

Rob blinked. 'Hey? Who's countin'?' he protested.

'Me,' said Granny. The kitten You leaped up onto her lap and curled up.

'Crivens, ye never said there wuz gonna be countin'!'

'Didn't I? The rules can change at any time! Two!'

Rob scribbled a passable M, hesitated, and then drew an R just as Granny said, 'Three!'

'There's gonna have tae be a "A" in there, Rob,' said Billy Bigchin. He looked up defiantly at Granny and added: 'I heard tell the rules can change at any time, right?'

'Certainly. Five!'

Rob scratched in an A and added another M in a burst of creativity.

'Six and a half,' said Granny, calmly stroking the kitten.

'Whut? Ach, crivens,' muttered Rob, and wiped a sweaty hand on his kilt. Then he gripped the pencil again and drew an L. It had a rather wavy foot because the pencil skidded out of his hands and the point broke.

He growled and drew his sword.

'Eight,' said Granny. Wood shavings flew as Rob hacked a rather ragged fresh point out of the pencil.

'Nine.' An A and a D were scribbled by a Rob whose eyes were now bulging and whose cheeks were red.

'Ten.' Rob stood to attention, looking mostly nervous but slightly proud, beside MRAMLAD. The Feegles cheered, and those nearest to him fanned him with their kilts.

'Eleven!'

'Whut? Crivens!' Rob scurried back to the end of the word and plonked down a small e.

'Twelve!'

'Ye can count all ye want tae, mistress,' said Rob, flinging down the pencil, 'but that's all the marmalade there is!' This got another cheer.

'An heroic effort, Mr Anybody,' said Granny. 'The first thing a hero must conquer is his fear, and when it comes to fightin', the Nac Mac Feegles don't know the meanin' of the word.'

'Aye, true enough,' Rob grunted. 'We dinnae ken the meanin' o' thousands o' wurds!'

'Can you fight a dragon?'

'Oh, aye, bring it on!' Rob was still angry about the marmalade.

'Run up a high mountain?'

'Nae problemo!'

'Read a book to the very end to save your big wee hag?'

'Oh, aye.' Rob stopped. He looked cornered. He licked his lips. 'How many o' them pagey things would that be?' he said hoarsely.

'Hundreds,' said Granny.

'Wi' wurds on both sides?'

'Yes, indeed. In quite small writing!'

Rob crouched. He always did that when he was cornered, the better to come up fighting. The mass of Feegles held their breath.

'I'll do it!' he announced grimly, clenching his fists.

'Good,' said Granny. 'Of course you would. That would be heroic – for you. But someone must go into the Underworld to find the real Summer Lady. That is a Story. It has happened before. It works. And he must do it in fear and terror like a real hero should, because a lot of the monsters he must overcome are the ones in his head, the ones he brings in with him. It's time for spring, and winter and its snow is still with us, so you must find him *now*. You've got to find him and set his feet on the path. The Path That Goes Down, Rob Anybody.'

'Aye, we ken that path,' said Rob.

'His name is Roland,' said Granny. 'I reckon you should leave as soon as it is light.'

The broomstick barrelled through the black blizzard. They usually went where the witch wanted them to go, and Tiffany lay along the broom, tried not to freeze to death and hoped it was taking her home. She couldn't see anything except darkness and rushing snow that stung her eyes, so she lay with the hat pulled down to streamline the stick. Even so, snowflakes struck her like stones and piled up on the stick. She had to flail around every few minutes to stop things icing up.

She did hear the roar of the falls below and felt the sudden depth of air as the stick glided out over the plains and began to sink. She felt cold to the bone.

She couldn't fight the wintersmith, not like Annagramma could. Oh, she could plan to do it, and go to bed determined, but when she saw him . . .

. . . *iron enough to make a nail* . . . the words hung around in her head as the stick flew on and she remembered the old rhyme she'd learned years ago, when the wandering teachers came to the village. Everyone seemed to know it:

> *Iron enough to make a nail*
> *Lime enough to paint a wall*
> *Water enough to drown a dog*
> *Sulphur enough to stop the fleas*
> *Potash enough to wash a shirt*
> *Gold enough to buy a bean*
> *Silver enough to coat a pin*
> *Lead enough to ballast a bird*
> *Phosfor enough to light the town . . .*

And on, and on . . .

It was a kind of nonsense, the sort that you never remember being taught but always seem to have known. Girls skipped to it, kids dib-dibbed it to see who was O-U-T out.

And then one day a travelling teacher, who like all the others would teach for eggs, fresh vegetables and

325

clean used clothing, found he got more to eat by teaching things that were interesting rather than useful. He talked about how some wizards had once, using very skilful magic, worked out exactly what a human being was made of. It was mostly water, but there was iron and brimstone and soot and a pinch of just about everything else, even a tiny amount of gold, but all cooked up together somehow.

It made as much sense to Tiffany as anything else did. But she was certain of this: if you took all that stuff and put it in a big bowl, it wouldn't turn into a human no matter how much you shouted at it.

You couldn't make a picture by pouring a lot of paint into a bucket. If you were human, you knew that.

The wintersmith wasn't. The wintersmith didn't . . .

He didn't know how the song ended, either.

The words went round and round her mind as the borrowed broom plunged onwards. At one point Dr Bustle turned up, with his reedy, self-satisfied voice, and gave her a lecture on the Lesser Elements and how, indeed, humans were made up of nearly all of them, but also contained a lot of narrativium, the basic element of stories, which you could only detect by watching the way all the others behaved . . .

'You run, you flee. How do you like this, sheep girl? You stole him from me. Is he all that you hoped for?' The voice came out of the air right beside her.

'I don't care who *you* are,' muttered Tiffany, too cold to think straight. 'Go away . . .'

Hours went by. The air down here was a bit warmer, and the snow not so fierce, but the cold always got through, no matter how much clothing you wore. Tiffany fought to stay awake. Some witches could sleep on a broomstick, but she didn't dare try in case she dreamed she was falling and woke up to find that it was true but soon wouldn't be.

But now there were lights below, fitful and yellow. It was probably the inn at Twoshirts, an important navigation point.

Witches never stayed in inns if they could help it, because in some areas that could be dangerous, and in any case most of them inconveniently required you to pay them money. But Mrs Umbridge, who ran the souvenir shop opposite the inn, had an old barn round the back and was what Miss Tick called FTW, or Friendly To Witches. There was even a witch-sign, scratched on the barn wall where no one who wasn't looking for it would find it: a spoon, a pointy hat and one big schoolmistressy tick.

A pile of straw had never seemed more wonderful, and inside two minutes Tiffany was inside the straw. At the other end of the little barn Mrs Umbridge's pair of cows kept the air warm and smelling of fermented grass.

It was a dark sleep. She dreamed of Annagramma taking off the De-Luxe Mask and revealing her face, and then taking her face off to show Granny Weatherwax's face underneath . . .

And then: *Was it worth a dance, sheep girl? You have taken my power and I am weak. The world will become frost. Was it worth a dance?*

She sat up in the pitch-black barn and thought she saw a writhing glow in the air, like a snake. Then she fell back into the darkness and dreamed of the wintersmith's eyes.

CHAPTER 11

EVEN TURQUOISE

Clang-clonk!

Tiffany sat bolt upright, straw tumbling off her. But it was only the sound of a handle clanging on the side of a metal pail.

Mrs Umbridge was milking her cows. Pale daylight shone through the cracks in the walls. She looked up when she heard Tiffany.

'Ah, I thought one of my ladies must've arrived in the night,' she said. 'Want some breakfast, dear?'

'Please!'

Tiffany helped the old woman with her buckets, helped make some butter, patted her very old dog, had beans on toast and then—

'I think I've got something here for you,' said Mrs Umbridge, heading for the little counter that was Twoshirts' entire Post Office. 'Now where did I—? Oh yes . . .'

She handed Tiffany a small bundle of letters and a

flat parcel, all held together by an elastic band and covered with dog hairs. She went on talking, but Tiffany barely noticed. There was something about how the carter had broken his leg, poor man, or maybe it was his horse that had broken a leg, poor creature, and one of the blizzards had brought down a lot of trees onto the track, and then the snow had set in so cruelly, dear, that not even a man on foot could get through, and so what with one thing and another the mail to and from the Chalk had been delayed and really there was hardly any of it anyway—

All this was a kind of background buzzing to Tiffany, because the letters were all addressed to her – three from Roland and one from her mother, and so was the parcel. It had a businesslike air, and when opened revealed a sleek black box which itself opened to reveal—

Tiffany had never seen a box of water-colour paints before. She hadn't known that so many colours existed in one place.

'Oh, a paint box,' said Mrs Umbridge, looking over her shoulder. 'That's nice. I had one when I was a girl. Ah, and it's got turquoise in it. That's very expensive, turquoise. That's from your young man, is it?' she added, because old women like to know everything, or a little bit more.

Tiffany cleared her throat. In her letters she'd kept right off the whole painful subject of painting. He must have thought she'd like to try it.

The colours in her hands gleamed like a trapped rainbow.

'It's a lovely morning,' she said, 'and I think I'd better go home . . .'

On the chilly river just above the thundering Lancre falls, a tree trunk was moored. Granny Weatherwax and Nanny Ogg stood on a huge, water-worn stone in the middle of the torrent and watched it.

The log was covered in Feegles. They all looked cheerful. Admittedly, certain death awaited them, but it did not involve – and this is important – having to spell anything.

'You know, no man has ever gone over these falls and lived to tell the tale,' said Nanny.

'Mr Parkinson did,' said Granny. 'Don't you remember? Three years ago?'

'Ah, yes, he lived, certainly, but he was left with a very bad stutter,' said Nanny Ogg.

'But he wrote it down,' said Granny. 'He called it "My fall over the Falls". It was quite interestin'.'

'No one actually *told* a tale,' said Nanny. 'That is my point.'

'Aye, weel, we're as light as wee feathers,' said Big Yan. 'An' the wind blowin' through the kilt keeps a man well aloft, ye ken.'

'I'm sure that's a sight to see,' said Nanny Ogg.

'Are ye all ready?' said Rob Anybody. 'Fine! Would ye be so good as to untie yon rope, Mrs Ogg?'

Nanny Ogg undid the knot and gave the log a shove with her foot. It drifted a little way and then got caught by the current.

'Row, row, row yer boat?' Daft Wullie suggested.

'Whut aboot it?' said Rob Anybody as the log began to speed up.

'Why don't we all sing it?' said Daft Wullie. The walls of the canyon were closing in fast now.

'OK,' said Rob. 'After all, it is a pleasin' naut-ickal ditty. And Wullie, ye'r tae keep yon cheese away fra' me. I dinnae like the way it's looking at me.'

'It hasnae got any eyes, Rob,' said Wullie meekly, holding onto Horace.

'Aye, that's what I mean,' said Rob sourly.

'Horace didna' *mean* tae try an' eat ye, Rob,' said Daft Wullie. 'An' ye wuz sae nice an' *clean* when he spat ye oot.'

'An' how come ye ken whut name a cheese has?' Rob demanded, as white water began to splash over the log.

'He told me, Rob.'

'Aye?' said Rob, and shrugged. 'Oh, OK. I wouldnae argue wi' a cheese.'

Bits of ice were bobbing on the river. Nanny Ogg pointed them out to Granny Weatherwax.

'All this snow is making the ice rivers move again,' she said.

'I know.'

'I hope you can trust the stories, Esme,' said Nanny.

'They are ancient stories. They have a life of their own. They long to be repeated. Summer rescued from a cave? Very old,' said Granny Weatherwax.

'The wintersmith will chase our girl, though.'

Granny watched the Feegles' log drift around the bend.

'Yes, he will,' she said. 'And, you know, I almost feel sorry for him.'

And so the Feegles sailed home. Apart from Billy Bigchin they couldn't carry a tune in a bucket, but that minor problem was dwarfed by the major problem, which was that they didn't bother with the idea of singing at the same pitch, or speed, or even with the same words. Also, minor fights soon broke out, as always happened even when Feegles were having fun, and so the sound that echoed among the rocks as the log sped towards the lip of the waterfall went something like:

'Rowaarghgently boat ouchgentlydoon boat boat ıoatiddley boat stream boatlymerrily boatarrgh …

CRIVENnnnnns!'

And with its cargo of Feegles, the log tipped and disappeared, along with the accompanying song, into the mists.

*   *   *

Tiffany flew over the long whale-back of the Chalk. It was a white whale now, but the snow didn't look too deep here. The bitter winds that blew the snow onto the downs also blew it away. There were no trees and few walls to make it drift.

As she drew nearer to home she looked down onto the lower, sheltered fields. The lambing pens were already being set up. There was a lot of snow for this time of year – and whose fault was that? – but the ewes were on their own timetable, snow or not. Shepherds knew how bitter the weather could be at lambing; winter never gave in without a fight.

She landed in the farmyard and said a few words to the broomstick. It wasn't hers, after all. It rose again, and shot off back to the mountains. A stick can always find its way home, if you know the trick.

There were reunions, lots of laughter, a few tears, a general claiming that she had grown like a beanstalk and was already as tall as her mother and all the other things that get said at a time like this.

Apart from the tiny Cornucopia in her pocket, she'd left everything behind – her diary, her clothes, every-thing. It didn't matter. She hadn't run away, she'd run to, and here she was, waiting for herself. She could feel her own ground under her boots again.

She hung the pointy hat behind the door and went and helped the men setting up the pens.

It was a good day. A bit of sun had managed to leak

through the murk. Against the whiteness of the snow all colours seemed bright, as if the fact that they were here gave them some special brilliance. Old harness on the stable wall gleamed like silver; even the browns and greys that might once have appeared so drab seemed, now, to have a life of their own.

She got out the box of paints and some precious paper and tried to paint what she was seeing, and there was a kind of magic there, too. It was all about light and dark. If you could get down on paper the shadow and the shine, the shape that any creature left in the world, then you could get the thing itself.

She'd only ever drawn with coloured chalks before. Paint was so much better.

It was a good day. It was a day just for her. She could feel bits of herself opening up and coming out of hiding again. Tomorrow there would be the chores, and people very nervously coming up to the farm for the help of a witch. If the pain was strong enough no one worried that the witch who was making it go away was someone you last remembered being two years old and running around without her vest on.

Tomorrow . . . might become anything. But today, the winter world was full of colour.

CHAPTER 12

THE PIKE

There was talk of strangeness all across the plains. There was the rowing boat belonging to the old man who lived in a shack just below the waterfall. It rowed itself away so fast, people said, that it skipped over the water like a dragonfly – but there was no one inside it. It was found tied up at Twoshirts, where the river ran under the coach road. But then the overnight mail coach that had been waiting outside the inn ran away by itself, with all the mail bags left behind. The coachman borrowed a horse to give chase and found the coach in the shadow of the Chalk with all the doors open and one horse missing

The horse was returned a couple of days later by a well-dressed young man who said he'd found it wandering. Surprisingly, then, it looked well fed and groomed.

Very, very thick would be the best way to describe the

walls of the castle. There were no guards at night, because they locked up at eight o'clock and went home. Instead, there was Old Robbins, who'd once been a guard and was now officially the night watchman, but everyone knew he fell asleep in front of the fire by nine. He had an old trumpet which he was supposed to blow if there was an attack, although no one was entirely sure what this would achieve.

Roland slept in the Heron Tower, because it was up a long flight of steps which his aunts didn't much like climbing. It also had very, very thick walls and this is just as well, because at eleven o'clock someone stuck a trumpet against his ear and blew on it hard.

He leaped out of bed, got caught in the eiderdown, slipped on a mat that covered the freezing stone floor, banged his head on a cupboard and managed to light a candle with the third desperately struck match.

On the little table by his bed was the pair of huge bellows with Old Robbins's trumpet stuck in the business end. The room was empty, except for the shadows.

'I've got a sword, you know,' he said. 'And I know how to use it!'

'Ach, ye're deid already,' said a voice from the ceiling. 'Chopped tae tiny wee pieces in yer bed while ye snored like a hog. Only jokin', ye ken. None of us mean ye any harm.' There was some hurried whispering in the darkness of the rafters and then the voice continued: 'Wee correction there: *most* o' us dinnae mean ye any harm. But dinnae fash yersel' aboot Big Yan, he disnae like anybody verrae much.'

'Who are you?'

'Aye, there ye go again, getting it all wrong,' said the voice conversationally. 'I'm up here an' heavily armed, ye ken, while ye're doon there in your wee nightie, making a bonny target, an' ye think ye are the one who asks the questions. So ye know how to fight, do ye?'

'Yes!'

'So you'll fight monsters tae save the big wee hag? Will ye?'

'The big wee hag?'

'That's Tiffany tae ye.'

'You mean Tiffany Aching? What's happened to her?'

'You'll be ready for when she needs ye?'

'Yes! Of course! Who *are* you?'

'And ye know how tae fight?'

'I've read *The Manual of Swordsmanship* all the way through!'

After a few seconds the voice from the high shadows said: 'Ah, I think I've put my finger on a wee flaw in this plan . . .'

There was an armoury across the castle courtyard. It wasn't much of one. There was a suit of armour made of various non-matching pieces, a few swords, a battle-axe that no one had ever been able to lift, and a chainmail suit that appeared to have been attacked by extremely strong moths. And there were some wooden dummies on big springs for sword practice, and right now the Feegles were watching Roland attack one with a great deal of enthusiasm.

'Ach weel,' said Big Yan despondently as Roland leaped about. 'If he never meets anythin' other than bits o' wood that dinnae fight back, he might be OK.'

'He's willin',' Rob Anybody pointed out as Roland put his foot against the dummy and tried to tug the sword point out of it.

'Oh, aye.' Big Yan looked glum.

'He's got a bonny action, ye must admit,' said Rob.

Roland succeeded in pulling the sword out of the dummy, which sprang back on its ancient spring and hit him on the head.

Blinking a little, the boy looked down at the Feegles. He remembered them from the time he was rescued from the Queen of the Fairies. No one who met the Nac Mac Feegles ever forgot them, even if they tried hard. But it was all vague. He'd been near-crazy part of the time, and unconscious, and had seen so many strange things that it was hard to know what was real and what wasn't.

Now he knew: they were real. Who'd make up a thing like this? OK, one of them was a cheese that rolled around of its own accord, but nobody was perfect.

'What am I going to have to do, Mr Anybody?' he said.

Rob Anybody had been worried about this bit. Words like 'Underworld' can give people the wrong idea.

'Ye must rescue a . . . lady,' he said. 'Not the big wee hag. Another . . . lady. We can take ye to the place where she bides. It's like . . . undergroound, ye ken. She's like . . . sleepin'. An' all ye ha' tae do is bring her up tae the surface, kind o' thing.'

'Oh, you mean like Orpheo rescuing Euniphon from the Underworld?' said Roland.

Rob Anybody just stared.

'It's a myth from Ephebe,' Roland went on. 'It's supposed to be a love story but it's really a metaphor for the annual return of summer. There's a lot of versions of *that* story.'

They still stared. Feegles have very worrying stares. They're even worse than chickens in that respect.*

'A metaphor is a kind o' lie to help people understand what's true,' said Billy Bigchin, but this didn't help much.

'And he won her freedom by playing beautiful music,' Roland added. 'I think he played a lute. Or maybe it was a lyre.'

'Ach, weel, that'll suit us fine,' said Daft Wullie. 'We're experts at looting an' then lyin' aboot it.'

'They're musical instruments,' said Billy Bigchin. He looked up at Roland. 'Can ye play one, mister?'

* 'Werk' . . .

'My aunts have a piano,' said Roland doubtfully. 'But I'll get into real trouble if anything happens to it. They'll tear the walls down.'

'Swords it is, then,' said Rob Anybody reluctantly. 'Ha' ye never fought against a real person, mister?'

'No. I wanted to practise with the guards, but my aunts won't let them.'

'But ye have used a sword before?'

Roland looked embarrassed. 'Not lately. Not as such. Er . . . not at all, in fact. My aunts say—'

'So how d'ye practise?' asked Rob, in horror.

'Well, there's a big mirror in my room, you see, and I can practise . . . the . . . actual . . .' Roland began, stopping when he saw their expressions. 'Sorry,' he added. 'I don't think I'm the type you're looking for . . .'

'Oh, I wouldnae say that,' said Rob Anybody wearily. 'Accordin' tae the hag o' hags, ye're just the laddie. Ye just need someone tae fight with . . .'

Big Yan, always suspicious, looked at his brother and followed his gaze to the battered suit of armour.

'Oh aye?' he growled. 'Weel, A'm no' gonna be a knee!'

Next day was a good day, right up to the point where it became a tight little bowl of terror.

Tiffany got up early and lit the fires. When her mother came down she was scrubbing the kitchen floor, very hard.

'Er . . . aren't you supposed to do that sort of thing by magic, dear?' said her mother, who'd never really got the hang of what witchcraft was all about.

'No, Mum, I'm supposed not to,' said Tiffany, still scrubbing.

'But can't you just wave your hand and make all the dirt fly away, then?'

'The trouble is getting the magic to understand what dirt is,' said Tiffany, scrubbing hard at a stain. 'I heard of a witch over in Escrow who got it wrong and ended up losing the entire floor and her sandals and nearly a toe.'

Mrs Aching backed away. 'I thought you just had to wave your hands about,' she mumbled nervously.

'That works,' said Tiffany, 'but only if you wave them about on the floor with a scrubbing brush.'

She finished the floor. She cleaned under the sink. She opened all the cupboards, cleaned them out and put everything back. She cleaned the table, and then turned it over and cleaned it underneath. She even washed the bottom of the legs, where they touched the floor. It was then that Mrs Aching went and found things to do somewhere, because this was clearly not just about good housekeeping.

It wasn't. As Granny Weatherwax once said, if you wanted to walk around with your head in the air, then you needed to have both feet on the ground. Scrubbing floors, cutting wood, washing clothes, making cheese – these things grounded you, taught you what was real. You could set a small part of your mind to them, giving your thoughts time to line up and settle down.

Was she safe here from the wintersmith? Was *here* safe from the wintersmith?

Sooner or later she'd have to face him again – a snowman who thought he was human and had the power of the avalanche. Magic could only slow him down for a while, and make him angry. No ordinary weapon would work, and she didn't have many extraordinary ones.

Annagramma had gone for him in a rage! Tiffany wished she could be that angry. She'd have to go back and thank her, too. Annagramma was going to be all right, at least. People had seen her turn into a screaming, green-skinned monster. They could respect a witch like that. Once you got respect, you'd got everything.

She'd have to try to see Roland, too, before it got dark. She didn't know what to say. That was kind of all right, because he wouldn't know what to say, either. They could spend whole afternoons together, not knowing what to say. He was probably in the castle right now. As she cleaned under the seat of a chair, she wondered what he was doing.

There was a hammering on the door of the armoury. That was the aunts for you. The door was four thicknesses of oak and iron, but they banged on it anyway.

'We will not tolerate this waywardness!' said Aunt Danuta. There was a crash from the other side of the door. 'Are you fighting in there?'

'No, I'm writing a flute sonata!' shouted Roland. Something heavy hit the door.

Aunt Danuta pulled herself together. She looked like Miss Tick in general outline, but with the eyes of the perpetually offended and the mouth of an instant complainer.

'If you don't do as you're told, I will tell your father—' she began, and stopped when the door was yanked open.

Roland had a cut on his arm, his face was red, sweat was dripping off his chin and he was panting. He raised his sword in a trembling hand. Behind him, on the other side of the grey room, was the suit of very battered armour. It turned its helmet to look at the aunts. This made a squeaking noise.

'If you dare disturb my father,' he said, as they stared at it, 'I shall tell him about the money that's being taken out of the big chest in the strongroom. Don't lie!'

For a moment – a blink would have missed it – Aunt Danuta's face had guilt written on it, but it vanished with speed. 'How dare you! Your dear mother—'

'Is dead!' shouted Roland, and slammed the door.

The helmet's visor was pushed up and half a dozen Feegles peered out.

'Crivens, what a pair of ol' corbies,' said Big Yan.

'My aunts,' said Roland darkly. 'What's a corbie?'

'I's like a big ol' crow that hangs around waitin' for someone tae die,' said Billy Bigchin.

'Ah, then you've met them before,' said Roland with a glint in his eye. 'Let's have another go, shall we? I think I'm getting the hang of it.'

There was a grumble of protests from every part of the armour, but Rob Anybody shouted it down.

'All right! We'll gi'e the lad one more chance,' he said. 'Get tae yer posts!'

There were clangs and much swearing as the Feegles climbed around inside the suit, but after a few seconds the armour seemed to pull itself together. It picked up a sword and lumbered towards Roland, who could hear the muffled orders coming from inside.

The sword swung, but in one quick movement he deflected it, stepped sideways, swung his own sword in a blur, and chopped the suit in half with a clang that echoed around the castle.

The top part hit the wall. The bottom half just rocked, still standing.

After a few seconds, a lot of small heads slowly rose above the iron trousers.

'Was that supposed to happen?' Roland said. 'Is everyone, er . . . whole?'

A quick count revealed that there were indeed no half-Feegles, although there was a lot of bruising and Daft Wullie had lost his spog. A lot of Feegles were walking in circles and banging at their ears with their hands, though. It had been a very loud clang.

'No' a bad effort, that time,' said Rob Anybody vaguely. 'Ye seem tae be gettin' the knowin' o' the fightin'.'

'It definitely seemed better, didn't it,' said Roland, looking proud. 'Shall I have another go?'

'No! I mean . . . no,' said Rob. 'No, I reckon that's enough for today, eh?'

Roland glanced up at the little barred window, high in the wall. 'Yes, I'd better go and see my father,' he said, and the glow in his face faded. 'It's well past lunchtime. If I don't see him every day he forgets who I am.'

When the boy had gone the Feegles looked at one another.

'That lad is no' havin' an easy life right noo,' said Rob Anybody.

'You've got to admit he's getting better,' said Billy Bigchin.

'Oh, aye, I'll warrant he's no' such a bunty as I thought, but that sword is far tae heavy for him an' it'll take weeks to ge' him any guid,' said Big Yan. 'Ha' we got weeks, Rob?'

Rob Anybody shrugged. 'Who can tell?' he said. 'He's gonna be the Hero, come what may. The big wee hag'll meet the wintersmith soon enough. She cannae fight that. It's like the hag o' hags sez: ye cannae fight a story as old as that. It'll find a way.' He cupped his hands. 'C'mon, lads, away tae the mound. We'll come back tonight. Mebbe ye can't make a hero all in one go.'

Tiffany's little brother was old enough to want to be considered older still, which is a dangerous ambition on a busy working farm, where there are big-hoofed horses and sheep dips and a hundred and one other places where a small person might not be noticed until it's too late. But most of all he liked water. When you couldn't find him, he was usually down by the river, fishing. He loved the river, which was a bit surprising since a huge green monster had once leaped out of it to eat him. However, Tiffany had hit it in the mouth with an iron frying pan. Since he'd been eating sweets at the time, his only comment afterwards was, 'Tiffy hit fish go bang.' But he did seem to be growing up as a skilled angler. He was fishing this afternoon. He'd found the knack of knowing where the monsters were. The really big pike lurked in the deep, black holes, thinking slow hungry thoughts until Wentworth's silver lure dropped almost into their mouth.

When Tiffany went to call him in she met him staggering up the path, much dishevelled, carrying a fish that looked as if it weighed at least half as much as him.

'It's the big one!' he shouted as soon as he saw her. 'Old Abe reckoned it was tucked in under the fallen willow, you know? He said they'll snap at anything this time of year! It pulled me over but I held on! Must weigh at least thirty pounds!'

About twenty, thought Tiffany, but fish are always much heavier to the man who catches them.

'Well done. But come on in, it's going to freeze,' she said.

'Can I have it for supper? It took ages to get in the net! It's at least thirty-five pounds!' Wentworth said, struggling under the load. Tiffany knew better than to offer to carry it. That would be an insult.

'No, it has to be cleaned and soaked for a day, and Mum's done stew for tonight. But I'll cook it for you tomorrow with ginger sauce.'

'And there'll be enough for everyone,' said Wentworth happily, 'because it weighs at least forty pounds!'

'Easily,' Tiffany agreed.

And that night, after the pike had been duly admired by everyone, and found to weigh twenty-three pounds with Tiffany's hand on the scales helping it along a bit, she went into the scullery and cleaned the fish, which was a nice way of talking about pulling out or cutting off everything that you shouldn't eat, which if Tiffany had her way meant the whole fish. She didn't much like pike, but a witch should never turn up her nose at food, especially free food, and at least a good sauce would stop it tasting of pike.

Then, as she was tipping the innards into the pig bucket, she saw the glint of silver. Well, you couldn't exactly blame Wentworth for being too excited to extract the lure.

She reached down and pulled out, covered with slime and scales but very recognizably itself, the silver horse.

There should have been a roll of thunder. There was just Wentworth, in the next room, telling for the tenth time about the heroic capture of the monster fish. There should have been a rush of wind. Barely a draught disturbed the candles.

But the wintersmith knew she'd touched it. She felt his shock.

She went to the door. As she opened it a few snowflakes fell but, as if suddenly happy to have an audience, more began to pour down until, with no sound but a hiss, the night turned white. She held out her hand to catch some flakes and looked at them very closely. Little icy Tiffanies melted away.

Oh, yes. He had found her now.

Her mind went cold, but crystal wheels of thought spun fast.

She could take a horse . . . No, she'd not get far on a night like this. She should've kept that broomstick!

She shouldn't have danced.

There was nowhere to run to. She'd have to face him again, and face him here, and stop him dead. In the mountains, with their black forests, endless winter was hard to imagine. It was easier here, and because it was easier it was worse, because he was bringing winter into her heart. She could feel it growing colder.

But the snow was inches deep already, in this short time. She was a shepherd's daughter before she was a witch, and at this time, in this place, there were more immediate things to do.

She went into the golden warmth and light of the kitchen and said: 'Dad, we must see to the flock.'

CHAPTER 13

THE CROWN OF ICE

That was then. This is now.

'Ach, crivens,' moaned Wee Dangerous Spike, on the roof of the cart shed.

The fire went out. The snow which had filled the sky began to thin. Wee Dangerous Spike heard a scream high overhead and knew exactly what to do. He raised his arms in the air and shut his eyes just as the buzzard swooped out of the white sky and snatched him up.

He *liked* this bit. When he opened his eyes, the world was swinging beneath him and a voice nearby said, 'Get up here quick, laddie!'

He grabbed the thin leather harness above him, pulled, and the talons gently released their grip. Then, hand over hand in the wind of the flight, he dragged himself across the bird's feathers until he could grab the belt of Hamish the aviator.

'Rob says ye're old enough tae come doon intae the

351

Underworld,' said Hamish over his shoulder. 'Rob's gone tae fetch the Hero. Ye are a lucky wee laddie!'

The bird banked.

Below, the snow . . . fled. There was no more melting, it simply drew back from the lambing pen like the tide going out or a deep breath being taken, with no more sound than a sigh.

Morag skimmed over the lambing field, where men were looking round in puzzlement. 'One dead ship and a dozen dead lambs,' said Hamish, 'but no big wee hag! He's taken her.'

'Where to?'

Hamish steered Morag up in a big wide circle. Around the farm, the snow had stopped falling. But up on the downs, it was dropping like hammers.

And then, it took a shape.

'Up there,' he said.

All right, I'm alive. I'm pretty sure about that.

Yes.

And I can feel the cold all around me but I don't feel cold, which would be pretty hard to explain to anyone else.

And I can't move. Not at all.

White all around me. And inside my head, all white.

Who am I?

I can remember the name Tiffany. I hope that was me.

White all around me. That happened before. It was

a kind of dream or memory or something else I don't have a word for. And all around me, whiteness falling. And building up around me, and lifting me up. It was . . . the chalk lands being built, silently, under ancient seas.

That is what my name means.

It means Land Under Wave.

And, like a wave, colour came flooding back into her mind. It was mostly the redness of rage.

How dare he!

To kill the lambs!

Granny Aching wouldn't have allowed that. She never lost a lamb. She could bring them back to life.

I should never have left here in the first place, Tiffany thought. Perhaps I should have stayed and tried to learn things by myself. But if I hadn't gone, would I still be me? Know what I know? Would I have been as strong as my grandmother or would I just be a cackler? Well, I'll be strong now.

When the killing weather was blind nature, you could only cuss, but if it was walking about on two legs . . . then it was war. And there would be a reckoning!

She tried to move, and now the whiteness gave way. It felt like hard snow, but it wasn't cold to her touch; it fell away, leaving a hole.

A smooth, slightly transparent floor stretched away in front of her. There were big pillars rising up to a ceiling that was hidden by some sort of fog.

And there were walls made of the same stuff as the floor. They looked like ice – she could even see little bubbles inside them – but were no more than cool when she touched them.

It was a very large room. There was no furniture of any sort. It was just the sort of room a king would build to say, 'Look, I can afford to waste all this space!'

Her footsteps echoed as she explored. No, not even a chair. And how comfortable would it be if she found one?

She did, eventually, find a staircase that went up (unless, of course, you started at the top). It led to another hall which at least had furniture. They were the sort of couches that rich ladies were supposed to lounge on, looking tired but beautiful. Oh, and there were urns, quite big urns, and statues, too, all in the same warm ice. The statues showed athletes and gods, very much like the pictures in Chaffinch's *Mythology*, doing ancient things like hurling javelins or killing huge snakes with their bare hands. They didn't have a stitch of clothing between them, but all the men wore fig leaves which Tiffany, in a spirit of enquiry, found would not come off.

And there was a fire. The first strange thing about it was that the logs were also of the same ice. The other strange thing was that the flames were blue – and cold.

This level had tall pointed windows, but they began a long way from the floor and showed nothing but the sky, where the pale sun was a ghost among the clouds.

Another staircase, very grand this time, led up to yet another floor with more statues and couches and urns. Who could live in a place like this? Someone who didn't need to eat or sleep, that's who. Someone who didn't need to be comfortable.

'Wintersmith!'

Her voice bounced from wall to wall, sending back '. . . ITH . . . Ith . . . ith . . .' until it died away.

Another staircase, then, and this time there was something new. On a plinth, where there might have been a statue, was a crown. It floated in the air a few feet above the base, turning gently, and glittered with frost. A little bit further on was another statue, smaller than most, but around this one blue and green and gold lights danced and shimmered.

They looked just like the Hublights, which could sometimes be seen in the depths of winter floating over the mountains at the centre of the world. Some people thought they were alive.

The statue was the same height as Tiffany.

'Wintersmith!' There was still no reply. A nice palace with no kitchen, no bed . . . He didn't need to eat or sleep, so who was it for?

She knew the answer already: me.

She reached out to touch the dancing lights and they swarmed up her arm and spread across her body, making a dress that glittered like moonlight on snow-fields. She was shocked, then angry. Then she wished she had a mirror, felt guilty about that and went back to being angry again, and resolved that if by chance she did find a mirror, the only reason she'd look in it would be to check how angry she was.

After searching for a while she found a mirror, which was nothing more than a wall of ice of such a dark green that it was almost black.

She did look angry. And immensely, beautifully sparkly. There were little glints of gold on the blue and green, just like there were in the sky on wintry nights.

'Wintersmith!'

He must be watching her. He could be anywhere.

'All right! I'm here! You know that!'

'Yes. I do,' said the wintersmith, behind her.

Tiffany spun around and slapped him across the face, then slapped him again with her other hand.

It was like hitting rock. He was learning very quickly now.

'That's for the lambs,' she said, trying to shake some life back into her fingers. 'How dare you! You didn't have to!'

He looked much more human. Either he really was wearing actual clothes or he had worked hard on making them look real. He'd actually managed to look . . . well, handsome. Not cold any more, just . . . cool.

He's nothing but a snowman, her Second Thoughts protested. Remember that. He's just too smart to have coal for eyes or a carrot for a nose.

'Ouch,' said the wintersmith, as if he'd just remembered to say it.

'I demand that you let me go!' Tiffany snapped. 'Right now.' That's right, her Second Thoughts said. You want him to end up cowering behind the saucepans on top of the kitchen dresser. As it were . . .

'At this moment,' said the wintersmith, very calmly, 'I am a gale wrecking ships a thousand miles away. I am freezing water pipes in a snow-bound town. I am freezing the sweat on a dying man, lost in a terrible blizzard. I creep silently under doors. I hang from gutters. I stroke the fur of the sleeping bear, deep in her cave, and course in the blood of the fishes under the ice.'

'I don't care!' said Tiffany. 'I don't want to be here! And you shouldn't be here, either!'

'Child, will you walk with me?' said the wintersmith. 'I will not harm you. You are safe here.'

'What from?' said Tiffany, and then, because too much time around Miss Tick does something to your conversation, even in times of stress, she changed this to: 'From what?'

'Death,' said the wintersmith. 'Here, you will never die.'

At the back of the Feegles' chalk pit, more chalk had been carved out of the wall to make a tunnel about five feet high and perhaps as long.

In front of it stood Roland de Chumsfanleigh (it wasn't his fault). His ancestors had been knights, and they had come to own the Chalk by killing the kings who thought they did. Swords, that's what it had all been about. Swords and cutting off heads. That was how you got land in the old days, and then the rules were changed so that you didn't need a sword to own land any more; you just needed the right piece of paper. But his ancestors had still hung onto their swords, just in case people thought that the whole thing with the bits of paper was unfair, it being a fact that you can't please everybody.

He'd always wanted to be good with a sword, and it had come as a shock to find they were so *heavy*. He was great at air sword. In front of a mirror he could fence against his reflection and win nearly all the time. Real swords didn't allow that. You tried to swing them and they ended up swinging you. He'd realized that maybe he was more cut out for bits of paper. Besides, he needed glasses, which could be a bit tricky under a helmet, especially if someone was hitting *you* with a sword.

He wore a helmet now, and held a sword which was – although he wouldn't admit it – far too heavy for him. He was also wearing a suit of chainmail that made it very hard to walk. The Feegles had done their best to make it fit, but the crotch hung down to his knees and flapped amusingly when he moved.

I'm not a hero, he thought. I've got a sword, which I need two hands to lift, and I've got a shield which is also really heavy and I've got a horse with curtains round it which I've had to leave at home (and my aunts will go mad when they go into the drawing room), but inside I'm a kid who would quite like to know where the privy is . . .

But she rescued me from the Queen of Fairyland. If she hadn't, I'd still be a stupid kid instead of . . . um . . . a young man hoping he isn't too stupid.

The Nac Mac Feegles had exploded back into his room, fighting their way through the storm that had arrived overnight and now, they said, it was time for him to be a Hero for Tiffany . . . Well, he would be. He was sure of that. Fairly sure. But right now the scenery wasn't what he'd expected.

'You know, this doesn't look like the entrance to the Underworld,' he said.

'Ach, any cave can be the way in,' said Rob Anybody, who was sitting on his helmet. 'But ye must ha' the knowin' o' the crawstep. OK, Big Yan, ye go first . . .'

Big Yan strutted up to the chalk hole. He stuck out his arms behind him, bent at the elbows. He leaned backwards, sticking out one leg to keep his balance. Then he wiggled the foot in the air a few times, leaned forward, and vanished as soon as the foot touched the ground.

Rob Anybody banged on Roland's helmet with his fist. 'OK, big hero,' he shouted. 'Off ye go!'

There was no way out. Tiffany didn't even know if there was a way in.

'If you were the Summer Lady, then we *would* dance,' said the wintersmith. 'But I know now that you are not her, even though you seem to be. But for the sake of you I am now human, and I must have company.'

Tiffany's racing mind showed her pictures: the sprouting acorn, the fertile feet, the Cornucopia. I'm just enough of a goddess to fool a few floorboards and an acorn and a handful of seeds, she thought. I'm just like him. Iron enough to make a nail doesn't make a snowman a human, and a couple of oak leaves don't make me a goddess.

'Come,' said the wintersmith, 'let me show you my world. Our world.'

When Roland opened his eyes, all he could see was shadows. Not shadows of things – just shadows, drifting like cobwebs.

'I was expecting somewhere . . . hotter,' he said, trying to keep the relief out of his voice. Around him, Feegles popped out of nowhere.

'Ah, you're thinkin' o' hells,' said Rob Anybody. 'They tends to be on the toasty side, it's true. Underworlds are more o' the gloomy sort. It's where folks end up when they's lost, ye ken.'

'What? You mean if it's a dark night and you take the wrong turning—'

'Ach, no! Like mebbe dead when they shouldn't be an' there's nae place for 'em tae go, or they fall doon a gap in the worlds an' dinnae ken the way. Some o' them don't even ken where they are, poor souls. There's an awful lot o' that kind o' thing. There's no' a lot o' laughs in a underworld. This one used tae be called Limbo, ye ken, cuz the door was verrae low. Looks like it's gone way downhill since we wuz last here.' He raised his voice. 'An' a big hand, lads, for young Wee Dangerous Spike, oot wi' us for the first time!' There was a ragged cheer, and Wee Dangerous Spike waved his sword.

Roland pushed his way through the shadows, which actually offered some resistance. The very air was grey down here. Sometimes he heard groans, or someone coughing in the distance . . . and then there were footsteps, shuffling towards him.

He drew his sword and peered through the gloom.

Shadows parted and a very old woman in tattered, threadbare clothes shuffled past, dragging a large cardboard box behind her. It bounced awkwardly as she tugged at it. She didn't even glance at Roland.

He lowered the sword.

'I thought there'd be monsters,' he said as the old woman disappeared into the gloom.

'Aye,' said Rob Anybody grimly. 'There are. Think o' somethin' solid, will ye?'

'Something solid?!'

'I'm nae jokin'! Think o' of a nice big mountain, or

a hammer! Whatever ye do, dinnae wish or regret or hope!'

Roland closed his eyes and then reached up to touch them.

'I can still see! But my eyes are shut!'

'Aye! And ye'll see more wi' yer een shut. Look aroond ye, if ye dare!'

Roland, his eyes shut, took a few steps forward and looked around. Nothing seemed to have changed. Perhaps things were slightly more gloomy. And then he saw it – a flash of bright orange, a line in the dark which came and went.

'What was that?' he said.

'We dinnae ken whut they call themselves. We call 'em bogles,' said Rob.

'They are flashes of light?'

'Ach, that one was a long way away,' said Rob. 'If ye want tae see one close up, it's standin' right beside ye . . .'

Roland spun round.

'Ah, ye see, ye made a classic mistake right there,' said Rob conversationally. 'Ye opened yer eyes!'

Roland shut his eyes. The bogle was standing six inches away from him.

He didn't flinch. He didn't scream. Hundreds of Feegles were watching him, he knew.

At first he thought: It's a skeleton. When it flashed again, it looked like a bird, a tall bird like a heron. Then it was a stick figure, like a kid would draw. Over and over again it scribbled itself against the darkness in thin, burning lines.

It scribbled itself a mouth and leaned forward for a moment, showing hundreds of needle teeth. Then it vanished.

There was a murmur from the Feegles.

'Aye, ye done weel,' said Rob Anybody. 'Ye stared it in the mouth and ye didnae take so much as a step back.'

'Mr Anybody, I was too scared to run,' Roland muttered.

Rob Anybody leaned down until he was level with the boy's ear.

'Aye,' he whispered, 'I ken that well enough! There be a lot o' men who became heroes cuz they wuz too scared tae run! But ye didnae yell nor cack yer kecks, an' that's good. There'll be more o' them as we go on. Dinnae let them intae yer heid! Keep 'em oot!'

'Why, what do they—? No, don't tell me!' said Roland.

He walked on through the shadows, blinking so that he wouldn't miss anything. The old woman had gone, but the gloom began to fill up with people. Mostly they stood by themselves, or sat on chairs. Some wandered around quietly. They passed a man in ancient clothing who was staring at his own hand as though he was seeing it for the first time.

There was another woman swaying gently and singing a nonsense song in a quiet, little girl voice. She

gave Roland a strange, mad smile as he walked past.
Right behind her stood a bogle.

'All right,' said Roland grimly. 'Now tell me what
they do.'

'They eat yer memories,' said Rob Anybody. 'Yer
thoughts is real tae them. Wishes an' hope are like
food! They're vermin, really. This is what happens
when these places are no' looked after.'

'And how can I kill them?'

'Oh, that was a verrae nasty voice ye just used. Hark
at the big wee hero! Dinnae bother aboot them, laddie.
They won't attack yet, and we've got a job tae do.'

'I hate this place!'

'Aye, hells is a lot more lively,' said Rob Anybody.
'Slow doon now, we're at the river.'

A river ran through the Underworld. It was as dark
as the soil, and lapped at its banks in a slow, oily way.

'Ah, I think I've heard of this,' said Roland. 'There's
a ferryman, right?'

YES.

He was there, suddenly, standing in a long, low
boat. He was all in black, of course in black, with a
deep hood that entirely concealed his face and gave
a definite feeling that this was just as well.

'Hi, pal,' said Rob Anybody cheerfully. 'How're ye
doin'?'

OH NO, NOT YOU PEOPLE AGAIN, said the dark figure, in
a voice that was not so much heard as felt. I THOUGHT
YOU WERE BANNED.

'Just a wee misunderstandin', ye ken,' said Rob, sliding down Roland's armour. 'Ye have tae let us in, cuz we's deid already.'

The figure extended an arm. The black robe fell away, and what pointed at Roland looked, to him, very much like a bony finger.

BUT *HE* MUST PAY THE FERRYMAN, he said accusingly, in a voice of crypts and graveyards.

'Not until I'm on the other side,' Roland said firmly.

'Oh, c'mon!' said Daft Wullie to the ferryman. 'Ye can see he's a hero! If ye cannae trust a hero, who can ye trust?'

The cowl regarded Roland for what seemed like a hundred years.

OH, VERY WELL THEN.

The Feegles swarmed aboard the rotting boat with their usual enthusiasm and cries of 'Crivens!', 'Where's the booze on this cruise?' and 'We're right oot in the Styx noo!' and Roland climbed in with care, watching the ferryman suspiciously.

The figure pulled on the big oar and they set off with a creak and then, regrettably, and to the ferryman's disgust, to the sound of singing. More or less singing, that is, at every possible speed and tempo and with no regard at all for the tune:

'Row row your row boat boat
row yer boat down the merrily stream
like a bird on the boa—'

WILL YOU SHUT UP?

'– bonny boat row stream stream
boat boat row yer boat down
the merrily stream row merrily merrily boat—'

THIS IS HARDLY APPROPRIATE!

'Down the boat boat down the merrily stream
stream stream merrily merrily
merrily merrily merrily merrily boat!'

'Mr Anybody?' said Roland as they glided jerkily along.

'Aye?'

'Why am I sitting next to a blue cheese with a bit of tartan wrapped around it?'

'Ah, that'd be Horace,' said Rob Anybody. 'He's Daft Wullie's pal. He's no' bein' a nuisance, is he?'

'No. But he's trying to sing!'

'Aye, all blue cheeses hum a bit.'

'Mnamnam mnam mnamnam,' crooned Horace.

The boat bumped against the far bank, and the ferryman stepped ashore quickly.

Rob Anybody scrambled up Roland's ragged chain-mail sleeve, and whispered: 'When I gi'e ye the word, run for it!'

'But I can pay the ferryman. I have the money,' said Roland, patting his pocket.

'You whut?' said the Feegle, as if this was some strange and dangerous idea.

'I have the money,' Roland repeated. 'Two pennies is the rate to cross the River of the Dead. It's an old tradition. Two pennies to put on the eyes of the dead, to pay the ferryman.'

'Whut a clever man ye are, to be sure,' said Rob as Roland dropped two copper coins into the ferryman's bony hand. 'An did ye no' think tae bring four pennies?'

'The book just said the dead take tuppence,' said Roland.

'Aye, mebbe they do,' Rob agreed, 'but that's cuz the deid dinnae expect tae be comin' back!'

Roland looked back across the dark river. Flashes of orange light were thick on the bank they'd left.

'Mr Anybody, I was once a prisoner of the Queen of Fairyland,' he said.

'Aye, I ken that.'

'It was for a year in this world but it only seemed like a few weeks there . . . except that the weeks passed like centuries. It was so . . . dull I could hardly remember anything after a while. Not my name, not the feel of sunshine, not the taste of real food.'

'Aye, we ken that, we helped tae rescue ye. Ye niver said thanks, but ye wuz oot o' yer skull the whole time so we didnae take offence.'

'Then allow me to thank you now, Mr Anybody.'

'Dinnae mention it. Any time. Happy tae oblige.'

'She had pets that feed you dreams until you die of hunger. I hate things that try to take away what you are. I want to kill those things, Mr Anybody. I want to kill all of them. When you take away memories, you take away the person. Everything they are.'

''Tis a fine ambition ye've got there,' said Rob. 'But we have got a wee job tae do, ye ken. Aw, crivens, this is whut happens when things get sloppy an' bogles take over.'

There was a big pile of bones on the path. They were certainly animal bones, and the rotting collars and lengths of rusted chain were another clue.

'Three big dogs?' said Roland.

'One verrae big dog wi' three heads,' said Rob Anybody. 'Verrae popular in underworlds, that breed. Can bite right through a man's throat. Three times!' he added, with relish. 'But put three doggy biscuits in a row on the groound and the puir wee thing sits there strainin' an' whinin' all day. It's a wee laff, I'm tellin' ye!' He kicked at the bones. 'Aye, time wuz when places like this had some pers'nality. Look, see what they've done here, too.'

Further along the path was what was probably a demon. It had a horrible face, with so many fangs that some of them must have been just for show. There were wings, too, but they couldn't possibly have lifted it. It had found a piece of mirror, and every few seconds it took a peep into it and shuddered.

'Mr Anybody,' said Roland, 'is there anything

down here that this sword I'm carrying could kill?'

'Ah, no. No' kill,' said Rob Anybody. 'No' bogles. No' as such. It's no' a magic sword, see?'

'Then why am I dragging it along?'

'Cuz ye are a hero. Whoever hear' o' a hero wi' oot a sword?'

Roland tugged the sword out of its scabbard. It was heavy and not at all like the flying, darting silver thing that he'd imagined in front of the mirror. It was more like a metal club with an edge.

He gripped it in both hands and managed to hurl it out into the middle of the slow, dark river.

Just before it hit the water a white arm rose and caught it. The hand waved the sword a couple of times, and then disappeared with it under the water.

'Was that supposed to happen?' he said.

'A man throwin' his sword awa'?' yelled Rob. 'No! Ye're no' supposed tae bung a guid sword intae the drinkie!'

'No, I mean the hand,' said Roland. 'It just—'

'Ach, they turn up sometimes.' Rob Anybody waved a hand as if mid-stream underwater sword jugglers were an everyday occurrence. 'But ye've got no weapon noo!'

'You said swords can't hurt bogles!'

'Aye, but it's the look o' the thing, OK?' said Rob, hurrying on.

'But not having a sword should make me *more* heroic, right?' said Roland, as the rest of the Feegles trotted after them.

'Technic'ly, aye,' said Rob Anybody reluctantly. 'But mebbe also more deid.'

'Besides, I have a Plan,' said Roland.

'Ye have a Plan?' said Rob.

'Yes. I mean aye.'

'Writted doon?'

'I've only just thought of—' Roland stopped. The ever-shifting shadows had parted and a big cave lay ahead.

In the centre of it, surrounding what looked like a rock slab, was a dim yellow glow. There was a small figure lying on the slab.

'Here we are,' said Rob Anybody. 'That wasnae so bad, aye?'

Roland blinked. Hundreds of bogles were clustered around the slab, but at a distance, as if they were not keen on going any further.

'I can see . . . someone lying down,' he said.

'That's Summer herself,' said Rob. 'We have tae be canny aboot this.'

'Canny?'

'Like . . . careful,' said Rob helpfully. 'Goddesses can be a wee bit tricky. Verrae image-conscious.'

'Don't we just . . . you know, grab her and run?' said Roland.

'Oh, aye, we'll end up doin' somethin' like that,' said Rob. 'But you, mister, will have tae be the one tae kiss her first. You OK wi' that?'

Roland looked a bit strained, but he said: 'Yes . . . er, fine.'

'The ladies expect it, ye ken,' Rob went on.

'And then we run for it?' said Roland hopefully.

'Aye, cuz probably that's when the bogles will try an' stop us gettin' awa'. It's people leavin' that they don't like. Off ye go, laddie.'

I've got a Plan, thought Roland, walking towards the slab. And I'll concentrate on it so that I don't think about the fact that I'm walking through a crowd of scribbly monsters that are only there if I blink and my eyes are watering. What's in our head is real to them, right?

I'm going to blink, I'm going to blink, I'm going to . . .

. . . blink. It was over in a moment but the shudder went on for a lot longer. They had been everywhere, and every toothy mouth was looking at him. It should not be possible to look with teeth.

He ran forward, eyes streaming with the effort of not closing, and looked down at the figure lying in the yellow glow. It was female, it was breathing, it was asleep, and it looked like Tiffany Aching.

From the top of the ice palace Tiffany could see for miles, and they were miles of snow. Only on the Chalk was there any sign of green. It was an island.

'You see how I learn?' said the wintersmith. 'The Chalk is yours. So there, summer will come, and you will be happy. And you will be my bride and I will be happy. And everything will be happy. Happiness is

371

when things are correct. Now I am human, I understand these things.'

Don't scream, don't shout, said the Third Thoughts. Don't freeze up, either.

'Oh . . . I see,' she said. 'And the rest of the world will stay in winter?'

'No, there are some latitudes that never feel my frost,' said the wintersmith. 'But the mountains, the plains as far as the circle sea . . . oh, yes.'

'Millions of people will die!'

'But only once, you see. That is what makes it wonderful. And after that, no more death!'

And Tiffany saw it, like a Hogswatch card: birds frozen to their twigs, horses and cows standing still in the fields, frozen grass like daggers, no smoke from any chimney; a world without death because there was nothing left to die, and everything glittering like tinsel.

She nodded carefully. 'Very . . . sensible,' she said. 'But it would be a shame if nothing moved at all.'

'That would be easy. Snow people,' said the wintersmith. 'I can make them human!'

'Iron enough to make a nail?' said Tiffany.

'Yes! It is easy. I have eaten sausage! And I can think! I never thought before. I was a *part*. Now I am apart. Only when you are apart do you know who you are.'

'You made me roses of ice,' said Tiffany.

'Yes! Already I was becoming!'

But the roses melted at dawn, Tiffany added to herself, and glanced at the pale yellow sun. It had just enough strength to make the wintersmith sparkle. He does think like a human, she thought, looking into the odd smile. He thinks like a human who's never met another human. He's cackling. He's so mad he will never understand how mad he is.

He just doesn't have a clue what 'human' means, he doesn't know what horrors he's planning, he just doesn't . . . understand. And he's so happy he's almost sweet . . .

Rob Anybody banged on Roland's helmet.

'Get on wi' it, laddie,' he demanded.

Roland stared at the glowing figure. 'This can't be Tiffany!'

'Ach, she's a goddess, she can look like anything,' said Rob Anybody. 'Just a wee peck on the cheek, OK? Dinnae get enthusiastic, we havenae got all day. A wee peck and we're offski.'

Something butted Roland on the ankle. It was a blue cheese.

'Dinnae fash yerself aboot Horace, he just wants ye tae do the right thing,' said the mad Feegle who Roland had come to know as Daft Wullie.

He went closer, with the glow crackling around him, because no man wants to be a coward in front of a cheese.

'This is kind of . . . embarrassing,' he said.

'Crivens, get *on* wi' it, will ye?'

Roland leaned forward and pecked the sleeping cheek.

The sleeper opened her eyes, and he took a step back very quickly.

'That's *not* Tiffany Aching!' he said, and blinked. Bogles were as thick around him as grass stems.

'Now take her by the hand an' run,' said Rob Anybody. 'The bogles will turn nasty when they see we're leavin'.' He banged cheerfully on the side of the helmet and added: 'But that's OK, right? Cuz ye have a Plan!'

'I hope I've got it right, though,' said Roland. 'My aunts say I'm too clever by half.'

'Glad tae hear it,' said Rob Anybody, 'cuz that's much better than bein' too stupid by three-quarters! Now grab the lady and run!'

Roland tried to avoid the stare of the girl as he took her hand and pulled her gently off the slab. She said something in a language he couldn't understand, except that it sounded as though there was a question mark on the end of it.

'I'm here to rescue you,' he said. She looked at him with the golden eyes of a snake.

'The sheep girl is in trouble,' she said, in a voice full of unpleasant echoes and hisses. 'So sad, *so* sad.'

'Well, er, we'd better run,' he managed, 'whoever you are . . .'

The not-Tiffany gave him a smile. It was an

uncomfortable one, with a bit of a smirk in it. They ran.

'How do *you* fight them?' he panted when the Feegle army were jogging through the caves.

'Ach, they dinnae like the taste o' us overmuch,' said Rob Anybody as the shadows parted. 'It may be cuz we think aboot the boozin' a lot, it makes 'em squiffy. Keep movin'!'

And it was at this point that the bogles struck, although that was hardly the right word. It was more like running into a wall of whispers. Nothing grabbed, there were no claws. If thousands of tiny weak things like shrimps or flies were trying to stop someone, this would be how it felt.

But the ferryman was waiting. He raised a hand as Roland staggered towards the boat.

THAT WILL BE SIX PENNIES, he said.

'Six?' said Roland

'Ah, we wasnae doon here more'n two hour an' bang went saxpence!' said Daft Wullie.

ONE DAY RETURN, ONE SINGLE, said the ferryman.

'I don't have that much!' Roland shouted. He was beginning to feel little tugs in his head now. Thoughts had to push hard to get as far as his mouth.

'Leave this tae me,' said Rob Anybody. He turned to look down on his fellow Feegles and banged on Roland's helmet for silence.

'OK, lads,' he announced. 'We're no' leavin!'

WHAT? said the ferryman. OH NO, *YOU* LEAVE! I'M NOT

HAVING *YOU* DOWN HERE AGAIN! WE'RE STILL FINDING THE BOTTLES FROM LAST TIME! COME ON, GET ON THE BOAT THIS MINUTE!

'Crivens, we cannae do that, pal,' said Rob Anybody. 'We're under a geas to help this lad, ye ken. Where he disnae go, we dinnae go!'

PEOPLE ARE NOT SUPPOSED TO WANT TO STAY HERE! snapped the ferryman.

'Ach, we'll soon ha' the old place jumpin' again,' said Rob Anybody, grinning.

The ferryman drummed his fingers on the pole. They made a clicking sound, like dice.

OH, ALL RIGHT THEN. BUT – AND I WANT TO BE CLEAR ON THIS – THERE IS TO BE NO SINGING!

Roland dragged the girl onto the boat. The bogles kept clear of that, at least, but as the ferryman pushed them away from the shore Big Yan kicked Roland on the boot and pointed upwards. Scribbles of orange light, hundreds of them, were moving across the roof of the cavern. There were more of them on the opposite shore.

'How's the Plan goin', Mister Hero?' said Rob Anybody quietly as he climbed down from the boy's helmet.

'I'm waiting for the opportune moment,' said Roland haughtily. He turned to look at the not-Tiffany. 'I'm here to get you out,' he said, trying not to look directly at her eyes.

'You?' said the not-Tiffany, as if the idea was amusing.

'Well, us,' Roland corrected himself. 'Everything is—'

There was a bump as the boat grounded on the further shore, where the bogles were as thick as standing corn.

'Off ye go, then,' said Big Yan.

Roland pulled the not-Tiffany along the path for a few steps, and stopped. When he blinked, the path ahead was a writhing orange mass. He could feel the little pulls on him, no stronger than a breeze. But they were in his brain, too. Cold, and nibbling. This was stupid. It couldn't work. He wouldn't be able to do it. He wasn't any good at this sort of thing. He was wayward and inconsiderate and disobedient, just like his . . . aunts . . . said.

Behind him, Daft Wullie shouted, in his cheerful way, 'Make yer aunties proud of ye!'

Roland half turned, suddenly angry. 'My *aunts*? Let me tell you about my aunts . . .'

'No time, laddie!' shouted Rob Anybody. 'Get *on* wi' it!'

Roland looked around, his mind on fire.

Our memories are real, he thought. And I will not stand for this!

He turned to the not-Tiffany, and said: 'Don't be afraid.' Then he held out his left hand and whispered, under his breath: 'I remember . . . a sword . . .'

When he shut his eyes, there it was – so light he could barely feel it, so thin he could hardly see it, a line in the air that was made up mostly of sharpness. He'd killed a thousand enemies with it, in the mirror. It was never too heavy, it moved like part of him, and here it was. A weapon that chopped away everything that clung and lied and stole. He smiled, and took a firm grip.

'Mebbe ye can make a hero all in one go,' said Rob Anybody thoughtfully, as bogles scribbled themselves into existence and died. He turned to Daft Wullie. 'Daft Wullie,' he said, 'can ye bring to mind when it was I told ye that sometimes ye say *exactly the right thing*?'

Daft Wullie looked baffled. 'No' that ye mention it, Rob, I dinnae recall ye ever sayin' that, ever.'

'Aye?' said Rob. 'Weel, if I had done, just now would ha' been one o' those times.'

Daft Wullie looked worried. 'That's all right though, aye? I said somethin' right?'

'Aye. Ye did, Daft Wullie. A first. I'm proud o' ye,' said Rob.

Daft Wullie's face split in an enormous grin. 'Crivens! Hey, lads, I said—'

'But dinnae get carried awa',' Rob added.

As Roland swung the airy blade, the bogles parted like spider webs. There were more, always more, but the silver line always found them, cutting him free. They backed away, tried new shapes, recoiled from the heat of the anger in his head. The sword hummed. Bogles curled around the blade and squealed, and sizzled into nothingness on the floor—

– and someone was banging on his helmet. They'd been doing so for quite a while.

'Huh?' he said, opening his eyes.

'Ye've run oot,' said Rob Anybody. His chest heaving, Roland looked around. Eyes open or shut, the caves were empty of orange streaks. The not-Tiffany was watching him with a strange smile on her face.

'Either we get oot noo,' said Rob, 'or you can hang aroound and wait for some more, mebbe?'

'An' here they come,' said Billy Bigchin. He pointed across the river. A pure mass of orange was pouring into the cave, so many bogles that there was no space between them.

Roland hesitated, still fighting for breath.

'I'll tell ye what,' said Rob Anybody soothingly. 'If ye are a guid boy and rescue the lady, we'll bring you doon here another time, wi' some sandwiches so's we can make a day o' it.'

Roland blinked. 'Er, yes,' he said. 'Um . . . sorry. I don't know what happened just then . . .'

'Offski time!' yelled Big Yan. Roland grabbed the hand of the not-Tiffany.

'An' don't look back until we're well oot o' here,' said Rob Anybody. 'It's kind o' traditional.'

On the top of the tower, the ice crown appeared in the wintersmith's pale hands. It shone more than diamonds could, even in the pale sunlight. It was purest ice, without bubbles, lines or flaw.

'I made this for you,' he said. 'The Summer Lady will never wear it,' he added sadly.

It fitted perfectly. It didn't feel cold.

He stepped back.

'And now it is done,' said the wintersmith.

'There is something I have to do, too,' said Tiffany. 'But first, there's something I have to know. You found the things that make a man?'

'Yes!'

'How did you find out what they were?'

The wintersmith proudly told her about the children, while Tiffany breathed carefully, forcing herself to relax. His logic was very . . . logical. After all, if a carrot and two pieces of coal can make a heap of snow a snowman, then a big bucket of salts and gases and metal should certainly make him a human. It made . . . sense. At least, sense to the wintersmith.

'But, you see, you need to know the whole song,' said Tiffany. 'It is mostly only about what humans are made of. It isn't about what humans *are*.'

'There were some things that I could not find,' said the wintersmith. 'They made no sense. They had no substance.'

'Yes,' said Tiffany, nodding sadly. 'The last three lines, I expect, which are the whole point. I'm really sorry about that.'

'But I will find them,' said the wintersmith. 'I will!'

'I hope you do, one day,' said Tiffany. 'Now, have you ever heard of boffo?'

'What is this boffo? It was not in the song!' said the wintersmith, looking uneasy

'Oh, boffo is how humans change the world by fooling themselves,' said Tiffany. 'It's wonderful. And boffo says that things have no power that humans don't put there. You can make things magical, but you can't magically make a human out of things. It's just a nail in your heart. Only a nail.'

And the time has come and I know what to do, she thought dreamily. I know how the story has to end. I must end it in the right kind of way.

She pulled the wintersmith towards her, and saw the look of astonishment on his face. She felt light-headed, as though her feet weren't touching the floor. The world became . . . simpler. It was a tunnel, leading to the future. There was nothing to see but the wintersmith's cold face, nothing to hear but her own breathing, nothing to feel but the warmth of the sun on her hair.

It wasn't the fiery globe of summer, but it was still much bigger than any bonfire could ever be.

Where this takes me, there I choose to go, she told herself, letting the warmth pour into her. I choose. This I choose to do. And I'm going to have to stand on tiptoe, she added.

Thunder on my right hand. Lightning in my left hand.

Fire above me . . .

'Please,' she said, 'take the winter away. Go back to your mountains. Please.'

Frost in front of me . . .

'No. I am winter. I cannot be anything else.'

'Then you cannot be human,' said Tiffany. 'The last three lines are: "Strength enough to build a home, Time enough to hold a child, Love enough to break a heart".'

Balance . . . and it came quickly, out of nowhere, lifting her up inside.

The centre of the see-saw does not move. It feels neither up-ness nor down-ness. It is balanced.

Balance . . . and his lips were like blue ice. She'd cry, later, for the wintersmith who wanted to be human.

Balance . . . and the old kelda had once told her: 'There's a wee bit o' you that willnae melt and flow.'

Time to thaw.

She shut her eyes and kissed the wintersmith . . .

. . . and drew down the sun.

Frost to fire.

The entire top of the ice palace was melted in a flash of white light that cast shadows on walls a hundred miles away. A pillar of steam roared up, stitched with lightning, and spread out above the world like an umbrella, covering the sun. Then it began to fall back as a soft, warm rain that punched little wormholes in the snow.

Tiffany, her head usually so full of thoughts, hadn't got a thought to spare. She lay on a slab of ice in the soft rain and listened to the palace collapse around her.

There are times when everything that you can do has been done and there's nothing for it now but to curl up and wait for the thunder to die down.

There was something else in the air, too, a golden glint that vanished when she tried to look at it and then turned up again in the corner of her eye.

The palace was melting like a waterfall. The slab she lay on half-slid and half-floated down a staircase that was turning into a river. Above her, huge pillars fell, but went from ice to a gush of warm water in mid-air, so that what crashed down was spray.

Goodbye to the glittering crown, Tiffany thought. Goodbye to the dress made of dancing light, and good-bye to the ice roses and the snowflakes. Such a shame. Such a shame.

And then there was grass under her, and so much water pouring past her that it was a case of get up or drown. She managed to get to her knees, at least, and waited until it was possible to stand up without being knocked over.

'You have something of mine, child,' said a voice behind her. She turned, and golden light rushed into a shape. It was her own shape, but her eyes were . . . odd, like a snake's. Right here and now, with the roaring of the heat of the sun still filling her ears, this didn't seem very amazing.

Slowly, Tiffany took the Cornucopia out of her pocket and handed it over.

'You are the Summer Lady, aren't you?' she asked.

'And you are the sheep girl who would be me?' There was a hiss to the words.

'I didn't want to be!' said Tiffany hurriedly. 'Why do you look like me?'

The Summer Lady sat down on the turf, which steamed. It is very strange to watch yourself, and Tiffany noticed she had a small mole on the back of her neck.

'It's called resonance,' she said. 'Do you know what that is?'

'It means "to vibrate with",' said Tiffany.

'How does a sheep girl know that?'

'I have a dictionary,' said Tiffany. 'And I'm a witch, thank you.'

'Well, while you were picking up things from me, I've been picking up things from you, clever sheep-witch,' said the Summer Lady. She was beginning to remind Tiffany a lot of Annagramma. That was actually a relief. She didn't sound wise, or nice . . . she was just another person, who happened to be very powerful but not frighteningly smart and, frankly, a bit annoying.

'What's your real shape?' she asked.

'The shape of heat on a road, the shape of the smell of apples.' Nice reply, Tiffany thought, but not helpful, as such.

Tiffany sat down next to the goddess. 'Am I in trouble?' she asked.

'Because of what you did to the wintersmith? No. He has to die every year, as do I. We die, and sleep and wake. Besides . . . you were entertaining.'

'Oh? I was *entertaining*, was I?' said Tiffany, her eyes narrowing.

'What it is you want?' said the Summer Lady. Yes, thought Tiffany, *just* like Annagramma. Wouldn't spot a hint a mile high.

'Want?' said Tiffany. 'Nothing. Just the summer, thank you.'

The Summer Lady looked puzzled. 'But humans always want something from gods.'

'But witches don't accept payment. Green grass and blue skies will do.'

'What? You'll get those anyway!' The Summer Lady sounded both confused and angry and Tiffany was quite happy about this, in a small and spiteful way.

'Good,' she said.

'You saved the world from the wintersmith!'

'Actually, I saved it from a silly girl, Miss Summer. I put right what I put wrong.'

'One simple mistake? You'd be a silly girl not to accept a reward.'

'I'd be a sensible young woman to refuse one,' said Tiffany, and it felt good to say that. 'Winter is over. I know. I've seen it through. Where it took me I chose to go. I chose when I danced with the wintersmith.'

The Summer Lady stood up. 'Remarkable,' she said. 'And strange. And now we part. But first, some more things must be taken. Stand up, young woman.'

Tiffany did so, and when she looked into the face of Summer, golden eyes became pits that drew her in.

And then the summer filled her up. It must have been for only a few seconds, but inside them it went on for much longer. She felt what it was like to be the breeze through green corn on a spring day, to ripen an apple, to make the salmon leap the rapids – the sensations came all at once and merged into one great big, glistening, golden-yellow feeling of summer . . .

. . . which grew hotter. Now the sun turned red in a burning sky. Tiffany drifted through air like warm oil into the searing calm of deep deserts, where even camels die. There was no living thing. Nothing moved except ash.

She drifted down a dried-up riverbed, with pure white animal bones on the banks. There was no mud, not one drop of moisture in this oven of a land. This was a river of stones – agates banded like a cat's eye, garnets lying loose, thunder eggs with their rings of colour, stones of brown, orange, creamy white, some with black veins, all polished by the heat.

'Here is the heart of the summer,' hissed the voice of the Summer Lady. 'Fear me as much as the wintersmith. We are not yours, though you give us shapes and names. Fire and ice we are, in balance. Do not come between us again . . .'

And now, at last, there was movement. From out of gaps between the stones they came like stones brought alive: bronze and red, umber and yellow, black and white, with harlequin patterns and deadly gleaming scales.

The snakes tested the boiling air with their forked tongues and hissed triumphantly.

The vision vanished. The world came back.

The water had poured away. The everlasting wind had teased the fogs and steams into long streamers of cloud, but the unconquered sun was finding its way through. And, as always happens, and happens far too soon, the strange and wonderful becomes a memory and a memory becomes a dream. Tomorrow it's gone.

Tiffany walked across the grass where the palace had been. There were a few pieces of ice left, but they would be gone in an hour. There were the clouds, but clouds drifted away. The normal world pressed in on her, with its dull little songs. She was walking on a stage after the play was over, and who now could say it ever happened?

Something sizzled on the grass. Tiffany reached down and picked up a piece of metal. It was still warm with the last of the heat that had twisted it out of shape, but you could see that it had once been a nail . . .

No, I won't take a gift to make the giver feel better, she thought. Why should I? I'll find my own gifts. I was . . . 'entertaining' to her, that's all.

But him – he made me roses and icebergs and frost and never understood . . .

She turned suddenly at the sound of voices. The

Feegles came bounding over the slope of the downs, at a speed just fast enough for a human to keep up. And Roland was keeping up, panting a little, his overlarge chainmail making him run like a duck.

She laughed.

Two weeks later Tiffany went back to Lancre. Roland took her as far as Twoshirts, and the pointy hat took her the rest of the way. That was a bit of luck. The driver remembered Miss Tick, and since there was a spare space on the roof of the coach he wasn't prepared to go through all that again. The roads were flooded, the ditches gurgled, the swollen rivers sucked at the bridges.

First, she visited Nanny Ogg, who had to be told everything. That saved some time, because once you've told Nanny Ogg you'd more or less told everyone else. When she heard exactly what Tiffany had done to the wintersmith, she laughed and laughed.

Tiffany borrowed Nanny's broomstick and flew slowly across the forests to Miss Treason's cottage.

Things were going on. In the clearing, several men were digging the vegetable area, and lots of people were hanging around the door, so she landed back in the woods, shoved the broom in a rabbit hole and her hat under a bush and walked back on foot.

Stuck in a birch tree where the track entered the clearing was . . . a doll, maybe, made out of lots of twigs bound together. It was new, and a bit worrying.

That was probably the idea. She took the back way, through the trees.

No one saw her raise the catch on the scullery door, or slip inside the cottage. She leaned against the kitchen wall and went quiet.

From the next room came the unmistakable voice of Annagramma at her most typically Annagrammatical.

'– only a tree, do you understand? Cut it up and share the wood. Agreed? And now shake hands. Go on. I mean it. Properly, or else I'll get angry! Good. That feels better, doesn't it? Let's have no more of this silliness—'

After ten minutes of listening to people being scolded, grumbled at and generally prodded, Tiffany crept out again, cut back through the woods and walked into the clearing via the track. There was a woman hurrying towards her, but she stopped when Tiffany said: 'Excuse me, is there a witch near here?'

'Ooooh, yes,' said the woman, and gave Tiffany a hard stare. 'You're not from round here, are you?'

'No,' said Tiffany, and thought: I lived here for months, Mrs Carter, and I saw you most days. But I always wore the hat. People always talk to the hat. Without the hat, I'm in disguise.

'Well, there's Miss Hawkin,' said Mrs Carter, as if reluctant to give away a secret. 'Be careful, though.' She leaned forward and lowered her voice. 'She turns into a terrible monster when she's angry! I've seen her! She's all right with us, of course,' she added. 'Lots of young witches have been coming to learn things from her!'

'Gosh, she must be good!' said Tiffany.

'She's amazing,' Mrs Carter went on. 'She'd only been here five minutes and she seemed to know all about us!'

'Amazing,' said Tiffany. You'd think that somebody wrote it all down. Twice. But that wouldn't be interesting enough, would it? And who would believe that a real witch bought her face from Boffo?

'And she's got a cauldron that bubbles green,' Mrs Carter said with great pride. 'All down the sides. That's proper witching, that is.'

'It sounds like it,' said Tiffany. No witch she'd met had done anything with a cauldron apart from make stew, but somehow people believed in their hearts that a witch's cauldron should bubble green. And that must be why Mr Boffo sold Item #61 Bubbling Green Cauldron Kit, $14, extra sachets of Green, $1 each.

Well, it worked. It probably shouldn't, but people were people. She didn't think Annagramma would be particularly interested in a visit right now, especially from someone who'd read all the way through the Boffo catalogue, so she retrieved her broom and headed on to Granny Weatherwax's cottage.

There was a chicken run out in the back garden now. It had been carefully woven out of pliable hazel, and contented 'werk's were coming from the other side.

Granny Weatherwax was coming out of the back door. She looked at Tiffany as if she'd just come back from walking around the cottage.

'I've got business down in the town right now,' she said. 'It wouldn't worry me if you came, too.' That was, from Granny, as good as a brass band and an illuminated scroll of welcome. Tiffany fell in alongside her as she strode off along the track.

'I hope I find you well, Mistress Weatherwax?' she said, hurrying to keep up.

'I'm still here after another winter, that's all I know,' said Granny. 'You look well, girl.'

'Oh, yes.'

'We saw the steam from up here,' said Granny.

Tiffany said nothing. That was it? Well, yes. From Granny, that would be it.

After a while Granny said: 'Come back to see your young friends, eh?'

Tiffany took a deep breath. She'd been through this in her head dozens of times: what she would say, what Granny would say, what she would shout, what Granny would shout . . .

'You planned it, didn't you?' she said. 'If you'd suggested one of the others they'd probably have got the cottage, so you suggested me. And you knew, you just *knew* that I'd help her. And it's all worked out, hasn't it? I bet every witch in the mountains knows what happened by now. I bet Mrs Earwig is seething. And the best bit is, no one got hurt. Annagramma's picked up where Miss Treason left off, all the villagers are happy and you've won! Oh, I expect you'll say it was to keep me busy and teach me important things and keep my mind off the wintersmith, but you still won!'

Granny Weatherwax walked on calmly. After a while she said: 'I see you got your little trinket back.'

It was like having a bolt of lightning and then not getting any thunder, or throwing a pebble into a pool and not getting a splash.

'What? Oh. The horse. Yes! Look, I—'

'What kind of fish?'

'Er . . . pike,' said Tiffany.

'Ah? Some likes 'em, but they are too muddy for my taste. In most stories it's a salmon.'

And that was it. Against Granny's calm she had nowhere to go. She could nag, she could whine and it wouldn't make any difference. Tiffany consoled herself with the fact that at least Granny knew that she knew. It wasn't much, but it was all she was going to get.

'And the horse ain't the only trinket I see,' Granny continued. 'Magick, is it?' She always stuck a K on the end of any magic she disapproved of.

Tiffany glanced down at the ring on her finger. It had a dull shine. It'd never rust while she wore it, the blacksmith had told her, because of the oils in her skin. He'd even taken the time to cut little snowflakes in it with a tiny chisel.

'It's just a ring I had made out of a nail,' she said.

'Iron enough to make a ring,' said Granny, and Tiffany stopped dead. Did she really get into people's minds? It had to be something like that.

'And why did you decide you wanted a ring?' said Granny.

For all sorts of reasons which never quite managed to be clear in Tiffany's head, she knew. All she could think of to say was: 'It seemed like a good idea at the time.' She waited for the explosion.

'Then it probably was,' said Granny mildly. She stopped, pointed away from the path, in the direction of Nanny Ogg's house, and said: 'I put the fence round it. It's got other things protectin' it, you may be sure of that, but some beasts is just too stupid to scare.'

It was the oak tree sapling, already five feet high. A fence of poles and woven branches surrounded it.

'Growing fast, for oak,' said Granny. 'I'm keeping an eye on it. But come on, I don't want to miss it.' She set off again, covering the ground fast. Bewildered, Tiffany ran after her.

'Miss what?' she panted.

'The dance, of course!'

'Isn't it too early for that?'

'Not up here. They starts up here!'

Granny hurried along little paths and behind gardens and came out into the town square, which was thronged with people. Small stalls had been set up. A lot of people were standing around in the slightly hopeless why-are-we-here? way of crowds who're doing what their heart wants to do but their head feels embarrassed about, but at least there were hot things on sticks to eat. There were lots of white chickens, too. Very good eggs, Nanny had said, so it would have been a shame to kill them.

Granny walked to the front of the crowd. There was no need to push people out of the way. They just moved sideways, without noticing.

They'd arrived just in time. A lot of children came running along the road to the bridge, only just ahead of the dancers who, as they trudged along with the Top-hatted Fool in the lead, seemed like quite homely and ordinary men – men she'd seen often, working in forges or driving carts. They all wore white clothes, or at least clothes that had been white once, and like the audience they looked a bit sheepish, their expressions suggesting that this was all just a bit of fun, really, not to be taken seriously. They were even waving to people in the crowd. Tiffany looked around and saw Miss Tick, and Nanny, and even Mrs Earwig . . . nearly every witch she knew. Oh, and there was Annagramma, minus Mr Boffo's little devices, and looking very proud.

It wasn't like this last autumn, she thought. It was dark and quiet and solemn and hidden, everything that this isn't. Who watched it from the shadows?

Who is watching now from the light? Who is *here* in secret? At which point, Granny Weatherwax took off her hat and placed You the kitten on the ground.

A drummer and a man with an accordion pushed their way though the crowd, along with the local publican carrying eight pints of beer on a tray (because no grown man is going to dance in front of his friends with ribbons round his hat and bells on his trousers without the clear prospect of a large drink).

When the noise had died down a bit the drummer beat the drum a few times and the accordionist played a long drawn-out chord, the legal signal that a Morris Dance is about to begin, and people who hang around after this have only got themselves to blame.

The two-man band struck up. The men, in two lines of three facing each other, counted the beat and then leaped . . . Tiffany turned to Granny as twelve hob-nailed boots *crashed* to the ground, throwing up sparks.

'Tell me how to take away pain,' she said, above the noise of the dance.

Crash!

'It's hard,' said Granny, not taking her eyes off the dancers. *Crash* went the boots again.

'You can move it out of the body?'

Crash!

'Sometimes. Or hide it. Or make a cage for it and carry it away. And all of it's dangerous and it will kill you if you don't respect it, young woman. It is all price and no profit. You are asking me to tell you how to put your hand in the lion's mouth.'

Crash!

'I must know, to help the Baron. It's bad. There is a lot I have to do.'

'This you choose to do?' said Granny, still watching.

'Yes!'

Crash!

'This is your baron who doesn't like witches?' said Granny, her gaze going from face to face in the crowd.

'But who *does* like witches until they need one, Mistress Weatherwax?' said Tiffany sweetly.

Crash!

'This is a reckoning, Mistress Weatherwax,' Tiffany added. After all, once you've kissed the wintersmith, you're in the mood to dare. And Granny Weatherwax smiled, as if she'd done all that was expected of her.

'Ha! Is it now?' she said. 'Very well. Come and see me again before you go, and we'll see what you may take back with you. And I hopes you can close the doors you are opening. Now watch the people! Sometimes you see her!'

Tiffany paid attention to the dance. The Fool had turned up without her noticing, wandering around collecting money in his greasy top hat. If a girl looked as though she'd squeal if he kissed her, he gave her a kiss. And sometimes, without any warning, he'd spring off into the dance, spinning through the leaping men with never a foot in the wrong place.

Then Tiffany saw it. The eyes of a woman on the other side of the dance flashed gold, just for a moment. Once she'd seen it, she saw it again – in the eyes of a boy, a girl, the man holding the beer, moving around to watch the Fool—

'Summer's here!' said Tiffany, and realized that she was tapping her foot to the beat; she realized it because a heavier boot had just trodden on it and pinned it gently but firmly to the ground. Beside it, You looked up at her in blue-eyed innocence that became, for the briefest fragment of a second, the lazy golden eyes of a snake.

'She's meant to be,' said Granny Weatherwax, removing her boot.

'A few coppers for luck, miss?' said a voice close by, and there was the sound of money being shaken in an ancient hat.

Tiffany turned and looked into purple-grey eyes. The face around them was lined and tanned and grinning. He had a gold earring. 'A copper or two from the lovely lady?' he wheedled. 'Silver or gold, maybe?'

Sometimes, Tiffany thought, you just know how it all should go . . .

'Iron?' she said, taking the ring off her finger and dropping it into the hat.

The Fool picked it out delicately, and flipped it into the air. Tiffany's eye followed it but, somehow, it wasn't in the air any more but *was* glistening on the man's finger.

'Iron's enough,' he said, and gave her a sudden kiss on the cheek.

It was only *slightly* chilly.

* * *

The galleries inside the Feegle mound were crowded but hushed. This was important. The honour of the clan was at stake here.

In the middle was a large book, taller than Rob and filled with colourful pictures. It was quite muddy from its journey down into the mound.

Rob had been challenged. For years, he'd thought himself to be a hero, and then the hag o' hags had said he wasnae, no' really. Weel, you couldn't argue wi' the hag o' hags, but he wuz goin' to rise tae the challenge, oh aye, so he wuz, or his name wasnae Rob Anybody.

'Where's mah coo?' he read. 'Is that mah coo? It gaes "cluck"! It is a . . . a . . . chicken! It is no' mah coo! An' then there's this wee paintin' o' a couple o' chickens. That's another page, right?'

'It is indeed, Rob,' said Billy Bigchin.

There was a cheer from the assembled Feegles as Rob ran around the book, waving his hands in the air.

'An' this one is a lot harder than Abker, right?' he said, when he'd done the circuit. 'That one was easy! An' a very predictable plot. Whoever writted that book didnae stretch himself, in ma opinion.'

'You mean *The ABC*?' said Billy Bigchin.

'Aye.' Rob Anybody jumped up and down and punched the air a few times. 'Got somethin' a wee bit tougher?'

The gonnagle looked at the stack of battered books the Feegles had, in various ways, collected.

'Somethin' I can get ma teeth intae,' Rob added. 'A big book.'

'Well, this one's called *Principles of Modern Accountancy*,' said Billy doubtfully.

'An' is that a big heroic book to read?' said Rob, running on the spot.

'Aye. Probably, but—'

Rob Anybody held up a hand for silence and looked across at Jeannie, who had a crowd of little Feegles surrounding her. She was smiling at him, and his sons were staring at their father in silent astonishment. One day, Rob thought, they'll be able to walk up to even the longest words and give them a good kicking. Not even commas and those tricksy semi-colonses will stop them!

He had to be a hero.

'Ah'm feelin' guid about this readin',' said Rob Anybody. 'Bring it on!'

And he read *Principles of Modern Accountancy* all morning, but just to make it interesting, he put lots of dragons in it.

Author's Note

The Morris Dance . . .

   . . . is traditionally danced on May 1st, to welcome in the summer. Its history is a bit confused, possibly because it's often danced near pubs, but it is now the English folk dance. The dancers usually wear white, and have bells sewn on their clothes.

I invented the Dark Morris for another book (at least, I think I invented it), reasoning that since the year is round the seasons might need more than one push. Once, when I was on a book signing tour a Morris side turned up all in black, just for me. They danced the Dark Morris in silence and perfect time, without the music and bells of the 'summer' dance.

It was beautifully done. But it was also a bit creepy. So it might not be a good idea to try it at home . . .

Terry Pratchett